Sir John
&
the Dragon's Boast

By
R.P. Edwards

Illustrated
By
David Paul Edwards

PUBLISH
AMERICA

PublishAmerica
Baltimore

ISBN: 1-4241-0634-6
PUBLISHED BY PUBLISHAMERICA, LLLP
www.publishamerica.com
Baltimore

Printed in the United States of America

LOVINGLY DEDICATED TO MY
FATHER JOHN, AND MY MOTHER DALLAS,
WHOSE CONTINUAL ENCOURAGEMENT
HAS SPANNED, WITHOUT WAVERING, O THESE MANY
DECADES.

ALSO, A VERY SPECIAL DEDICATION TO MY
ELDEST BROTHER,
THE STOUT-HEARTED FREDERICK.

Table of Contents

"I should have seen that coming," Sir John thought to himself as he lay face down, his cheek pressed against the brittle black stubble—all that remained of a once fragrant field of clover. "First the fire, then the tail…first the fire, then the tail," he mumbled to himself as he spat out soil and root. "Where is my shield?"

Slowly, to hands and knees the wounded knight arose. His strong left arm—the bearer of the shield—was now naked of not only the warrior's protection, but of most of his garment and large portions of flesh as well. Never before had he lost his shield in battle. But never before had he faced such a dragon.

"H-U-U-C-C-C," through the veil of steam and smoke the rumblings of the beast were heard. Like a giant unearthly bellows, the creature seemed to stoke its inner furnace with successive draws of air, punctuated, as it were, by the clapping of some sort of hellish valve.

"That sounds like number nine," mused the knight as he painfully pivoted on bended knees, and then, reaching down, lifted, then thrust the blade of his battered sword into the smoldering earth in front of him. Finally, with head bowed, eyes closed, and both hands grasping the hilt of his weapon, he waited for the deadly blast. It wasn't the thought of dying that bothered him. All must die, and he knew that death was but a door to his master's table. No, it was that he had failed to stop this evil. He was a knight! And for this he had trained, and sweated, and labored. For this he had deprived himself of dainties and damsels and all manner of earthly pleasures. For this he had lived, and now, sadly…for this he would unceremoniously die.

Chapter I

The lesson found in Eden's plight
Is that evil lives in beauty's sight
Yet it cannot play its wicked part
Until it finds a willing heart.

Alexander looked back at the pea-green orb jutting up from the freshly-turned soil and his usually straight row, number sixty-six of an estimated five hundred, was edging, ever so slightly, off course. "Whoa, Jezebel!" the old farmer yelled to his equally ancient plow horse. "Take a break, you ol' nag," he said without affection. Jezzy, a not so gray and slightly overweight mare, welcomed the pause with a head-wag and snort and then proceeded to munch on a dandelion clump that had avoided the fate of being plowed under, only to now be eaten for lunch.

"Not another one of these things," grumbled the fifty-five-year-old as he trudged back the ten paces to the grapefruit-sized sphere, punctuating each step with a curse—each one more vile than the last. Finally, with labored breath, he stood over the odorous nodule and paused a moment to gather strength.

"*Lift with your legs, son,*" he recalled the instruction of his long-dead father as he prepared to bend. "*It'll save your back.*"

"If my knees didn't hurt so much," he replied through clenched teeth, "I would!" Then, after a brief tirade directed at an injury and illness-prone ancestry, he began the time-tested technique that he had developed to pick up the accursed things without too much pain or the possibility of falling on his back to resemble a leg-churning, bottoms-up snapping turtle—a condition only remedied by rolling onto one's stomach (no small feat), then crawling to a sturdy vertical structure for the purpose of using his still-strong arms to pull himself up. Unfortunately, on the few occasions when he found himself thus, the only "structure" available was his temperamental horse...who had a tendency to kick first and ask questions later.

After a moment of painful reflection, Alexander began the process. First, with appropriate grunts and groans, using his right foot he nudged the five-pound sphere from the bottom of the furrow (where they *always* gravitated) to the top of the closest rim. Then, standing in the trough, he faced the thing and, like a predator-wary giraffe, he slowly began spreading his straightened legs which, in turn, lowered his bulging grotesque torso and brought the orb—with only a slight bend at the waist—into arm's reach.

"You're mine!" he uttered through a pained grimace as he quickly snatched the sphere and began to slowly close the gap between his legs. It took a series of little sideways baby steps to complete the task, and as he rocked back and forth he held the green pest close to his face.

Oh, there had been a time when he wouldn't dare touch the nasty things with his bare hands. But now, after so many, he had grown quite accustomed to the weight and feel and yes, even its putrid sulfurous fumes had a certain familial air.

"Why so many this year?" he wondered as he hobbled back to the plow and threw the orb into the converted potato sack that hung from Jezzy's port quarter. "That makes an even dozen today already."

Alexander pulled the scarlet mop-rag from his brown coveralls' front chest pocket and wiped, in a swirling clockwise motion, the sweat from his tanned wrinkled forehead—a forehead which now extended decidedly aft. "Why so many this year?" he puzzled again as he gave the reins a snap and Jezebel slowly plodded forward with one last dandelion remnant protruding, in desperation, just beyond the reach of her grinding ashen molars.

The spheres, pods, orbs, seeds, dragon droppings—they went by many names—had been a thorn in his side, and in the side of most of the valley's farmers, for as long as he could remember. Some said they were a leftover of the time when the land was under the control of *another* king. Others insisted that air-born demons dropped the things during their midnight excursions—when, after the western horizon had received a reluctant sun, the sound of huge horrible bat-like wings could be heard high above the peaceful valley. A dragon launched, no doubt, from the upper caverns contained in the volcanic peaks that separate this realm from the next. And that "armor-plated fool," as Alexander referred to him—the king's knight, Sir John, who was assigned this quadrant as his area of influence and protection—*he* suggested that the influx of these *poison pills* could be a reflection on the general increase of all things ungodly. "Fool!" Alexander uttered crisply, along with a few choice adjectives not generally accepted in polite company. Whatever the cause, each one of these *things* stunted or killed the growth of even the hardiest of crops for a radius of three meters. They had to go, and the king's command said there was only one way to properly do it and, as with much of his advice, it came in a rhyme or riddle.

> *Touch not long the unclean seed*
> *Or surely harvest hate and greed.*
> *To the water quickly go*
> *Or evil's place will surely grow.*

"Surely grow…Bah," grizzled the sour old man, punctuating his disgust by spitting groundward as he unhitched Jezzie from the plow. "What does a king know about farming? What does *His Royal Highness...*" he said, emphasizing his disdain by crinkling his bulbous pockmarked nose and speaking with a high-pitched nasal inflection, "*...he who knows nothing of dirt under the fingernails or pains in the back,*" and then in a loud, almost shouting voice, "WHO IS HE TO TELL ME WHAT TO DO?!"

—Now, it should be noted that Alexander had not always been such a bile-driven malcontent. Indeed, if one had made his acquaintance just a few years prior, they would have seen no semblance at all to this acid-tongued troll. But, such is the nature of deception, and Alexander, to be sure, was quite deceived.—

Free from the plow, Jezzie, by sheer instinct, started meandering towards the river—a good half mile hence. It was this river, as the king's message suggested, where these vile crop-killers would quickly dissolve and thus be rendered harmless. But, some time back, Alexander had decided that the journey was too long.

"Get back here, you idiot!" the farmer uttered, hands on hips. The old horse stopped, turned her head, and proceeded to give Alexander a look that spoke louder than Balaam's donkey.

"I will kill you if you take another step," the old farmer said coldly, moving his gnarled right hand across his body to grasp, and draw, the half-sword he used to slaughter smaller livestock.

Jezebel—*not* an idiot—stood motionless. She'd seen this behavior before. And she knew that *that blade* meant death…and not a death of the merciful kind. Her master had become quite sadistic in recent years. Indeed, once described as a man of compassion and noble character—now he was known, and deservedly so, as heartless and cruel.

* * *

The Sower stood on the edge of the lofty granite crag that was his usual launching point. Behind him, the cavern of his keeping, where he waited out the patrolling of the sun, and where he dined on human flesh—"Only fresh will do," he'd tell his fellow dragons. "The blood must still be warm and the screams still ringing in my ears."

As he surveyed the *hated land* before him, he could, through the pale light of a quarter moon, make out the silver ribbon that enclosed the holdings of his enemy. The *ribbon* was the river, of course—the boundary that encircled those in league with that *other* king. The one who had—and he shivered at the thought—so brutally humiliated his master. This was his assigned target, his *only* target, ever since its birth, many years ago.

A cold easterly wind began to press gently against his back, as if trying to push him off the precipice. But it wasn't yet the moment for that. He first had to inventory his wings and his wares. There would only be enough time for one pass, and his sovereign was most unforgiving of mistakes.

With deliberate effort he unfolded his massive membranous wings. The term "bat-like" had been used before, and it was fairly accurate in that these structures contained not a feather, but rather a skeleton covered with smooth dark reptilian skin. Other than the wings, the Sower looked much the same as the other dragons—scales, stout hind legs, smaller, more adept forelegs—each possessing four of five razor-sharp talons—an elongated face with a protruding tapering snout. The mouth contained many pointed teeth—perfect for tearing—and, as you might expect, a slight division of the tongue, which gives the voice of each a curious serpentine raspiness. Oh yes, the tail of this *flying dragon* differed from the *Ganab*, the *Shachaths*, and the *Muths*—rudimentary classifications of the *Earth Walkers*—in that, while all dragons need a tail for stability, *this* creature's was long and thin and provided not

14

only the service of a rudder, but it also contained the agility of another grasping appendage. Many a time had he used it to disable or disarm an opponent who was too busy guarding against tooth or claw.

The wings were ready. The foul fluids of the beast coursed freely through the many sections of these enormous air-catchers and he pumped them up and down to achieve their full extension in a slow, pre-flight idle. Now it was time to inspect the cargo. Around his protruding midsection—slightly paunched due to a recent human appetizer—he wore a wide leather belt. Mind you, he didn't care for the taste of cattle flesh, but their tanned hide was much more durable than the skin of man. Attached to the belt was a two-bushel pouch, also made of leather, with a heavy flap that could be fastened to prevent unwanted spillage. And beneath the flap were three easily accessible compartments, each a temporary womb for the seeds—yes, the very same mentioned previously, but these, rather than being the size of a grapefruit— these more closely resembled the dimensions of dust, even yeast, or as some say—leaven.

Prior to his ascension to the ledge and prior to his pre-flight feeding, the Sower had descended through a dark and twisting passage into the bowels of the mountain. Here, in a great sweltering cavern were three huge piles of the stuff. There was a label for each and, although his master said a mixing in the pouch was acceptable, even preferred, his lord did not, for any reason, want a *seeding run* to be made without all three present.

"What are they, Master?" he had meekly asked at one point, being sure to lay prostrate with eyes always downward.

"They are weapons, fool!" came the irritated reply. The words were clothed in a low, reverberating tone that had a most unnerving quality to it, and the Sower, though evil himself, felt very much inferior to this father of his kind. "They are the seeds of my enemies' destruction," the voice continued, hovering, so it seemed, just above the head of his servant, as if contemplating yet *another* death. "These seeds, when joined with the tainted soil in man's heart, will produce death. And this death will wound my enemy."

The Sower lay silent for many moments, fearful of disturbing his lord further. Finally, he heard the sound of a great earthen hatch opening and he saw, as if by chance, just a glimpse of his master descending to a lower level. He had a peculiar appearance—as if unstable and elusive—as if he were not one form, but many. And the flying-one pondered why the visage of his ruler seemed to take on the likeness of a serpent, then dragon, then man, then some sort of bright illuminated being. "And why," he wondered out loud, "does he hold his head, as if bruised?"

And so, before each run, he would fill his pouch with the "weapons" of his master's design. "Curious names," thought the Sower as he put equal portions into his pouch. "*Lust of the eye. Lust of the flesh. The Pride of Life*...most peculiar."

* * *

Jezebel resisted, ever so slightly, as her master led her in the direction of the depository. She, though not considered an enlightened creature, certainly had enough sense to avoid obvious dangers such as holes, and snakes, and open fires. But her owner, for some inexplicable reason, could not discern the smell of death that emanated from *that* place.

"C'mon!" he demanded, as he leaned against the reins which he had slung over his right shoulder as he began the ascent to the barren mound that occupied the center of his property. "A little closer, you four-legged demon!" he shouted, pulling hard now as he leaned backward, having shifted to face the rebellious beast.

It was no use. Alexander knew that even the threat of the blade would not compel his animal to edge even one step closer to his destination. He tied her off to an aging iron post—leftovers of a barrier of some sort—and angrily pulled the warm, weighty bag from Jezzy's side. He noticed a growing, weeping sore at the spot where the bundle had lain. "Serves her right," he muttered. And he began the short trek up the desolate outcropping.

Funny, he hadn't thought much of this curious rise when he started farming here years ago. Plainly seen from all areas of the fields, it stood a mere two meters high—a height easily attained via a gentle slope—and the summit (if such minuscule mounts can be said to have one) was a paltry fifty meters square. It was obviously rock-laden—certainly not good for crops or grazing. But, some time back, when he first balked at the idea of disposing of the orbs in the distant river and had collected quite a number—it was then he seemed strangely drawn to explore the top...an exploration that yielded the uncovering of a cave of sorts. Perhaps it was an old animal den, or simply an unexplained pocket of air created by an ancient shift in the underlying earthen layers. Whatever the cause, it was here—an opening that was shielded by a sizable flat stone—a slab large enough for a pig, or a child of eight—which, although appearing to be made of the durable grayish granite that was common in this valley, had the many unmistakable marks that told a story of butchering, and there was a downward channel that no doubt directed the draining fluids to pool somewhere out of sight—into the half-meter opening below the stone. It was into this cavity that Alexander threw the spheres.

"I wonder how many will fit in there?" he pondered as he reached into the sack with his arthritic right hand and heaved the last *seed* into the dark. "There must be at least three hundred by now."

The Ganab

Chapter II

The sword and shield are tools of war
To battle dragons...nothing more.

John fidgeted a bit. The large, moss-covered stone—his seat for the night—had a few most-annoying protrusions and he didn't want his partner to detect any discomfort.

"I told you that was a bad choice," came the soft baritone utterance from the man who sat directly opposite in words that barely exceeded the volume of the crackling fire that sparked between them.

"I always prefer a piece of fallen wood—a little on the rotten side," he continued, stirring the embers with a stick and still not looking at his young protégé. "Of course, I'm sure *my* behind is not nearly as tough as yours."

John managed a grin—which was returned by his aging teacher—and the knight-in-training stood, rubbed his sore posterior, then joined his elder—sitting down on the *fallen wood* which, of course, had room for two.

"Sir Peter..." the teenager began, then stopped when his companion turned his head and gave him that stern "don't you remember?" look. "That's right..." he thought to himself. "He wants me to call him just *Peter* now."

"Peter," he said, feeling quite uneasy about the familiarity of the name. "How far is it to our destination?"

"Not far...John...not far."

This, too, sounded strange to the younger one...having his master and

18

mentor not refer to him as *child* or *lad* or *whelp* or *pup* or a host of other substitutionary names—names always preceded and modified by the phrase "my young." For ten years he had been the warrior's helper, squire, page, servant—whatever term you prefer—and for ten years he had *never* heard his name spoken alone. Granted, some of the monikers were a bit humorous like "my young dalmatian," or "my young screech owl" when his complexion and vocal cords were going through pubescent turmoil. And some of the names like "my young champion," or "my young warrior" when spoken after an adequate performance indeed caused a swelling of pride and gratitude. But…what was it he had said as they were crossing the river just one day prior?

"This is your last journey with me before your *Quest of Proving.* You are now of a man's age and I'll not demand a title from someone who is my equal. I shall call you…John, and you shall call me Peter."

"His equal?" thought the seventeen-year-old. "Ridiculous. Equal perhaps to one of his arms or legs, or perhaps equal when we are both asleep. But I *am not* equal to the king's knight, Sir Peter."

"Peter," John said coyly…looking slightly away while rubbing the back of his neck with his right hand. "I feel most uncomfortable referring to you in this manner. Is there anything else I can call you?"

At this request the old fighter looked intently into the fire and, with his left elbow planted firmly on his knee he began stroking—grabbing his own face as one might grab a melon and slowly pulling outward—the long gray and red matting that was supposedly a well-kept beard.

"Oh, no," thought the enquirer. "Not another rhyme!" And, as the elder knight's response was slow in coming…John remembered back to their first encounter.

* * *

"Peter…?" The wall-builder felt a gentle tapping on his left shoulder and remembered at once the appointment, made days earlier, by the concerned parents of a little boy whose only ambition was to be one of the "king's knights." The middle-aged warrior slowly turned his head and, looking behind and above (he was currently laying the foundation for a property line barrier—where precision is key—and had been kneeling in a most unflattering position) and saw the large, dark-haired, modestly dressed woman who, previously joined by her farmer-husband, had begged his assistance. And there…peering around her homespun ankle-length dress stood a little blonde-haired boy who wore a most disappointed look on his face.

"Ah yes," said the knight, standing quickly and brushing off his dust-covered faded-gray coveralls (the kind supported by thin shoulder straps—sometimes accompanied by a shirt—but not this time). "I was so busy with the task at hand…I had neglected the moving of the shadows."

"Peter," said the mother—ignoring the excuse as she reached behind her and pulled the boy forward with an adeptness that revealed much practice at herding little men, "this is John."

The two looked intently at one another. The boy, pressing slightly backward on his mother's immovable palm…gazed in disbelief. "This is a knight?" he thought as he raised his eyes skyward to take in this burly, hairy, unkempt, and not-a-little odorous…man.

In the boy's defense, Sir Peter was not what most envision as a Champion of the King. At six foot, his height was not unusual, but donning the apparel of a common laborer and stacking rocks in a row certainly was. For, although such as he were allowed a royal stipend to assist in their living expenses…he would have none of it.

"*If I use my back to earn my pay, I'll not by pride be swept away*"—was the first of a thousand rhymes that were prompted by an inquiry from the young learner and, as his mother's figure slowly faded from view—she having answered the usual questions—

"Has he achieved the age of knowing?" (different for each individual)
"Yes."

"Has he sworn allegiance to the king and been washed in the river?" (necessary for a place in the realm)
"Yes."

"Does he walk in his sleep?"
"No."

"Is he allergic to gruel?"
"No."

"So…as previously agreed. You'll be wanting him back one weekend a month and on the Holiday of Release?"
"Yes."

—the child perceived that perhaps in choosing "Sir Peter" as the guide—perhaps his parents weren't too thrilled at his seeking a vocation other than farmer.

"C'mon, my young donkey," said his teacher, minutes later—noticing a lag in rock-lugging production—"you'll have plenty of time to reflect when you're in the stable tonight." Of course, the boy couldn't see the smile, nor know of the score of other *knight wannabes* that had failed to stay even one fortnight under the tutelage of "Sir Slavedriver, Sir Backbreaker, Sir Bore-a-lot, Sir Need-a-bath," or a host of other less-than-kind titles bestowed upon him by those who quickly quit his instruction. But John was not a quitter.

* * *

Peter returned his left hand to his side, sat more erect (so as to aid in his voluminous delivery), cleared his throat and said, "*Besides my name, there is one other...if you don't like 'Peter,' then call me 'Brother.'*"

"Brother Peter, then?"

"No, my young..." Sir Peter stopped himself, embarrassed at the near blunder. "No...John...it's 'Peter,' or 'Brother.' You may call me either name—but not linked together."

"Why not...Peter?" asked the apprentice with a slight tinge of mischief.

"Because, my inquisitive friend, long ago, when our king liberated our land he, in the process, abolished all nobility. We were instructed that no man is higher than another—regardless of talent or vocation. The insistence on titles or labels implies a superior—of which there are none."

"But...Brother...Peter..." John said in a soft childlike tone, being sure to inject an adequate pause between the words so as to follow the new stipulation, all the while concealing his delight by doodling in the soil at his feet with a half-meter branch that had escaped the initial combustion pile but was now being used as a prop in this impromptu comedy. "If none are superior," he continued—sensing, but not seeing the growing tension in his master's frame, usually exhibited by bulging veins in the neck and forehead and reflected in a heightened tone and volume in speech, "then why are not all men knights? For surely being the king's knight is a most enviable position—a station, no doubt, merited by an *inner* worthiness?"

—Now, it should be noted that John knew full well the answer to his question. He could quote it verbatim. For, you see, over the course of the last decade he had become quite accustomed to his instructor's agitation points and, on occasion, he was more than willing to try them...and this was such an occasion.—

"Because, my young..." Sir Peter stopped, nearly growling.

"Because…" he continued, pulling firmly on John's left shoulder to force a face-to-face dialogue, "…as the king has said…*all* abilities come from our Great Lord…" Peter paused, snatched the branch from his smirking associate, snapped the palm-width staff like a twig and, as he threw the wood to the flame, concluded, "…and the measure of a man's achievements are not in his eye-catching trophies, nor in the accolades dripped upon him by a fickle populace, nor in the great number of dragon he has slain, but in his *obedience* to his individual calling!"

"I see," said John through a wide toothed smile that informed Sir Peter that the pupil had, once again, successfully baited the professor.

John slowly sat up. The blow from Sir Peter had, as always (at least when not successfully avoided) sent him flying. It was, for the most part, a congratulatory back-slap…but as with all the elder knight's efforts—it was done with gusto. John tilted his head from side to side—realigning the neck—and tried to ignore the uproarious laughter as he slowly crawled back to his previous perch.

"I shall miss you, John," Sir Peter sighed, producing an off-white handkerchief and slowly wiping his eyes of laugh-induced tears. "You've been like a son to me these last few years. I'd have adopted you…if not for the technicality of you having parents."

The old veteran placed his hand on John's shoulder and the two warriors sat in tender silence for a few minutes—the sobering thought of the impending separation having dwarfed any concern over what life-threatening beastie they might face on the morrow.

"Not much to look at, these two," thought the dragon as he beheld the pair of armored humans from his shadow-covered vantage point—a mere ten meters away. This particular creature, named Cower, had been trailing them for quite a while…ever since they distanced themselves from the *accursed* river. His mission was, of course, to kill. But, at the very least he must separate, discourage, dissuade, dishearten. Perhaps he wouldn't have the pleasure of tasting blood's first gush, but, if not, he could at least aid in the victory accomplished by his brothers…the Muths. And then he'd have his fill. "Yes," he thought. "Second-hand is better than nothing…better than nothing."

"John," said the older man while he stood, stretched, and reached for his shield that lay within arm's reach, "you'll have the first watch. There's a

Ganab nearby. He'll most likely test the waters before long. You know what to do."

Sir Peter arranged a thin layer of dry leaves by the fire and proceeded to assume a most restful repose. John looked down on the aging one and paused a moment to engrave the scene into his memory. This would be their last mission together, and he wanted to recall the details for his inner journal.

As the teenager took the Stance of Defense, some of Sir Peter's rhymes bubbled into his consciousness.

Men see the copper, polished bright...but miss the gold just out of sight.
Shining armor makes not the knight...takes sword and shield to win the fight.
Be not impressed by those who crow...the battle's won by those who know.

"How true," he thought as he gazed briefly at the slumbering warrior. Years before—noticing the substantial difference in appearance of his simply attired mentor when compared to that of *other* knights—he had asked why so many of the King's Champions donned such *conspicuous kettles* (as Sir Peter called them.)

"Because they fear attack from behind," was the answer given between rhymes. "Or they're interested in using their skills against other knights, in contests of contempt." Sir Peter further divulged that his armor—fashioned after the king's own—was meant only for a forward attack. Rear protection was not necessary...for the enemy doesn't see these parts—unless you're running, of course. "Besides, my young chatterbox," he said at one point, "when a knight fights rightly, the only death he'll suffer on the battlefield is the one administered by man...not beast."

On the ground, Sir Peter, and his likewise-attired sentry, wore a simple cloth garment with dull brass armor covering only the front part of the legs, chest, and shoulders. A rather inornate helmet, also of brass, covered the crown and temples of his head, and a shield—a full meter wide, and half again in length (adorned with the mark of the king) covered the upper part of his body like a blanket. Within moments he was asleep—the shield gently rising and lowering to the scratchy melody produced by this "Builder of Walls."

Meanwhile, John paced a prescribed circumference...his shield, held securely by the left arm, and sword—slightly more than a meter in length (rather small compared to some of the fancy weapons of the more visible knights), double-edged, razor sharp, hardened steel of the king's own stock—was gripped tightly by the right hand and half-raised in a forward position…ready to strike.

Cower eased his way, ever so slowly, toward the pair of outsiders. "The elder is asleep…good!" he thought as he tailored his delusions to the younger, more impressionable mind.

As Sir Peter had sensed, this particular dragon was a Ganab—the smallest of the *Earth Walkers*. Usually not more than two and a half meters in height, lightly armored, very little flame (if any), yet considered by the old soldier as the most dangerous class of evil beings.

Fear not the Ganab's claw or tooth; depend not on your strength or youth,
For he'll use his words to mold your will…and when you bend—he'll have his fill.

John, too, had perceived that a murderer was in the wood. For, as they emerged from the invigorating wash of the river on the previous day, it didn't take long to detect a more potent scent of sulfur. True…the whole area beyond the river's edge (which the people of the redeemed kingdom referred to as *Tebel*) had the slight smell of brimstone…but the dragons themselves seemed to reek of the stuff, and each particular type had its own distinct flavor. The Ganabs had a sickeningly sweet aroma—like a funeral pyre dipped in honey and, due to its close proximity…the stench was almost overpowering. "Funny how the locals don't seem to notice it," John mused. "But," he concluded, "as Sir Peter has said on more than one occasion…*A feather is felt by tender skin, but a calloused hand feels not the pin.*"

"The Muths are coming…they know you're here…very soon you will die…very soon you'll feel their claws…ripping…tearing…"
It had begun. Sir Peter said it wasn't telepathic—that is, it isn't a mind-to-mind transfer. He said these chameleon-type creatures have a way of matching their utterances to the background noises that fill even the most quiet of spaces. It's as if the wind whispers, or the cricket speaks, or the moth wing repeats…lies, lies, lies…the language of the Ganab.

"Why should you die?…You *will* die if you continue…leave the old one…run…run…back to the river…the Muths are coming…you will die."

The words were almost hypnotic. John looked about anxiously. No one there. Nothing moving…but the words continued…smothering like a fog.

"Why should you die?...you're young...you want to live...but you will not live!...the Muths are coming...you will die...tomorrow you'll fill their bellies...run...run...run to the river..."

Cower was almost within a talon's touch of the near-knight. He had been spinning his wares for almost an hour and the youngster showed signs of weakening. John's pace quickened. His head moved erratically from side to side. Like a fish on a line the dragon played him perfectly.

First fear...then escape...fear...escape...die...live...die...live. How utterly predictable these humans were. True, the warriors took longer to crack. But crack they will. "Give me enough time," he'd boast to his wicked companions, "they'll soon bare their neck. They'll surrender their children. They'll offer their very soul."

And then it was over. John's shield clattered on the ground and his horrified steps could be heard tearing through the brush. The Ganab had won. The two were divided.

"Easier to kill this way," thought Cower as his dark greenish-brown form emerged from the shadows. This dragon, the embodiment of the monster imagined beneath the bed or just outside the window, glided towards Sir Peter as the sounds of John lessened in the distance. "I'll pursue him in a moment," he hissed. "But first an appetizer." Cower stood over the sleeping knight and pondered the best way to remove this oyster from his shell. True, if he bore the mass of his larger relatives—the Shachaths and Muths—all he would have to do is step or sit on this invader's shield. Then it would just be a matter of joyfully removing the helmet and toying with the fool as he screamed for mercy. "Oh, I'd describe in detail all my most notable meals—the women and men, and the children and infants—moanings and pleadings and grovelings and screamings. Not to mention the knights I've eaten, Ha!" A tablespoonful of foul spittle dripped onto Sir Peter's shield as Cower fantasized this ending. "But," thought the beast, coming to reality, "I contain not the weight or strength to finish it this way. Besides...if those oafs came within fifty meters, this warrior would be up, sword ready. I wonder," he paused, quickly scanning the campsite, "where that weapon is?" For, although he had eaten his share of knight flesh (usually killed by someone else), he had also had a half-meter of tail removed by a too-close encounter many decades prior.

John could no longer be heard...the fire dwindled...and overhead, moonlight—reflected off the Crystal Sea—danced on the underside of a high- flying cloud. Cower hesitated for a moment as he considered leaving this one for the *professionals*. "No," he concluded. "This old one is ripe."

The dragon, ever so gently, used his blood-red claws and lifted the shield that protected Sir Peter's upper body. "If I can get to his neck before he wakes..." he thought, his eyes widening in anticipation.

But, as the covering was slowly pealed away—in one fluid motion the war-worn blade of the Champion rose to within a centimeter of the dragon's throat. The Ganab stopped—as if frozen—and saw Sir Peter, eyes open and his face sporting a smirk which then mouthed these words...

The Ganab, known for stealth and speed, will fall because of pride and greed.

You might call it a feinting move. Like the lizard that sacrifices its tail so that the greater part may live. Cower lunged at the knight's head with his right foreleg. It only traveled a quarter meter before it was severed at the wrist by Sir Peter's quick blade. But that painful diversion gave him the window of escape. The dragon twirled away from the arcing of the sword and darted back towards the foliage that had concealed him earlier. Forgotten was his intent to follow and kill John. Forgotten was his boasting and arrogant predictions. And, within another few meters...forgotten was everything. For, as he passed the moss-covered side of a great oak, John appeared and, with a lightning-quick upward motion, he expertly removed the demon's head from its clueless body. Indeed, the mindless hulk traveled a good three paces before it finally slammed to earth. Cower...who had consumed a thousand souls in his long, wretched life—was dead.

Back at the campsite, John arrived in time to see his companion throwing the ineffectual claw into the flames. "Nice touch with your shield," said Peter, making sure the dragon part was completely consumed. "Very convincing."

"I was just following your advice...with a slight twist."

"We'll call it *artistic license* then," said the elder as he stood, stretched, and finally resumed a horizontal position.

"Um, Sir...I mean...Peter," stammered a most tired John. "Isn't it *my* turn to rest?"

Peter opened one eye, looked at the lad and said, "Ah, if only it was. But you must remember...(a pause, to yawn)...we agreed that I went first, and surely you don't think my little charade was in any way restful?"

John capitulated to this logic, but he also knew that the old rhymer had an uncanny ability to doze and yet be alert at the same time.

The Muth

Chapter III

The dragons rage.
The people sing.
Behold! The emblem of the king!

"I thought there might be two," whispered Sir Peter as he and John paused at the edge of the forest and took in the unsettling sight of a pair of Muths parked between them and their objective—a simple two-room earthen hovel that contained the precious treasure that true knights seek to save and nurture—human souls.

John noticed that the tone and demeanor of his elder had changed, as it always does, as they had neared the place of decision. No more rhymes. No more jovial banter. And the dark blue eyes of the warrior, framed by brows and beard of gray and red—which often had in them a twinkle of mischief and mirth—were now fixed, resolute, unwavering.

John turned to ask a question, only to discover his elder kneeling, his sword piercing the earth in a perpendicular fashion, and both hands grasping the cross-bar of the hilt...palms down. The younger quickly assumed a like position and Sir Peter, with head bowed, began an earnest prayer.

"Oh, Great Lord...God of the Crystal Sea...God of our benevolent king...whom you sent to bring release of the Living River...whom you sent to free us from the shackles of our former masters—the dragons..."

John knew well the progression of the coming events...first the prayer...then attack. As his mentor continued his supplication the teenager slowly lifted his head and gazed at the beasts that were their destiny. "Strange," thought he, "before Sir Peter's intercession the creatures seemed at rest. Now they appear most anxious."

A stony silence awakened John from his dazed state. Sir Peter had stopped praying and was sternly looking at his wayward companion. "Why don't *you* continue...John," said the elder in a disciplinary tone.

John bowed his head, cleared his throat, and tried to focus his thoughts and heart on the omnipotent being he had never seen...yet *knew* existed. "Lord," he said in a timid whisper.

"Louder, bolder!" exhorted an agitated Sir Peter, cupping John's chin in his strong right hand while riveting him with his eyes. And then, moving the hand to the back of his fellow warrior's neck, he gave it a firm squeeze and said, tenderly, "We're here on the king's business, lad. Our success depends on much more than steel and shield."

The two bowed their heads again and John began anew, "Lord," he said, in a stronger, more authoritative voice, "thank you for releasing us from the dragon's chains. Thank you for allowing us the privilege of trying to bring your release to others. Our great king, your servant, has sent us on this mission...and although we have skill in the ways of battle...our victory is only assured if you fight with us. Please Lord, guide our steps, strengthen our arms, and protect the people in that house from the jaws of death as we struggle to reach them. In the name of the king, we ask."

For perhaps a minute more there was a gentle, sacred silence. Finally, through the dingy handkerchief that had been retrieved to dab the eyes and wipe the nose, Sir Peter added... "Amen...yes...Amen."

John, as only the young can do, sprang to his feet and offered a welcomed hand to his fellow pilgrim. Sir Peter, feeling the wear of years, arose with a slight grunt and then, with a fatherly look at his former pupil said, "Well, John, shall you test the fire...or shall I?"

* * *

To destroy the Muth...test the fire.
If you skip this step...you will expire.

John had to reach his eleventh year before his instructor, Sir *All-in-Good-Time*, would even *begin* to teach him the rudiments of his call—that is, the actual physical aspect of being a warrior. Up until this time he was, in his own mind, anything *but* a future champion. For…day in, day out, he was a blonde-haired pack mule, camel, carrier pigeon, mole, waiter, dish washer, stable cleaner and a host of other non-knightly job descriptions. Not to say that he didn't have lessons to learn, or that he didn't accompany his master on non-dangerous outings of exhortation but, plead as he might, Sir Peter would not yield the sword until nearly *four years* had passed from that first fateful encounter by the wall. On occasion, usually out of tired frustration, the boy would beg, "Why may I not begin to train as other apprentices do?"

Sir Peter would often respond, "All in good time," or, as might be expected, he offered a rhyme, thus—*Any fool can wield the blade…but a knight of finer stuff is made.*

After the basic maneuvers were learned—concerning the marriage of shield and sword—Sir Peter added instruction on the defeat of particular dragon types. "The Muth," he would say, "is specialized to do one thing…kill. He does not plague the mind and will, as the Ganab…he does not wreak havoc by destruction and torment, as the Shachath. No…he is a killer. For this he is designed and, when you see one, know this…he will seek to slay you or, failing that…he will seek to slay those you are in search of."

"Do not all dragons seek to kill?" said the boy at one point.

"Eventually, yes. But though these fiends draw nourishment from the flesh and souls of humankind, theirs is a need for domination, power, fear. The crop of man is something they carefully cultivate…drawing every last drop of horror from their victims is just as important as draining the blood from their veins…perhaps more so.

"Now…pay attention my young tinder box," said Sir Peter, "and I'll instruct you on the proper way to *test the fire.*"

Over the course of his pre-fighting years, John had been forced to memorize many a rhyme to aid in his future endeavors. Some of these had to do with the dragons he'd encounter.

> *One good thrust…the Ganab dies.*
> *The Shachath takes a few more tries.*
> *But the Muth's hide will make you tire.*
> *Yet before the blade…you must test the fire.*

On a stubbled, barren field—it was early autumn and the corn crop had been harvested just days prior—the veteran had the boy walk twenty paces from himself and then turn to face his *enemy*. In John's right hand—the sword of training (a weapon of fighting weight and length, yet not commissioned of the king), and on his left arm—a full-sized shield (*full-sized* in Sir Peter's eyes. Some knights did not use a shield at all, and some used different shapes and configurations—dependent on preference or, sadly…fashion sense).

"I am the dragon," bellowed the instructor. "Come towards me, you knight…champion of the king…I am a Muth, and one of us will die this day."

The boy walked toward Sir Peter, sword raised and shield held level with his chin—a little to the side. "You're dead," spoke the elder, bouncing a pebble off the boy's helmet. "Try again."

This time the apprentice ran towards his master—shield held high, both arms and head protected as he approached. He came within five paces… "You're deceased," said the knight. Another pebble angled off the boy's foot.

Finally, supposing that the pebbles signified a fiery burst, the page approached slowly and then crouched fully behind the shield as the stones came at regular intervals. Then, having made his way close enough to strike, he awaited another pebble and, immediately after it bounced harmlessly over his head he stood, raised his weapon, and then heard… "dead again."

John slumped to the ground, exhausted from the burden of the puzzle and his wares and asked between gasps, "What have I done wrong?"

"Well, for being your first time," said Sir Peter, continuing to annoy with pebbles to the noggin, "you did quite well. You remembered, *finally*, that the Muth's fire comes in regular intervals. You remembered to protect your whole body behind the shield—any significant gap can be fatal. Unfortunately, when nearly close enough to strike, you forgot that with most Muths (there are exceptions, of course) the tail immediately follows the flame. I suppose it's a recoil action of sorts. Whatever the reason, if you're not ready for it—that spiny thing can knock your head off."

* * *

John considered a response as he cast his gaze towards the huge dragons that, although neither advancing nor retreating, were nevertheless moving legs, necks and heads in such a manner that suggested extreme fury. "Since there are two," he said, pausing to look at his mentor, "…shouldn't we separate and do our own testing?"

Peter momentarily removed his helmet with his left hand and scratched the matted underbrush with the other. "Quite right…John," he said, replacing the cover and taking up sword and shield, preparing to engage… "I'm so used to one Muth that I had forgotten the protocol for more. Very well, then," he said, walking towards the larger of the two which, upon seeing a hated knight, started roaring and spewing fire and smoke… "I'll take the ugly one. And, if you don't mind…please lead that infant away…I don't want you interfering with my artistry."

John shook his head and smiled as Sir Peter approached the nearest beast. "The ugly one? Is that what he said?" thought the younger as he skirted the edge of the field—going in the opposite direction of his companion in order to separate the two flame-breathers. "I've never seen a dragon that was anything less." And, as he prepared to *test the fire*, he couldn't help but notice that the old warrior's tone had lightened considerably since the request for divine assistance. Yet, from many past observances, he knew, without a doubt, that Sir Peter's determination would not be denied. He would either conquer, or die.

After distancing himself from his teacher, John paused briefly to survey the expanse of this battlefield that had been their destination. It was a farm—of the share cropper variety, and there, across this barren plain that had been a wheat field—most likely destroyed by a Shachath in recent days—was the house where three humans were waiting to escape. Between he and they stood the Muth. This particular monster, though only smaller by decimals, was *hardly* an infant. Standing erect on hind legs as thick as hundred-year-old trees, this creature towered at least six meters. His forelegs had a length of a man's span, and although slow in the grasping of his prey—if successful, even the thickest of armor would not resist long the pressure of those bloody talons. But, as John had been taught, and knew from experience—the primary weapons of this demon were the fire and the tail.

* * *

Fredrick, or Fren, as his parents called him—a nickname from obscurity most likely taken from the child's long-ago mispronunciation of the word *friend*—looked out the small, paneless opening that was one of only two windows in this impoverished dwelling. "Father, Father…look…they come…knights!" said the excited twenty-year-old, pointing out the half-meter square portal with his right arm, and beckoning his father with his left.

Alexander looked up from the simple pine table where he had been sitting, his face resting upon calloused palms…exhausted from worry and dreading the intentions of the two giants that had made their presence known in the darkness of the pre-dawn. He managed a smile at his innocent man-child and stood slowly to join his wife, Mary, who was also now at the window.

"I thought they'd never come," he half whispered to himself as the sight of the two armored warriors confirmed the words of his only son. "You're right, Fren...You're right!" said the forty-something farmer (considered old in the land of dragons) as he wrapped an arm around each loved one and hoped against hope that these mere men could free them from their earthen prison.

John stood motionless opposite the ashen-brown murderer that blocked his path. This Muth, unlike the recently vanquished Ganab, was extremely well-protected. Thick bony plates, layered neatly, encased every part of his enormous body like fire-baked tiles on a steeply slanted roof. Twice the size of an elephant—in height, length, and tonnage—these creatures were designed to harvest great quantities of souls, or, as in the present case—two well-armed knights.

On the edge of his peripheral vision, the armored and eager youth could make out the familiar orchestrated battle of his elder. Sir Peter had wasted little time in his attack and, although the sights and sounds of the contest— great bursts of yellowish-blue flame, sickening sulfurous fumes, the pounding of the large reptilian tail, the distinct crack of steel against scale, and the deep, guttural howls of demonic pain—were, to the unschooled...maddening, to John they meant another Muth would soon be dead. But...he had his own battle to win and, not knowing the fate of the prisoners...he quickly focused all his resources on the task at hand.

To make the dragon, fire bring...show the emblem of the king.

Not knowing the extent of his adversary's reach (the twenty paces in his youthful lesson were, he learned later, an elementary step for an unskilled apprentice), John stood approximately forty meters from the fuming leviathan. Then, after drawing the beast's full attention (usually accomplished by a pregnant hesitation—something these monsters are not used to...most victims either run or faint), the future knight held high the shield and there, in clear view, etched into the shining brass rectangle (although most of Sir Peter's—and therefore John's—armor was *not* polished—he insisted the opposite be true on that which bore the king's mark) was the emblem of their Sovereign…an upside-down crimson sword. Upon seeing this the creature's head shook violently and he let out a high-pitched, ear-splitting shriek. The dragon then firmly planted both forelegs on the ground in front of him and, taking a good fifteen seconds to stoke his inner fire, he finally spewed forth a powerful maelstrom of flame and smoke. John noted that the stream reached a little over half way to his position. "Perhaps this is an infant after all," he thought as he remained steadfast. Another burst gave him all the information he needed—the range of the fire, the time-period between blasts, and the manner of the tail.

* * *

"Was it five or ten thousand?" These were the early-morning thoughts of the smaller of two Muths as it plodded behind its larger cousin while they bulldozed their way through a defenseless countryside. They had been suddenly ordered to destroy a pair of thieves.

"It could have been more…much more…much more," he growled to himself, regretting being pulled from a city that was ripe for harvest. "Oh, it had been a classic deception," he thought, recalling the history of the crop. "A band of these hated insects, seduced to exalt themselves to godhood. Then utterly defeated and destroyed…well…almost destroyed." He paused to fell a small stand of ancient hardwoods—using his armored and daggered eight-meter tail as an unholy scythe—slashing, effortlessly, through that which took centuries to produce.

His companion, hearing the destruction, turned its hateful gaze towards the youth. The younger Muth, without seeing, felt the rebuke and quickly fell in line behind the older. There was no love between these two (*Love*, the real kind, is unknown among the dragons. Their emotions and actions center only on the perverse gratification that comes from living to fulfill one's own lust at the expense of all. Though they sometimes work in tandem—as is the case here—it is only grudgingly at the command of their ruler.), but their mission was the same, and the lead Muth had proven, upon their meeting some time back, that he was the superior.

As the dawn quickly approached, the two monsters saw the place of the snare. It was an unimpressive mud nest…the kind they step on without a second glance. But their lord had given them explicit orders to "hurt not the worms" and they knew that these were but bait for the armored robbers that had come to steal their treasures…human souls.

33

* * *

John looked intently at his adversary as the Muth prepared to send another blast. The adjoining battle, between Sir Peter and the other creature, although growing in intensity, started to fade from the young man's consciousness as his focus heightened.

The dragon in front of him was fully braced—all talons tightly gripping the hard clay earth. The brute then raised its head, as if cocking the string on a crossbow and with one violent forward thrust—the fire was loosed! Like a high-pressure stream from a punctured dam, the flames of sulfurous blue approached the warrior in an ever expanding plume of destruction.

John, waiting patiently just out of range, knew that the force of the hellish geyser increased as one neared the beast. Even with the protection of the shield, no man can stand long adjacent the demon's foul vent. But, as he had been taught, and knew from previous endeavors with his teacher, if a knight took proper care he could not only survive the consuming onslaught, but he could, if not double-minded, turn the monster's own powerful ingrained mode of attack against the killer itself.

After a span of some five or six seconds the roar of the blaze ended as quickly as it began. The dragon's head swung backward in a recoiling type action—with a slight angling to the right (no doubt the involuntary relaxing of muscles needed to anchor the beast during the attack). Simultaneously, the creature's body pivoted with the neck—the talons having been released—and the monster's tail followed suit, resulting in a whipping action reaching some yards to the front of its station.

John tensed himself, as a sprinter before the call. He knew that after the tail the creature would most likely begin anew the process of fire-building. The procedure, once begun, could not be stopped until it climaxed in yet another explosion. And it was during this brief window of opportunity— when all of the murderer's systems were focused on the flame—that the warrior must strike. Unfortunately for most (many unschooled knights, having tasted victory against Ganab and Shachaths, assume the same tactics will work on the fortress that is the Muth), the precise technique, though quite effective, is brutally unforgiving in the hand of the novice.

The teenager anxiously paused as his enemy's tail followed its course and returned to its passive state. The dragon then regrouped to prepare another salvo. This was John's queue. Quickly he ran right up to the monster's exposed chest. Though carrying armor, sword and shield, the distance was covered in mere moments. To his left and right the powerful forelegs of the beast quivered under the stress of grasping the earth for the coming blast. Five seconds had passed...he only had ten more. In front of him the great furnace of the monster swelled as it took in oxygen to stoke the fire of hell. (There had been much conjecture as to the make-up of the dragon's flame. Some believed it was the result of quarried sulfur. Some, the oily fat of its prey. But whatever the source, the fuel was ignited by hatred and sent forth with rage.)

John raised his sword (this weapon—issued before this latest mission—carried the king's commission, was perfect in balance, tempered by truth and, when used in the cause of righteousness, seemed to almost glow with the very countenance of the one who forged it) and, with a powerful swift stroke, he brought it down sharply upon the armored plates immediately in front of him. This tightly woven barrier (each scale in this area—they vary by location—was approximately one-third meter in width, and slightly more than that in length) seemed to chip, ever so slightly at the three blows this brief period would allow. Then, with time nearly exhausted, he turned and ran a straight course from the demon's mouth.

The bewildered dragon (he had never experienced an attack like this before) quaked violently as the pressure for another blast mounted in his hellish combustion chamber and he saw, with twisted delight, that the youth would *not* escape the reach of his next vile discharge. The creature, now at the point of eruption, opened wide his hideous jaws and threw his head and neck forward in one great convulsion of all-consuming fury. The semi-liquid torrent of bluish-yellow flame surged relentlessly forward and the insolent human was enveloped by the unquenchable wave.

The Muth—destroyer of tens of thousands—recoiled backward as his cycle of blazing destruction took its course. In his mind the images of fallen armies—charred, screaming, begging for mercy—emerged from his memory as he turned to face, again, the remnants of one of his attacks. "I hope he's still alive," the demon thought, expecting to see another disfigured human writhing in pain...his skin blackened, blistered and smoldering. "I want to make his death excruciatingly slow and painful."

But, as the killer turned to face his victim—as the pungent black and grey smoke of the blast slowly dissipated—instead of seeing another defeated *insect*...he saw John, unscathed, unbent, unyielding—holding high, in polished brilliance, the emblem of the hated king!

For a moment the mountainous creature froze in disbelief. Then, with teeth towards heaven, the monster let out a great rumbling cry. Like a horrible merciless avalanche of stone and ice, the utterance started low and then, with ascending pitch and volume, culminated with the Muth charging the one who dare survive his onslaught.

—Now, it should be noted that of the *Earth Walkers*, the Muth, although undoubtedly the most powerful and destructive, is also the slowest of the three. Like a large seething lava flow, nothing (or so they themselves tend to think) can stand in their way. However, a human not paralyzed by fear, and being fortunate enough to have an open expanse…can easily outrun one.—

The young warrior, seeing the advance of the enraged enemy, backpedaled without sign of anxiety or alarm. Step for step he maintained the same distance…never turning…perpetually holding the symbol of defeat in full sight of the impotent beast. Finally, realizing the folly of this tactic, the dragon stood still and submitted himself fully to his instinctive hellish drive to destroy by fire.

John, noticing immediately the change, ran to the creature and gave five well aimed blows to the plates already marked. There seemed to be little damage, but the teenager knew…that like the stone-cutter's wedge and the woodsman's axe, his persistence and precision would eventually fell this giant and split its wretched heart.

On and on the two engaged…the titan and the flea. A blast of fire…the crack of steel. A blast of fire…the crack of steel. The dragon roared…he charged…he tried to use his horrid tail…but he always, *always* returned to the fire. And the fire *always* led to the steel. Finally, after what seemed an age, the monster spun back once more to prepare another blast. But, instead of seeing that accursed shield…there were two!

"John!"…It was Peter, nearly out of breath, running to join his companion just before the torrent of flame. They joined the edges of their shields and the superheated tempest rushed harmlessly around and over them. "John!" Peter shouted over the roar of the flame. "Run to the house! Quickly!"

The sulfurous flow ceased, and the tail cut its swath, but instead of both warriors attacking the beast…the younger continued around him and sped towards the faraway dwelling.

"Mary! Mary! It's me…let me in!" Mary, distraught over the horrendous battle outside, went towards the front door while her husband and son continued to peer out the window.

"Alan, is that you?" she whimpered…her face pressed against the rough-hewn wood—her right hand trembling at the latch.

"Yes! Yes! It's me!…Let me in! Hurry! I'm afraid!"

"Oh, Alan!" she sobbed. "I thought you were dead…I thought you were dead…tell me you're not dead…tell me you're alive." By now, tears were flowing freely down her swollen cheeks.

"Yes, it's me!…I got away…It's me!…Let me in!…I'm afraid!"

Mary, delirious from worry, lack of sleep, and confronted with the thought of a reunion with her long lost brother—firmly gripped the iron and started to lift.

"NO MARY!!…What are you doing!" her husband shouted as he dove across the room and resecured the door moments before it opened.

"It's Alan, husband!…He's alive…he's outside the door…I have to let him in…he's in danger."

Alexander firmly grasped his wife's sloping shoulders and gazed into her reddened eyes. He pulled her close to him and tenderly whispered, "No dear…it's not Alan…Alan's dead…taken long ago by a winged dragon…we saw him taken…we heard his cries."

Mary buried her head into her husband's chest and trembled as great heart-wrenching sobs accompanied the torrent of tears. She finally crumpled to the floor and pressed herself against the wall, her hands over her ears to try and block the continuing voice. "Make it stop!" she screamed. And then, in diminishing tones… "Make it stop…make it stop…make it stop…"

"GET AWAY FROM HERE, YOU DEMON!!" Alexander shouted into the door. "YOU'RE NOT COMING IN!!"

A moment later a horrible face was at the window…it was a Ganab! Fren jumped back and screamed as a long hideous foreleg thrust in and thrashed wildly about trying to rend a throat. "Stay back, Fren!" the father shouted, pulling his son out of reach. The boy…their dear innocent son…injured at birth and retaining the mind of a child…clung to his father as a two-year-old might squeeze a parent's leg. "It's all right, Fren…It's all right." Alexander gently patted his terrified boy's back…and then the scratching began.

* * *

"If the Muths fail…kill the worms." These were the simple instructions the Ganab had received one day prior to the arrival of the thieves.

"Our master must be concerned about these two," whispered one murderer to another as the pair backed away, being sure to stay in a submissive pose—bowed, with eyes to the floor. "Two Muths…two Ganab…yes, very concerned." The speaker, a sixty-year-old (young for those with dragon blood), could not utter another syllable for, as soon as the duo left the mountain chamber where they had been summoned, the older turned and fiercely grasped his companion's throat with the razor sharp talons of his battle-scarred forelegs. The pressure and pain caused the youth to buckle as he tried frantically, in vain, to remove the powerful clamps that were beginning to penetrate the skin.

"It's not up to you to interpret our lord's reasonings…" rasped the older Ganab some minutes later as he, with black forked tongue, slowly licked the warm liquid from his claws after having thrown his *partner* to the ground. "These thieves have killed many of our kind…and stolen many of our treasures. They will steal no more."

* * *

"I almost had her," the elder Ganab thought as it frantically splintered the hard-wood barrier that separated him from his meal. Inside, the three humans—Mary, on the brink of madness—Fren, weeping and clinging to his father—and Alexander, the provider, the protector, the leader…feeling utter despair at his impotence in this situation—all radiated an almost pure essence of terror that was quite intoxicating to the demon at the door.

"If only I had more time," the fiend fantasized, "I'd drag this out for days…weeks. Then I'd kill them." Visions of past atrocities danced across his perverse mind and then, awakened, he paused to curse the Muths who had botched such a trivial task. "Imbeciles! Idiots! Armored morons!" he shouted out loud. Then, sensing the flow of fear thickening, he began anew, like a famished terrier ripping apart a rabbit's lair. He could *almost* taste them.

"FATHER!! LOOK!!" Fren screamed to his wilting parent who had knelt to comfort his tormented spouse. Alexander quickly stood to his feet and saw, in the adjoining room (a small sleeping chamber for he and his wife) *another* Ganab who was frantically widening the opening that had been the other window.

"Fren! Quickly…the table!" The doorway, covered only at night by a simple fabric curtain, could, at least temporarily, be sealed by the upturned table. The two men held it in place and awaited the jolt of the enraged monster. They didn't have to wait long.

The younger Ganab, eager to deny his companion of the kill, slammed himself against the impromptu barricade. The two men were thrown back, for just a moment—but long enough for a clawed appendage to reach in and rake across Alexander's leaning shoulder. "Aarrgh!" the wounded father screamed, but he continued to push the table against the creature's arm, even as his blood filled in the crooked grain of the wood on its way to pool on the floor. Finally, the Ganab pulled its foreleg—having been painfully squeezed against the door frame—back into the bedroom. The humans were safe for the moment.

"I'm all right, Fren," Alexander, panting for air, assured his distressed son. "It's not as bad as it looks."

"*Alexander…*" a pleasant, almost melodic voice seemed to emanate from the very walls and act as a balm on the tortured nerves of the father. "Alexander…I'm here to protect you…I'm here to stop that other Ganab…let me in…I didn't mean to hurt you…let me in."

The farmer shook his head as if trying to repel a swarm of gnats and then shouted, "LIAR! LIAR! LIAR!"

The voice changed instantly to the natural grating rasp of these deceivers. "I'll kill you last!" it hissed. "You'll watch the boy and your wife dismembered…and your death will be slow and oh, so painful." Then this monster, like the first, began to shred the wood. The only difference…this was soft pine. In a moment an opening began to appear.

At the same time, the Ganab at the front also penetrated the door. He, with a horrid glance, looked in at the petrified occupants and then, in an instant, thrust in a grisly leg to let himself in.

They say, at such moments of ultimate danger, that the procession of events, though taking only seconds, seem to those intimately involved as a much greater span. So it was for the human participants in this nondescript dwelling in the land of the dragons. Alexander, still pressing against the table even as his strength quickly drained away, watched in horror as the Ganab that had tormented his dear wife reached in as if to raid an earthen pantry. Then…suddenly…the noonday sun burst through the opening causing the humans (those still coherent) to shield their squinting eyes. But…the stream of light was not the result of the door following its normal arc. No…it was as if the weakened timbers disintegrated under a terrific unseen force. Another moment passed, and Alexander—even as splinters from the frenzied ripping of the monster behind the table bounced off his unshaven face—saw two uneven, and still spurting halves of a Ganab fall through the doorway, followed closely by an armored youth carrying a gleaming sword. In one fluid motion the future knight, using both hands, then thrust his weapon through the remnants of the table and into the other wretched beast. It too, like its horrid companion, fell to the ground...dead. Mary...free at last from the tormenting voice...looked up briefly at the three men in the room and, as her precious son knelt beside her...she fainted into his arms.

Meanwhile, one hundred meters distant, and at the same exact moment, another anointed sword was piercing the now unprotected flesh of a mighty Muth. The mass murderer raised its hellish head one final time and let out a roar of disbelief as the blade of Sir Peter successfully rent the barrier between the chambers of blood and fire. The two vile substances explosively mingled and the unbeatable Muth...conqueror of all things human...made the earth tremble as its huge, weighty, lifeless carcass bowed, forever, before the emblem of the king.

Chapter IV

Before the prisoner can be free
The prison walls his eyes must see.

Mary, using a pair of dry dish rags (lovingly decorated by her son), carefully lifted the heavy copper kettle from the hearth and poured boiling hot water over the dinner dishes that rested in the bottom of a large porcelain basin. As she returned the half-empty kettle to its place of warmth, she turned to see the last wisps of steam rising from the wares. "It reminds me of the river," she whispered, and her mind traveled back to the day of *her* release.

* * *

"Hurry now!" the somewhat gruff commands of the older knight—even though he had just risked his life for their sake—didn't quite sit well with Mary who considered herself, though poor, a woman proper in the ways of etiquette. Of course, she didn't understand that the experienced warrior had seen more than one instance when the initial victory was followed by near calamity. Indeed, they wouldn't be safe until they were at the river's edge.

"How's Alexander?" Peter nearly shouted as he led them a different way back, which involved, at times, cutting through the underbrush which lay in their path.

"He's fading quickly," replied John, as he and Fren supported the semiconscious farmer.

"We're nearly there," uttered the trail-blazer, and with a final swipe of his sword…the river appeared before them.

"It always seems much closer on the way back," said John as he and Fren lay Alexander down for a moment's rest.

"Yes…" said Peter thoughtfully, reaching down to cup some of the crystal flow in his hand to take to the injured party. "The truth is…" he continued, as he gave Alexander a much needed drink—which seemed, amazingly, to the eyes of Fren and Mary—to effect an immediate partial strengthening of their loved one, "…the river is never that far away from those who seek it."

Rushing, roaring, restless wave
Brings freedom to the dragon slave.

The Living River: It had been Peter, some months before, who had told a weeping Mary about its existence. He, dressed in his knightly attire, had been walking the countryside proclaiming another kingdom where the dragons did *not* rule. In his journey he happened across this portly, round-faced farmer's wife…weeping over, of all things, a family pet—killed, so it appeared—by a Shachath's tail.

"Why?" she asked as she wept, cradling the poor dog's lifeless body (it was some sort of collie mix) as she rocked back and forth in an unfenced field used for grazing. "…that beast went out of its way to do this…just when you love something…*they* come and take it away."

It was this impromptu meeting that opened the door for the knight to show some kindness and tell this family about another life they could have—a life not dominated by dread and fear. And it was this encounter, along with many more, that convinced them that they must try to reach the river.

* * *

For a moment, as Sir Peter was preparing to enter the water (a procedure which involved strapping the shield and sword to one's back), John gazed at the three weary escapees who, sitting on a small patch of ragweed surrounded by purplish thistles, were taking in the sight and sounds of the Living River.

"Look how calm it is," uttered Mary, marveling at the smooth glistening iridescent water that seemed unaffected by the breeze that gently swayed the trees behind her. And, although the sun was now high into its midday flight—a velvet white mist, like an early-morning fog, seemed to hover above the midpoint—obscuring the view of the other side. "Is that mist always there?" she said softly to no one in particular and then, as if awakened... "Listen!...I hear the sound of a flood! Quick! Let's get back before we're swept away!" The matron and her family, having experienced a destructive deluge before, started to stand and retreat.

"Mary..." The voice...though not much louder than a whisper...was easily heard above the oncoming torrent and...inexplicably...something in that gentle word immediately disarmed the fear that had so suddenly gripped them. Alexander and his haggard family paused to look at one another, and then slowly turned to face their rescuers, who were now both standing heart high in the tranquil water—an arm's length from shore.

"There's nothing to fear here," continued Peter in a comforting fatherly-like voice that was so much different than his barking commands of mere moments before. "Only evil need dread this place..." he said, raising a hand of invitation. "Come...take a drink."

"But..." Alexander stammered, "the flood!"

"Yes." Peter smiled, resisting the temptation to laugh. "Yes, there is a flood, a mighty torrent, and wave upon wave of purposeful power. But, as I told you before, this river finds its birth in the crystal sea. And this," he continued, as he swept his outstretched hand in the direction of the flow, "is the path you must take to enter the land of our king." He paused a moment as the sound of the great unseen force seemed to pass immediately behind them, yet, as far as could be observed...the water remained still...and only the mist seemed to dance as the intangible *something* rushed by.

Mary, Fren, and finally Alexander—reassured by the words of the knight and the decreasing sounds of the flood—slowly inched their way over to the beautiful flowered bank which stood only a hand's breadth above the water.

—It should be noted that along the dragon side of things there was approximately a six meter clearing that ran the length of the river and, as one approached the flow, the ground cover became more agreeable. Thus, by the river—flowers. By the forest—thistles.—

Each, now on hands and knees, paused and looked up at the warriors for an encouraging nod...and then, individually, each looked into their own reflection as they slowly reached down to touch the mysterious shimmering plane.

"Why…I've never seen a mirror with such clarity," Mary whispered to herself as her aging brown eyes focused on the sharp picture in the river beneath. She paused a moment, taking special note of the white stormless clouds—blissfully sailing high above—that framed her portrait in the wondrously still water. Then she turned to her own reflection. She sighed as she beheld her once black hair, now retreating before an onslaught of gray. The skin on her face—once delicate and smooth—was now sagging and giving way to the inroads of years and, as she noted the tattered collar of her homespun red and yellow dress…she gasped. For suddenly, the visage in the water transformed to that of a beautiful dark-haired infant…it was her as a baby! And not only this, but she was being cradled in the arms of her long-dead mother. (This cherished parent was a tender sort, hardly beautiful, but possessing the pioneer qualities usually associated with those who wrestle the land.) And as Mary smiled at the memory of this precious loved one, she then saw a pair of pulsing fire-red eyes materializing over the shoulder of her dear mama. A moment later a weeping seven-year-old Mary stood at a graveside…laying a single daisy on the fresh-turned sod.

On and on the visual images of her life progressed. And, for every moment of joy…for every moment of happiness…there was a pair of eyes, or a claw, or a bloody fang interrupting—as if cruelly pruning and harvesting the essence of her very soul. Finally, with tears beginning to well and then quietly overflowing down her reddened cheeks, she saw her current state…but the hideous eyes were still there…pulsing…waiting.

Mary's hand gently touched the water and her reflection disappeared. It had only been a moment—in the very brief span it had taken to reach down for a portion. But, with the drink forgotten, Mary leaned back on her heels and, with her hands to her face, the despair of her heart once again overflowed in great mournful sobs.

"So much pain," John, moved with compassion, uttered to his mentor as he beheld this tormented soul—and his resolve to help these, and those like them, grew deeper still. And although Fren and Alexander didn't display their grief as openly, it was obvious from their expressions that a great weight was upon them…a weight caused by revelation.

"Mary, Alexander, Fren…look at me." The older warrior, with gentle words and a tender voice, sought to awaken them from the trance. Alexander and Fren looked up, but Mary continued to weep. Finally, after a few moments, Peter moved to the river's edge and softly placed his rugged hands on those of the trembling woman. "Mary," he said, slowly pulling her palms from her swollen eyes. "Mary…it's going to be all right…I need you to hear what I have to say." She reluctantly raised her head and found comfort in the kind expression of the grizzled old knight and, wiping her eyes on the hem of her dress, she nodded that she was ready to listen.

"When I visited you before," Sir Peter began, moving back slowly to stand beside his apprentice, "I told you there was another land…another kingdom…where the dragons do *not* rule. All this is true. But…" he continued, his voice and expression taking on a more deliberate tone, "I needed you to look into these waters to see the depth of your bondage. For, you see," he said, pausing a moment to accentuate this truth, "the evil lord of the dragons does not just rule you…he *owns* you."

An expression of horror quickly appeared on the faces of the three refugees…and Alexander spoke the question… "What do you mean…*own*?"

"I mean," spoke the knight, coming one step closer to the wounded farmer, "that your very soul is not your own. The creatures who have tormented you for so long have merely worked within their rights. They own you…and the branding of that ownership is, even now, on your hearts."

"How? How did this happen? I don't remember any…" Alexander's confusion flowed out in a torrent of words until, at last, Sir Peter raised his open hand for silence.

"It happened long ago," the warrior began, lowering his arm. "Our race, in an act of treason, sold their souls and their heritage to all that is evil. The chains of that ownership are wound tightly around your spirit, and even death will not bring release. You, of yourself, cannot break the shackles…even if you slay a dragon…your fate remains the same."

"What must we do then?" said Mary, tears again beginning to well. "Why are we here? Surely you didn't bring us to this spot to tell us there is no hope."

"Yes," said Peter, his face and voice displaying the joy of a treasure to be unveiled. "Yes, hope…but much more than this. Truly, I tell you…" he said, raising his bent arms above the water—his hands pressed together as if holding one hundred precious pearls. "Not just hope…but deliverance, freedom, redemption."

At that very moment a whispering from the wood began. It was like the rustling of the autumn leaves or the gentle hum of a busy hive. "What is that?!" Mary blurted out, turning to look towards the dense forest behind them.

"It is the dragons," said John. "They have come to dissuade you from your path. It is as Peter has spoken," said the young one, turning to receive his mentor's approving glance. "Your soul is owned by these evil creatures…you are their prize…and we are considered thieves."

The three, frightened, started to stand, uncertain of what to do. "It's all right," reassured Sir Peter, motioning them to sit back down. "They will come no further. To them, the river is death. But to you…it is *life*. At this point they have only words to woo you. But listen now to a better message that will offer you true liberty."

Alexander, Mary, and Fren all seated themselves once again and paid close attention even as the dragons spoke from the shadows.

"In the distant past," began the teacher, "the Living River coursed freely throughout this region. Not just the blessed flow that you see here…but everywhere. And wherever the river coursed…there was life, beauty, freedom. But the lord of the dragons, through cunning deception, convinced our ancestors to reject the river and it's glorious source…the God of the crystal sea. And, when these fools boldly declared their rebellion—a great unscalable wall erupted from the earth—separating humankind from the life-giving waters."

"Yes, I've seen it!" uttered Alexander as the knight continued.

"You three have known much of sorrow, and pain, and despair. Your food has been hardship, and your drink…bitter tears. All your lives you have been subject to the cruel and merciless rule of creatures who consider you as nothing more than a crop to be harvested, or a lamb to be slaughtered. But," he emphasized, "if you renounce your allegiance to the dragons, and join yourselves to our great king—the one whose victory caused the Living River to spring forth once again—these waters will bring you release."

"That's it?" said a puzzled Alexander. "Just like that?"

Before another syllable could be uttered…GAWOOSH!!…Fren, excitedly, and in a most ungraceful manner, plunged head first into the river and, as the remnants of the wave dripped off the warriors' helmets, the men in armor gazed at the remaining two—who had the look of utter, open-mouthed surprise on their faces—and then these sober soldiers turned to each other and began laughing uproariously.

"Where's my baby?!" shouted Mary, noticing that Fren had disappeared beneath the surface and now, a good two minutes later, could still not be seen.

"It's all right, good lady," said Peter, striving to retrieve his breath from the extended outburst. "As I told you…" he continued, pausing to wipe the joy induced tears from his eyes, "only evil need fear this river. Your son will pop up any time now."

Sure enough, a moment later up surfaced an exhilarated Fren. He quickly made his way to the bank and said, with childlike enthusiasm, "Mother, Father, I saw the king!...He hugged me!...I saw the king! Oh, Mother...you must come in. I feel different...better...much better!"

"What's this he's saying?" asked a skeptical Alexander. "What does he mean—he saw the king?"

"As I told you before," spoke the old knight, using two burly hands to squeeze the remnants of the wave from his beard, "this is the *Living River*. Although we speak of it as merely a transport of water—it is not made of the stuff you pull from a well. No," he continued, fluffing the matted red bush with an outward flicking motion, "it comes from the Crystal Sea...which comes from the God of all. I figure it's made of spiritual stuff...although I try not to overanalyze things. I just know it brings life, and will..." he said, having finished primping and now looking directly at the farmer, "...bring *you* release from those chains that hold you still."

"You didn't answer my question," Alexander replied, somewhat annoyed. "What does Fren mean...he saw the king?"

"Oh yes," Peter continued, as Fren, his face beaming with delight, made his way to the knight and flopped his arm on the warrior's shoulder, "since this flow comes from an eternal source...it has different attributes than that of any river you've ever known. For instance...have you noticed that my companion, young..." he paused and gave his fellow laborer a mischievous glance, "...I mean, have you noticed that John and I, though of different heights, seem to be equal in these waters?"

Alexander took a closer look and, sure enough, Sir Peter, John, and even Fren, though of different stature (Fren being the tallest, and Peter the shortest), all seemed to be the same height in the tranquil flow. "I assure you," continued Peter, noticing Alexander's puzzled expression, "that we are not standing on different foundations. No, there is a oneness to this place...a commonality I don't quite understand. And not only this," he said, pausing to tilt his head slightly to dispel a last remnant of moisture, "but I've been told there are many currents, effects, eddies. So...did Fren see the king?...I believe he did."

"I did," said a smiling Fren, arms folded, with an accentuated nod.

"I'm ready," came a gentle voice from the shore. It was Mary, kneeling, as if in prayer. "I want to come in."

Peter walked to the bank, extended his hand, and asked, "Do you renounce your allegiance to the dragons, and claim the Great King as you sovereign lord?"

The aging farmer's wife, barely hearing the empty promises of the demons behind her, took the hand of the kindly knight, sat down on the flowered edge, and said, "Yes, your king is now my king," and slipped into the water.

Now, those who observed the process would say the dear lady was only under the surface for a few seconds. But, if asked, she would say something like this—"I expected the water to be cold, or hot, or in some way shocking...but it was as if I slipped into an embrace—a loving, all-encompassing welcome. And all the hurts, the pains, the fear and despair...went away. It simply went away. But, it wasn't a decrease in me...no...as the bad departed...a love came in. An unconditional love took residence."

Mary, like her son, rose from the water a new person. From her countenance, Alexander could tell something was different—a weight had been removed. And oh, how he wanted to be free from that which crushed his very soul.

"*Alexander...*" The voice was sweet, enticing, and coming from the wood. "Alexander, don't go. Come back from that place. You don't need that stuff. You're stronger than that. You've always gotten by. No need for help. No need for a handout."

The four in the water looked on as Alexander sat silently with a dazed expression on his face. Shortly after Mary had joined them, Peter had offered his hand and the invitation to the farmer also. But there was a battle going on, and the warriors had seen it before.

"Why is it always the older men who seem to struggle so?" John spoke in a whisper.

"It just seems that way, John," said Peter, standing, his arms crossed, watching. "I've seen all types hesitate at the edge of freedom. But yes, it does seem a greater struggle for the male of our species."

"Is it pride?" asked the younger, also now crossing his arms.

"Yes...that's probably it. It's the source of the original rebellion and," he continued, scratching the whiskers on his chin, "it is still the fertile soil for destruction. Even for those released. Look, he's getting up."

Alexander slowly stood and started to walk towards the dense forest—oblivious to the call of his wife and son.

"*Yes, that's it,*" said the voice. "You don't need that superstition. Come back to the farm *you* built. You can marry again. Have more children. Your line of descendents will grow, prosper. You are a great man, Alexander. We've always seen it. You've passed every test—all your hardship was a test. Those *others* are not worthy…but you are…and now you will be exalted. Come back. That's it." The farmer edged, in half-steps, past the delicate lilies and into the thorny thistles and, just as he came nearly within a talon's reach, he heard, "Well done, faithful one. Come back…and no harm will visit you again."

And, as this last hiss pierced his ear…as the appeals of his loved ones vanished in his self-absorption…he felt something run down, and drip from his fingers. He paused and raised his left hand before his face. There, the crimson flow of his life's blood—having flowed steadily from his gashed shoulder—filled the channels of his rugged palm. And…as he shifted his focus beyond the appendage and into the shadows…he saw the hate-filled eyes…pulsing…waiting.

Alexander slowly shook his head at his own foolishness and, turning his hand so the dragons could see their handiwork, he screamed, "LIARS!" He then turned and quickly hobbled back to the bank where both Sir Peter and John—as Mary and Fren wept for joy—helped the embattled former slave into the healing flow.

The Sathar

Chapter V

The seeds are sown for good and ill.
The ones you tend bring life...or kill.

Like a gentle nudge, the simple sweet melody awakened Mary from her daydream of remembrance. She smiled as she retrieved one of the dishrags and quietly began drying the silver flatware while listening to Fren play his hand-carved wooden flute as he sat in the midst of the garden he loved.

—It should be noted that several years have passed since Mary and family had escaped the Land of the Dragons. Sir Peter, the king's instrument of invitation, has since been called to another task, and John, now *Sir* John, has assumed his mentor's former post as protectorate of this quadrant.—

"Who knew he had such a talent?" she thought while placing another plate in the ornate cupboard nearby. "But, I suppose the river releases us from more than just chains. It also releases the expression of our soul."

The dishes done, Mary gazed out the open window (located just above the basin—and this one *had* glass panes) and began to quietly sing along with the tune.

When I ponder where I've been...lost in sorrow, dead within
And the tears I cried each day...longing for love.

Fren, sitting on a backless pine bench located in the middle of the half-acre garden, turned slightly as the delicate voice of his mother added color and substance to the solitary notes. Together, their outpouring merged as a peaceful canopy over the thatched-roofed dwelling…a canopy that kept something sinister at bay.

* * *

One might compare it to the birth of a foal, or a calf, or even a human. The *womb*, however, that produced *this* offspring was not a place of blessed growth. No…it was a residence of the opposite—a hellish chamber where evil combined with evil, and the thing that oozed from beneath the stone—having forced its gelatinous oversized form through that tiny opening—lay prostrate, breathing great heaving breaths while its members gained strength and its armor solidified. Yes, it was a dragon. But not of the types known beyond the river. None of those fiends would last even a moment in the life-giving torrent—should they be foolish enough to attempt such a thing. No, this creature (known as a *Sathar)* was by invitation—born and nurtured by a disobedient heart and, though it would, if left unchecked, cause destruction to spread in a peaceful valley—it's first order of business—it's overpowering compulsion—was to seek out the human hand that lent its touch. And having found it…to kill.

* * *

As the sun slowly disappeared behind the wall of separation, Alexander, reins in hand, led a weary Jezebel back to her stall for the night. If he had cared to look, a brilliant orange sunset bathed the king's castle (the majestic outline of which rose above the wall) with a most beautiful backlight. But, though in years past he would relish this view of where the river was born (indeed, it was a high point of his day), now it gave him no joy. Rather, it had become merely a reminder that he could labor no more in the field. No more planting and reaping. No more harvest to gather and hoard.

The old farmer opened the door of the twice expanded barn. Years before, when they had first crossed over, they were greeted by a loving community that had provided land—*and* a barn—both of which had been more than adequate for their needs. But, as the orbs were gathered, and his *wisdom* increased, he found that he had a desire for a greater container—a larger vault.

"That's better than you deserve," the miser muttered to the horse as he placed the feedbag roughly on the four-legged slave. "I'll work you twice as hard tomorrow. Those blasted spheres slowed me down today." Jezzy ignored the venom of her owner and began slowly chewing the substandard grain that was her daily ration.

It was quite dark by now and Alexander lit the crude oil lantern that was his guide when daylight waned. At such a time, most men, after a hard day's labor, would be more than content to seek the warmth of home—where the treasures of loving companionship served many purposes—both motivational and medicinal. At one time he himself, with an overflowing heart, had said to his wife and son, "*You* are my wages...of greater worth than gold." But, that was long ago, and now he busied himself in his servitude to *things*.

Mary, having finished her duet, and having summoned her son in for a cup of herbal tea (herbs grown and lovingly tended by Fren), tentatively opened the decoratively carved front door (built for beauty and simple function—unlike the barrier of their previous dwelling which was built as a fortification) and gazed, longingly, across the huge barren expanse that separated the house from the barn. Even at this great distance she could see the solitary yellow flame of the lamp as her husband of so many years scurried about in his delusion. A tear came to her eye and a great sigh escaped her lips, then she felt a man's hand tenderly touch her left shoulder.

"I prayed for father today," said a concerned Fren as Mary turned, quickly wiping the tear with a corner of her apron.

"Yes...I have prayed for him also," she whispered, receiving a hug from her gentle grown child. "We must continue to do so." Then the two went to the main living area, which contained a few comfortable chairs in front of a large granite fireplace and, while a modest blaze melted into warm glowing embers, Mary occupied herself with needlework, while Fren continued to play the melodies of his heart.

Hours had passed since the sun had set. Having meticulously inventoried his goods and counted his coin, the farmer sat down, at last, on an old three-legged stool and began working the pedal that, in turn, caused a vertical, circular, well-worn sharpening stone to rotate. He expertly lay the blade of his half-sword to the wheel and, as had been done for years, he watched with delight as the sparks shot into the darkness. This was his final task before retiring and, in an inexplicable way—it soothed him. Indeed, his eyes widened as the stream of glowing particles attacked the night, and the slight burning aroma given off by stone, steel, and oil also brought him a degree of strange satisfaction and, rubbing his shortened right thumb (reduced by a slaughtering mishap some time back) against the razor edge, he turned to look at the only remaining animal in what had been, at one point, a full and chaotic menagerie.

"You're next," said the farmer coldly as he watched the old mare sleeping in the shadows. "More trouble than you're worth...and I'll find a replacement easy enough." He, feeling a sudden urgency to do the deed tonight, walked over to the animal and began thinking of the logistics of the thing. "No...not now," he reasoned, placing the weapon back in its sheath. "Too messy, here. I'll wait till I get another day's work out of you."

"*Alexander...*" It was a low, raspy voice coming from the dark interior of the massive storehouse. The farmer, startled, placed his right hand on the hilt and with his left he extended the lantern in the direction of the sound.

"Who...who's there?" he stuttered, feeling an ancient wave of dread washing over him—a terrifying emotion associated with an old enemy...an enemy he thought long gone.

"You remember me...don't you, Alexander?" the voice, a bit louder, but somewhat familiar, continued.

"No...no, I don't know you," said the old man. And then, in confusion, "At least I don't *think* I know you." By now the blade had reemerged and the hoarder of things felt compelled to investigate this person who was, by their very presence, threatening *his* treasures. "Who are you!? Why are you here!?" Alexander's voice was stern (not unlike the growl he used when trespassers dared cross his property), yet it also had an element of timidity (he knew this was no ordinary intruder). "What do you want?" By now the ancient miser, having crept past the finely crafted timbers of the original structure (fashioned with love by those who built it), stayed squeezed to the right of the narrow hallway (narrow—so that there would be more room for storage) as he shuffled through the first extension (this add-on, by paid contractors, was well-built but lacked the detailed finery of the first. The last addition, build by Alexander himself [too tight-fisted at that point to pay another] was rough and crude, yet suitable to hold the wares of his obsession). He, holding high his lantern and gripping tightly his slaughtering blade...entered the final chamber of his storehouse.

Alexander knew intimately every part of this place. His *possessing* demanded knowledge, and he *knew* everything that was his. However, in this final room—filled with piles of hoarded grain—as he swung slowly the light…he could see nothing. Yet, there was a presence here…something dark…and the fragrance of sulfur was unmistakable.

In an instant the miser found himself on the unswept barn floor! *Something* had knocked him off his feet and both the knife and the extinguished lantern were out of his frantic reach. "*I'm so sorry,*" said the voice with dripping sarcasm. "Let me help you up." Suddenly, Alexander felt something like a thick solid rope—such as might be used to moor a giant vessel—thrust underneath him. Like a relentless anaconda, this *thing* rushed quickly past and then proceeded to coil tightly around the farmer's rotund middle. In a moment the four-hundred-pound man was dangling upright…yet unable to even scream due to the ever tightening snare.

"Come closer…*Father,*" hissed the creature. Alexander, face and eyes bulging from the pressure, could smell and feel a foul, warm, sulfurous breeze as the words were spoken. "Look upon your child…*Father,*" said the darkness, and then two slanted, egg-shaped eyes—just one meter from the human's terrified and helpless form—began glowing ever brighter as the beast took in great quantities of fire-enriching oxygen.

Alexander, barely conscious, stared in horror as the creature paused, turned its head, and then, with a violent forward thrust, spewed a geyser of blue and yellow flame into a great heap of the farmer's precious grain. The fuel, made of some sort of flammable gel, stuck to the target and burned fiercely.

The old man, seeing what he cherished destroyed…squirmed wildly. Then, with hatred—seeming to forget his precarious position—he turned to face the beast. But, before he could gather even the enormous amount of strength necessary to whimper, his mouth opened in disbelief as he gazed upon his conqueror.

"Don't you recognize me…Father?" hissed the monster, flaming spittle dripping from its horrid jaws.

—Now, Alexander had observed many dragons before. But this *thing* was like none he had ever seen. Larger than a Ganab—though smaller than the Shachath and Muth—it seemed, somehow, to have the characteristics of all three—the cunning and conversation of the Ganab, the armor and flame of a Muth and, clearly, the propensity for destruction of the third. But, as he had sadly experienced, this one had a tail that seemed longer and more deft and deadly than those of the others and, along with its most disturbing blood-red hue—there was something *so* familial about this murderer.—

The creature, before stoking its furnace for another blast, saw the question on Alexander's now discolored face. The dragon lifted its elongated snout to the ceiling and laughed even as he raised the old troll high to the rafters and then threw him violently down in the direction of the door. The farmer, so infirm to begin with, landed with such force that both ankles shattered against the hard-packed floor. And, in agony, he lay on his side and observed a second blast to yet another gathering of his wealth.

As a terrified Jezebel thrashed in her stall—as ever increasing portions of his beloved *vault* burst into flame—and as burning sections of the roof rained down in a shower of spark and embers…the creature paused a moment in his mayhem and, encircled, yet unharmed by the fire and smoke, spoke again to the dying man.

"Don't you understand…Fool! That it was you who gave me birth?" Alexander, unable to speak, could only motion his head from side to side in desperate denial. "Surely you know," continued the monster, pausing a moment to loose another stream, "surely you know none of my kind can cross the accursed river. But," the dragon raised its teeth skyward and let out a screech of delight, "but…*you*…by your delay and disobedience—you nurtured me. And," the fiend, bringing its foul mouth within an arm's length of the helpless invalid, "I must destroy *all* things which you have touched. *All things that you hold dear.*"

Alexander, ever weaker, closed his eyes…expecting, and half hoping, that the dragon would finish the job he had started.

"Not so fast…Father," chuckled the beast as he picked up the now limp ogre and threw him—with much less force—out the barn door. "I'm saving you for last," he said from within the inferno. "I want you to see everything you love, everything you care about, utterly destroyed before I fill my belly with your bounteous blubber." Alexander, facing the barn—his legs twisted in unnatural positions—could only lay and watch as his life's work, his life's passion—his life!—went up in flames. And, a few moments later, as the walls blackened and started to collapse, he heard the creature laugh one more time—just before a free and unharnessed Jezebel bolted through the door and off into the night.

* * *

Be mindful of remembered dreams
They may be more than what they seem
They may a needful truth convey
So do not quickly throw away

Young John, rock in hand (roughly a ten-pounder, mostly gray with some streaks of white) stood behind a kneeling Sir Peter who, dressed in his frayed wall-building coveralls, was slowly stroking his matted red beard with his left hand, while leaning slightly on a meter-length steel pry bar, held by the right. The boy, nearly nine, and certainly able to carry this load for an extended period of time (after all, he had been the good knight's *mule* for well over a year now, and as such he was intimately acquainted with the tasks of lifting, lugging, laying…and waiting), nevertheless he felt three minutes was definitely long enough to determine a rock placement and, in order to get the *old man* back on track…he let out a little "ahem."

Sir Peter, awakened by the gentle sound, let his left hand drop to his side and, without turning said, "Put the rock down, boy. We're done working for the day."

"Done working?" repeated the youth with surprise. In all the many months that he had toiled for the knight, he had *never* known him to put in less than a ten-hour workday. And here it was, shortly after daybreak, and they were quitting already? "Why, Sir?" he said meekly, hoping against hope that this detour did not lead to an even more unpleasant task.

"Come here, lad," said the burly supervisor in a most soft and uncharacteristic tone. John, a bit wary, slowly bent at the knees (Sir Peter, long ago, had instructed his new beast of burden the proper way to lift and lower things—*"Keep you back straight and lift with your legs. I don't want you to wear out too quickly."*), and set the rock down. He then, hesitantly, inched his way up to the left side of his instructor. And there, midst the other perfectly placed stones, was a shimmering orb.

—It should be understood that John had seen many of these nasty things before. Indeed, one of the tasks of a king's knight (to which John was attached and dutifully followed) was to exhort those in the realm against the incursion of such *seeds* and, when found (well, not really *found*—as if something looked for—but rather discovered in one's ongoing routine), to provide instruction as to their proper disposal. But he had never seen one in his daily attendance to the labors of Sir Peter.—

"It has a certain beauty to it, don't you think, boy?" said Sir Peter, prying the sphere from the wall, causing it to roll and come to rest in the grass nearby.

"I suppose it does," said John, noticing that the green color of the object had a shimmering movement to it—as if it were somehow alive. However, with a slight change in wind direction, the apprentice added, "Eeww! It stinks!"

"That it does!" bellowed a rising Peter (seeming to take on his former bluster). "Go fetch me the leather glove and the burlap sack, my young refuse remover. We have an appointment with the river."

"Gone so quickly," said John softly to Sir Peter after seeing him effortlessly toss the offending sphere into the crystal flow. "You say it dissolves. But I say it rather vaporizes."

Sir Peter looked down at his observant assistant, who was still transfixed on the spot of disappearance. He then leaned close to the boy's ear and whispered, *"How it's destroyed, I do not know. The important thing…is that it goes."*

A bit startled at the words, the youngster turned to find himself face to face with his smiling, hairy-faced mentor. Sir Peter stood upright and then, placing a hand on the boy's shoulder (a sign of affection he usually reserved for his horse), he said, "I want to spend time in the presence of the king today. Come along, my young pilgrim."

At the sound of their destination, all of John's foreboding took flight. To spend time in the king's presence, John had learned, was a delightful place to be and, strangely, when one determined to go there…the journey, though on a narrow straight path, was really quite short.

"Isn't it funny, Sir?" offered the apprentice, trying to dislodge the somewhat grim expression from his master's face.

"Hmmm? What's that?" said the knight, looking down at the boy (who was taking oversized steps to keep up with the elder's lumbering gate).

"Isn't it funny, that no matter how far we seem to be from the king's castle…it seems only a very short time till we reach it?"

Sir Peter, upon digestion of the youngster's words, slowed his pace, smiled down on the lad, and again placed one of his calloused hands on a shoulder.

"Young John," he said, in a rather fatherly tone.

"Yes, Sir."

"Do you remember when you reached the age of knowing?" (Basically, the age of knowing is that point in a child's development when the abstracts of good and evil, right and wrong, become tangible entities, not just indistinguishable labels thrown at them upon certain actions. Since each individual develops at a different rate...the age of such revelation is also different.)

"Yes, Sir...I mean, not exactly. I recall it was several years back, before I became your apprentice, and on one of my family's weekly visits to the river—which were normally delightful—well, it became quite distressful."

"What do you mean, distressful?" said the elder, somewhat amused at John's attempt at adult speech.

"I mean, Sir, that when I gazed upon my reflection—as I had done many times before—I saw something this time that was dark and wrong. I also saw a pair of glowing red eyes. It was as if there was more to me than just me...if that makes any sense."

"Then what happened, my young orator?"

John didn't know what *orator* meant, but he continued anyway. "Well, my parents explained to me that, on the inside, there was the mark, or brand, of the Lord of the Dragons. Which meant I belonged to him! And let me tell you...I didn't like that at all!"

"And what else?"

"Well, if that wasn't bad enough..." by this time John's formality had evaporated and he began expressing himself with descriptive arm movements to accentuate the dialogue—much to Sir Peter's amusement and growing affection, "...my parents said there was *nothing* they could do to help me...nothing! Well, let me tell you (a much repeated phrase of the lad in his earlier years), I cried like a baby. There I was, doomed to have my soul collected by some dragon...and there was nothing they could do."

"So...?" Peter stopped, faced the speaker, crossed his arms and gave the boy a sincere look of interest.

"Well...well," John stammered a bit, regaining a little of his subservient composure, "I learned about the king, and the river, and how the enemy was defeated..." and then, softly, "...and then I said I wanted no part of that dragon, and that I wanted only to follow the king."

"And...?"

"And I dipped in the river—which I had done many times before—but this time I came back up different somehow and—and this is the best part!—that dragon thing was gone from the inside."

"Yes," said Sir Peter thoughtfully, placing his right palm upon John's shaggy head and jostling the blond nest approvingly. "And it was the same for me."

"The same for you?" asked the boy, looking up at his teacher as they continued walking.

"Yes, the same for me, though I was a little older, and I came from beyond the river."

"No kidding!" said John excitedly. For not only was he learning a little of his benefactor's past (of which, up until this time, he knew next to nothing), but Sir Peter actually came from *beyond* the river! (a place the youngster knew of—but had never gone—and was therefore quite curious about). "Tell me about the land beyond the river…please, Sir."

"In the coming years, my young professor, you will accompany me to the other side to try and rescue those who are in the dragon's grasp. I will teach you much before then. But, for now…" he continued, trying not to ramble, as was his habit, "…do you recall the odor of that green sphere?"

"Yes…it was awful," John replied, along with a grimace to drive home the point.

"Well, my boy, that foul smell is everywhere in the land beyond the river."

"Everywhere?"

"Yes, even in the soil and the food and the water drawn from the well."

"Yuck!"

"Yes…yuck, indeed. However, let me tell you the source of that ill wind." Sir Peter stopped and gazed seriously at the child. "It is the very essence of the rebellion that brought the original curse that banished our kind. It is the stuff that dragons are made of, and," pausing for a moment, as if contemplating whether he wanted to open this door or not, "it is the stuff, when joined with the human will, that must bring death. On the other side of the river…it is everywhere, in everything. Those who exist there have it imbedded in their soul. Only the river can free them. And, my young citizen, even those born on *this* side—as you know from experience—even here, the seed of rebellion has taken residence in each newborn's heart. And only…*only* the conscious acknowledgement of the root—the forsaking of the same—and the cleaving to our king…" Peter authoritatively raised his right hand to eye level, index finger extended (a sure sign of an important point—usually accompanied by a volume increase), "…only this can bring release!"

The two stared at one another for a moment longer, then the elder took the lead once more.

"But what of the orbs?" said John, hurrying to catch up. "You were going to tell me about the orbs."

"Yes, that's right," said the knight, slowing a bit for the continued lecture. "Well…as I said before…on the other side of the river that foul stench is everywhere. But here, in this realm, where the king rules supreme…only the orbs (or their offspring—a subject Sir Peter chose not to discuss at this time) give off the odor of rebellion."

"But where do they come from? Didn't you say the king rules this place?"

"Yes, my young inquisitor. But as I've already said, those who dwell here (aside from the freshly born, of course) do so by choice. And those smelly spheres are a result of *choice*."

"Choice? Who would choose to have such nasty things?" John, who was beginning to feel more and more comfortable in this dialogue with his superior, continued with a touch of sarcasm. "Did *you* choose to have that ball of stink placed in the wall you were building today?"

The two walked on for a good half minute and the question that John thought rhetorical…became anything but.

"Yes…I suppose I did choose," said Sir Peter, somewhat subdued, but not slacking in his pace and continuing to gaze straight ahead.

The nine-year-old, going on thirty, grabbed the crook of Sir Peter's arm and proceeded to pull and stop at the same time. "What do you mean, Sir…" he said, looking at the elder's face that was now looking at him, "what do you mean…you did choose?"

The warrior gazed down at this future knight and sighed the sigh of those who are willing to rend their heart for a more intimate walk with another.

"I mean this, my young champion…even though the dragons do not rule here…the seed of their very nature still exists. It is small, and in itself, harmless. But, if someone dare turn their affections away from the king and his God, even for a short time…well, the seed feeds off this rebellion and blooms. That orb, the very one that initiated this needful detour, was fed…" a slight pause—the length of which could be compared to a shield being lowered, "…by me."

It took a moment for this delicate revelation to penetrate the boy's understanding. When it did, Sir Peter again found himself stopped and facing his pupil, whose expression was sad and unsettled—like the long-time owner of a perfect gem, who is told by a jeweler that the *perfect* is, and always has been…flawed.

"What do you mean…*you* fed it?" the child said in a near whisper.

Sir Peter smiled tenderly at the boy while gently turning him back to the path with his strong left arm, which he left draped, lightly, over the lad's downcast shoulders. The two walked on, at a much slower pace. And the now *very human* instructor…concluded the lesson.

"Young John," he began, in a tone both firm, yet clothed with care, "yes, I fed that nasty thing. You see, I, of late, have become quite full of myself. Simply…I had taken the eyes of my affection off the king, and placed them on me." After this statement, a troubled silence let the knight know that the words were not being understood.

"Let me put it another way. As you now know," he continued, "all, born of woman, carry the seed of rebellion. It is treason in waiting. It is the ongoing tainted remnant of our ancestors who rejected the rule of a good God for the enslavement of a deceiving dragon. When we who, through the efforts of our great king, have been freed from the dragon's chains…when we choose again to follow the evil one's ways…"

"Wait a minute," interrupted the boy. "I never saw you following any ol' dragon!"

The two abruptly stopped…again…and the knight, facing his apprentice…*again*…concluded by saying, "My young theologian…you began this inquiry by stating that the way to the king's castle, when one determines to go there…is a short distance. The reason that is so…is because in *this* kingdom…it is in the heart that reality is birthed. It is in the heart that the chains of the dragon are broken when allegiance to the king, by an act of faith and will, is forged. It is in and through the willing heart that the Living River rushes and purges and purifies. And, when someone, such as myself, becomes full of pride…it is in the heart that the offense begins and, if left unchecked, it will grow until the heart…indeed, the very life…is destroyed. That is why, my young seeker, we have turned our hearts to spend time with the king. And," he said, turning the boy to face forward once more, "having done so…we are there."

John's eyes widened as he, with Sir Peter's words still in his ears— and although they had not walked one step during this last exchange— turned to see, not two meters away, the bridge that led to the castle gate. Up until this time, the castle—a grand structure made of some sort of translucent stone that seemed to radiate (though in measured intensity) the very colors of the Crystal Sea—had been clearly seen in the distance. But here, due to the life-giving torrent that violently gushed out from the castle's foundation (the Living River), the king's residence, though close indeed, was perpetually obscured by a great swirling cloud of mist that continually enveloped the simple structure that offered access, on foot, for those seeking audience.

Of this bridge, *homely* is the word that quite adequately describes its appearance. Made of simple hand-hewn timbers connected by crude iron nails, this transport was only wide enough for one individual at a time. Yet, as young John was beginning to grasp, this bridge, though narrow, and only one in number, could somehow be traversed by a myriad—at the same time! It was as if each individual had his *own* bridge to cross. Rather confusing if you chose to think about it. Which is why the future dragon-slayer chose not to...at least not now.

Invigorating...that might be one of the words a grown-up would use to describe what was felt when walking on the bridge towards the castle. But, if asked, John would say it was just *Wow*! For, along with the coolness of the spray, came a joyful refreshing to the soul and, along with the roar of the river below, an overwhelming chorus of voices seemed to both sing blessings and, at the same time—shout praise. It was as if all creation—once held in bitter, dark, heavy bondage—was, perpetually, at this moment...released!

As the boy exited the cloud on the other side of the bridge he saw, just ahead, Sir Peter facing and smiling at him. "C'mon, lad," uttered the older, with a touch of childlike wonder in his voice, "let's go to the inner parts of this place and watch our beloved king hold court."

—It should be noted here that *all* citizens of the realm had access to the enormous hall (which will be described in greater detail later) where the king carried on the business of rulership. Before entering this inner chamber, however, one had to first pass through a great outer courtyard filled with all sorts of beautiful growing things. Of particular interest were the dazzling lilies, and the breath-taking roses, of which there were many. And, before this outer court, one had to pass through the towering arched gate that provided the only access on this side of the enormous outer wall. This gate (ten times a man's height, and wide enough for a multitude) was never closed.

Young John and Sir Peter turned towards the castle to walk the short distance from the polished gold platform (where the bridge on this side was anchored) to the gate previously mentioned. It was—to their horror—blocked! And this barrier that repelled them—this intruder that kept them from audience with their blessed king—was not made of steel, or stone, or ordinary brick. No...this thing seemed very much like the wall of separation that already encircled those beyond the river and, indeed, used to occupy *this* area before the day of release. It was cold...and black as pitch...and to touch it...was to touch something akin to a gravestone.

"Oh no!" cried the child, as Sir Peter, no less anxious, began pounding on the heartless barrier as he yelled, "Let us in! Let us in!" and finally, with his sword hand clenched in a fist, he continued to administer powerful, yet ineffectual blows, as he shouted the words in a helpless cadence. "Let us in! Let us in! LET…US…IN!!"

* * *

It was only a half-meter fall, but the confusion of being awakened in such a rude manner caused the already exhausted knight to begin a rather jerky defensive move that resulted in a face-first encounter with the somewhat unkempt stone floor. As Sir John slowly pushed himself up from this embarrassing recline, he heard again the pounding that had invaded his dream.

"Sir John!…Help!…A dragon!…My father is hurt!" It was the familiar voice of Fredrick, yelling at the door as he pounded with both hands. Quickly the knight let in the distraught neighbor and, as he put on his armor and readied his sword, he listened intently as Fren recounted what events had preceded this visit.

"Mother and I were in the house," he gasped, still out of breath from his twenty-minute run. "Father was in the barn, like always. We smelled something terrible…like sulfur…like the dragons from before…" By now John had untied and saddled his powerful plow horse, named Amethyst (not a common name for a black and brown gelding, but this particular beast of burden had one sightless eye that displayed a most interesting violet hue) and, with the two men aboard, this capable creature galloped off in the direction of the ominous amber glow in the distance.

Only, only, only…you. Love forever, love so true…

Mary, tears streaming down her face, stroked the thin gray fibers—all that remained of Alexander's once thick and wavy auburn hair, and continued to sing the love song *he* had written to her shortly after crossing the blessed river, just a few years before.

Who can make an old heart new…only, only, only…you.

She, continuing her lullaby, gently cradled the head of her disfigured and dying husband. He, unnaturally bent and twisted due to his injuries—along with the disease associated with continual contact with the orbs—was oblivious to the woman who so lovingly tended to him while his possessions were, one by one, destroyed.

Loneliness…was all my life…

The dragon, having incinerated the great hulking vault—the barn—was now, methodically, ripping, tearing, and burning the elegant home that Alexander had built to house his former treasures…his family.

Who could make this old heart new?

The monster, finishing the structure with a final burst of gelatinous fire and a wall-toppling swipe of its powerful tail, turned to seek its father's face. Intending, of course, to kill and eat this ogre in a tortuously slow process.

Only, only, only…you…

The beast, still standing amidst the flames of the former dwelling, shuddered as the music of the matron reached its ears. Indeed, it had been this soothing sound that had repelled him as he made his way earlier. For, although it acted as a balm for a human soul—it had just the opposite effect on a dragon. "I can't stand that horrid chatter!" he bellowed. "Shut up!" he screeched, along with a litany of curses that need no repeating.

Now our years are old and gray…

Mary continued the song, oblivious to the murderer's threatening. She had had enough of fear in her lifetime and was determined not to have it rule her ending. She gently placed her hands on Alexander's ulcerous cheeks and turned his head so that their eyes could meet.

Counting down our final days…

Alexander, having seen the *things* that had possessed *him*…consumed— tried to focus on the figure above him. It had been so long since he had felt a human touch…so long. And, as the pain in his body began to wane due to shock and injury…the pain in his heart became acute. Like the near-frozen limb as it starts to warm…the sorrow that he had caused this precious woman, the love of his life, began to emerge and gush out of him in great uncontrollable waves. Meanwhile, the dragon—who could not—due to the repulsive sound—bear to get close enough to chew—began to stoke its inner fire for a long-distance kill.

With one more hour…what would I do?…

The demon, only five meters away, let loose his fiery venom to fulfill his hellish mission. The roar of the blast overpowered the sweet sounds of the lady and, as the beast recoiled and returned to view its handiwork…he screeched in rage. For there, between he and his fill—stood Sir John—shield raised, sword ready.

The next few moments were a blur of violent intensity. This *thing* was no Muth and, although it contained a conglomeration of evil expertise, the knight—himself overcome with righteous fury—ran to the creature's very heart and began mercilessly hacking at the mark. The monster, shocked at such a course, flailed wildly at this intruder. But *every* weapon of his attack…the tooth…the claw…the tail…were met with the razor sharp, hardened steel of the sword commissioned by the Great King. And, as the beast—roaring, screeching, hissing—was dismembered one piece at a time…Mary, her tears mingling with those of her beloved husband…finished the song.

I'd spend it, dear, with only you…I'd spend it dear with only you…

Alexander, who had joined his wife in mouthing these final syllables, now averted his eyes to see this royal knight—whom he had so often cursed—whom he had ignored, week after week—fighting on behalf of he and his family. The tears of repentance, so long in coming, finally joined those that had flowed for his wife. He had rebelled against the king…he had betrayed his family…and now he would die. And, as he felt his strength slowly draining…he saw his precious son, Fren, standing in the distance…weeping.

A few moments later the blade of the king pierced the heart of the monster and, as it gurgled in low diminishing repulsive tones, the weary knight walked over to the aged couple. John gently placed the blade of his sword in the charred earth and leaned upon it as he knelt, on one knee, beside the fading Alexander. The knight removed his helmet and quickly put his ear close as the dying man strained to speak two things.

"For…forgive…me," he whispered, as more tears flowed and, grabbing weakly the knight's sleeve, he wheezed, "Please…please…take me…take me…to the…river."

The Sower

Chapter VI

Beware the wing that beats at night.
Its drink is fear; its food is fright.

Like a great diving bird of prey, the Sower plummeted earthward in, what appeared, a suicidal freefall. From his lofty perch—an outcropping near the very top of what many humans called *Dragon Peak* (The tallest, and most ominous pinnacle in a jagged range that seemed, in some degree or other, to extend throughout the whole Earth. This particular mount was rumored to be the primary dwelling place of the Lord of the Dragons and, curiously, although *not* of volcanic origin, sulfurous fumes, nevertheless, seemed to perpetually ooze from the cracks and crevices)—the winged demon, on his nightly run, would begin by standing on the edge of his habitat (a solid, and mostly level granite ledge, where this monster's taloned feet had worn indentations—so long had he engaged in this practice), fold his huge wings close behind him (except for the very tips, which were used for small navigational adjustments), and simply lean forward. In a moment his rigid body would be just inches from the sheer rock face, dropping like the proverbial stone until, a split second before splattering on the rocks below (an end many had prayed for, no doubt), he'd quickly extend his grotesque air-catching membranes and swoop, unharmed, into the innocent night sky. And, although a casual observer might consider this a spectacular display, when one contemplates that this run was just the latest in a half million—then such mind-boggling precision is quite understandable.

At a dizzying speed the flying dragon skimmed just above the tips of the tall mutated evergreens that sprouted near the base of the accursed mount. These, like everything associated with the evil, were twisted into grotesque shapes—far from the stately beauty that was their intended design. Then, angling upward, the Sower would brace for the turbulence experienced when crossing—even though he flew high above—the Living River. Curiously…in the beginning, this invisible barrier, and the subsequent buffeting associated with flying over enemy territory, nearly prevented a seed run of any kind. Now, after a millennia of work, it seemed the air currents above the flow were just as tumultuous, but the sky covering the land enclosed by the ribbon…this seemed more placid…weaker…anemic. Indeed, the demon imagined himself, some day, walking the lanes and byways of the wretched kingdom…devouring, at will, all those he called *traitors.* "But," he thought to himself as he reached into the worn leather pouch (the latest of many) and let the first fistful of poison be carried downward by gravity and a midnight breeze, "I dare not set foot upon that soil too quickly. I've never seen one of my kind survive such an incursion…and I shall not be so careless as to be numbered among *those* fools."

Slowly, in a well-established pattern, the Sower—his huge taught-skinned ashen wings beating with great pulsing downward thrusts—crisscrossed the blessed land and let his wares take flight. In the early years—just after the establishment of this *horrible hemorrhage* (one of the many phrases this creature used to describe the area of his attack)—the *seeds*, the vast majority, anyway, would encounter an unseen resistance and burn up long before reaching the earth. Indeed, the *shield* (as good a name as any) previously compelled this rabid destroyer to maintain such a height that houses appeared as dust, and humans could not be seen at all. But now, after so much toil, the covering had been diminished to such an extent that the Sower could make out the facial expressions of the prey, and oh how he wished he could cross that chasm—that he could make that final progression from *sight*…to *bite.*

On and on he flew…and on and on he sowed. Past the boundary of the river (where virtually *all* the droppings were quickly incinerated—a fact he had once pointed out to his Lord—whereupon he received a blow that, when he awakened, convinced this winged monster to *never* openly question his master again). Past the massive interior of the kingdom—originally somewhat barren and merely a place to be visited for a brief exploitation of the earth, but—and the Sower rejoiced at this—in recent centuries many of the treasure seekers stayed and now there abounded cities and towns, and each of these were replete with great stone universities, cathedrals, and palaces and, even though this *bounteous blister* (the land enclosed by the river, whom the Great King referred to as *Ekklesia*) was huge, it was dwarfed—a thousandfold—by the area still under darkness. And, as the Sower, having flown some hours—his muscles of flight beginning to ache and his belly complaining for another human treat—he, one final time, reached deep into the vile bag to scoop out the last putrid remnants to let fly on that acreage which ran adjacent to the castle of his enemy.

This mighty fortress, made of some sort of radiant stone, appeared long ago, when his master was defeated. It separated the Dark Wall as a sword might displace an opponent's ribs, and oh, how this demon wished it were gone. Of the Wall, from which the castle so rudely protruded, it should be noted that its color was that of the grave. Its texture was smooth, like a serpent's belly and, though it had been tried countless times before, this barrier could not be breached by man *or* dragon. And beyond all this, even though the Sower was capable of flying nearly into the stratosphere, he had never been able to peer *over* it. Indeed, it always seemed just beyond his reach. Only the reflection on the clouds gave testimony to the sea beyond…vexing him with a constant, eternal…taunting.

"How I hate him!" the flying demon seethed, watching every molecule of this last discharge quickly vaporize as it encountered the huge billows of mist that always obscured the castle entrance. The Sower hovered, growled, and then quickly turned, not wanting to get too close to the shimmering castle walls that were, of themselves, poisonous to his kind. He proceeded north— (though not exact by degree, Dragon Peak lay roughly due east, the king's castle—due west)—the quickest route to his Lord's domain and, as he had hoped, he saw, far below, a pair of the foolish crossing the Living River to spend time in the Land of the Dragons. Upon closer scrutiny he discerned they were definitely *not* knights, and although their flesh would not be quite as satisfying as his usual fare (their souls belonging to the enemy), they would serve, rather nicely, as an appetizer.

Sure of his course (he had done this many times before), the murderer ceased his flapping and glided gently to a spot just beyond the forest line. A few minutes passed, and then two horrifying screams were heard, pleading. A moment later, one wounded human dove back into the river. And the other?…His silhouette was last seen writhing in pain against the backdrop of a starlit sky, held, mercilessly, in the talons of a winged dragon.

Chapter VII

Real love transcends the tie of skin.
The heart is where the bond begins.

"Tell me again, Father," said the voice, tinged with a bit of playful mischief, "why is it that you work the soil?"

Sir John, from the waist down covered in sticky, dark brown mud, slowly turned his head to the right and gave a squinty-eyed glower to his adopted son, also likewise covered...Albert. The two, along with the valiant efforts of Sir John's horse, Amethyst, were struggling to remove a rather large portion of an old maple tree that had rudely chosen to fall across part of the good knight's corn field. It was nearly time for planting and though the soil was a bit damp (Ha!), the thing had to go. Up until this moment the laborers had spent some days sawing and removing much of the giant, but now the largest, most obstinate member remained and, with a stout rope secured to the gelding's rig, the threesome combined to give one more united...umph!

"It...(grunt)...keeps...(grunt)...me...(large grunt)...grounded!" the knight sputtered as the log gave way and its quick release sent him splattering to earth and, as he slowly arose—now *completely* covered in goo—he put his hands on his hips, shook his head, and grinned as he saw Amethyst, log in tow, and Albert to one side, reins in hand...laughing.

Several years have passed since the incident with Alexander's *sin child*. The poor man died shortly thereafter, but had made his peace with God. His error, however, as is so often the case, affected more than just the offender. The fallout from his folly left an aging widow and dependent son. These, thankfully, were immediately taken in by their compassionate overseer…Sir John.

It wasn't long after this family extension (John now referred to Mary as *Mother,* and Fren as *brother*), that Sir Peter stopped by with a young injured lad. The ten-year-old was all that remained of a family of five. The elder knight had fought courageously to deliver them from the dragons, but all save this child had died in the struggle. And he, gravely injured by a Shachath's tail, had received a head wound that would result in a partial paralysis of the face. When he smiled, only one side would respond, but the twinkle in his eyes more than made up for the showing of teeth. For it was through these soft, blue-green windows that the heart was revealed…a heart noble, brave, and true.

As John slowly plodded back to the simple home he had painstakingly constructed years before, he waved to his *son* who, having released the grateful Amethyst to a nearby field, was running to intercept his adopted father as the knight made a straight course towards the dwelling.

"He leaps like a deer before the hounds," thought the elder as the fifteen-year-old bounded towards him, seemingly unhindered by the pounds of mud caked onto his olive-green coveralls and, as the warrior played the part of one unsuspecting (knowing full well that the boy would strive to tackle his "Pop" for an additional dose of dirt), he, in the blinding quickness of memory, scrolled the scenes that had led to the boy's adoption…

* * *

"Will he live?" whispered Mary, as she gently dabbed the ten-year-old's brow as the boy, unconscious, breathed in shallow, irregular breaths.

"Yes," said Sir Peter, holding his helmet in his left hand while combing back his matted red and gray hair with the fingers of his right. "I believe he will."

"You should have had me come with you," said John, kneeling beside the lad, tending to his other injuries.

"No, John. Your place is here. Besides," Peter continued, pausing a moment to lean, gingerly, into a waiting wicker chair, "besides, I was joined by one of the nobles."

"Oh…" John responded, with an affirmative head nod. He knew that by *nobles*, Peter was referring to some of the more polished knights who—contrary to the simplicity of the king's ways—preferred the lance to the sword, and chose encumbering full-body armor to the less restrictive protection prescribed by their Lord. To be fair, many of these were zealous and loyal to the king but, somewhere along the line, they had been caught up in the attention they, as knights, received (a natural progression considering their *calling* was to lead and defend) and began—as they were instructed by other like-minded warriors—to expect the pomp and privileges lavished upon those of their kind [more on this later].

"He was able enough, I suppose," said the elder knight as Fren handed him a glass of refreshment. "There was only one Muth and a pair of Shachaths about (Shachaths—the *in-between* of the Earth Walkers—less mass than a Muth, more than a Ganab—usually of a dark-green hue—like pond scum, and specializing in the destruction of *things* [both living and non], either by force, fire, or disease [of which they reeked]. In the grand scheme of terror, these dragons were like the husbandman—pruning the crop for a better yield.) and my partner was, rather ably I might add, disposing of one with that long pointy stick."

"But," interrupted John (knowing full well that the *one* of which his mentor spoke was a Shachath, as the *lance* is virtually useless against a Muth), "while he was doing *that* the other was destroying what you came after."

Sir Peter took another sip, wiped his lips with his left hand, mouthed the words, "Thank you," to Fren (along with a wink)—which made Fredrick smile widely (for he *always* sought to please), and continued. "Yes…and no. True, using the lance hinders greatly one's ability when faced with multiple foes, but in this case," a pause as Peter glanced at the boy, whose breathing had become normal, "the lad's father had convinced the family to try and save some of their possessions." John hung his head slightly, shaking it in disbelief. "This one," Peter said, motioning towards the boy with the hand that held the glass, "tried to dissuade and rescue the others." A pause as the scene replayed in his mind. "They were crushed as their home was destroyed…and *he* was flung clear by the beast's thrashing tail. By the time I had finished with the Muth, and with one Shachath dead, and the other in flight, and even though this poor pilgrim had lost much blood…he continued to plead on behalf of his family."

"Poor dear," whispered Mary, tears streaming down her face.

"Yes, he has been through much," said Peter, rising to his feet, preparing to depart. "But he still had the presence of mind, even as I carried him, to make the good confession at the river. Indeed, we went below the waves together and," using both hands to squarely secure the helmet, "I suspect the Lord has preserved this one for a purposeful life." Sir Peter walked to the door, opened it and, before crossing the threshold, turned and said, "Farewell, dear lady and good sir." At this Mary smiled and gave a glancing wave as she continued to tend to the child. Fren then shuffled over to his rescuer and gave him a hug. Then, a moment before closing the door behind him, the elder poked his smiling face back in, looked at his former pupil, and recited a poem… *"So serious was John, about his call, he vowed 'in love' to never fall, but the Lord had decreed a family life…mother, brother, and son, but alas…no wife*. Goodbye, *Papa*."

* * *

Albert was nearly upon him when he snapped back to the present. The agile, two-hundred-pound youth (the boy liked to eat—what teenager doesn't?—but Albert was stout and strong, such was his love for labor, especially farming) leaped with arms extended…envisioning, no doubt, a perfect up-ending of his father. However, Sir John, quite agile himself, merely stopped one step shy of the target area. A surprised look flashed across the youngster's face as he flew, headlong, into the muddy earth…burrowing a good distance.

"I prefer that my furrows run north to south," said Sir John, between deep belly laughs. Albert, still buried, slowly rolled over to reveal he had acquired a striking earth-tone beard on his formerly whiskerless chin. This was too much. Sir John hunched over and began slapping his knee to accentuate each burst of laughter.

Of course, it wasn't long before there was a chorus. A chorus of rollicking guffaws as the two wrestled in the dirt. Which, as usual, ended up with a slow walk back to the house, arms overlapping on one another's shoulders.

"Oh no you don't!" came the warning as the pair neared the entrance. Mary, by now quite silver-haired, but ageless in her persuasion, stood in the doorway—her left hand on hip, and the right pointing towards a stream that ran nearby. "Get your dirty selves down to that steam and don't come back till you're presentable." At this she threw out replacement garments and promptly slammed the hard-wood door. The duo, stopped in their tracks by the onslaught, turned their faces towards one another, whereupon the sight of each produced another round of laughter. After which they did an about-face and, as they headed towards a bath, they heard the distinct sound of the protective front door *bolt* being thrown. (It would, no doubt, take a full inspection before admittance was granted.)

Later, that night, as peace again reigned between the matron and the masses, Albert sat down with his adopted father at the simple circular table (enough for a seating of five) that served as the centerpiece of the living area of this modest dwelling. In front of them the fireplace sported a lazy flame, and off to one side they could hear the gentle clatter of Mary finishing the dinner dishes. As usual, she was engaged in a song of some sort, alternating between humming and verse, and this time, though not always the case, she was following the lead of another…it was the sweet haunting sound of a flute being played in the garden.

"Father," began the boy, taking a drink of hot herbal tea from his oversized checkered mug (a gift given by his new parent when this custom began years before), "tell me again of the Day of Release. I know you've told it a hundred times (both here and at the gatherings), but could you tell it again…please?"

Sir John, elbows on table, cradling his own *cup of fellowship* just below the lips, looked across at his son…a lad, dark of complexion, round of face with curly black shoulder-length hair… "So different than I at that age," he thought briefly before responding. Not referring, of course, to their obvious physical differences, but rather to the direction of the heart. For, when John was Albert's age, he was heavy into his apprenticeship to Sir Peter. His focus was on his *calling*…the calling of a champion…warrior…defender…the high calling of one of the king's knights. And, for the briefest of moments, he felt just the shadow of disappointment. For, as genuine, and pure of heart that Albert was…he leaned not in the direction of his father's vocation. In fact, although he delighted in assisting his parent, he would much rather tend to the mundane tasks of the farm.

John, shaking off the discomfort, lowered the still-steaming cup gently to the polished pine and gazed, with true fatherly affection, at his son (who had since placed his chin upon the backs of his overlapping hands which, along with his muscular forearms, now lay flat against the table) and said, softly, "Very well, my son. Remember with me…the story of our release."

Chapter VIII

From death...new life.
From torment...peace.
When all was lost...he brought release.

Elizabeth, attired in her usual tattered-brown peasant's dress, pounded—as she had for many minutes—against the cold, black, Wall of Separation. In desperate futile unison, hammering with the sides of her now cut and bleeding fists, she leaned her graying head against the barrier and continued, in lessening volume, to ask the same questions she had been uttering from the start—at first screaming—and now as a broken whisper, "When...when...when will you send a deliverer? Why won't you help us? Why..." she whimpered, slumping to her knees, her arms too weak to continue, "...why won't you help us?" And then...only mournful sobs.

As the hot midday sun beat down upon the broken woman, to her right—a hundred meters' distant (a spot, somewhat lower in elevation, and therefore a pooling place for the ever-present defilement that permeated the soil), at the spot of execution (where those condemned by the dragons were publicly run through and left to be feasted upon by the masters), her only son lay dead, his body and soul awaiting consumption by the Ganab that gathered nearby—she suddenly felt a cooling shadow move across her sun-scorched shoulders, offering just the smallest measure of relief.

"There, there," a soothing, fatherly voice purred. "It will be all right, daughter."

Elizabeth, dazed and dehydrated, looked hopefully up and, focusing on the creature above her, she saw, what appeared, as a shimmering being. Angelic, you might say, except for one feature she hadn't noticed...the eyes. The eyes had a pulsing red quality to them.

She, near delirium, asked, "Are you the one? Have you come at last? Have you come to save us from the dragons?"

"Yes," the figure indulged. "I will solve *all* your problems...trust in me...believe in me." The words were like warm honey...easily digested. But there was something unsettling about this *savior* and his next utterance confirmed the presence of the poison. "Worship me!"

The woman slowly raised her right hand to shield herself from the distraction of the sun. Upon doing so she recoiled at the revelation of this *imposter's* eyes.

"I know who you are," she whispered through parched lips, as she, trembling, made herself as small as possible in the place where the wall met the earth. "You're...you're the one who ordered my boy killed."

For a few moments all was still, save the whimpers of the woman and the caustic breathing of the *thing* over her. Then, suddenly, a tail (long, thin, and snake-like in appearance) emerged from behind the creature. The slithering crimson appendage made its way up the woman's side and wrapped quickly around her throat—lifting her to eye-level, where she beheld, face to face, the Lord of the Dragons.

"Have mercy," she gasped as the noose tightened and she struggled, in vain, to loosen it.

"Mercy?" the creature said, its voice taking on a dark cavernous quality. "Yes...I will give you mercy. I am *very* merciful."

The woman, who had clenched her eyelids together in terror after the initial confrontation, opened them slightly as her captor released his grip and she fell hard to the barren soil beneath. She...so very weary...so utterly alone and in agony of heart...watched as the Dragon *King* slowly made his way to the feasting horde who were fighting over the last remnants of her beloved son. Then, as the outer fringe bowed before their leader, she saw him point a claw in her direction. Whereupon two red-faced murderers came stalking, drooling, screeching while bearing their fangs and, just before the fatal slash—she, who had, as a child, seen her father slaughtered in an old riverbed that was legend to be a place where living water once flowed—she, who, as a tender young mother, had held a sick and dying babe as the reflections of a distant and unobtainable sea beckoned her from a midnight sky—she, who had cried day and night as everything she had ever loved was painstakingly defiled and destroyed by the dragons, all the while hoping against hope that the promised warrior knight would someday come—in this last moment before the bloody talon struck, she looked briefly beyond the ravenous pair to see the eyes—the cold and hideous eyes—the eyes that insatiably hungered for so much more than mere flesh and, turning to behold her attackers, she bravely bared her neck and, without emotion whispered, "Yes...death...is...mercy."

* * *

The generation that had walked in fellowship with the God of the Crystal Sea—the generation that knew what it was to lay on the golden shore, and play in the glistening surf, and feel the washing of the waves that spoke a continual chorus... "love...peace...joy." The generation that paused too long to listen to a lie and, having listened—the generation that exchanged truth for terror. It was at that moment—the moment the humans turned their back on the God of the Crystal Sea—that the horrid wall arose. No, not completely at first, but just high enough to be unscalable—just high enough to see the omnipotent walking away—just high enough to hear the last faint whispers of the waves. And, as the realization hit them—as they saw the waters evaporate from the land even as the deception evaporated from the beast, the faintest of sounds was heard from the unseen waves crashing against the wall. And it was from these, as the wall grew ever higher, and the chorus ever fainter, that the promise of a deliverer was birthed, for the waves spoke, "compassion...compassion...compassion."

Soon, the generation that bowed was dead...but the wall remained. The rebellion—much more than a transient thing—was ingrained in the breed. It passed from father to son, and mother to daughter. And since this seed was *not* of the holy God—it produced all that was unholy...murder, deception, lust, pride, arrogance, and an endless list of variations. And just as successive generations did not remember life before the wall, even so they knew nothing of the righteous God and his ways. They only knew the torment of the dragons, and that whatever hope there was—hope to live free from fear and pain and eternal bondage—since it could not be found in *this* terrible land—

it must, *must* (if it can be found at all) be found on the other side of that accursed wall.

But, as the countless sought to breech the barrier, they discovered that no weapon born of man could penetrate, or even mar the surface of that which was made of some sort of other-worldly stuff. And, having miserably failed in this (indeed, some humans had spent their whole existence in the attempt [much to the amusement of the dragons who would, in fact, whisper encouragement to the drones as they abandoned all for the hope of even a pinhole]), others sought to climb above and over the thing. These (many, likewise, using one's whole life in the pointless pursuit) would build great towers of wood or masonry, or would use catapults and other gravity defying devices to try and *fly* beyond the reach of the black obstruction. But, as each ultimately discovered (though most never learned from), just when victory was within a finger's touch…the goal would rise still higher. The poor fools didn't realize that the wall was merely a reflection of the rebellion within. If the *sin* was there…the wall was there. And the sin was *always* there.

And so, as long centuries passed, the great throng of humans tried in desperation to erase all knowledge of the wall. Though it stood ever before them, the powerful sought distraction through debauchery and oppression. And the weak, on a smaller scale, did the same. But the dragons—those hate filled creatures who seemed to revel and thrive on all things opposed to the true God that they had betrayed in eons past (another story), these, like malevolent shepherds, would lead the human sheep into paths of maximum torment…all the while plucking and slaughtering, at will, whomever their black hearts desired. But amidst all this…midst the war and famine and plague and fear and endless weeping…when many, in despair, lay prostrate on the foul floor of their living dungeon…when these would look up and, through sullen swollen eyes, see the reflection of the Crystal Sea in the bitter dark night that was their existence…these, prompted by something (they knew not what) within…would plead a prayer for deliverance. And that prayer…that insignificant, poorly worded, ignorant prayer…was heard.

* * *

"Who's this?" rasped the old Shachath (named *Scab*, due to his specialty in dispensing disease that adversely affected the skin), having just finished secreting his vile transparent venom on the door of a tenant farmer's impoverished home (where the terrified family of four cowered behind the barricaded entrance) and having turned to see a warrior of some sort standing defiant—ten meters distant.

"Another fool, no doubt," offered *Rot,* a Ganab who paused from whispering lies through a cracked window. "What are you waiting for? Finish him, you idiot!"

Though rarely do dragons willingly partner in their onslaught of men (at least not in this time period), these two were the exception. Like the jackal and the vulture they often combined their *talents* to totally destroy and consume their two-legged prey and, even as these scions of hell paused to stare at this intruder, the Shachath's poison had slithered its way into the dwelling and the helpless humans inside commenced to scream as the skin of each began to decay.

"Oh, he's a curious one," said the smaller villain as he came along side his larger accomplice. "Look at the armor and...*my*, what a big shield and sword," whispered the deceiver into the simple, fist-sized ear opening of his slime-green cousin. "Be careful, my pungent friend...this insect means business."

The two demons wheezed a laugh between them and then the Shachath took a moment to stoke its inner fire while the Ganab stood poised to add his teeth. Meanwhile, the unknown warrior said nothing, but remained in a fighting stance—sword and shield raised.

A few seconds later the fire was loosed (remembering that Shachaths are less potent in this area, though still quite lethal for most human encounters) but, before the sulfurous fumes had even dissipated, the Ganab, who had been peering expectantly towards the *fool*, heard a sickening thud and gurgle even as he was violently shoved from his position by something large. He turned his head quickly and there, beside him, lay his partner...prone. Indeed, it had been the falling Shachath's body that had so rudely displaced him, and a simple glance down the torso revealed why. The armored stranger, in mid recoil, had made his way up the remnants of the fire and thrust his weapon, effortlessly, through the dragon's heart. The warrior now turned to face the other fiend.

Rot, shaken by this never-before-seen sight, raised up on his hind legs and hissed loudly as the *dragon killer* approached. With blinding quickness the polished blade came down, but instead of extinguishing the demon's spark, only its tail was removed. (The Ganab, fueled by fright, had wasted no time in making his retreat—a retreat to tell his cruel Lord of a *human* like no other.)

79

His weapon sheathed, the knight walked up and over the still-bubbling carcass of the Shachath and made his way to the front entrance of the dwelling. "It's all right," he said, removing his helmet and speaking in a low gentle tone. "It's all right...you can come out."

Inside, the father—an emaciated, balding man of middle age, his arms wrapped around his fear-stricken and dying family as they huddled in a corner—whispered to his weeping wife, "Did you hear that? Someone's at the door." They then heard a gentle knocking. "Whoever it is...they're *knocking* at our door." A pause as all eyes looked at the father, whose own seemed to be fixed on something beyond sight. "I'm going to open it," he said suddenly, standing and beginning to hobble towards the entrance.

"No, Gregory!" the wife screamed, clinging to his old worn and faded garment. "It's a Ganab! I know it is!" The father, unhindered, continued...driven, so it seemed, like a thirsting deer to a distant crystal stream.

"It's all right...come out," the muffled voice continued. "These dragons will harm you no more."

"Please husband! Don't go...we'll all be killed," the wife, sobbing now, begged as she was slowly dragged along for a few feet, then, finally, she released her hold and lay, quaking, on the hard clay floor.

The man quickly removed the simple furniture that had been their protection and, as he placed his right, trembling, hand on the latch, he turned to see his two five-year-olds (sandy-haired fraternal twins, their skin being quickly covered by foul oozing sores) stroking their mother's matted black hair and whispering words of childlike comfort, "It will be all right, Mommy. The man at the door is good...I know he is."

Gregory, afraid, but desperate for even the slightest promise of hope, opened the door a crack (enough for one eye) and peered into the unknown. What greeted him was beyond his wildest expectations, for instead of a small army (what else could drive off a pair of dragons?) there stood a man—a lone solitary man—not unlike himself in appearance—except for one thing...his eyes. His eyes had a certain glimmer that looked familiar. "What does it remind me of?" he puzzled, staring awkwardly for some time as this *deliverer* stood motionless and said nothing. "I know!" the farmer excitedly, but with some foreboding, concluded. "His eyes are as the reflection of the Crystal Sea!"

"Gregory," said the warrior softly to the startled farmer, "lead your family out to me." By now two more sets of small eyes were peering from behind their father at this mysterious savior and, upon hearing this request they attempted to awaken their still-shocked parent by administering some firm tugs to his shirt-tail.

"Daddy!" they said, in near unison as the boy—a fearless inquisitive lad aptly named *Emunah*—wedged himself into the small opening between his Papa's body and the door, even as his sister, *Yachal*—herself accustomed to the role of accomplice—scooted, on hands and knees, out the small porthole afforded by her brother's efforts.

"Wait!" shouted the distraught adult, seeming to snap out of his dazed state as he beheld his beloved heritage, having slipped past him, running into the waiting arms of this smiling (nearly laughing) stranger. Gregory opened the door wide and, with mouth agape, stood, as if anchored in stone, pausing, periodically, to rub his eyes with one hand (not believing what these organs were relaying) while motioning to his now standing wife with the other. She, trembling, and with small, sliding, weighted steps, slowly made her way toward the light and, finally leaving the darkness of their dwelling, she stood at her husband's right side and then, clinging with both hands to his arm, she rested her tired head against his shoulder and joined him in quiet weeping. For there, before them—in the brightness of a new day—they saw the horrible affliction of the dragons—not only the disease, but the very pale of despair that accompanied all in this life—literally melt off the skin and countenance of their joyful children as they sat, one on each knee, of this unknown warrior knight who paused, for only a moment from his *very* important conversation with the youngsters, to look at the adults and say, with words that seemed to contain both power and peace...

"Won't you join us?"

* * *

"Who is he?" The words...quiet, calm, cold...were spoken a mere hand's breadth from the trembling grimacing face of *Rot*, who lay prostrate, his throat feeling the ever-tightening vise-like grip of his master's blood-red talons. The Ganab had understood, before coming into this secluded inner chamber (where his master dined) that audience with the *King*, the Lord of the Dragons, was hazardous at best...but being *uninvited*...this was suicidal. Indeed, the wounded wretch (his barren posterior rudely bleeding all over the royal floor) considered himself quite fortunate that *he* had not already become a part of the dessert menu.

The servant, beginning to convulse from the lack of fluids to the brain and smelling the foul remnants of his master's last meal wash over him, replied in a whisper, "I...don't...know...sire. But (his Lord loosened the hold to speed up the response—he could always kill him later), he's not like any other...(a pause to clear the throat via a muffled hack)."

"You were saying," (the Master, not appreciating the needful hesitation, began closing the gap, once again, between his opposing crimson-stained digits).

Near unconsciousness, *Rot* abridged his message by rasping, with his final ounce of strength the words, "Crystal...Sea."

"What?...What did you say?" The Dragon Lord immediately loosed his grip and instinctively stepped back as if encountering a heretofore hidden danger.

"His eyes, sire..." the Ganab, with gaze still lowered, dared to rise, just enough to massage his throat with his right appendage while balancing with the left. "The look in his eyes was as the reflection of the Crystal Sea."

The Dragon King's countenance changed, in an instant, from demanding to distant. He half stumbled back into his large opulent throne (constructed of human bones—femurs mostly, except the arching crown of the back, which had a large number of forearms—wrists and hands still attached, pointing upward—all painstakingly overlaid with pure gold—rather beautiful if viewed from afar, yet hideous if examined closely) and whispered a nearly forgotten prophecy...*Among the feeble, one shall rise, and conquer all...beware his eyes.*

Rot dared a glance at his silent Lord. He angled his head slightly to one side and upward and, continuing to massage his bleeding throat (that last squeezing had broken the skin), he scanned this creature he feared above all others. As usual, his Lord's visage was hard to pin down—fluctuating, as it were, between creatures described earlier—but he had the added air of uncertainty...a most unsettling condition the Ganab had never observed before. Then, the squinting red eyes of the *King* suddenly opened wide (as if a single course had been decided upon) and the evil one's appearance solidified to that of a great, crimson serpent. The forked tongue of the thing (long, thin, shimmering black) darted in and out between nearly closed ashen lips which were bracketed, on either side, by long, sharp, brilliant white fangs (which seemed to constantly exude a crystal clear venom—a poison, of course, but, for some reason, *humans* seemed ever attracted to the stuff), then he looked at his groveling servant and hissed a command.

"You…" the triangular head of the serpent was now hovering above the trembling, prostrate Ganab, "…my repugnant fellow," the dragon felt the abrasive scales of his master's hind parts rub up against his sides as the huge snake coiled around this helpless morsel. "You…" he continued, flicking his tongue against the tightly shut lids of the near-fainting underling, "my stubby intruder…" the words were more distant, and the constricting sensation was gone. "You…may go."

Rot, not believing what he had just heard, opened one eye and saw, in front of him, jutting out from the throne, the familiar sight of dragon's feet. "I will need many of your kind," his master continued. "Round them up, and bring them here."

* * *

At first it was like the felling of an ancient, immovable Sequoia. *Carnage*, a dragon of the original murderers who adeptly devoured great hordes of the helpless human worms and was, at the time of his end pausing to extinguish, for momentary amusement, the inhabitants of an insignificant hamlet—he was the first of the Muths to tremor the earth with his demise. And, like the original meeting of the giant tree and the axe wielded by man— the destroyer fell as the mysterious warrior's blade hacked its way past the withering flame and the impenetrable scales coming, finally, to the demon's wretched heart. And the expression—the utter bewilderment on the dragon's face—as it tottered and finally succumbed to the draining of its life's blood— was that of utter disbelief.

Disbelief. This, too, described the countenance of each human—those old enough to comprehend anyway—who had just beheld this frightening spectacle. "A Muth…killed by a mere *man*."…This was the thought (with understandable variation) that flashed across the minds of all present and, as the warrior—standing erect beside the fallen mountain—beckoned the people to come, they, like timid doves, slowly made their way to stand before this *deliverer*. And, though all were amazed and rejoiced at the result of the man and the blade…his next action amazed them still more.

"Come…come here," he said with tenderness. "All you who bear the dragon's mark…come to me." Then, sifting slowly through the crowd (many more than just the small hamlet's inhabitants had now come to see this *dragon slayer*) the lame, the blind, the deaf, *the infirm*…indeed, all whose outward diseases displayed exquisitely the curse that *all* bore within…these stood before him…vulnerable, exposed, helpless…drawn by his words…his simple, penetrating words.

The warrior, slowly sweeping his gaze from right to left, silently beheld this wretched semi-circle that now knelt before him. He then, without speech, walked over to the first of the outcasts—an old blind one that the self-righteous called *Parasite*—and raised his dragon-destroying blade high overhead. The crowd gasped in disbelief! Perhaps this was some sort of Ganab, and the Muth merely feigned death to enhance this treachery! Then, after that lingering moment before the blade came down…in the time it took for eyes to widen and chins to drop…the multitude saw the blade turned sideward and the flat part of the steel brought gently down on the afflicted's thinning scalp. It alighted like a feather and remained but an instant. Then, quickly, the warrior went down the row and touched the blade softly to each. And, like a bountiful harvest that appears almost immediately after the seed is planted…one by one the formerly lame, blind, deaf, *diseased*…arose…whole, healed, delivered…and praising the unseen God of the Crystal Sea for sending them a champion.

Well, naturally, one can rightly imagine that such a person would be desperately sought out by the many who despaired under the cruel bondage of the dragons. And so it was. From all quadrants of the land they came—each having a tale of horror and heartache and, though dragon upon wretched dragon tried to defeat this knight…none could. Indeed, most—those foolish enough to test the sword and ignore the history of its flight—were quickly and unceremoniously dispatched. A few, however—usually the Ganab, sometimes a Shachath, but *never* a Muth—would stand back and threaten from afar, all the while reporting their observations to their ever-plotting Master. And what they observed was indeed grievous for the evil one, for not only did the best of his fiends prove powerless against this warrior…it became apparent that this stranger was training *other knights* to bear the armor and wield the blade.

Surprisingly, however, not all humans were delighted at the doings of this *savior*. Many—those accustomed to the rule of the ruthless—who aided the dragons in exacting misery from the masses—feared that their earthly kingdom would be dissolved. These, mainly those numbered among the *strikers* and the *climbers* [as mentioned earlier, there were collections of humans who spent a lifetime in nothing other than seeking a way through {*strikers*} or over {*climbers*} the wall and, although their efforts were useless, they were viewed by many as wise, and holy, and many followed their *rituals* and *rules*, supposing that arduous—though fruitless attempts—somehow equated to piety] sought and found grounds for their disdain in that this impertinent warrior made grandiose statements about the unseen God and—the pinnacle of arrogance—he also claimed that only *he* could breach the horrible barrier.

Indeed, when this warrior knight made such claims, it no longer mattered *how many* dragons were destroyed. For, as they reasoned among themselves, his lofty claims were now eroding "their place and their power" and, although they had for some time been thoroughly in the camp of the *great deceiver* they now, more than ever, gave a ready ear to the Ganab who—with fresh instructions—shadowed, with delicate steps, the leaders among men and planted…carefully…craftily…the poisonous seed given by their master.

* * *

"He must die," rasped the slippery Ganab into the willing human ear.

—The place: a great temple hall where a multitude of *climbers* and *strikers*, dismayed at the actions of the upstart knight, angrily gathered.—

"He must die!" repeated the finely dressed religious drone as he, standing behind an elevated golden podium, thrust his right clenched fist into the humid, smoke-filled air that patrolled the bejeweled ceiling overhead.

"Yes! He must die!" echoed the room full of like-minded conspirators.

"We must find a way," the dragon tickled…his tongue dancing on the ear.

"We must find a way!" the elder repeated…slamming his now open palm on the unholy pulpit.

"We *will* find a way!" the chamber echoed…voices rising in volume.

"He's standing in our path," the yellow-brown fangs of the fiend now brushing the dangling gray locks of the speaker.

"He's standing in our path!" the high priest shouted, echoed, as before, by his bloodthirsty peers.

"It's time for us to act!" The forelegs of the beast were now on the shoulders of the fleshly puppet—the dragon head above the human head, the eyes of one like the eyes of the other…glowing red.

"It's time for us to act!" repeated the dark-hearted pawn, both arms raised, his face flushed with rage.

"It's time for us to act!" said the frenzied mob as they turned and seethed out of the chamber…the eyes of each also glowing red and, intermixed among them a legion of Ganab…whispering, whispering, whispering.

85

And, from that moment onward, the warrior knight—he who would not raise his blade to strike a fellow human—found himself surrounded by two groups who sought his destruction. The dragons—some still foolish enough to physically encounter him (surprisingly, many [a prideful lot] deceived themselves into challenging this unbeatable foe)—and some humans, who, although the message of deliverance was to them as well, these chose instead to listen to the deceptions of the Lord of the Dragons which were delivered so exquisitely by the ever-present Ganab. And, it was one of these humans, one who was listed among the inner circle of those who attended the warrior knight…it was one of these who betrayed this champion into the waiting snare of his enemy.

* * *

The procession to the place of execution was a collage of contrasts. As the two-legged *champion* walked with labored, weakening steps (he had been stripped of his armor and sword through the betrayal of a *friend* and, being held by *those* he came to deliver, he had suffered great injury by the spray of the Shachath and the claw of the Ganab who would reach past the human restrainers to deliver blows they would not have dared attempt previously), the sound of cheers and wails of despair mixed, unevenly, above this unholy parade. Those holding, and immediately following the man…these were those who, like the dragons, sought his death. And at a distance, staying just beyond the reach of the mob, were other humans who had been set free by the blade of this knight. These wept and pleaded.

Finally, at the place of execution (as mentioned previously, a horrid indentation located against the black wall of separation) the condemned, who would normally be forced to stand—back against the wall—and be thrust through with some sort of cruel instrument…*this time* the Lord of the Dragons motioned that the knight be temporarily put to one side.

"Bring them," the ruler hissed, his blood-red talons pointing to the spot of death. Then, like single-minded ants, a multitude of brutes (representing, as it were, every human tribe), each carried upon their back a rough-hewn timber. And, as they came to the place of horror, they dropped their cargo, whereupon other slaves quickly constructed, using long iron spikes, a crude platform…a platform (approximately three meters in height, with enough area for four to stand [the victim, two restrainers, and the executioner], all supported by dark crisscrossed timbers) where *all* could see what was to be done to this *savior.*

"Prepare him," ordered the *King* while his grotesque triangular head and thickening body rose in a sickening sway, having transformed, once again, to that of a huge crimson serpent.

Two barbaric humans, men of muscle and malice, who followed effortlessly the familiar voice of the dragon and having roughly drug the wounded warrior up the newly constructed steps, faced the knight, one on each side, and with the outward hand grabbed a wrist, and with the other they, in a violent pushing and lifting motion, shoved and slammed this nearly unconscious deliverer against the black wall of separation. The knight's head, having struck the barrier, hung down for a moment. Then, with effort, he slowly lifted it to behold, without fear, the face of the serpent, which hovered an arm's length away. The two locked eyes—one, pulsing hateful red—the other...a perfect reflection of the Crystal Sea.

The Lord of the Dragons, not averting his gaze (indeed, the very sight of the knight's countenance seemed as fuel to the cruel one's all-consuming hatred) rasped a command to the executioner. "Get the weapon."

"Yes, Lord," said the ogre of a man, being sure to keep his eyes lowered and his back bowed.

—It should be noted that, of course, the dragons had no need of intercessors to carry out their murderous ways. However, the Dragon King, from time to time, would make an *example* of those who rebelled, even going so far as to have a human executioner use the very device that the offender had wielded.—

This executioner, named Paul, had coldly extinguished many of his brethren over the years. If he had had any remorse...its delicate song had been silenced long ago. Indeed, knowing the misery of his people, he even considered his occupation a *service*...an avenue of escape, or at least a change of venue for his subservient suffering race. However, as he made his way down the steep rough-hewn steps to retrieve the *instrument* (held, barely, by a terrified child who had been cruelly conscripted for just this purpose), he reflected upon what he knew of this present victim. A knight...undefeated in battle, a healer, a breaker of chains and curses, yet (his thoughts began to center as he approached the small girl, attired in a simple tan peasant's dress [homespun, coarse fibers, ankle-length, short sleeves with a thin knotted cord for a belt]) like *all* those who had preceded him, even this *speaker of lofty things* had proven false. And this...this terrible deception (so apparent by the knight's present predicament) began to stir this civil servant beyond his normal pitiless state.

"What's your name, child?" said Paul, in an uncharacteristic pause of caring.

"Y...Y...Yachal, Sir," the youngster stuttered, her upper body arching backward to compensate for the heavy blade that rested across her slender forearms.

The executioner glanced briefly up and back to note the focus of his master, then looking forward again, he observed that the weapon—though obviously sharpened to a razor's edge—drew no blood from the girl's delicate skin. Then, quickly, before his Lord took notice, he knelt before her on one knee while gently taking the sword by the dark leather handle and laying it on the lifeless ground before him. The child, standing with slouched shoulders—the red marks of the blade still visible on her arms, breathed in sharply punctuated gasps—the kind associated with great heartfelt sobs. Paul, from somewhere finding a feeling of concern, could see from the channels lightly etched on her soft rose-colored cheeks that she had been crying for some time and, as he gently cradled her chin in his calloused right palm, he whispered... "You need to go now. Quickly. Run as fast as you can."

"NO!!" The voice—dark, deep, and right in his ear—caused the executioner to quickly prostrate himself before the serpent's head which was now a hand's breadth away. "She will witness this death...yes (the long black tongue of the beast arching first up, then down, as the demon spoke)...*all* will witness this death."

The thin tapered end of the demon's tail coiled suddenly around the child's midsection and then, like a flower, plucked her kicking and screaming body from the earth and suspended it two meters off the ground. A simple squeeze...and the screams were reduced to a whimper.

"Dip the blade...fool!" rasped the enormous snake to the executioner who now stood, head bowed, with the weapon held groundward in his right hand. "Dip the blade, long and full...hurry, before the enemy dies of other causes."

As stated earlier, this spot...this loathsome hollow...was a pooling place of the *sin* that permeated...lived and coursed...through all that dwelt on this side of the wall. In the brackish oozing that puddled here was, not only the remnants of murders past (bones, rottings, tears) but also a liquefied form of treason, rebellion, lust...indeed *all* the manifestations of what was *not* holy. It was all here...in a half-bubbling-acre of repulsive horror...and it was here that the warrior knight...he, *above all,* who seemed *not* of this place...it was here he would die...die like the rest.

Paul, aware of his master's impatience (indeed, chastising himself for foolishly testing the tyrant), quickly took the weighty blade and attempted to thrust it beneath the thick repulsive liquid. Strangely, it seemed to resist the immersion. The executioner, whose experience had been that *all* mortal things were ravenously swallowed when touched to the nasty stuff, marveled that this instrument of steel seemed to buoy on the surface. But, not wanting to join the damned this day, he quickly placed both hands on the blade and put his full body weight (a hefty three hundred pounds) on the weapon. After some moments, like a slightly cracked cask, the thing grudgingly sank. However, as it was pressed down into the swill—the resisting force lessening as it absorbed the enveloping evil—Paul felt a trembling. Like the orange-glowing metal from a blacksmith's fire when thrust into the tempering wash...the blade seemed to violently vibrate beneath the watery waste. Finally, after some minutes, all was still...and the executioner carried the dripping sword up the blood-stained steps to his waiting master.

The human-slayer paused a moment as he reached the summit. Although not of great age (rarely attained by *any* human), the constant dealings with death and dragons had taken their toll and, the ascent, though not lofty, had nevertheless caused his heart to race and his breathing to thicken.

"When you're quite ready," the serpent sarcastically hissed—his eyes not wavering from those of the victim. He knew this faithful human slave was nearly spent and had determined, in his black heart, to gratuitously end his service after this last cruel obedience.

"Yes...Lord," Paul gasped, arching his back to facilitate another breath, while the sword, feeling of slime, lay rigid across his powerful forearms and, as he prepared to deliver the weapon for his master's *blessing*, he briefly took in all that surrounded him. To his immediate right...the knight, a shadow of his former self, his body beginning to swell and fester from the blows of beast and man. He, in turn, was being held, securely (though it did not appear that he was in any way struggling), by two muscular brutes—each pinning an arm against the unforgiving wall. To the executioner's left, where he now shuffled in subservient fashion, was the sight of the cruel snake...the form of choice for the murderer of old. This manifestation was huge...the majority of the serpentine body was coiled in the waters beneath...only the head and tail (still clutching the little girl, who quietly sobbed) appeared above the platform. And beyond the evil Lord...the masses. As far as the eye could see, a swirling chaos of humanity. Some...mostly those who, like flies on decay, huddled next to this unholy altar...these were filled with caustic hatred and shouted in frenzied tones for death. Others…those at a distance, were drawn to the spectacle as to a carnival. These were oblivious to the meaning of the moment…wishing only to occupy a few minutes of their dreary lives with a distraction. And…gathered far to one side…a grouping of those who recognized this knight as one sent from beyond the wall…sent to heal and deliver. These…so few in number…wept and prayed.

Paul, as he had done many times before, bowed the head and lifted the weapon for his *King's* inspection and, though not looking upward, he could tell, from the drippings at his feet, that the *Lord of the Dragons* was coating the hated sword with his own vile venom.

"Stand ready!" barked the creature, and the executioner turned and stationed himself. And though this elevated theater was indeed different from what he was used to…his procedure for exacting death was a matter of reflex…so long had he done it. First, he angled himself towards the soon-to-be dead warrior. With his left leg forward, and somewhat bent at the knee, he then leaned back and slightly down—his right foot nearly perpendicular to his torso. The weapon, coated and saturated with evil, was held securely by both hands gripping the hilt, which was itself resting against the executioner's lower right chest, the point aiming at the victim's heart with the cutting edges directed towards earth…and heaven. Thus, with this position of leverage and at the Dark Lord's command, the sword would then be thrust quickly and powerfully—having the benefit of the full force of Paul's muscle and mass—and, as the *instrument,* in a moment's time, having already gone through the most vital organ and striking the impenetrable wall…it would then, just as quickly, be removed from the screaming and blood-gushing subject. Whereupon the cruel attendants, no doubt enjoying the whole ordeal, would release their grips and the *dead man* would crumple into a lifeless heap…to be consumed shortly thereafter. Yes, it was always a cruel and violent spectacle…but today…for some reason…the Lord of the Dragons insisted that *all* creation observe and recognize, once and for all, that *he*, the Dragon King, was indeed master over the souls of men.

The warrior knight—much of his physical strength having been depleted by the abuse of his captors—through swollen eyes looked out at those arrayed before him.

First, he beheld the sword…his trusted weapon, forged by an unseen hand in a faraway furnace of all-consuming purity…positioned and dripping now just inches from his heaving breast. Never before had it been used to shed human blood. *Always,* it had been a source of death for the dragons…and healing for the helpless. Now it was *held* by a human and seemed weighted down by all the remnants of rebellion. Indeed, the horrid pond in which it had been violently immersed…this was the very spot where the first traitor had turned his back on his Creator…so many years ago. And now, this instrument of right and righteous seemed to reek of all things *unrighteous.*

Next, he beheld the gaze of Paul, the executioner. A stone of a man, hardened by years of exposure to cruelty…himself an instrument of the dragons…adept at his duty…oblivious to the serpent's no-frills retirement plan which awaited him upon completion of this last grisly act.

Beyond this professional human-killer, who had since donned a ceremonial crimson hood, was the Great Snake of the same color. Hovering just two meters above the edge of the platform…his horrid head…eyes pulsing red, mouth agape with flicking black tongue and brilliant white fangs which bracketed the foul opening and continually dripped venom. The monster seemed to exude…not just evil…but a hunger—an insatiable, ravenous lust that would consume, if it could, even the whole world…the whole of creation…rather than occupy a place of subservience. If *he* could not be God…he would be master of all things made of God and, just below the reptilian face of this enemy, coiled tightly in ringlets that squeezed the middle part of her delicate body…was Yachal. The warrior tried to smile at this precious child who—with arms hanging limp outside the snake's cruel snare while tears silently flowed from puffy blue eyes, was among the first delivered when he began his mission…what now seemed long ages ago and, although it had only been three years since she first giggled on his knee…his acquaintance with her family had continued. Indeed, their dwelling had often been a place of rest for he and his disciples and she, living up to her name— always greeted him as a beloved uncle. Always, upon his return, leaping to his arms and filling his ears with the light-hearted observations of an innocent soul. And now, this child, whom he loved as a daughter, was held by pure evil…the fingerlike tip of the demon's tail stroking her long auburn hair even as his vile poison dripped upon…destroying…the single white lily that she had carefully placed among the beautiful locks…placed there just for him.

"Thrust! Thrust! Thrust!"…the taunting of the frenzied crowd wafted up from the earth like a foul mist and drew the warrior's gaze past the platform. Before him, in a living, convulsing carpet of shoulders and heads—as far as a mortal eye could see—the bloodthirsty mob beseeched their heartless master for the one-word command that would end another's life. This knight, sent on a mission of mercy, now beheld, not just the blurred grouping of the thousands...but...in this culmination of his cause...he saw all...every human...every traitorous heart...every dragon slave—both those churning before him—and those who have been, and those who will come. And, in this omniscient moment...as he scanned before and beyond the horizon...every human face...*every* human eye—even those of his followers—even those of the weeping beloved child—every window to the soul reflected the same pulsing red glow that spilled with rebellion from the orbs of the Dragon King.

"It is time," hissed the serpent as its grotesque head cocked up and back in preparation for the deadly strike. However, unlike its smaller cousins—from which it was modeled—or even the dragons of lesser stature...this lightning-quick impending delivery would not administer death through fire or venom. No...the lethal discharge would simply be that of a simple, one-syllable...word.

"Ironic...don't you think," rasped the murderer as he looked down and into the iridescent eyes of the victim. "I understand that all things began with a word. How fitting..." the creature panted, seeking to milk every last drop of misery from this *failure* from beyond the wall, "...that you should perish through a word."

The knight said nothing...no sign of fear...no begging or bargaining...only a steady, silent focus on the eyes of the evil one and, as nothing more could be added or taken...the air was split.

"THRUST!!" the word flew out of the monster's throat even as the head violently jerked forward as if striking an invisible foe. And, as the snake's shadow darted over the poised executioner...Paul, with all the strength and skill attained through years of practicing his ghastly art and aided, this time, by a deep desire to rid this fallen world of one more hope-destroying imposter—even before the creature finished the biting command...the sword had pierced the warrior's heart.

And the scream of agony which followed began as that of any other man. Indeed, at the very moment of violation the knight's head jerked backwards and, with every fiber convulsing, a great cry of pain was desperately raised towards the reflecting sky. But, as his life's blood violently gushed from around the blade (the weapon, its flight only halted by the now-released hilt which, along with the sword, remained mercilessly and horribly imbedded), the utterance of the warrior took on an other-worldly tone. Yes, what began as a cry of the flesh—that desperate plea that sounds when the defenses of skin and bone are hopelessly breached—became something much deeper and resonated on an unseen level of soul and spirit. It was as if all that was unholy and impure and unclean was suddenly, viciously, pushed upon, injected into…that which was clean, and pure, and good. Then, as this final plea for release faded without remedy, the knight—the last remnants of his essence draining from the wound—lowered, with eyes shut, his head. And, for a brief span, in that smallest of moments between life and death, all—every fallen creature on this side of the wall—beheld the pain-twisted features that revealed utter defilement and defeat. And, just before the final falling of his wounded brow, the knight, one last time, opened his eyes. But instead of revealing a light birthed from a distant shore…instead of a mirror of a being from beyond and within…his eyes now, like those of the very serpent himself…beamed a glowing, pulsing…red.

And then…it was over. With nothing more to give…or receive…the warrior knight finally yielded up his spirit and his swollen head slumped heavily forward even as his tortured breast slowly expelled the last wheezing breath. And, for a very few seconds…all was silent. It was as if all the observers…all who had formerly seen this stranger succeed in every battle he had ever engaged in…it was as if they could not, no matter how desperately some desired (and there were many who desired it), believe that he was at last dead. But, as the great vile Dragon Lord puffed wide his hoary neck and, with dripping fangs towards the clouds let out a great bellow of victory…it was as if a huge wretched dam had broken and the majority of the multitude joined the evil king in a wave of irreverent jubilation. Conversely, on the edge of this seething mass…a minuscule island of believers, seeing that their champion was now hopelessly gone…these huddled quietly together…their tears and muffled sobbing joining as one.

But, as the air was filled and the earth vibrated with the clamor of fools…there was one whose station was somewhere between horror and hope. Paul, the executioner—he who had struck the deadly blow—knelt, trembling before the lifeless body that, although slumped, was still firm against the wall. And, though one might guess that the cumulative carnage this killer had been exposed to (indeed, his knees and hands were covered with this latest victim's blood) had driven him to near madness…it was not this that was destroying his foundations. No…it was that he…Paul…he who had willingly done the dragon's wishes…it was *he* who first saw and knew that the blade—that instrument of righteousness, now twisted to *slaughter* the righteous—had done what no other weapon fashioned by man could do—IT HAD PIERCED THE WALL! And so he knelt, trembling, his layers of unbelief peeling quickly away…and, through teary eyes he stared at the blade—that weighty deliverer of *justice* which, having delivered its death blow, could *not* (though he had strained momentarily to do so) be removed—and he looked at the man. And, not surprisingly, it was he who first saw the water.

It started as a droplet…a trickle…a shimmering bead. Where the blood had once flowed from around the cutting edges…now an iridescent rivulet began. Paul, oblivious to the riotous sounds of his contemporaries, reached out to touch that which he had only seen as a reflection in the sky or in the eyes of the perfect warrior and, as his gnarled fingers neared the flow—the Great Serpent suddenly stopped his celebration. He…he who was victor!…now felt a piercing of his own. It was a deep, concealed injury…a long forgotten and covered wound…and suddenly it began to ache anew.

—The following events, though myriad, occurred with an indistinguishable quickness…like the blinking of an eye.—

The Dragon King, having predetermined to cap his victory by devouring *all* on the platform (starting with the executioner and his assistants, then the child, and finally the corpse of the knight), stood, momentarily paralyzed with fear as his human servant barely touched the delicate stream. Then, a rumbling began. It started in unseen regions and can be compared (only barely, as no earthly comparison is adequate) to giant trees being violently uprooted, thick iron chains being hopelessly shattered, huge mountains instantly humbled and deep canyons just as quickly filled and whole continents ripped from their station to hurriedly move to another place.

The Great Serpent—thoughts of victory, conquest, and power fading quickly—started to lunge towards the fallen knight. Perhaps, if he could consume this enemy, no more damage would be done. But, before any movement on his part was discernable, the wall—that hideous barrier, birthed in the heart of man and an ever-present testament to his treachery—suddenly split upon the line created by the blade. And the sword—that holy weapon used to deliver that which was its perverse opposite—vibrated, as if under the pressure and power of a great unseen force and, like a lightning strike from the heavens, it shot out of the fallen and delivered a crushing blow to the head of the snake.

Now…the river was loosed! In a roar of a thunderous deluge it came and, as it gushed violently through the opening, the wall…which no man could mar or move…moved! Wider and wider was the breach as wave upon wave of crystalline purity invaded and, such was the tumult, that a swirling white blinding mist enveloped the spot where the waiting sea made its relentless charge of reclamation.

It could be described as an explosion of sorts…a deep, horrifying shaking as the waters from beyond the wall overwhelmed and consumed the horrid pond from which the platform arose. And, as the wooden theater was violently dismembered by the blast, the flow became a wave. Much like those greatly feared tidal surges that breach the normal barriers between soil and sea…this wave, too, rushed unstoppably forward. However, unlike the natural phenomenon which seeks to envelope all…*this* wave had the two-fold desire to push and pursue. For, as it came upon the mass of humanity that had, only moments before, cried for the blood of the innocent…these the water pushed. Back, back…gathering like foam on the crest, the horde of the faithless tumbled mindlessly on the streaking edge of that for which they proclaimed a desire…yet through their actions…revealed a disdain. Onward the luminescent liquid relentlessly pushed…plucking, picking, and sifting the seed of man as it utterly destroyed the many hovels where they hid. Down came the lofty towers that were built to peer over the wall. Crushed and scattered were the engines designed to burrow or pierce. Destroyed were great kingdoms and castles and corrupt colleges built to exalt the creature instead of the creator until, at last, the millions upon millions were deposited in a great scattering…a dispersion beyond the ancient riverbed.

Meanwhile, the dragons in the midst—those horrible murderers who intermingled with their human prey—these, seeing the coming of doom…turned to flee. But, only those closest to the ancient boundary survived. The others, like vile droplets of fat thrown into a blazing furnace…these momentarily burst into flame and then were instantly vaporized by the relentless force of purity that was, by nature, their exact opposite. And the Dragon King? He had just barely escaped the crystal flow by transforming into a flying demon and flew, with wounded weighted wings—towards his lair of the ancient mountain and, with one foreleg cradling his bruised and bleeding brow, he uttered curses as, below his talons, the beachhead of his enemy was irreparably established in a land he had thought forever his own.

* * *

Paul...the executioner...knelt, trembling, hands over eyes...weeping greatly as he gently rocked back and forth much like a grieving father on the grave of his beloved son. "What have I done? What have I done?" he whispered between sobs. "How...could...I?" the quaking and remorse seeming to intensify with each passing moment. "How...could...I?"

"Paul..." It was a voice, gentle, yet piercing...like a golden sun-ray through an overcast sky. "Paul...look at me." The words, though soft, were like the key to a dungeon door...a shackle's release...a physician's healing touch. "Paul...look at me."

Slowly, timidly, the former executioner slid his calloused fingers down the channels of his tear moistened cheeks. Still bowed, he placed his now clean palms upon his knees and stared into the delicate clover on which he rested.

"Paul...brother...look at me."

The former dragon-slave was slow to respond...he thought himself in a dream or delusion. "Where is the platform?" he thought, as his labored breaths began to ease at the soothing words of the stranger.

"Paul...friend...look at me."

Hesitantly, like a man testing the surface of an ice-covered pond, he raised his gaze. First, looking forward, he saw a carpet of fragrant clover—bathed in an undiluted sun and moving to the rhythm of a tender breeze. Then, perhaps three meters' distant, he saw a pair of legs—wearing the armor of a knight...but which knight? Finally, sitting back on his heels, Paul looked up to behold the warrior he had, just moments before...slain. "Ohhh," he sobbed, hands over eyes, again bowing down to his knees, "...please, forgive me."

And for a few moments—though the knight still spoke—the great heart-wrenching cries of the penitent drowned out the words. Finally...when it seemed such pain could only lead to death...Paul felt a touch. And, from that simple intrusion...a sudden peace seemed to calm the raging sea in the soul of this former prisoner. And...with the peace...he heard the words anew... "Paul...son...look at me."

The former executioner...the former slayer of dreams and hopes...looked up and grabbed hold of the hand which had touched him, and was now extended to help him up. And, as he—with some effort—rose to his feet...there...before him...stood the warrior knight. And, though in many ways he appeared the same as he had before his final battle...now, the iridescent blaze of his eyes seemed to radiate beyond the confines of his body and, instead of the simple helmet of a knight…he wore a crown.

Paul again slumped to the ground, this time in homage to the ruler of all. But as he did, he heard the words, "Brother…you've spent enough time on your knees for one day. Rise and join me. I have much to tell you." And then, in a raised and sweeping voice, "I have much to tell *all* of you!"

And, as Paul slowly stood erect, he felt a delicate little hand curl around the index finger of his left hand. It was Yachal! And she—looking up at him and smiling said, "C'mon…let's follow him!" Then, as quickly as she came, the little pixie skipped away in the direction of the knight who was walking towards a rough-hewn bridge. Soon, the stationary man was gently passed on either side by those who had, only moments before, been the outcasts on the edge of the mob…many of these pausing to exhort him to come.

Finally, still anchored by shame, Paul watched as the king turned at the edge of the bridge. Beyond him…a cloud of crystalline mist caused by the rushing river. And beyond this…a great rising castle which split the horrid wall and, as the people gathered close to their sovereign, the warrior knight raised his strong right arm and lifted skyward his great sword. But, instead of a shimmering blade which formerly had the appearance of polished silver…now this wonderful/horrible weapon…this instrument of unwavering justice…had the unmistakable glimmer of crimson. And, as all eyes turned toward Paul, the former spiller of human blood, once again he heard the words of invitation… "Come, Paul…I have need of you. Come join your king." And…with tears of gratitude overflowing…he came.

Chapter IX

Some seek gold
Though cold and dead
But the wise seek living things...instead.

"Ah...it does my heart good to see such impressionable young men engaged in honest and honorable labor."

Sir John, sporting a sweat-stained pair of dark-green coveralls along with a humorous-looking, though functional, wide-brimmed straw hat...looked to his left and squinted to focus upon the speaker who leaned against the property wall which ran parallel to his rows...a strong stone's throw distant. If there had been any uncertainty as to the identity of this *stranger*...the following spoken verse removed all doubt.

If out of mischief you wish to keep...work the young men hard...and at night they'll sleep.

"Uncle Peter!" exploded Albert, dropping his bag of seed and bounding over the furrows like a hurdler on his way to a trophy.

"Whoa, Amethyst," Sir John spoke to his faithful work-engine while gently pulling back and tying the reins to the rig. "I didn't want to labor any more today...did you?" he whispered into the gelding's left ear after securing a feed-bag and firmly patting the horse's muscular neck. Amethyst, letting

98

out a slight snort and rocking his head as if in agreement, slowly began to chew as he watched his master trudge towards the two in the distance.

"What a fine wall you have here," said the aging knight as he leaned, elbows and forearms resting in a crisscross fashion on the flat granite surface even as an enchanted Albert—sitting atop the structure, back facing the field with legs dangling—looked down at his ancient and hairy deliverer (Sir Peter, never one for fashion, was now adorned with an even *greater* mane of mostly gray) with an expression of pure adoration.

Sir John, approaching the duo while lifting his unwarrior-like straw bonnet with his left hand and wiping his sweat-beaded brow (alas, *another* forehead expanding with time) with his right, replied, "Yes, it was built to the specifications of an old master."

"I see you mated the stones perfectly…no movement and no mortar."

"Yes…my teacher impressed upon me the need for precision. He would say…*Mate the stones…like man and wife. If you place with care…they will last for life.*"

"I notice the surface is smooth…most inviting to the touch." Sir Peter was now rubbing his calloused palms in opposing circular motions even as John came within an arm's length of the barrier.

"Yes…my old mentor insisted it be so. He would say…*Make the surface smooth, and gentle to the skin. A wall that causes pain…is a wall that invites sin.*"

"And I notice…" Peter, leaning again on elbows with his hands clasped and forearms perpendicular to his torso, "that the wall is just the right height for leaning."

"Yes," John replied, now himself leaning in a similar fashion…directly opposite Sir Peter, "my old dear friend would say…"—And at this *all three* spoke the words in unison:

Not too low for an idle seat…not so high that your eyes won't meet. But make it such, that you can pause and share. At a wall thus built…you'll find friendship there.

As the verse concluded, as one might expect, there was a riotous outburst of laughter, along with the grasping of hands and necks and, though none present could claim to be a proper *blood relation* to the others…an observer would have to conclude that these three were obviously family. And so they were.

"So, Peter," John continued, leaning again and watching as the visitor playfully tried, with both hands, to jab young Albert—who skillfully deflected each attack, all the while grinning with delight. "I see from your attire that you are being sent on another mission."

—It should be noted that since Sir John occupied the place of protector of this quadrant (a position Sir Peter formerly filled until commanded, by the king, to another station) that his former teacher would often stop by his abode as he traveled to and from the harvest field beyond the river. These visits were usually quite short (a pause for a refreshment and a few words) until, some years back, the elder's wife...died. Now, on those few occasions of his coming (although still a match for any dragon, the diminished mobility of the warrior limited his excursions) the good knight usually set aside an extra day so that he might replenish not only the storehouse of the body...but, by the company of the caring...fill the heart, as well.—

"Yes, John," said the elder, ceasing his attack and feigning complete attention to his former pupil. "I've just come from the king's presence with direction for an urgent mission...deep into the dragon's lair. AH HA!"...the ruse was successful and the teenager, having been broadsided by the knight's powerful left arm, lay, laughing, on the ground near Sir John's feet.

"I could have told you that was coming," uttered the warrior/farmer in a fatherly tone. "I only hope such tactics are not used against the Ganab that are met beyond the river."

There was a moment of tender silence as Albert regained his footing and the two adults gave thought to the implication of the last spoken sentence.

"Would you like me to go with you?" John, more serious now and with a heartfelt concern for his elderly *parent*, said in a gentle tone.

"Has the king given you such a command?"

John's expression said, "No," and since both understood that success in the ways of the king must always begin with obedience...Sir Peter merely smiled and said—though such a pairing would, no doubt, bring him great joy—"maybe next time...my young sod-buster...maybe next time."

The three, for some minutes, began to fill the air with such questions and answers that effortlessly flow from the hearts of those who genuinely care for one another. Then...the trumpets were heard.

It was a faint sound...yet distinct and well-known by all those present. Still quite far in the distance, yet heading their way...a procession of the *nobility* and, from the fullness of the blasts...it appeared to be quite a contingent.

"I wonder what brings *them* here?" puzzled Sir John, oblivious to the presence immediately behind him.

"Oh, I've heard there's some trouble in the inner realm...some sort of beastie wreaking havoc. By the way," Sir Peter continued, without emotion, while pausing to reach into his front hip pocket to produce a half-eaten carrot, which he held out towards his old apprentice. "Are you embarking on some sort of agricultural experiment whereby plowed rows crisscross like a woven basket?"

Sir John's opened-mouth puzzlement at such a bizarre change of subject was answered when Amethyst, who had been steadily *plowing* across the rows to get to an old friend, rudely nudged aside his master to receive the treat from Sir Peter's hand. This was another occasion for laughter and, as the voices of the three diminished, and the trumpet blasts became more evident, Sir Peter made a suggestion.

"Why don't you fellows go home now and prepare for my eventual arrival. I so look forward to another evening in your presence and in the presence of the Lady Mary...and the stout-hearted Fredrick." And, as the soil-tenders succumbed to this wisdom and commenced their trek back to the house, Sir John briefly looked back over his shoulder...knowing that there would soon be a confrontation of sorts. A battle of words between a time-tested, rough-hewn champion...and a polished gathering of the *chosen*.

* * *

Before the coming of the wave...before the blood-caused breach in the accursed wall...before the emergence of a haven of hope...the land of slaves (for *all* humans, whether they acknowledged it or not, were slaves) was filled with many levels of delusion and oppression and servitude.

In the desperate attempt to escape the finality of the wall, man—helpless to comprehend, much less effect a way of escape from his chains—would turn against his own kind in order to construct a many-tiered system of worth. Thus, the strong were positioned over the weak...the intelligent were above the dull...the educated were over the ignorant...the tall over the short...the thin over the stout...the shrewd over the naive...the handsome over the homely...the healthy over the infirm...and on and on, in, and by every imaginable distinction—layer upon layer of judgments and calculations were used to elevate one's self above his neighbor...even to go so far as to employ bloodline or breeding or variant hues of color…all in a fruitless vain attempt to justify or exalt or merit one's worth over others as if, by standing upon the human *rungs* of those deemed *inferior*, one might attain a position high enough to go over the barrier.

This perverted mind-set…this grossest of errors…was not, of course, limited to those few who had abilities or attributes deemed by the masses as distinctly superior. No, *every* human heart engaged, either consciously or unconsciously, in this struggle for exaltation. Indeed, no matter how debased or loathsome an individual might be or appear…even these…in their soul of souls…would place themselves upon a lofty throne and call themselves…king.

However, when he who was innocent was forced…no…when he *chose* to receive the sentence of death deserved by the whole human race…the wall of condemnation *had* to open and, having done so…the Crystal Sea violently stormed through the rift and every lofty non-living thing…every tower and castle and kingdom, as well as every mud-hut and pride-soaked hovel, was destroyed…made low…reduced to rubble. And, as mentioned previously, every human whose Lord was not the warrior knight—those who would not place their hopes on the merit of *his* work—these were mercifully pushed, transported…removed to a place beyond the boundary of the river. Where, without pause or reflection, they began anew their struggle for dominion and exaltation. And where, perhaps, in a future time, they would have opportunity to hear and, hopefully receive, the word of deliverance which would cause them to seek the river…and the true king.

In the *new* kingdom—that which was birthed by the washing of the wave—the Lord commanded and decreed that the *nobility* of old be abolished. He *alone* was king and there would be no others. Indeed, no more kings, princes *or* peasants. Since *all* owed their lives to him…all were equal…all were, you might say…brothers. But, since the soil of man's heart was still prone to selfishness (unfortunately, even those freed from the dragon lived in a body of flesh that *cannot* be redeemed [a subject for another time]), over the years distinctions were made among the equal and, perhaps quite naturally, those whose abilities, talents, vocations, *callings*…were those of leader, or protector, or proclaimer—indeed, any office which put an individual over or in front of others…these, when not careful, were tempted to ascribed the attention associated with their position…to a divine right…a worthiness and favor above that of their charges. Thus…over time…a hierarchy evolved. And…in the reborn land scoured flat by the wave (meaning *level* by way of equality and dependence, not necessarily topography) there arose high places, towers, castles...walls...cathedrals.

* * *

Sir Peter reached down and carefully selected a strand of half-brown prairie grass which—when determined and harvested (a process that could take a minute or two...*Take time to pick...you won't get sick*)—the smooth end of the same was then promptly placed between the well-worn bicuspids in the right side of the warriors mouth. He slowly righted himself, turned to face the rutted clay road and, with a sigh, crossed his arms while gently leaning against the property wall...hearing and feeling a gentle grinding of the granite against his shield as he rocked to a place of comfort.

Ta, tooooo...the chorus of the horns, off to Peter's right, was coming steadily closer. The elder turned his head and squinted—shielding his old, yet still keen eyes from the hot, overhead midday sun—to look down the somewhat winding corridor to see the beginnings of the *Prissy Parade*. (Never one to mince words, Sir Peter had labeled such outward displays thus, long ago. But, trying harder now to guard the leavings of his bearded gateway [his mouth], as was the desire of his sovereign, he endeavored to be less critical than in years past...but sometimes...it was *so* terribly hard.)

Ta, tooooo...the horns, like a rude early-morning rooster, blasted their message faithfully every half minute. One short low note, followed by a much higher note of quadruple length. When queried by a curious John—while still an apprentice—as to the purpose...Peter had said, "It's meant to get your attention, lad. It takes the place, yet has the same meaning, as saying (Peter, gruffly singing the words in the same pitch as the horns)...*Hey you!...Look here!...It's Me!...Bow down!...I'm great!...You're not!*...whereupon he finished the discourse with a voluminous expulsion of collected spittle. Followed, immediately, by a wiping of the mouth on the right sleeve while uttering an under-his-breath chorus of his own.

Ta, tooooo...Peter could, in the lazy blur of the summer air, just make out the gleamings of the first row of trumpeters. Five abreast, the horn-blowers—arrayed in a slight V pattern, whereby the middle musician, blowing a golden instrument, was followed on either side by two others playing trumpets of silver, which were, in turn, followed on either side by two more playing horns of brass—all sitting atop stately mounts of brown and black which occupied the whole breadth of the roadway. Other travelers on the road—of which

Peter saw a half-dozen—when encountering this juggernaut, were forced to move their feet or wagons to the unkempt and rocky side. These, as the procession slowly passed, would bow the head (men removing the hat) and stay in this submissive pose till the *nobility* had passed. Not far from the aging knight, and hobbling towards him on his side of the road, was an old acquaintance that Peter recognized from his days as protector of this quadrant. As the procession nearly overtook him, the old gentleman—who was hard of hearing—finally recognized the buzzing in his ear and nearly stumbled getting to the shoulder to avoid the hooves. Once there, he quickly snatched the worn leather cap from his thinly carpeted gray crown…and then stood, motionless, with head bowed. The lead trumpeter, from the corner of his eye…gave the old *fool* a look of disdain.

Ta, tooooo…the procession was nearly parallel the chewing champion and, such was the number of *tooters* (Peter had alternate names for *everything*) that he promptly placed an index finger in each ear hole and grimaced at each irritating blast.

Ta, tooooo…One, two, three, four, five…six! Six rows of horn blowers. Each on an impressive beast. Each trumpeter (and mount!) adorned in the colored finery of their prospective house (of which there were many). And, behind these noise makers…were the standard bearers and, just as there was one trumpeter for each house, so too, a banner (usually consisting of at least a square meter of fine fabric containing an embroidered symbol unique to each fiefdom, along with, to some degree or other, the symbol of the king) was raised on a towering staff to announce the presence of an official of the same. And, as each musician had a place of prominence or submission, so too, each flag bearer rode in an order of importance.

Ta, tooooo…finally the *fluttering fancies* were past and the first row of shining knights made their regal entrance. As with the preliminary procession, these *warriors* were also in the peculiar pecking order. The middle lead knight, who wore an impressive suit of polished armor (the finest steel plate, extending from head to toe—as were they all—except that this *defender* had a helmet overlaid in gold leaf, signifying that he was the current champion of the *games* that were held every year) and, as he came parallel to the unkempt figure against the wall who did *not* bow…the lead knight raised high his gauntleted left hand and the huge procession instantly stopped.

By this time, Sir Peter had not only plugged his hairy ears (alas, with aging came new annoyances…such as uncivilized hair growth) but he also closed his eyes to avoid the glare of the knights…all the while chewing the blade of grass like a contented cow. Meanwhile, the offended noble directed his steed (a brilliant while stallion…the usual choice of the riding knights) to within a lance's thrust of the still oblivious Peter.

For a moment their was an irritable silence, and then, from behind the polished face-plate of the leader came a muffled, and then unmuffled (as the grill was lifted) "AHEM!" Peter, sensing a change in atmosphere, opened his left eye and looked up to see the towering unmasked figure.

"Well, if it isn't Sir Peter?" said the rider, his sudden ease causing the other knights to relax as well.

"Reggie, is that you?" The elder shielded his eyes with his left hand even as he punctuated the question with a bite and spit.

—Now, those in this procession were not used to such displays, and Peter's *obvious* lack of protocol caused a few of the underlings to scowl and fidget until Sir Reginald held up his hand to dissuade any advance.—

"Yes…it's me, old master. How long has it been…ten…fifteen years?"

"More like twenty, I reckon (chew…bite…spit)."

—Sir Peter knew that these dandies thought little of his kind and he decided to "sculpt his speech" to more closely match their preconceived notions.—

"That's a mighty fine animal you have there (pointing his staff of grass towards the well-dressed beast)."

"Yes…we've bred out all the impurities," said Sir Reginald, puffing up slightly at the attention given *his* creation. "You won't find a single spot on any of our war horses."

"I don't much care for the things, myself. They ain't much good against a Muth."

"One has to change with the times, old friend," said the lofty one, ignoring the reference to the dragon type he had *never* slain. "We can travel ten leagues in the time it takes you to waddle one."

"*In such a hurry? Not for me. I'll miss the flower, and the buzzing bee* (bite…spit)."

At the sound of the rhyme an inner and ancient discomfort began to swell within the bosom of the younger. "I see you haven't lost your *talent* for fine lyricism," said the protector sarcastically as he glanced over his shoulder to gather the approving expressions of his fellow knights.

"Well," Peter rubbed his beard thoughtfully with his left hand, "I suppose if it's good enough for the king…it's good enough for me."

After a sobering pause, Peter continued. "So, tell me Reg…I notice you have a right fancy chapeau (chew, bite, spit…again pointing with the ever-shortening blade of grass)…what's up with that?"

"It's from the games, old teacher. You remember them, don't you? The contest to hone the skills and better the craft?"

"Foolishness! (hard bite and spit)" Peter nearly losing his composure at this sensitive subject.

"Foolishness? Why, Sir Peter…I happen to know that you, on more than one occasion, had nearly earned the title of *Exalted Knight.*"

"Yes…" Peter responded, reigning in his emotions and speaking loudly and clearly as he locked his gaze on the eyes of his *superior*. "…but I also used to soil my diaper and swallow pap."

At this, a great agitation rippled through the procession (such was their esteem for the *games.)*

Now, equally intense, Sir Reginald, desiring to have a contest of his own…right now!…moved his right hand slowly across his body to grasp the bejeweled handle of his sword (mind you—this *was* the original instrument given upon the king's commission. However, since it was so plain…many knights embellished it to their own liking) and said with clenched teeth… "I think it would benefit both of us to test our skills against one another…don't you think? I'm sure the younger knights would learn much."

At this, Peter, holding up his opened left hand (palm forward) while his face contorted as if to resist an outburst of some sort. (In this case it would be uproarious laughter, but the warrior turned it into an onslaught of near-gagging coughs…the kind associated with a pesky tidbit caught in the throat.) Finally, he stood (having been doubled over for a good half minute), said quickly, "Scuze me," and then proceed to clear his nasal passages in the very effective, yet outwardly repulsive manner of closing one nostril while venting the other. At last, after a collective groan circulated through the gathering, he said, while wiping his face on his sleeve. "You win, Reg. I wouldn't stand a chance against your swordplay. But then…" pausing to primp his whiskers "…I only know how to fight dragons."

The moment of anger had passed and Sir Reginald turned his mount to rejoin the procession. "I don't have time for any more foolishness. Goodbye, *Sir* Peter."

"By the way, Reggie" said the crude one as the golden knight resumed his position at the head, "where are y'all headed?"

"To see the king. To speak to him of the dragon in the inner realm."

"Funny," Peter puzzled, scratching his scalp with his left hand to accentuate the point, "I was just there. He didn't say a thing about it."

106

"No…" said Sir Reginald with upturned nose while slowly lowering his faceplate and raising his right hand, "I don't suppose he'd trouble you with such an important matter." And then, facing forward, he quickly lowered his glove and shouted, "Onward!" and, as the procession grudgingly began, and before the first trumpet blast, a disrespectful murmuring accompanied by low scornful laughter was heard, starting at the front and filtering back through the ranks…*Sir Need-a-bath…Sir Bore-a-lot…Sir Slavedriver* and then, as the last row of knights passed the wall-builder, the outward warrior—one who was lowest in rank among these elite…the one closest to Sir Peter…turned his head and, looking into the eyes of the one he had once accompanied, years ago, on a quest that had saved a boy…he mouthed the words…*Sir Noble Heart.*

Ta, tooooo…the horns, the banners, the knights, the supply wagons…all finally made their way past Sir Peter who was again resting against the wall with crossed arms and only the seeded head left of the once long stalk of grass protruding from his mouth. He spat the thing out, shook his head as he watched the *parade* amble into the distance, and then noticed that a figure had stopped on the road in front of him…head bowed, hat in hand.

Peter smiled and nearly shouted, "Put your blasted hat on, Ralph!"

At this, the old gentleman raised his head and, with a twinkle in his eye to accompany his toothless grin, he held his arms wide to receive a welcome embrace from his old friend.

Chapter X

Near the river, always be. Near the river...close to me.

After the crystalline wave destroyed and delivered...after it pushed the unwilling and after it pursued and consumed the broken...the kingdom...that place reclaimed and ripped from the destroyer's claw...this new domain, free from the roaming and rulership of the cruel dragons...this became as it was originally intended...a land vast in beauty and wealth. For, in the flat land...that enormous plain which rimmed the new kingdom...where once the sterile soil reluctantly—through the strain of man's muscle along with the watering of sweat and tears—produced only the bare minimum...now, especially near the river, the dark earth was fertile and, with much less hardship (though not totally devoid of it) the blessed ground amply responded to the human touch. And, in the inner quadrants, where once there had been barrenness and jagged horrid peaks (of the same mountain type previous mentioned), now, these lofty granite mounts that once served as platforms of domination—outlets for dragons as they seethed back and forth, like bees from a hive, to dishearten, destroy and devour—these were humbled, broken, smoothed down to the point of being a great latitude of gentle, rolling hills. Hills, where the treasures of the earth lay just below the surface...easily mined and, between these...valleys of rich fertile soil...able to support and enhance the growth of any seed planted. However, not *all* seeds are beneficial. And some...to be sure...are downright deadly.

Be wary of the temple built
Though motives...pure and true
For when the builder passes on
What will the children do?

After the kingdom was established and the population (due to a vigorous execution of the king's command to *seek and save*) grew, many, although admonished to make the river a regular part of their sustenance...many settled in the inner regions of the realm and began to draw freely from the treasures of the earth and soil. At first, wisely, these sojourners were careful to make regular pilgrimages to the river's edge. However, over time, many became weary of this trek that was added to the toils of there daily pursuits and, out of necessity (so they thought)...a remedy was fashioned...a remedy birthed from concern and compassion...a remedy born of human reason and sculpted by the hand of man.

To be sure...it was a glorious edifice...mirroring, on a much smaller scale (though still huge by human standards), the magnificent chamber where the king held court in the castle that was birthed through his victory. To those who had seen the royal dwelling (and *all*, upon swearing allegiance have seen it...at least once) the substitutionary gathering place, though lavish by earthly measure, appeared as a shadow of the perfect—giving merely an outline without the fullness of the form. For, when one traverses the rugged narrow bridge to reach the king's abode...when one goes through the all-enveloping mist which rises from the Living River and then passes the first arched gate into the massive flowering courtyard, there is, towering before you, a huge inner dome, made, as it were, of some sort of shimmering other-worldly stone and, if one cares to examine the make-up, it can be discerned that this wonder is one piece...made without mortar or seam, and from it radiates all the delicate hues, in ever-changing patterns, of the closer and closer Crystal Sea. However, though the outer gate to the castle can accommodate the many...the entrance beyond this inner wall—to a more intimate place— is, curiously, a doorway for one. Stranger still, this path to the king's court is made of a simple, and seemingly out-of-place construction. Indeed, it appears as the access to a peasant dwelling...two rough-hewn crimson doorposts and a lintel, of the same color, atop. Rough to the touch, yet inviting nonetheless...this doorway, like the bridge, is an avenue for one, yet, there seems to be no delay to those who would seek entrance. But *seeking* is the thing…and a step inside reveals that not many (after their initial introduction) do.

Once beyond the outer layers, a gasp is expected when first viewing the sights within. For, farther than the eye can discern, a great chamber sprawls before you. Oval in shape…the narrow end (though *hardly* narrow [is the horizon narrow?]) is where one enters, and the other is off straight ahead in the blurry place (due to distance) where there appears to be some sort of unrecognizable motion. The walls, which rise sharply and angle inward gently (such is the great height of the dome) are of the same brilliant material as the outer, yet, there appears to be emanating from them a chorus…not just of song and word, but a story of sorts…as if the great history of the defeat and triumph associated with the fall and rescue of humanity were perpetually played, celebrated, displayed before an adoring universe. Then, as one scans along the wall there is, suddenly, where the midpoint must surely be…huge towering windows. These, without glass or any other human fashion, give place to the reflections that must be the emanations of the Crystal Sea which surges without. No doubt, since this castle lies squarely in the breach of the accursed (and now forever debased) wall…this place, where the windows begin, is where the wall ends and, if one goes directly inward from the beginning of these (they rise on both sides of the dome), on this very center line, in the exact midpoint of this architectural wonder, is the place where the Great King holds court. It is here, on a small, slightly elevated platform midst a broad level plain, where the conqueror directs the affairs of his kingdom.

—It should be understood that the hall, similar to an amphitheater, slopes, ever so gently down to a certain point—much like an enormous balcony that can accommodate millions—and where, after coming just so far, one is greeted by a simple railing of uncut common stone (approximately a meter in height) which serves as a restriction to prevent entrance to the king's level (a four meter straight down drop). However, at the king's discretion, an opening sometimes appears in the wall and a citizen, who is chosen, is escorted by one of the king's attendants down a nondescript masonry stairway to afford a closer audience, and the possibility of a personal dialogue (a rare, and highly sought after honor) with the great ruler.—

The edifice of man, however, as stated earlier, was, in its beginnings, and when not closely compared to the dwelling from which it was patterned…glorious. In the very center of the inner quadrants…in that place that was, from every corner, equidistant (since the architecture of the age could not properly imitate a *dome* of any great size, a lofty structure, rectangular, was made using the technology of the time [buttresses, etc.]) from the blessed river…in a gentle indentation…a valley of sorts (round, like a fine porcelain saucer, a full kilometer in diameter, the remnants of a volcanic crater humbled and filled long ago)…like a giant hub from which all other domains radiated as spokes on a massive wheel…it was here where the *wise* decided to construct this common convenience that would serve to unify the many in their pursuit of service to the king.

For it was here, situated and surrounded on all sides by carefully attended blooms of red and white, that the leaders laid the foundation upon the hard-packed clay. "Only the finest materials will do!" was their command to the laborers. And soon, from the surrounding quarries and hills and canyons came the abundance of the earth. Marble, red-granite, gold, silver, copper, and all manner of precious stones and hardwoods were joyfully brought and laid at the feet of the craftsman and, in the quickness of zeal, and in the beauty of man's eye…the meeting place arose.

From a distance, when reaching the top of the gentle rise that is the outer rim of this nearly perfect circular valley, one would first see the spires…a multitude of impressive, unbelievably high pinnacles (reminiscent of the towers built by the *climbers* of old) that would nearly reach the clouds in a silent chorus of hands-raised celebration. These spires, however, rather than a homogeneous grouping, were each uniquely different. Indeed, each of the various groups of peoples who gathered here added their own distinct part and, accordingly, each tower was overlaid in the finery of their choice.

Closer, walking midst the delicate flowers, one would then see the three, enormous, fluted marble columns which guarded the entrance of the tabernacle (the structure was arrayed east to west, with the entrance being toward the rising sun). Along the outer walls on either side were a great number of polished, dark-stone buttresses which, along with the columns, rose to support and complement the many-angled, and multicolored, layered slate roof. And, in that spot where the two met…along the rim of the cathedral…a multitude of figures (statues of the king, *and* dragons, in action poses) would play out the final battle. Behind the columns there were three massive doors (three times an average man's height and able to allot entrance to ten abreast)—hardwood, exquisitely carved and, in the beginning…always open.

Upon entering this gathering place one would first be struck by the many beautiful colors which seemed to cloth all within. A great hall…ample for thousands…filled with vibrant, *moving*, color. Indeed, it was as if the reflections of the Crystal Sea (once only seen as in a mirror from the clouds overhead) were now (as in the king's chamber) transported to this hallowed spot. However, after the initial pause to wonder, one would realize that this radiant flood was due to sunlight being cleverly transformed as it passed through a great many exquisitely crafted stained glass windows (tall—nearly to the roof—and narrow) and, due to a great many polished reflectors placed some distance from the building, there was *always* [while there was day] sunlight available for the journey.

Once one became accustomed to the brilliance, a person could then scan and see the simplicity of the structure…as stated earlier…a great hall. It was an enormous open space (interspersed with stout granite pillars) where a great multitude could gather (at first sitting on the polished wood floor [wood, because there was a basement below for storage] and then, as a matter of economy, simple benches were provided to more efficiently accommodate the masses.) And, when the house was full, the perfect parallel rows of the faithful had the appearance of wheat in a farmer's field…moving…ever so gently, as they faced a rather ordinary open spot (sporting a very slight platform) at the west end where the leaders (aided by a shell-like sound directing and amplifying curvature of the back wall) would exhort them as to the king's desire.

And…at the first…it became as it was intended…a place to gather, hear, remember, rejoice, receive instruction, and…very importantly…it was a place to lay down, for weekly removal to the river, the *dragon seeds* that were beginning to be found with greater frequency among the peoples of these inner quadrants. However, over time, as is so often the case with the inheritors of fortunes…the methods of the early citizens were changed to accommodate the desires of a later breed. And, where once there was a humble rise from which the leaders would lead…soon there was built a lofty platform where the *chosen* (knights, who, over time, abandoned their simple warrior attire for a finery befitting royalty) began to dictate. Indeed, these warriors, who, at the first were careful to pattern themselves after their victorious Lord in that they were defenders and teachers and guides…soon these fellow pilgrims—though hardly seeing themselves as such—soon these began to imitate their king in a way not commanded…they began to *rule*. And, although the seeds of destruction were still summoned for disposal, the leaders decided to implement a new pattern whereby the horrid things were not even brought into the sanctuary for revelation and removal, but were, instead, sent down an outside chute to be stored in the basement for a later trip to the river…journeys which, over time…ceased to occur.

* * *

Edward Hershel, known simply as "Hersh" by his fellow treasure seekers, paused a moment to catch his breath before making the final assent up the well-worn path that led between the ever-encroaching brambles to the rim of the circular valley that contained, in its very center—the *dumping place.*

"Why do *I* always have to carry the accursed things," was his periodic lament to his odious cohorts as they loaded the many nodules (usually one or more per man) into the filthy burlap sack that was strapped upon his bowing back.

—At one time he could simply lift the load and sling it over his shoulder. Now, with the increase of the foul things, he would have to stand, crouched—like a dumb donkey—as they, not gently, loaded his pouch with a weight that his legs could still bear...but not his arms.—

"Because *you* live the closest...idiot!" was one of the many replies he received at such times (usually accompanied by a tweak on the cheek, or a punch in the arm, or a slap to the top of the head). "Now, on with you (a rough turning and shove in the direction of the dump) and give our regards to the fair Lady and the little Hershel!"

Edward could, in his mind, still hear the laughter of his so-called *friends* as he pushed aside the final scratching sticks that guarded the summit of this ominous ring and, for a moment, he pondered the life he had chosen. For, at one time—what seemed long ages ago—he had felt the call of a knight. He had even begun to train and associate with the others of that vocation...John, Peter, Bartholomew, Erick...many others. He had even crossed the river and aided in the very important task of seeking and delivering the oppressed. "Yes," he thought, looking down at the battered sword strapped to his side (battered...by way of being used as a digging tool)...that was a long time ago."

Eddie (the name preferred by his young wife, Delilah, a beautiful redhead who had stolen his heart a few years past and who, quite frankly, was the main reason he moved to the inner quadrants [*Be wary of the eyes and curves...these things will cause your path to swerve.* A saying he once heard from, you-know-who]); *Eddie* tried to straighten up a bit (the load was *very* heavy) and as he did so he scanned the length and breadth of this horrid place that could be compared accurately to the repugnant hole in the lowest spot of a crematorium. For, all around and through this gentle indentation, as he scanned left to right, he could see nothing but gray, steaming ash. It was as if this valley were the giant leavings of a burning place…nothing green…nothing moving…nothing alive…only dead, irreclaimable ash. "Hard to imagine," he thought to himself as he made his way slowly down another well traveled path (being careful to align his body in such a way as to compensate for the load *and* the incline) that led to the only spot in this miserable bowl that had a structure of sorts…the center, "that this used to be a paradise." And, as he neared the jagged skeletal walls (a partial frame of a once huge edifice) he, usually aware of the stench of sulfur that was, at times, almost overpowering, wondered to himself why the aroma of the enormous mass of putrid seeds (surely thousands upon thousands upon thousands—the byproduct of a million soiled hands and hearts that had been deposited there) was now, for some reason, not nearly so present. He eased himself over to the edge of the still-standing northern wall. There, next to a half-buttress and the few remaining shards of a once magnificent stained glass window, he pulled the hanging cord dangling from his chest, which served as the release mechanism for the increasingly hotter load which pushed relentlessly against his back. With a heavy *thunking* sound—like a clashing of moss-covered stones—the bag slammed to the earth and Edward, temporarily freed from the burden (and oh, so grateful to be so), extended his arms outward and commenced to stretch and swivel until the pain in his cramping muscles had eased.

"First the gloves," he mumbled to himself, grabbing the communal pair of leather sheaths that hung from his corded belt. "Then (Umph!) through the window with you!" The words, spoken only on the first throw, were accompanied by a sideward heave-ho as he crouched, bow-legged, over the open bag and, like a human pendulum, with straight arms grabbed and flung the nasty byproducts, one by one, through the adjacent broken window.

—By now the reader must suspect that the building to which Edward has dutifully come is the very same described earlier in this chapter. As mentioned previously…in its beginnings it was a blessing…used as intended…a place to purge and purify. However, due to the imperfections of man, many self-exalted knights abandoned the corporate meeting and established their own *gathering places* in their own appointed realms of influence. But…even with the diminishing of the congregation…it was not this that led to the destruction of man's temple. No…it was a shifting…a heaving…a twisting in the very structure itself that caused it to become uninhabitable. Some say it was simply poor planning to build upon a hard packed crater's bed. But, much more than an architectural misstep was in play here. For, as the seeds gathered in the basement, even as the faithful gathered above...there was a calling. It was an unheard drawing...a yearning...a beckoning...it was an unholy reaching out from that which was above—in the belly of the building—to that which was far below...in the bowels of the earth. And, as that which was below struggled to mingle with the other...the foundation tottered...the spires fell...the windows cracked and shattered, and the doors...once always open...were closed and locked...never to be disturbed again. However, even though the once beautiful thing was now left unattended (along with the gardens without)...still the people came to discard their wayward offspring. And thus the little miner stood outside the northern wall and did as the many others have done...for many, many, years.—

Though, during such mindless labor, it was not unusual for Edward's mind to wander far while his body did its task...there was something...even as he went through the motion of lifting, swinging, throwing...that called his attention back. "What is it?" he began to question. "Something's not quite right." He paused to straighten and stretch (the bag half empty) and, with hands on hips, he looked slowly about. "What is it?" he murmured out loud.

After a slight shrug of the shoulders, he stooped to begin anew. However, when the first orb arced through the ancient opening, Edward stopped again...the blood draining from his face even as his heart quickened with fear. "The s-s-sound," he stuttered. "The sound is different."

He picked up another seed and let it fly. Yes!...it was different. Indeed, what used to be a muffled splatter—like a stone thrown into the sticky gumbo left by a receding river—now there was a greater length of time before *anything* was heard. And, what *was* heard was like that of a pebble dropped into a very deep dry well. The little man started towards the edge of the building...understanding that he, in times past, had been prevented from a closer inspection due to the unbearable concentration of sulfurous fumes that hovered and pooled and, occasionally, splashed over the ancient walls. However, now, as the increasingly anxious Edward approached the rim...his fears began to solidify in that, on previous occasions, when he, standing on an adjacent slanted rock (a former reflecting stone), sought to peer into the inner realm of this ghastly depository...he could only view the seething, bubbling mist that hovered just below the window's edge. Now, bravely (or foolishly...for the vapors could kill, as evidenced by the barren valley) he shuffled to the very edge and, leaning, he looked in and down.

"It's...g-g-gone," he stammered. "Why...why is it gone?" The little man turned and paused a moment, leaning against the former foundation. He quickly (though not known for quickness) analyzed the data his brain had just received. "Before…a great pool of deadly vapor (*so* much more than vapor…but that's all that *he* could see). Now…" he unwisely touched his unshaven chin with his gloved right hand, "Now…only a great hole." He stood for a minute more, ignoring the slight burning from the glove's leavings, and then, perhaps gleaning from the conversations of knights he had known…he started walking, forgetting all about his task and leaving the half-filled bag, towards the eastern entrance.

"Something is terribly wrong," he whispered to himself, his steps quickening as he made his way toward the place he had seen only a handful of times.

—Edward's dwelling was a mere one kilometer south of this valley. The place of the mines, where he and others scratched in caverns for precious stones (there was a sizable market for such baubles in the inner quadrants) was just north. He was indeed the closest to this horrible hole and, since his family resided a bit west of center—he almost never bothered to circle around the front. Only his introduction to this graveyard (by a co-worker) and subsequent tours for his wife and a few curious friends had caused him to circumnavigate the huge structure. Usually he would do his business, then skirt the partially standing western rear wall, then, lighter, continue on his way over the rim to be joined to his beloved Dell.—

Panting, with hands on knees (he was not used to running, or any other activity that required purposeful endurance), he beheld the front of the structure, or, rather, what *used* to be the front. For, as his memory replayed, the front *used* to have two giant supporting pillars (a third, the middle one, lay prostrate, perpendicular to the entrance) and behind these, three doors, of great age yet still intact though slightly askew on the hinges, accompanied by a weaving of brass chains firmly secured to prevent any human entrance. However, as Edward's terrified expression gave evidence…something human did not enter. Something *else*…something *not human*…had exited. For, not only were all three pillars humbled to earth…the doors and chains were obliterated, pieces, splinters.

Whatever it was…it was *huge*. And its *stench*…the smell that had, in times past, *only* wafted from the pit…this foul perfume was almost overpowering at this spot and, horribly, it seemed to be coming *not* from the dumping place, but it seemed to be coming from a long line of enormous claw-prints (*dragon-prints!*) in the ash…claw-prints that led in the direction of Edward's home.

Chapter XI

All that have beginnings.
All you see and know.
Nothing...suddenly appears.
Its birth was long ago.

"Excuse me, miss...I was hoping I could have a word with you." The high-pitched gravely voice made Mary, who had been dutifully attending to the tasks of the kitchen, squeal and jump back from the window...causing, along with her feminine yelp, a chorus to be sounded from the hanging copper pots that served as a backstop to the frenzied movements of this normally unflappable house matron.

"Miss? Miss? Is everything all right?" The peculiar voice, coming, apparently, from the mouth of a fluffy white (plump, rather) cottontail (head and forelegs propped on the polished maple sill.)

(This window, *her* favorite, opened to the garden—lovingly tended by Fren...in fact...even now she could see her boy shuffling [He was not one for running and, when he *did*—only on occasions of extreme emotion—it appeared as an awkward shuffle] towards the house, coming from the river. Apparently he saw something, or *someone*, that invoked great excitement.)

"Miss, is everything all right?" the rodent repeated. And, as it spoke, it seemed to quiver a bit, as if there were an unseen arm attached that was itself attached to a man (no doubt a gray-haired adult [though by his actions you'd never know it!]) who was doing all he could to restrain his laughter.

Mary straightened herself, took a deep breath, and ran her hands down the front of her disheveled turquoise apron (a recent gift from an old acquaintance) and, calmly, clearing her throat, spoke to the gifted rabbit who had invaded *her* space.

"Oh…I'm fine," she, still a bit flustered, said, patting her gray mane (a nearly subconscious act, usually done when a certain nervous heart-fluttering takes place) which she had hastily arranged (including the addition of a splash of violets) upon hearing that a certain *someone* was coming for dinner. "Thank you for asking, Mr.? Mr.…?"

"Mr. Bunny, is fine," answered the rabbit…hopping a bit to the middle of the sill. "Normally I'm not one for titles or formalities but, since this is our *first* meeting…you may call me Mr. Bunny."

"Mr. Bunny, then. Fine." Mary started to remove some already washed dishes from the basin that lay, nearly full (holding not a few liters of sudsy, warm water), just below the jabbering Jack. "My name is Mary, but…I'll not tolerate any titles or exaltations attached to it. Just call me Mary."

At these words the rabbit leaned sideways a bit, as if in contemplation (actually, the puppeteer, Sir Peter, who was kneeling on the ground [on one of Mary's flowerbeds!] below the window was, at hearing these words, *himself* sporting a thoughtful expression [head cocked slightly to one side, lower lip protruding a bit as he nodded in agreement, as if to say, "Somebody finally gets it!" and, while in this position he noticed a smiling Fredrick coming quickly towards him, whereupon Peter waved and then held his left hand to his mouth to convey the universal *shhhh* signal.])

"Mr. Bunny? Mr. Bunny? Is there a problem?" Mary, knowing her well-aimed remarks had caught her furry opponent off-guard (both Sir Peter *and* the rabbit were abundantly hair endowed [no pun intended]), she then, as she continued to empty the basin and sensing a slight advantage, asked, "Mr. Bunny? You were saying?"

"Ah, yes," Peter said in his normal voice. "I mean…*Ah, yes* (the falsetto returned and, as Fren giggled and watched, the elder knight tried to counter attack), I've heard that you're the finest cook in the kingdom. Is this so?"

"Well, I…I…don't know if I'm the *finest*." (Mary, who prided herself on her culinary skill, started to blush and let down her defenses.)

"Well, (the rabbit continued, hopping to the right side) I was instructed to come to this house to offer myself for dinner…and that to be prepared by such a cook as ye…would be a great honor."

Mary snapped out of her daze. "He's doing it again!" she thought to herself. "Here I am, tirelessly preparing a favorite meal (certainly not one of *my* preferences) for *Sir* Peter...and he shows up with a menu change!"

"Well...*Mister* Bunny," she purred, pausing briefly to roll up the sleeves of her flower-print dress, "and how, exactly, would you like to be fashioned?"

The old knight, quite pleased with himself, scratched his bearded chin with the fingertips of his left hand and, noticing that Fredrick's eyes seemed to be widening with expectation, decided to offer one more jab. "Oh, I don't know...perhaps in one of your delicious vegetable stews, or maybe a scrumptious fricassee." Sir Peter turned his head slightly and, with the fingertips now covering his lips....he bobbed in accentuated silent laughter as Fren seemed to be getting into the spirit of things by clapping his hands together in short quick strokes. "And one more thing...*Mary.*"

"Yes (muffled *umph*)...what is it, *dear*?"

"Since we're acquainted now, and since you'll be getting to know me in the most intimate way (Peter imagined her eyes rolling at this statement...and so they were)...please refer to my by my first name."

"And what might that be...*dear*?"

"You may call me, Honey."

"Honey?"

"Yes...Honey."

"Are you telling me your name is, *Honey...Bunny*?"

"Yes." Peter could hardly restrain his laughter and, from the looks of things...Fren was in the same state. He was clapping *and* hopping.

"Well, *Honey Bunny*, I have one request before we begin our *relationship*."

"Oh...and what might that be, darling?"

"You simply must take a bath."

Sir Peter, not the quickest of minds (especially when matching wits with a woman), looked up just in time to see the deluge of soapy water arc out the window...slamming into his upturned, open-mouthed, bewildered face.

A moment later, as he sat, drenched, cradling and petting the curious rabbit...and as Fren, a few meters away, lay on the ground laughing and Mary, her smirking face peering over the maple sill...in obvious triumph...Sir Peter offered this final thought. "You missed the rabbit entirely...*He's* not wet at all."

* * *

Edward…tired, bewildered, very much afraid…ran in the direction of the awful footprints. "It *must* be a dragon," he thought as he struggled up the incline that preceded the rim. Panting, exhausted, he barely noticed that *whatever it was* had cut a huge swath through the brambles that led to this spot. However, he did notice the following: For, as he straightened slightly (his heart racing and his lungs screaming) and, as he raised his calloused right palm to shield his eyes from the waning summer sun he felt within him an ancient foreboding…the remnant of a time when, though merely a babe, he recalled the terror his parents displayed when a black-hearted creature passed nearby. And, as he looked down and beyond the path (normally no larger than a deer trail, winding midst the thorny undergrowth till it vanished into a forest of towering pine) he saw…not the usual standing of trees, but a wide shearing of the wood…as if a giant scythe had effortlessly mowed down a fifty-meter swath and, added to this, there was a horrible stench…like a mixture of sulfur and sewer and, as Edward stumbled (at first, due to shock) toward his dwelling, he perceived that much more than brute force had been at work for, everything growing (that which was mowed down, and that stretching far beyond the effects of the unknown cutting instrument) was decaying, shriveling, dying.

"Dell!" the word was desperate, a call into the dark. "Dell…I'm coming! Little Deb…I'm coming!" Edward ran…stumbled, jumped over the fallen trees and frantically pulled himself out of the snags created by the mayhem. "Dell…I'm coming! Little Deb…Daddy's coming!"

—Edward Hershel, enticed and entertained to seek the "good life," was now a father. Little Deb, or Debbie, was merely six months of age. Red of hair, like her mother, her hazel eyes and toothless smile controlled him in the most disarming and delightful way. In fact, it was *her* birth that had caused him to consider returning to the riverside…to a simpler, purer, existence.—

"Dell…I'm coming!…Go into the wood! Run into the woods!" (It was a reflexive plea…something he remembered from the blur of infancy when such warnings were given as large dragons approached). Edward, his dwelling within sight (a rather eloquent log structure…something he had contracted others to construct [he could afford it]), built in a large clearing, not far from a clean running stream. Now, in the twilight, it appeared merely as a shadow…though still distinguishable as the daylight waned and moon glow began to dominate. He paused and sighed as the path of destruction—

that which he had followed with all his might—seemed to vanish when it met the open ground. "Whatever it was…perhaps it took to the air, or went another direction…or perhaps it wasn't a dragon at all; perhaps it was a tornado of sorts (he *had* known of such occurrences [a storm lowering, destroying, then rising] but in choosing this explanation, he ignored the other elements of the equation…the claw-prints, the stench, the horrible turmoil in his spirit.)

Edward, noticing that the canvas bag which held his pickings from the mine (uncut gems…sapphires, rubies, emeralds) which normally hung from his belt…was now gone…slowly shook his head. "Perhaps another sign," he thought, walking towards the home that evidenced the slightest flicker of a candle in a bedroom window. "Perhaps I *should* return to the river."

Then, as he came within a stone's throw of his home…he heard it. It was a clicking…a steady clapping…a most disturbing cadence that ended at the count of ten. Edward paused, straining to sift the cool night air for another sound…but there was, for the briefest of times…none. No clicking, no owl, no cricket…no sign of life whatsoever. Then…in an instant…he felt a wave of pressure, as if something horrible had been loosed and all other things— even the air—fled before it. Immediately after this he was assaulted by a mighty roar—like the torrent at the base of a giant waterfall—it washed over and around his dwelling only a millisecond before the structure was totally…all at one time…instantly…engulfed in blue and yellow flame.

At the mind-numbing sound he had, instinctively, slammed his palms over his ears, and then, with the sight of his home…*and* family (he thought he could make out the slightest scream of anguish as the inferno consumed) going up in an unholy offering…he crumpled to his knees, screaming, even as the roar of *whatever-it-was* kept coming, and coming, and coming. Finally, after what seemed an eternity…the roar ceased…but then…an instant later…something indiscernible sliced, from right to left, through what little structure was left standing.

It was maddening. It was impossible! "I must be dreaming…I must have fallen in the mine and now lay unconscious." Edward, still on his knees, trembling and grasping for an explanation…wrestled with this horrible event that wiped away…in mere moments…all on which he had based his existence. "I must be dreaming," he slowly repeated, choosing to close his eyes as if to close the book and begin anew. "No dragon I've ever heard of could do such a thing," he reasoned, shaking his head, trying to stir himself to awaken.

"*Father…*" a voice, not unlike his own in pitch…yet cavernous in depth…with a dark, spiritual quality that chilled the bone. "*Father…*"

Edward opened his eyes. Before him, walking slowly (with earth-trembling weight) into the very flames that now occupied the space that *was* his home…there emerged an enormous dragon! The human stood, paralyzed by fear, and beheld the creature that had done this horrific deed.

"*Father…I've come for you. Come to me…Father. Join me…Father.*"

"H-H-How?" the gem-digger stammered, his mind unwilling to accept the presence of such a creature on *this* side of the river. For, unlike the human-nurtured villains that sometimes pop up among the citizenry of the king (the *dumping place* was supposed to prevent such happenings)…this *thing* was gigantic! Fully twice the size of a Muth…this creature—whatever it was—*could* speak, and, as it chose to sit back—its enormous armored hind parts smothering much of the area that *was* Edward's home—it spoke again.

"*Father…I've come for you,*" it rasped, beckoning with the upturned broadsword-like talons of its lifted right foreleg. "*I've come to thank you for giving me life. Come to me, Father. Come to me.*"

Edward, realizing that this was *not* a dream, instinctively reached across his body and drew the battered sword with his right hand. "What have you done with my family…you demon!" said the flea.

"*I…am your family,*" hissed the dragon, its huge red eyes squinting as it lowered its dripping jaws (some sort of flaming gelatinous substance oozing from between the jagged teeth) to within three meters of the man.

"Aaaayyy!!" it was a scream of anguish. It was the guttural yell of a man who had lost everything and no longer considered even his life of value. Edward ran past the wretched head (this orb, alone, was taller than he) and, planting himself one meter in front of the enormous plated belly of the beast…he began swinging wildly his dull digging tool that had been, at one time, the sword of a future knight.

The dragon slowly lifted his head to a tree-top height and peered down as the little man exhausted his strength and words against this foe he was incapable of wounding…let alone kill.

Finally, the man, utterly spent and defeated, his mind slipping into madness—even imagining that he could still hear the cries of his dead child—slumped forward against the unscathed crimson scale of the beast. But this moment of repose was brief for, with blinding quickness, the adept tip of the dragon's tail wrapped around the vanquished and held him over the gaping hole that would be his end.

"*Father…*" the dragon hissed, its foul breath steaming over Edward's body in a cruel caress. "*Father…join me…Father.*" And…in that brief span that it took him to fall head-first into the demon's craw…the little treasure-seeker thought he could still hear the wailing of his wife and child.

"I'm coming," he whimpered as his body quickly dissolved in the caustic wash. "I'm coming."

But…as fate would have it…Edward was *not* as mad as he thought at his final gasp. For…somewhere beyond the treeline…in the shelter of the dark…a red-haired woman (hastily aroused by the sounds of a beast and the pleadings of her now-deceased husband) held a screaming infant and wept as she saw this enormous monster devour her dear and then sift through the embers of her fallen home like a bear clawing and digging a garbage heap.

Suddenly, the dragon raised its head. At this the woman roughly placed her hand over the mouth of her bereaved child. And, for a few moments, there was that frenzied tension akin to the hounds before the hunt. The dragon's head swiveled in all directions, its enormous plated nostrils taking in great draws of midnight air. Then, looking directly to where she hid (no more)…the creature spoke.

"*Mother…*" (It *now* had a feminine wail!) "*Mother…I'm coming for you. Come join me, Mother.*"

Delilah trembled as fear surged through her members. "What can I do!" she whimpered.

"Run into the wood,"…the last words of warning her precious Eddie had screamed. "Run into the wood!"

She turned and, like the fox before the ravenous pack, she, holding little Deb tightly against her chest, weaved in an out of the thick-trunked pine…running…running…running. But, try as she might, the thunderous steps and the sound of shattering trees came closer and closer.

—As told earlier, the larger dragons (in particular, Muths) have limited speed. Although able to dispense with any sort of growth that may serve to impede them…this, in turn, slows them down still more. *This* creature, however, though no faster than a Muth (remember…a man of normal aptitude can outrun one), the trees (though huge) served as *no* hindrance whatsoever. Indeed, the winding way slowed down the prey.—

She, near exhaustion, could hear the demonic pleading right behind her. "*Mother…come to me…wait for me…join me, Mother.*" Delilah heard the horrible cracking as the trees shattered and fell at her heels. Finally, exhausted and unsteady in the dark…she fell…and, hearing the monster stop

123

just behind…she found the strength, somehow—a moment before her sure demise—to jump up and run again.

Never had she felt such terror. Her mind, devoid of reason, only played the primal thoughts of survival…*run…must live…run…must get away!* But, after a few minutes had passed, and she realized that the creature had paused from his pursuit…Delilah noticed that her arms, which moments before had grasped her precious child…were now vacant. Then, crumpling to the ground…and hearing in the distance the pleadings of a baby who could only speak in tears…she, she who had prodded and pushed her husband to abandon a knight's vocation and seek, instead, the temporal things of this life…she began to grind her teeth, and pull out her hair, and make incomprehensible screeching noises as she heard from a distance…

"*Thank you, Mother…thank you.*" And…the faint wailing that evidenced the precious life of an innocent little babe once adored, and kissed, and tenderly caressed…suddenly ceased.

* * *

"Most peculiar," mumbled the night flyer as he, his pouch half full of the poison, spiraled downward in the airspace high above the central location. He, as usual, had been *seeding* the land of his enemy (as he did every night) however, something was very different about this center spot over which he now descended. Although not privy to the plots and plans of his Master (he was told little, and he dare not ask), he *did* know that this hole was a gathering place for the harvested orbs. And he *did* know that this pleased his leader and that it did somehow fit into the Great Plan. Yes, very familiar was he of this spot where the *barrier* seemed weakest of all. But tonight was different somehow. For, just as he crossed into that invisible cylinder (the area rising above the middle) he felt an ease…a freedom…a sense of *home.* Indeed, over this little dark hole, it was as if he were flying over the mount of his master…as if he were over the blessed lands *beyond* the cursed river.

"Perhaps that last human morsel was tainted somehow?" he mused as he crisscrossed back and forth over the confusing coordinates, thinking about the terrified aging *snack* (too old to escape) he had retrieved from a town square on the other side. But, as he reached the edge of the invisible circle…the pain of the shield—that piercing that normally repulsed those of his kind if they flew too low—returned, and he, like a rat in a maze, then naturally turned in the direction of less resistance. Yes…it was definitely gone when over the center…no!…even a bit *beyond* the black middle.

The heart of the monster quickened! Forgotten was his task to sow the seeds. Somehow, someway, there was an opening to the land of his enemy and, descending lower and lower, he was determined to explore it. Finally, he hovered just above one of the few remaining buttresses that rimmed the dumping place and, prepared to ascend at the slightest twinge, he gingerly alighted on the man-made structure…his talons grasping tightly the highest stones…and then, ceasing his efforts to remain aloft…he folded his wings and let his full weight balance on the tower.

"Nothing," he thought to himself. "Nothing!" he rasped audibly. So often had he felt the power of the shield…the realization that it was gone (at least in this little area) almost short-circuited his twisted brain. "What has happened! Why is it so?" he pondered, scratching his pointed chin with two blood-stained claws. And then…gazing down into the cavernous hole and then following, with his eyes, the trail of destruction that led out to the rim of this unholy sacramental bowl…all the little things said and whispered by his master…all the things he had overheard from the higher ranked of his brothers…began to make sense. *"When he is ready…when he is born…when they're done feeding and nurturing and delivering!"*

The Sower, emboldened by his deduction, extended his giant bat-like wings and swooped down to touch the soil that none of his kind had touched in over a millennium. "Yes!" he screeched, as his talons sank into the ashen earth and he felt no resistance whatsoever. "It is time!" Then, after some moments of devilish dancing he stopped to ponder his next step. "I wonder where *it* is," he muttered, flying to the edge of the valley to the spot where the scarring of his new-born relative went over and beyond. "I must take a look at this *deliverer*."

The flying dragon, having long forgotten that his seeding task was half done, leaped into the night air, his wings churning and pulling his weight high into the heavens. "I will find you, brother," he said, following the moon-lit trail south until he felt the *barrier* at a spot just beyond the dying embers of a human's destroyed nest. "Oh," he drooled, "If I could just partake of one of these worms." His mind refocused as he assumed a counter-clockwise course, staying just inside the point of pain as he followed a path of destruction that seemed, although steady in a circular course, to vary only in small degrees to pause at now-destroyed insect dwellings.

"There he is!" the demon screeched, his eyes widening as he beheld, far below, a huge plume of oily blue and yellow flame engulfing a dwelling (delightfully, he also saw some two-legers running ablaze and then falling and writhing before being quickly gobbled up by this brutal behemoth.)

The Sower hovered a moment, his ghoulish emotions peaking as he saw this cancer eating at the heart of his enemy. "Perhaps I should introduce myself?" he thoughtlessly mused as he descended, almost unconsciously, towards the largest of his kind he had ever seen. Then, just a few meters above the monster's towering head...reason reemerged. For, the Earth Walker, rumbling onward in its steady purge, suddenly sensed the flitting of his tiny cousin. Then, raising its horrid head, it gave the Sower a murderous gaze while, at the same time, almost swatting the flyer with its whip-like tail.

"No," the Sower whispered, avoiding another lash as he climbed to the altitude of planting, "introductions will have to wait. But," he continued, heading back towards the granite peak of his beginning, "surely my Master will wish to know. Yes...surely he will be pleased with the news."

* * *

"Why have you returned so soon?" the words were monotone, cold, and punctuated by the steady squeezing of talons on the neck of his servant who lay prostrate, trembling, bleeding, and still carrying a pouch, not yet empty.

"He is born...sire." The reply...almost inaudible due to the pressure...was, nevertheless, heard.

"What did you say!" the Sower was now lifted to eye level with his King.

"He is born...I have seen him! He is destroying the land of our enemy! Where he goes...the barrier is gone!" The words, excitedly spoken with eyes tightly shut (gazing directly into the Dragon King's orbs was in itself a death sentence) brought release of the claws. Whereupon the Sower fell in a heap before his merciless Lord.

After a full minute had passed without sound or assault, the trembling underling (still with eyes closed) finally heard the words... "Have you touched it?" And this time the tone was not piercing, but almost civil. "Have you touched it?"

"Sire?"

"Have you touched...the soil?"

"Y-yes," was the cautious reply (not knowing if this was an offense or not.)

126

A long pause ensued, as if thoughts of centuries ago, when dominion was absolute, were being replayed in the mind of the humbled tyrant.

"Go...tell your brothers," the words, fading as the monarch walked away—his talons clicking on the hard stone floor and echoing off the walls of the cavern to the attentive ears of the *not dead* Sower. "Go tell your brothers that *he* is born. (the sound of claws and then, without pause, the soft shuffle of slithering scales)...And then finish your seeding run."

The sound of a great hatch, mingled with the crackling of flames, obscured, only slightly, the final utterance. "Tell them he is born...yes...he is born...yes...*We* are born."

Chapter XII

Treasures...pleasant to the eye
Care nothing
If you live...or die
But treasures born of love...endure
And last...eternal
Strong and Sure.

Sir Peter leaned back, pushing away from table that had served, so often, as the mingling place of food, fellowship, friendship...family. It had been, as usual, a glorious banquet. No, not fancy as the world esteems cuisine, but hearty, and robust, and so satisfying to the appetite of a man who, in his own lonely dwelling, often made due with just a loaf of bread, some cheese, and perhaps a tankard of cool well-water and, on occasion, some donated ale. As before, being one of the king's knights, he was still entitled to the royal stipend but, as before, he had chosen not to take it...feeling, perhaps, that his deeds of love and devotion to his monarch would be somehow cheapened if he took what was rightfully due. And, unfortunately, with his complaining joints and slower step, he was no longer capable of long hours of wall building which had been his engine of sustenance...although, on occasion, he would assist in smaller projects and these, few as they were, provided him with an income that provided the barest of essentials.

The aging knight caused the front legs of his sturdy captain's chair (*My arms need a place to sit, as well*, he'd say) to leave the floor and, although done without so much as a whisper, this maneuver brought a correcting glance from a distant Mary (who was attending to the dishes in the adjoined kitchen). Peter, feeling the weight of her eyes, smiled sheepishly and leveled the chair to its previous state.

Across the table, his back to the fireplace (always, in these cooler months [it was not quite summer], a fire was gently murmuring in muffled crackles and pops in a rather large stone hearth which, in turn, bathed a cozy sitting area [a simple couch and some chairs angled inward] where many weighty discussions…and light-hearted banter…had often taken place) Sir John, his elbows and forearms resting on the table as he mindlessly rubbed his thumbs along the irregular grooves of his drinking mug (a homemade gift from Albert, years before [with the aid of the Potter]. Not fancy, by any means [a shiny black and gray, the handle, large, a bit crooked, along with some indistinguishable markings throughout ["That's you and me and Amethyst!"], but, being made with love…it made all liquids put therein— that much sweeter). John, thoughtful (something was stirring…something terribly deep) looked across at his mentor (who was exchanging curious expressions with Mary as she stood [immovable, head slightly cocked, with a whimsical glint in her eyes] drying a small copper pot that had been used for some homegrown vegetables).

"He *is* flirting!" he thought to himself (having suspected for some time that Peter and Mary [both *so* very different] were becoming a *little more familiar* in their discourse of late.) The younger knight nudged (using his knee, under the table) the leg of Albert (the teenager, seated to his right, who was on his third helping [not unusual]) who then stopped his voluminous intake, glanced at his father (who was side nodding with his head [while pivoting his eyes in Peter's direction], and then the boy whispered (leaning inward to his father's waiting ear,)

"I know. Isn't it weird?"

"What'd you say, lad?" bellowed Sir Peter, whereupon both Albert and John straightened in their seats and displayed, in unison, the most innocent of expressions.

"Nothing, Uncle," the boy offered, beginning afresh his left-handed fork action. "Nuffing at all."

A moment later, Sir Peter, again drawn (like the proverbial moth to the flame) to the damsel in the doorway, got up, started walking in the direction of the kitchen and, as if needing a proper excuse, reached back to grab his drinking mug. And, as both Sir John and young Albert (who had paused, mid-stroke) fixed their wondering eyes on him…Sir Peter awkwardly stuttered, "I…I…believe I shall have some more of that delightful tea." Whereupon he eased his way in the direction of his heart.

The elder gone from view, Sir John, ever so slightly, shook his head while slowly bringing, with his right hand, a drink to his lips. "Who'd have thought," he whispered while taking a long draft and rolling his eyes upward to gaze into the lazy yellow flames of the oil lamp which hung from the rafters above.

Albert, nodding in agreement even as he brought a decorative cloth napkin to his mouth (napkins, drapes, color, cleanliness…all the result of the woman's touch), again leaned toward his father and said in a scholarly tone, *"Though the ashes…be cold and gray…deep within…an ember lay."*

Phhhhhhhttt! Out came the mouthful of drink as John exploded at the unexpected musings of his son. Meanwhile, Albert, quite pleased with himself, *he* began snickering violently (trying ever so hard not to laugh out loud) as his *Dad* commenced to wiping the table (and *himself*) with a hasty gathering of other napkins that lay nearby. What a sight as John, the *king's knight*, himself fighting off tremors of explosive laughter, bustled about wiping, lifting,…and nearly knocking the table over in his efforts. Finally, after a minute of this frenzied action, he settled, with a sigh, into his chair and both he, and son, simply smiled widely at one another as this new, most unusual chapter…opened before them.

* * *

Sir Reginald leaned back into his cushioned oversized throne which stood elevated atop the highest of three stepping-tiers of polished white marble at the western end of a giant hall in the very center of the great walled city known as, Alazon.

—In the realm of the Warrior Knight there are many cities, towns, hamlets, villages. The closer to the river…the population centers are free from barriers (speaking, of course, not of boundary markers, but rather of defensive bulwarks). As one travels inward, however, the cities are surrounded by walls. Some are simple…wood, earth. Others are more elaborate and ominous…high granite barriers, complete with towers and surrounded by moats. One would suppose, in a land free of dragons, that there would be no need for such fortifications. However, *these* walls are not made to keep reptilian devils at bay…No, *these* walls are made to keep *some* men in…and other men…out.—

"My Lord! My Lord,"…it was the frenzied call of Sir Robert (one of the lesser knights who, although *barely* of the royal class, and although thoroughly inadequate in the arts required for promotion to the upper levels [as evidenced by the games], he was, at least, a competent servant and he was…at this point…disheveled…obviously upset and out of breath and, as he quickly made up the distance from the large decorative brass doors (from which he had just burst through) at the other end of the hall and came to a hurried stop a few meters from his lord…he assumed the proper position of kneeling on the right knee (as was required when addressing the high knight), and spoke again.

"My Lord!…"

Sir Reginald held up his bejeweled left hand to silence the gush. "What is it now, Sir Robert?" he said with near disgust. "Another sighting of a dragon? A rumor of wings in the wind?"

"No, my lord," said the inferior knight, barely pausing to recognize the slight. "A woman…mad…quite mad…at the gates…she's asking for you. She says you know her."

"A woman, you say?"

—Sir Reginald, although ever faithful to his childhood darling (at least in body), fancied himself a man to be desired and, when in the presence of the fairer sex, he was not above a flirtatious remark or gesture.—

"Who *is* this woman?" the ruler leaned back into the softness of the throne, his arms cradled by the form-fitted armrests. "What is her name?"

"Delilah, Sir Reginald. She says her name is Delilah."

Sir Reginald, for a moment puzzling at the information even as he fixed his gaze mindlessly on the sparkling bobbles (he was especially drawn to the crimson sapphire) which adorned each finger of his left hand and, suddenly making the connection, said, "Yes…I know who she is (words spoken with a slight rising of emotion, as if this person had some sort of connection to that which he held dear.) She's the wife of that fellow who brings the gems."

—Sir Reginald, long before, had made an arrangement, not only with Edward, but indeed with *all* the treasure seekers that they would bring their wares *first* to him…that he might pluck the very best for the adornment of his many prized possessions…not the least of which was…his body.—

"Yes, Delilah," he muttered, stroking his clean-shaven chin as he recalled a woman, fair of form…quite beautiful to the eye. "Yes, go fetch her,

Sir Robert. I find it curious that her husband has not been by recently with his merchandise. I must enquire as to the state of her family and if there is trouble in the house. By all means…let her in."

"Sire?" Sir Robert, now standing, discerning that his full message had not been properly digested, cautiously sought to clarify. "Sire?" he said again.

Snapping out of his daze of memories past, Sir Reginald looked harshly at the servant. "What is it, Sir Robert? Why do you delay?"

"Sire," the messenger said calmly. "Whatever this woman was…she is no more. The creature at the gate is quite mad. Her appearance is most unsettling (a slight pause as the words at last penetrated) I wanted you to be prepared, my lord."

Sir Reginald, for all his bluster, appreciated, from time to time, the loyalty of this lesser knight. "Thank you for the warning, Sir Robert. Now, please…let her in."

* * *

Peter and Mary returned to the dining area, he…carrying the additional plates and silver, and she…cradling in a protective cloth a hot breaded delicacy (that she had *just* placed in the oven when *Sir Honey Bunny* had made his appearance some time before.)

"How natural they seem together," thought Sir John as the couple (who were ever exchanging the light-hearted nonsense of the smitten) approached the table and began distributing the steaming treat to the fortunate who had gathered that day.

"Fredrick, it's time for dessert!" shouted Mary in the direction of the garden (knowing, of course, that if her son was not in sight, he was either in the garden or had gone to the river.)

"Coming," came the faint reply, and before long the *family* of five were enjoying, not only the pleasures of the palate, but even more so…the feasting of the heart.

* * *

Behind the brass doors one could discern a frantic shuffling…the sounds not unlike an animal of the field which was used to the freedom of *all* directions…but was now required to travel only one. There was a shriek…more frantic shuffling…and then…an opening of the doors and the presenting to Sir Reginald of a creature…like none he had ever seen before.

"Yes, she *is* a woman," he thought, as he beheld her from afar (this was evidenced by a bruised [and in no way appealing] body which was covered by the barest of remnants of a once fine garment), "but could this really be Delilah?"

Sir Reginald motioned that the frightened waif be brought closer (she, surrounded on three sides by able servants, was constantly, nervously, looking over her shoulder even as she cradled *something* in her arms). "Come here, child," he spoke in a fatherly tone. "You've nothing to fear here…come…come." He held out his hand as if beckoning a skittish rabbit. And, perhaps in response to the tenderness of his voice, and the familiarity of the place…she seemed to settle a bit…and walked, a little more surely, to the edge of the stair.

The high knight looked down on this loathsome thing that trembled at his feet. "Could this possibly be the miner's wife?" he silently puzzled as he stood and descended (ever so slowly, so as to inspect without causing flight). "Delilah," he said, in a tone reminiscent of an afternoon tea. "So good to see you."

The woman, upon hearing the words, seemed to stabilize still more and subconsciously began stroking her few remaining hairs (the rest had been yanked out.) "Yes, my lord. It is good to see you, as well." The response seemed reflexive, as if a more sober part of the brain had been activated and had achieved, for the time being, temporary sway.

Sir Reginald paused at the last step, now just an arm's length away. "Oh, my lord!" he thought with revulsion as the odor exuded from this troubled being assaulted his nose which was accustomed only to the finest concoctions derived from his personal perfumer. "What has happened to this woman that she has attained this horrid state?"

—Delilah, as Reginald had recalled, was a young, sensuous, impeccably dressed woman of character. This *thing* which stood before him—if it was indeed her—had undergone an amazing transformation. For, where once there were polished locks of flowing red…now there was a nearly bald scalp, covered with scabs, with only a handful of strands that appeared darkened by congealed blood. Her face, once shining, smooth and perfect…was now sullen, scarred and gaunt. The rest of her body was emaciated and covered with sores and, her once manicured and enviable nails…were now broken and filthy (as if used to dig for grubs). Finally, peculiarly…there was, what appeared, as perhaps a sleeping baby, tenderly cradled beneath a ragged blanket in the crook of her left arm. As Sir Reginald glanced [trying not to be obvious] at the bundle, he *did* recall that his favorite jewel provider had said something about having a baby…but he was sure the child would be much older by now.—

"Delilah, (he kept his tone light…as if passing pleasantries at an informal function) how is your fine husband, Edward…that's his name, isn't it? I so would like to examine some more of his wares."

The sound of her departed husband's name seemed to change her countenance like a dark cloud's shadow moving quickly across a sun-bathed reflective pond. "Edward?" Her voice trembled…her eyes widened and took on a deep wildness even as she began looking over her shoulder…looking for something…something terrifying. "Edward is fine," she said with little faith. "He's at the mine…yes…he spends so much time there…such a hard worker…working for Debbie and me."

Reginald, aware that a threshold was approaching, decided to push a little further. The truth had to be known. "Little Debbie? Yes, your husband spoke of his most prized jewel. *You can't have her*…he'd say to me in jest. (A little laugh and then a pause…the knight noticing an ebb in emotion as the little girl was mentioned.) Is *this* your daughter?" His right hand reached for the soiled pink rag.

"No! You mustn't!" Delilah twisted her body away sharply, frantically. "She's asleep…she needs to rest…(turning her face to the bundle) There, there, child…it's all right, baby…Mommy's got you."

Sir Reginald paused, wanting to go further…wanting to do *something*…and then he saw it…something fell to the polished crimson floor…something white, which wiggled. He quickly, before she could resist, snatched the soiled threads from her arm. Then, as all eyes were on the baby…a menagerie of shouts and shrieks rose from the room. For, in the crook of her arm was *not* a human baby…but a pig. A dead, decaying, worm-eaten baby pig.

Delilah sobbed as she dropped to her knees, stroking the animals hideous eyeless face. "It's all right, baby," she consoled as she rocked. "Mommy's got you…Mommy's here."

Sir Reginald, who had jumped back at the revelation, now, as the shock began to lose its grip…beckoned to Sir Robert, who dutifully rushed to his side. "Retrieve the animal from this poor woman…and then we must try to help her."

"Yes, my lord," was Robert's reply as he motioned with his eyes to the others in attendance.

"NO!…WHAT ARE YOU DOING!!" Delilah screamed as two servants restrained her and the carcass was quickly pulled and placed in a bag for disposal. She struggled for only a moment and then, no doubt from her extremely weakened state…she crumpled to the floor and curled into a fetal position.

As one of the attendants left with the refuse, the others stood behind as Sir Reginald stooped to try and talk to this tortured soul. "Delilah." His words were gentle, compassionate, genuine. "What happened to your husband…what happened to your baby?"

The poor creature on the floor sobbed a constant stream. Her tiny body quaked under a horrible unseen weight and then, she whimpered an answer. "They're dead…both dead…a dragon…a huge talking dragon…it killed them…it *ate* them. Oh! My husband! (Her cry increased in volume even as she closed her eyes tightly and pulled out the last strands of her hair.) I'm sorry I made you move to the center…I'm sorry I made you move." There was a pause…long deep breaths…and then more words. "I'm sorry, little Debbie…Mommy's sorry."

Sir Reginald stood, with Robert by his side. Turning to his fellow knight, he instructed, "Take some of your brothers to the center. Check out this story." And then they heard, rising from the crumpled mass on the floor…a poem in the form of a song:

From the center, rounding round
Father, Mother, bring
Then to Master, we present
The perfect empty ring
The perfect empty ring…

The voice of the maid faded in repetition and then, taking one last deep breath, she seemed to drift into unconsciousness.

"Sir Robert, fetch my personal physician for this pitiful child."

The servant knelt beside her, touching lightly her wrist as he leaned his ear close to her slightly opened mouth. "No need, my lord," he spoke quietly as he turned his gaze above. "She's dead. Quite dead…poor creature."

Chapter XIII

To find a man
Look past the skin.
The heart reveals,
"We now begin."

The empty plates (stacked neatly in the center), the mugs—full and steaming (Fren had made another pot of his famous herbal tea and hovered nearby, ready to top-off any cup that needed fullness). The men of the table leaned in, and (although Mary frowned on such practices) they all had their elbows anchored…acting as pivot points to aid in the quest for nearness.

"Oh, *Sir Peter*," the words were followed by a slight girlish giggle (Sir John and Albert were simply *amazed* at what love had done to the *general* of the house) came from Mary who, sitting on Peter's left, took the opportunity to pat gently the rough, overlapping hands of the old warrior as he told of yet another amusing episode from his extensive travels.

The gray-haired knight, still quick of hand, grabbed hers tenderly and, while holding it (she did not resist) said, "Dear Mary…please call me Peter."

The damsel blushed a bit as she smiled. "I'll try, Sir…I mean *Peter*. But it seems so awkward."

Sir John looked down into the slowly swirling foam in the recently refilled mug which he held with both hands. He recalled the episode, long before, when Peter made such a big deal over the business of the name.

Indeed, he himself had no problem with a title…after all he *was* a knight and besides, people were so used to calling him thus…he surmised it would be more trouble breaking them of the habit.

"Uncle Peter?" The voice of Albert, who, as a pre-man, was *expected* to use titles of respect; however, due to their closeness, instead of *Sir Peter…Uncle* was acceptable. The lad's deepening voice brought his father back to the present. "Uncle Peter," the boy repeated, causing the love-birds to unlock eyes, "please tell me again about that time and the name."

"Yesss," Peter settled back in his chair, both hands (lovingly relinquished by Mary who, smiling, stood to attend to the dishes) now holding the warm mug, which balanced on his belly. "Yes…let me recall for you that day."

Around the table there was a quick acknowledgment with eyes that they were entering a new phase of the evening. Peter would tell a story…so you'd better settle back and let him tell it. Besides…such times were relished by the four. And each, in their own way, put their minds in a calm receptive mode. It might be short, or long…but one thing was certain…it would not be boring.

"I was still a young, inexperienced protector," he began, the right hand cradling the cup while the left thoughtlessly sifted through his coarse gray beard. "Oh, I'd been trained properly enough…Sir Timothy had made sure of that." (A slight pause as Peter's eyes glanced to the ceiling and his mind appeared to take a slight detour [no doubt concerning his former mentor]…the hearers wondered if this road would also be traveled [it wouldn't be the first time that a single story turned into many] but the elder's next words put their minds at ease.) "Where was I? Yes…I was a young protector. Full of zeal. Strong, skilled…even (a sip of tea, a portion of which dribbled on the chin, which was followed by a sleeve) a bit cocky. And, you understand, this was even before that most stabilizing element, God rest her soul (the hearers added, in unison, "Amen.") entered my life. Sooo…a call went out from the king for a great expedition."

Peter leaned in now, elbows and forearms on the table, hands grasping the mug. Likewise, John and Albert also leaned in (Fren, not wanting his mother to toil alone, excused himself in order to aid in the task of clean-up [but, while performing their chores, both were attentive, nonetheless]). "There must have been fifty of us," he continued. "I'd say thirty good strong knights and a variety of assistants and helpers."

—On a larger and longer expedition there was, naturally, a need for the underpinnings of any successful army. Not just those who specialized in combat (The knights…although, truthfully, *all* were required to attain a certain level of skill in this area), but also those who supply bread, water, and the basic necessities. On this particular assignment the king had said that a *whole town* had petitioned him for citizenship, but their escape to the river was blocked by many dragon.—

"Well, let me tell you, (Peter gazed intently into the hungering eyes of those at the table, especially Albert), I had never seen such a gathering of the accursed creatures. As you all know (with the words a pointing of the right hand index finger along with a sweeping glance that caught each individual's gaze) these monsters are not known for fighting as one. Usually they're a selfish lot—cruel, territorial, vicious—even amongst themselves (another sip, dribble, wipe). Truly, there's been many a time I've run across the stinking carcass of one of these devils and the cause of death appeared to be nothing more than the result of a family spat (a pause to snicker, then slowly shake the head from side to side while bringing near the mug for a draft. Then, placing the mug down he added, under his breath)…idiots."

"Peter," John interjected, knowing that a little nudging would be necessary to keep the storyline singular, "what did you say the place you were going was called?"

This time the right hand scratched vigorously the back of the elder's head and then, as he briefly went through his memory log, it continued down the neck and ended between the shoulder blades (the elbow, thus, pointing straight up). "Kol…Kol…(it was as if he were pulling a resistant night-crawler from its hole)…Kolleb! That's it! (The right hand quickly joined the other around the base of the nearly empty mug. Fren, noticing [he *always* noticed such things] quickly filled it. Whereupon, Peter paused a moment.) Thank you, brother." He said, looking up and giving Fren his customary wink.

* * *

Sir Rob, riding his spotted stallion, Rammak (the royals, usually very attentive to appearance [except, on occasion, when exclusively with their own kind] had rejected this particular horse due to its imperfect colorings. Sir Rob, however, rather than see it destroyed [a disturbing practice…the imperfect were killed rather than given, or even bartered, to those who have great need, but little means, in which to purchase such an animal], had rescued the foal and discovered this creature to be intelligent, strong, and even protective of its master. Of course, when the royals parade en masse the lowly knight had firm instruction to leave this beast in the stable), now, a day after the episode with Delilah, Sir Reginald's servant led a small band of his fellow knights (four others) to the place where Edward the miner was last known to live.

"Come now, children...this way," said Robert sarcastically to his four lagging companions. Riding abreast, these *warriors* busied themselves in pointed banter, as if intimate siblings. Yet, at these words, the four ceased their heated discussion (they were *always* debating something) and each looked coolly (yet without malice) to the lead horseman who had since turned his head forward and, unseen by his companions, now sported the slightest of smiles.

An interesting grouping these five...Sir Gustov (a giant of a man), Sir Francis (skilled in the bow), Sir Gerald (somewhat of a poet/singer), Sir Joseph (a light-hearted sort) and, of course, Sir Robert. These, the lowest in the ranks of the Knights of Alazon, were often assigned many of the tasks that did not involve the spotlight or the catching of the eye. And, although as one man they thought little of the "games" and the many inventions of nobility (thus, they never excelled at these man-made contests) they did, however, like to be associated with the prestige of the city...and this little tether of pride...it was this that anchored them to the inner realm (although they, unlike most of their brethren, still made *the river* a part of their regular devotion.)

"How much further...*old man?*" offered Joe (as with many of equal station, these knights, among themselves, almost *never* used proper titles. Thus, Sir Joseph was *Joe,* Sir Gustov was *Gus,* Sir Gerald was *Jerry,* Sir Francis was *Frank,* and Sir Robert was *Rob,* or, in an attempt to annoy and exploit his greater years...he was sometimes referred to as, *old man.* And, of course, there were often other names given that, depending on the circumstance and provocation, were less flattering and sometimes, downright nasty.)

"Oh, we've another day's ride, my young pup," said Sir Rob, taking no offense at the words of his brother. "The miner's abode is very near the center in the outskirts of a stately forest. I've been there once or twice. His dear wife (a slight pause as he remembered her horrid end) would entertain from time to time..."

The sentence stopped abruptly as Sir Rob, who was a good five horse-lengths in front of the others, came to the peak of a slight rise in the trail.

Normally, from this vantage, a rider could see a great deal of the coming countryside—not only a broad panorama of the many hills that dotted this most inner of regions, but also a small portion of the very valley that contained the *dumping place.* However, Sir Rob (evidenced by his silence and a dropped-jaw expression) saw something terribly unexpected and, as the others, sensing that *something* was horribly amiss, hurried to join their elder…they too saw the unthinkable. For, where once there was forest and field and wildlife in abundance, now it appeared as an enormous, barren, ashen sore…a huge, expanding, circle of decay.

* * *

Sir Peter planted both elbows squarely on the table, his burly hands embracing the steaming mug. "As one," he said, his expression bearing witness to an inner focus, "each knight emerged from the mist, zealous, eager, determined. I, positioned somewhere near the middle, looked to my left and right and felt a great swelling of pride and wonder. I," he sat up slightly, momentarily removing his right hand from the warming mug to pat his breast, "I…a novice—in regards to practical experience in the ways of our king—had been selected to join a great expedition. It was a crusade…a rescue…an opportunity to show my fellow warriors my skill. And I," pausing for a quick draft and wipe, then assuming his first position, "was determined to do just that."

* * *

After the initial shock had worn off and the expected unanswerable questions of, "What happened? How could this be? How long has this been going on?" had been asked, the five made their way to the edge of the fouled ground, determined to continue toward the last known location of the miner's dwelling.

"Yuck," offered Sir Gerald, as the stench of the defiled land wafted and washed over them.

"Is that the best you can do, my young poet…*Yuck?*" said Sir Robert in a half-attentive tone, his gaze not departing from the path they were preparing to take.

These knights of Alazon, for the moment still and thoughtful, sat quietly upon their agitated steeds (especially Rammak, who was most disturbed at the prospect of placing even one hoof on the ashen pavement before them) until the leader spoke once more.

"It smells very like our enemies' land," said Sir Rob, pausing a moment as his mind sifted the scent. "But in some ways it is more penetrating...more vile."

"Yes...I agree, brother," offered Sir Gus. (This common dilemma united, as it always did, the five squabblers. Now, at least until all were at ease...they were *brothers.*)

"Do you think we should return and report this to Sir Reginald?" said Sir Francis who, like they all (to some extent), wanted to remove himself far from this disturbing landscape.

"No, little brother," Sir Rob turned his gaze to the eyes of each. "We've come to unravel this mystery. And that is what we will do."

* * *

"Uncle Peter?" young Albert interrupted. "Were any of the royals among you on this quest?"

—Again...there must be an understanding that this story had been told before. However, it is only natural that individual listeners would like certain parts expanded and embellished, something the aging knight was more than willing to do.—

"Oh, yes...my young farmer." Peter paused to take another draft. "Yes...there was a grand mix of the nobles and the nobodies. Indeed, some of the mighty warriors among us rode the finest of white stallions...tall, shimmering, visions of regality they were."

Albert and Sir John quickly glanced at one another with raised eyebrows and wide eyes, as if to say, *"Regality?*...I've never heard him use that word before."

Sir Peter took another sip. (During his storytelling the old rock-hauler normally consumed an amazing amount of the tasty brew [as if it were fuel for the fire]. Therefore, Fren always stood at the ready.) "Of course," he continued, "on the other end of the spectrum, there were a fair amount of the simple folk...those knights garbed only for the necessity of the task...those *ignorant, uninspiring, not pleasant to look at...barely-knights.*" A slight chuckle escaped Sir Peter's lips...joining those of his listeners.

"As for me," again, he sat up, patted his breast, and then raised his right arm (at a ninety-degree angle, the index finger pointing towards the ceiling),

"I was a young knight with a vision. I had done well in the games and my aspirations were to join the elite in the halls of Alazon. Indeed, I had begun polishing, religiously, my simple armor and, I had hoped, with an adequate showing, I might fall under the good graces of the *fancy ones*. But..." he assumed his previous position as Fren again filled his mug, "for the time being I knew I would have to prove myself and oh, how I wanted to do just that."

* * *

The five—this time *all* riding abreast—entered, with much foreboding, the circle of decay. For a time, until their sense of smell was numbed by the onslaught, each held a handkerchief to their nose. (All had their own set of embroidered hankies with gold letters...one of the many perks of a knight of Alazon.)

For a few minutes there was nothing but silence, save the crunching of the hooves on brittle, apparently burnt, grass. However, upon closer examination, it could be seen that this *burning* was not from flame but, rather, some sort of chemical. Whatever it was, all the foliage it touched seemed to wither in a smoldering cry. It did not matter if it was a delicate blade, or a towering oak...all growing things touched by this *stuff*, died.

Perhaps one kilometer in from the edge of the defilement, Sir Gus was the first to notice the tracks. "Easy, *Mighty One*." (Sir Gus, a man of great stature [and girth] needed a mount that could function under these weighty conditions. *This* stallion, being more than able to handle the load, was given a name that reflected its great strength. However, if, for some reason Sir Gustov was out of favor with his mates, the horse's name *also* changed. Thus, along with any derogatory name the knight might receive, his horse became...*Garbage Hauler, Royal Barge*, etc.) The knight gently pulled back on the reins even as the others continued on.

"Wait!" Sir Gus cried out. "Come back. I think we've found the source of this calamity. At least *part* of the problem anyway."

By this time Sir Gus was on the ground squatting next to the obvious indentation made by a dragon's foot. "It's huge," offered Sir Joe, stopping along side his companion. "I've never seen one of that size, and look," he said, pointing to another one some meters away. "If that's its counterpart, this *thing* must have an enormous gate."

Staying on his horse, Sir Robert, with a sober expression, joined the pair and, looking down at the track said, "Our plans have changed, gentlemen. We shall follow this unholy trail until we find its creator." The leader urged his steed in the direction of the claw-prints and, as the others looked with uncertainty at one another they heard, "Mount up, my good knights. I trust your hearts and weapons are ready for what lies ahead."

* * *

"The forest on the other side was dark and heavy. You all have been there…you know what I mean." Peter looked at the eyes of those attending his words. All, even Albert (though only in a limited fashion) had experience from the other side. "Yet," he continued, "the pungent smell of the dragons was more intense…they were waiting." A pause for emphasis. "They knew we were coming."

"How many days, Uncle Peter?" Albert's expression betrayed complete absorption in this story. "How many days did it take you to reach the city?"

"Well, lad," Peter, leaning in, now giving his full attention to Albert as if to an audience of one. "Thirty days, child. Thirty hard-fought days and nights. And the *Ganab*," he paused to roll his eyes, "from the first these demons seemed to be behind every sizable tree or lurking in any dark hiding hole…whispering their damnable lies…whispering, whispering, lying, lying."

"Did any turn back?"

"Lad?" Peter, finishing another drink, queried.

"Did any of your number turn back? Run away?"

"No…not one," said the elder, a triumphant tone in his voice. "And I'll tell you why." He raised his mug as if in the giving of a toast. "It was unity." His words softened a bit as he reflected on a truth that was not so quickly grasped at the time. "We each—so different in so many ways—we each had a commission from the king, every one of us…from the slinger of slop to the lance-toting dandy…and we each, for the most part, remembered that we were a team…dependent and supporting of one another."

—There were many lessons learned in the liberation of Kolleb…one of which is emphasized here. A more in-depth account is given in Sir John's *Quest of Proving.*—

"I remember when we broke from the forest and entered the barren plain," he continued. "There…snorting, stomping, fuming…were no less than five Muths! Each of these beasts were fifty meters apart, and between them…if you can believe it…" By now Albert had his head in his hands (his elbows in a planted pyramid formation). Sir John, enjoying the story no less (although he had heard numerous variations over the years) was leaning back in his chair…his hands clasped behind his head. "If you can believe it," Peter repeated for emphasis, "there were at least two Shachaths between each behemoth. And…to our rear…a dozen Ganab clawing from the wood."

* * *

The five followed the dragon tracks for half a day's ride. From time to time they'd come across a burned out home or hovel. And, although the tracks were fairly singular in one direction…the decay, which they presumed had something to do with the beast, seemed to fan out…like the wake from some sort of unholy plague-ship.

Finally, the evening sun slipped behind the barely seen silhouette of the king's castle to the west and, as the shadows lengthened and then disappeared into the oneness of dusk…the five made camp…choosing by lot the order of the watch. However, before these weary warriors made due on the tainted soil, they could just barely make out…far, far ahead…an almost indiscernible flashing of light…like a distant eruption. And they all wondered if, like the spewing volcano that seems so innocuous at a distance…they wondered if, when found, this *beast*, too, would be a deadly fountain that no mortal can contain.

* * *

Peter's oration of some of the high-points of his youthful adventure occupied the good part of the evening. And, by the time he came to the gist…Fren and his mother were both seated near the fire (Mary, attending to a quilt, and Fredrick, gazing thoughtlessly into the once robust blaze that was now only dying embers).

"Yes, lad," Peter focused tenderly on the young man before him (whose position remained unchanged during all this time), "I, so I thought," he continued, "had accomplished my goal. Of all the knights present…whether they were the lance-toters or the simple…*my* total of vanquished dragon exceeded them all. Indeed, it was as if Sir Timothy had *tailor-made* my training for the many tasks this arduous endeavor required. And so…" he patted himself (again) on the breast, "it was with great pride that I led the procession of the rescued and the rescuers through the river and to the gates of the king's castle."

"So?" uttered Albert, using a pause created by Sir Peter's mug being refilled *again*. "So...what was it the king said to you?"

"All in good time, child," said the elder, placing the mug gently down on the battle-weary table. (He had noticed that his beloved Mary was beginning to nod off.) "First, after we all made our way across the bridge and into the courtyard and, as the new citizens quickly made entrance into the inner sanctuary...it was at this spot, midst the beautiful blooms, that many of the other knights lavished great encouragement to me."

"*Fine job, Sir Peter*," said one. "*The king will surely reward you.*"

"*You're on your way*," said another. "*No doubt a distinction of honor awaits.*"

"Yes, on and on my fellow laborers were free with their praise. And I, being so young, and full of myself (a slight pause to shake the head), I puffed up like a decaying sow." At this description Albert crinkled his nose. (He had run across a few bloated beasts in his time.)

"Anyway, young pilgrim," he continued, "as each passed with a kind word...and I stayed to receive it...all went into the sanctuary before me. Finally, I snapped out of my self-absorption—just a little—and made my way into the huge inner chamber."

At this point, Sir John stood, stretched, and made a path, quietly, to the hearth in order to add another log and encourage the coals.—Although some might consider such an unannounced departure an act of rudeness...it had been established, long ago, that the necessities of this family could be done, when appropriate, without the added burden of some time-wasting protocol.—

"Son..." Peter, his eyes meeting those of the child. "Son...have you noticed, that when one enters the great chamber of the king, that the atmosphere...the colors...the sounds...the very presence of the place...seem to diminish greatly the outward trappings of those who enter?"

Albert, perceiving that the slight pause after this query meant that the elder actually desired a reply...said, "Yes...although I haven't dwelt on it...but, yes...it's as if all the clothing, or armor, or frills and fancies...are cancelled out in some way. It's like we're all equal...or something."

"Yes...quite so," said Sir Peter as he gazed a moment into the warm, dark liquid which swirled lazily in his cup. There was another brief silence as the elder perceived that a little thought had begun rising up from his heart and, if it persisted (as these things, if genuine, inevitably do) he would be sure to not hold back the divine utterance. But…there had to be a greater unction and this, too, would be clarified soon enough.

"Yes, son," he continued, looking into the questioning face of the boy. "Yes, it is as you say. And, even though there is an equality in the royal chamber…even more so the closer you get to the sovereign…I, in my mind, was still rehearsing the tally of the previous battle. So, being thus distracted, it took me a long time to be invited to the king's level. Indeed," Peter made a broad sweeping motion with his right hand, "*all* the others of our expedition crossed the inner barrier before I. And so…as I stood at the wall…I saw, first, the rescued invited to be welcomed by our Lord. Then, as I tried to tame my selfish thoughts, I saw the knights of the crusade invited to attend, and then, one by one, I recognized that even the lowest of the attendants…the *non-knights*…were given place by his side."

For a moment the old fighter gazed upward into the flame of the lamp. "So foolish was I…" he half mumbled as he slowly brought the mug to his lips.

"Excuse me, Sir?" Albert interjected, now himself straining to see *whatever-it-was* that his elder perceived in the flame.

"I was very foolish, lad," Peter's and Albert's gaze locked once again. "…in the ways of the king…in the nature of honor, worth…so many things." Peter could tell that he was a bit beyond the boy's reach so he stopped to add, "Now, where was I?"

"I believe you said you were at the wall."

"Yes…quite right…at the wall. Well, there I was at the barrier. And, I suppose, through the passage of time and perhaps a weariness on my part, I finally started to focus on the king and, as you know," Albert slightly nodded in the affirmative (his head, once again cradled by his hands), "it is desire and focus…or," Peter unthinkingly stroked his chin whiskers, trying to define more closely the obvious secret of entrance, "perhaps surrender and yielding would be more accurate. Anyway, I was finally invited down and soon stood mere meters away from the Great King."

Albert fidgeted at what he *knew* was coming.

"So, lad, eventually…long after all of my party had had their time with our Lord…at last *I* was beckoned to come and kneel before him."

"How was he dressed?" Albert blurted out…not trying to be rude…but just so excited to hear this part again.

"Hmm?" Peter questioned, peering over the brim of his cup as he took another drink.

"How was he dressed...Sir?"

"Well..." Peter put down the mug and began stroking his beard again. "He, of course had on the royal robes...the finest flowing colorful fabrics I've ever laid eyes on. This garment actually seemed to emanate some sort of light and warmth. But...and I know you know this..." Albert's eyes widened, "what he wore was not fixed. I mean...it seemed to change subtly. Oh yes...the royal robes were always there. But, I also saw him as a knight...an armored, unbeatable knight. And, of course, on his head he wore a gold crown with every precious stone I can think off, and on his feet...not that I could see them very well...but it seemed they too were adorned in gold."

"And the sword?" Albert added.

"Yes, of course, the wonderful, terrible, glorious crimson sword was at his side."

There was another pause. This one, however, was not due to drink or distraction but, rather, the elder, still a child at heart, was playfully setting the hook, so-to-speak. He sensed Albert's excitement and knew a slight delay would be most irritating. After a few moments he started to rise from his chair.

"Uncle Peter?" Albert pleaded, sitting upright with the most pitiful expression on his face. "Uncle Peter...aren't you going to finish the story?"

"I have finished, haven't I?" the elder grunted as he stretched and swiveled as one preparing to retire.

"Aren't you going to tell me about what comes next...the children...the *lesson*?"

The gray-haired knight smiled widely, reached over and jostled Albert's hair and then, sliding his chair beside the youth's he sat down and leaned in to continue the tale.

"Well," he began, "there I was, kneeling, expecting at any moment a ribboned medal to be draped over my head or perhaps even an anointing from the crimson sword on each shoulder. But...after what seemed an eternity...I heard, instead, the monarch's gentle voice calling.

"'Peter,' he said. At first I wasn't sure it was he speaking...so familiar was the tone. 'Peter, Peter,' he repeated and finally I dared to lift my gaze and there he was, the Great King of the Universe, sitting on his throne (a rather simple affair...hardly exorbitant...a high-backed armed chair with gold overlay) and on his lap...a child!"

"Tell me about the child!" Albert blurted out. Albert, who had placed his head on his overlapping hands to listen (leaning on his left cheek since Sir

Peter had assumed a closer position) had lifted his head for this retort, whereupon Peter placed his leathery left palm on the lads crown and gently pressed it down to its previous position.

"Of course I'll tell you of the child," he said smiling. "He was toddler, perhaps two or three. Able to walk, and run—after a fashion—but still quite dependent, innocent. He was a dark-haired fellow wearing a simple white robe of sorts and there he was running his fingers through the beard of our king! (who seemed rather delighted at the whole thing).

"Well, I must have been a sight…mouth agape, stiff, glassy eyed, and the next thing I know…the king motions with his right hand and *another* throne—identical to his!—is brought in and placed just to his right.

"'Have a seat,' he says to me.

"Now…let me tell you, my young sod-slinger," the knight said, assuming a position similar to his audience (Peter, hands overlapping, leaning on his *right* cheek), "I had heard of such an honor, but even I, in my youthful arrogance, had not imagined that I would experience it so soon. So, I stood, straightened my attire, bowed, and then sat down (in an *oh so dignified* manner)…all the while, the king is having a conversation with this miniature.

"'*Good!*' says the king. '*Here you go.*'

"The next thing you know, our sovereign is passing the child to *me*. And not only this," Peter sits upright as Fren fills his mug, "but he then had one of his shining attendants bring a bowl of pudding."

"What kind!" interrupted Albert (who liked pudding).

"Butterscotch, I think…no matter…anyway," Sir Peter swatted at the air as if this distraction were a gnat, "there I am, one of the king's royal knights, the *champion* of this last crusade, spoon-feeding this slop to a kid. And he, hardly a refined diner, is getting it *everywhere*. Finally, the child wipes his mouth with his sleeve, jumps down to the floor and, before he toddles off he motions that I bring my ear down for a question.

"'What's your name?' the little pudding-breathed shorty whispered. And I, still topped off with pride, sat up, began wiping the goo off myself and replied, '*Sir* Peter.'

"After this, the child began waddling off to the *far* side, but, every few steps, he would turn around and, with his pudgy hand, wave and yell, 'Goodbye, Sir Peter!' He must have done it ten times. Finally, less distracted with myself (only momentarily) I realized exactly *where* he was going and, as I turned to question the king…I could see that his eyes were following the child…and that there was a great sorrow in his expression."

—It should be noted here that on the lower level of the royal chamber there is, off to one side, an archway. From this archway, from time to time, there appear people (children mostly) who come directly from the river. And, as the castle is built above the life-giving torrent, all who enter the great hall...if they care to be still...can discern its great power vibrating the place. The archway, which truly is available to all citizens, is also a portal to those not yet of age who untimely die. These, as Sir Peter had discovered, after meeting with the king...go on to the other side. The flesh-bound return to the river.—

"When I saw his countenance," Peter continued, "I dared not speak and, even if I had...a moment later *another* child appeared. This one was a little girl who possessed the most beautiful blue eyes and hair as red as my own. She, without hesitation, reached up into the waiting arms of the king who greeted her with a kiss and embrace. Then, he turned, once more, to me and said, as he held her little giggling body out, 'Here's another, *Sir* Peter.'

"Well, young Albert," Peter's voice softened and became full of tender emotion, "when he spoke my name in that way...I realized that it was not he, upon my knighthood, who had given me a badge of exaltation. No...(the old fighter's voice wavered a bit as he shook his head slowly and, with his left hand, wiped moisture from his closed eyes) No...he had given me a commission of servanthood. It was *I* who ascribed royalty to the call. So foolish...so foolish."

Peter pulled an old handkerchief from a back pocket and, in a roughshod fashion, wiped his eyes and blew his nose. Then, looking at his young attendant (who was using one of Mary's prized napkins to accomplish the same thing), he smiled and said, "Now...where was I?"

"The red-haired girl."

"Yes...she was a beauty, and," Peter's voice began to waver a bit as more emotion flowed from his heart, "and...she too was brought a bowl of pudding."

"What kind?" whispered Albert, half laughing, half crying.

"I don't know..." offered the old wall-builder, with a slight smile (appreciating the deflection), "but I will tell you this...this time I focused more on her than on myself. This time...as she prepared to depart," the knight touched his left cheek with his fingertips (as if remembering the location of a kiss long ago), "she asked me my name, and I, falling into those beautiful eyes, said, 'Peter...my name is, Peter.'"

A moment of silence passed between the pair at the table and it was understood that the story had concluded. However, there was something more that needed to be said. Something more that needed to be birthed.

With an expression of warm affection the old warrior smiled at his young companion and then, as if a door had been suddenly opened, his countenance became serious and he asked the boy a question. "Albert…when you look at the king…what do you see?"

The boy, feeling the weight of the moment, lifted his head, sat up, and replied, "When I see the king…I see everything you've described…the robe, the crown, even a glimpse of the armor…but…" then he…who had, until this time, been looking into Sir Peter's eyes, dropped his gaze.

"But?" the elder lifted the chin of the lad to return the focus.

"But…I also see him as a servant…sometimes he seems to dress even as I."

There was then an intangible *something* that was felt by all. Like the wave that breaches the dam, or the sun-burst that parts the night…the house was filled with a presence…a covering…a newness. Peter, his form more rigid and his eyes ablaze…reached for the mug and stood…slowly, solemnly. And, as the legs of his sturdy chair scraped along the stones, Albert sat up straight, eyes wide and…as a moment passed and Peter stood there, motionless…the boy became aware that around and behind him were Mary, Fren, and Sir John…each with a lifted cup and an expression of purpose.

"From this day forward," began the elder, his mug lifted to chin level by his right hand, approximately a half meter from his face. "From this day forward…you, Albert," Peter looked into the puzzled (and not a little startled) eyes of the younger, "you shall call me, Peter. For…on this day you are a man, and I'll not demand a title from he who is my equal." Then, looking about at the others (who also had raised mugs [including Albert—thanks to a tap on the shoulder from Sir John]) he took a drink of tea (as if the declaration itself were consummated by the deed) and the others dutifully followed suit.

A few minutes later, as Mary and Fren prepared the home for slumber, Sir John—leaning back in his chair—said, "You know, old teacher…*I* was *seventeen* when you made the pronouncement."

"Yes, quite right," smiled Sir Peter, also leaning back (Mary was out of sight) with his hands behind his head. "But maturity comes to all at a different time…and I figured I couldn't wait forever in your case."

After a slight chuckle by all, Albert, clearing his throat, said—in a very grown up fashion, "Peter…how long do you think it will take the royals to get to the king's castle?"

The old knight looked past the young man into the renewed flame of the hearth and, pausing to take one last drink, he said,

To find His way...be low and meek. But the strong may find...
when they're tired and weak.

"I imagine it will be quite some time," said the knight, looking once more into the eyes of the teenager, "...quite some time, indeed."

Chapter XIV

*Those who heed
the monarch's call
must be prepared
to give their all.*

Sir Robert looked to his right. There, in the distance, was the castle of the king and, as the royal parade made yet *another* wrong turn and headed away…he sighed a great sigh. Yes…the castle *was* their destination. And yes…there it stood (as it had a half dozen times before) but…it is simply not proper for one of the lowly (and among the Knights of Alazon…he was near the bottom) to suggest a different course than the one set by the warrior with the golden chapeau. And so they would continue their trek…on…and on…and on…until (and he knew this all *too* well) weariness had humbled the lead navigator. "Alas," the under-knight thought to himself, "Sir Reginald has been in an excellent condition of late. This could take a very long time."

* * *

"Sir John?" The knight, who had been momentarily distracted as yet *another* invisible wave rumbled through the mist of the Living River (*They seem to be coming at an ever-increasing frequency*, he thought to himself) felt a gentle tapping on the breastplate of his armor. "Sir John?" the little voice said again.

"Hmm?" said the teacher as his eyes followed the evidence of the power as it stormed into the unseeable distance. He stood there a moment longer...his mind still dwelling on the wave when he felt a tapping once more. Then, reeling in his thoughts he looked down to see Mark, a rambunctious six-year-old, dressed in oversized armor, holding a wooden sword in his right hand and a light-weight shield (made from stretched cloth over contorted sticks) in his left.

"Is this right, Sir John?"

The elder, himself adorned in full armament, knelt down on one knee and looked eye to eye into the miniature warrior's face. The boy stood before him, head slightly cocked to one side with one eye squinting in resistance to the rays of the rising eastern sun. "Well, Sir Mark," he said, sounding quite serious while straightening the boy's wares a bit, "everything seems to be in order."

At this the lad smiled a great gap-toothed smile (he was always quick to tell his overseer when one tooth came out or another arrived) and turned to run back to the gathering of other likewise dressed students.

"Oh, Mark?" said Sir John before the boy waddled too far. "Aren't you *left-handed*?"

"Oh, yeah," said the youngster, accompanied with his own infectious trademark chuckle. He then quickly switched the sword and shield and proceeded to skip back to a waiting line of smiling older students (who couldn't resist patting the boy on top of the helmet, which left it somewhat askew).

The rest of the morning of this fine *King's Day* was very much like the many that had preceded it...the people of the quadrant gathered (not all, but many) at the Living River and, while there, there was time set aside for remembering, rejoicing, repenting, restoring...renewing. Sir John, being the overseer of this quadrant, was given the responsibility of urging the many under his care to reacquaint themselves with the ways of the king and the river. (Sadly, once crossing this life-giver, some were hard pressed to return.) Also, it was a time for fellowship, of bearing another's burden, for instruction in the use of the sword and shield, and of stepping again into the healing waters. All this was centered and firmly anchored in the victory the warrior knight accomplished at the wall...so many years before. But, as the proceedings began to wane and the faithful offered their farewells, Sir John, sitting on the bank by the river, his feet dangling just above the crystal flow and noticing that Fren, who had been bobbing up and down near the center of the waters the whole time was now missing (not unusual)…his thoughts turned to the previous morn when his old mentor said a different kind of goodbye.

It had only been a few moments since the shadows of the eastern peaks had quickly given way to the rising conquering sun. Yet, on this early daybreak…as lazy puffs of mist still gathered in the hollows and each precious blade of grass was beautifully adorned with dew…it was at this time…the day after Peter's proclamation (concerning Albert) that the old warrior, dressed in full armor, stood on the walkway, just outside the main entrance, and seemed to breathe great lingering breaths…as if he were trying, if possible, to absorb everything about this place that he had grown to love.

John, dressed for labor in the field, walked out to his old teacher carrying two mugs of steaming tea. For a moment he stood along side, looking in the direction of the quest. Then, after a gentle nudge from his elbow, the gray-haired warrior on his left turned to see his *son*, smiling, and offering one last cup of fellowship, which he gratefully embraced.

"You won't stay a little longer?" offered John in a near whisper, "I could use a little help on the south wall."

Peter, turning again to peer off towards the river while holding the warm cup in both hands, took a drink and then smiled a broad smile even as he turned to look into John's questioning eyes. "Oh, you need my help, do you?"

John sheepishly returned the smile and, as they both turned to walk back to the house (where Mary had prepared a simple breakfast) he asked his *father* about this last commission from the king.

"It was most strange," said Peter, as he the crossed the threshold in front of John and sat down, giving Fredrick an acknowledging nod and wink, "I've been spending more time in his presence, of late," he continued, after bowing the head for a moment in silent thanks to the God of the Crystal Sea, "and, since I'm not young and robust like you," he said, one cheek full of scrambled eggs and pointing to John with his fork, "I didn't expect any great assignment. But, (another bite) as others around me were being given written instructions by his attendants…they passed me by completely!"

—It should be noted here that, although there are known duties that *all* in the realm are expected to follow, regardless of station…it is not unusual for those who seek the presence of the king to receive personal, intimate details of some task that their sovereign has tailored, just for them.—

"The next thing you know…he's calling for me!" Peter started to wipe his mouth with his right sleeve but was almost immediately intercepted by Mary's sure hand, which stopped the elder's arm and thrust one of her decorative napkins into the palm. "Thank you, dear," said the knight meekly, wiping his mouth and taking deliberate effort to fold the used cloth and place it to one side. As Mary walked off, Peter leaned in and continued the account.

"Well, it had been so long since I was given direct audience, I couldn't imagine what our Lord wanted of me."

"What *did* he want, Uncle?" came a voice from out of the kitchen where a slightly disheveled Albert (his hair resembling a wheat field after a pounding rain) approached with his own mug of mild stimulant.

"As I was telling your father…*oh, fellow laborer*," Peter pulled out the chair to his right as an invitation to the boy. "I could not recall a face-to-face assignment from the king. But there I was, kneeling, head bowed, expecting who knows what. And, as before, he spoke in the most gentle fashion." Peter's voice tapered off a bit as he wiped his mouth and seemed to look past his present company.

"What did he tell you?" interrupted Albert, who was now half way through his morning meal.

"He said that he had a special task for me, brother. That there was a great evil beyond the river. A practice most heinous. He said it demanded his attention and, although he had urged and assigned many to attend to it. Most, for one reason or another…would not."

John leaned back in his chair, measuring the elder's words. And, as he did, he was reminded of not a few instances when he *himself* seemed to fall short of the king's command.

"But what he said next was most peculiar," Peter said, both elbows on the table as he gazed into the design of his own personalized mug. "He said," (a long pause), "…he said there was great danger involved and that I didn't have to go if that was my choosing. But just as he said it, from the distant archway…" John and Albert both leaned in to hear more precisely, "came a steady stream of children whom our king turned to greet with embracing arms and, as he attended to these he turned his gaze, for only a moment, in my direction."

"What did you say, Peter?" It was Mary who, with Fren just behind, had made her way to the side of her new beau.

"I said I would go," the old warrior replied as he gazed lovingly up into Mary's eyes even as he tenderly grasped her trembling right hand. "I said I would go."

A few moments later Albert, John, and Fren, having all given Peter expressions and gestures of farewell, stood back near the house as, a bit further on down the path, the two older love-birds spoke their tender goodbyes. John could see that Mary, nervously petting the rabbit that Sir Peter had brought the day before (*not* a meal, *now* a pet) was being comforted by the old knight and, although they couldn't hear the words, they knew he spoke of a future joining in marriage. Then, seen to grasp her right hand, Peter bowed and gave it a kiss and, as they all waved and shouted their devotion until the warrior's form faded from view, Albert turned to Sir John and said, "Father...will we ever see him again?"

Still gazing in the direction of his departed mentor, John recalled the answer given to another young man, many years before...

> *Though parting oft does sorrow bring*
> *We'll soon unite before our king.*

* * *

It must have been two full weeks....two draining, arduous weeks but, at last, through the weary eyes of Sir Reginald...the castle was now seen and the great company of knights (their attendants were commanded to make camp in the large field which precedes the bridge) made their way through the mist and eventually into the great sanctuary. Sir Robert, patiently waiting his turn at the end of the line (knowing full well that if he had come alone...he could have come and gone in one day's time) thought back to the instance, three years prior, when he first laid eyes on the dragon.

* * *

"*What...is that!*" the words, quite animated, of Sir Joe, accompanied by a rigid pointing of his outstretched right arm along with a facial expression of utter amazement. He, the youngest of the five, had ridden somewhat ahead on this morn following their discovery of the expanding circle of decay. The others, catching up to their comrade, joined him at the top of the small rise and looked in the direction of his leading.

"Most peculiar," offered Sir Jerry.

"I've never seen anything like it," added Sir Gus.

"What do you make of it, Rob?" asked Sir Francis, turning his gaze away from the spectacle to look at his elder captain.

"Hmm…I, too, have never seen the likes of this…but, seeing as how the land is untouched beyond it…and defiled behind…I'd say that this *thing* is the object of our quest."

—In front of these *detectives*, perhaps an arrow's flight away, was, what appeared as a great steaming mound. Crimson in color, having the appearance of a layered stone dome, this three-story aberration seemed to vibrate with a very low and unsettling resonance. All around this curiosity was a circle of rotting and stinking decay (this *had* been a woodland). On the other side of the mound, however, past the ring of defilement, a few trees remained. And beyond these…there was a town of some size. In fact it was the largest settlement closest to the center. A place known as *Philautos.*—

For a few moments the five warriors sat upon their somewhat agitated steeds and wrestled with their next step. It was, as usual, Sir Gustov who broke the stalemate by gently prodding his horse in the direction of the anomaly.

"Where are you going, Sir Gus?" offered Rob, dryly…as if he didn't know. (This scenario had played itself out time after time in the many years of their acquaintance.)

"While you *ladies* sit here puzzling over your next move…I'm going to check this thing out."

"Wait, my large friend," said the leader, somewhat amused at the word, *ladies.* "I think it best we test the mettle of this mound. Sir Francis?…" Rob turned to his acquaintance, on his right, who was unmatched in the skill of archery, "let fly your sharpest arrow. Aim, if you can, at one of those delicate lines that may reveal a breach in the stone."

Sir Frank drew back on the string, aiming the shaft skyward to compensate for distance and wind and, as he made the final adjustments—his clenched right hand firmly against his cheek—he muttered a response as he let the missile fly… "*Sharpest arrow…*indeed. They're *all* sharp. *If you can?* Ha!"

The group watched with interest as the delicate sliver raced along its arch to the curious mountain in their path. True to form, the arrow was placed perfectly on one of the many creases of the mound. Yet, as might be expected when attacking a granite face or a barrier of steel…the arrow shattered and the remnants tumbled down the side.

The five, seeing this, were satisfied that this thing, if it *was* alive, was like no creature they had ever seen or heard of (for even the scale of Muths are not totally impenetrable). Therefore, with just enough confidence to step tepidly into the unknown…they cautiously made their way towards the base of this most unusual hill.

Coming within a stone's throw…the smell of the object was almost overpowering. "Phew!" said Sir Gerald. "This stench is more vile than even a rotting Ganab!"

"Yes," muttered Rob, thoughtfully, "its offense goes deeper than the nostrils…there is a soulish quality to it. Most disturbing."

By now, having been emboldened by the arrow and the passage of time…the warriors each took their own course around the perimeter of the thing. "Perhaps it's some sort of volcanic bulge," shouted Gus, as he headed towards the edge which directly faced the city. "Wait a moment!…What's this?!" The others, noticing an urgency in the voice of their comrade…each stopped and looked in his direction. "Come here!" he shouted. "There's something on this side that I want you all to see!"

* * *

It had taken two long weeks to get here and now, for what seemed another uncomfortably protracted period, the great assembly of knights—with Sir Reginald in the center—now rigidly assembled in single file against the barrier that separated this level of the sanctuary from that which afforded a closer audience with the king. It should be noted that, from time to time, the wall *did* open in front of individual knights but these, not wishing to go before their leader, would refuse to descend and, eventually, the wall would close again. This was the case with Sir Robert for, almost immediately, upon his reaching this hurdle, the intentions of his heart were drawn to his distant monarch. He could have, if not hindered by the protocols of Alazon, walked smoothly down the staircase provided but, turning his eyes to see that none of his brothers had yet an open door…he declined. And, as his opportunity, for the moment, was removed…he rekindled the memory of that first encounter.

* * *

"Most peculiar," uttered the leader as he, and the other three, joined Sir Gus in front of the *thing*. (They supposed it was the front…as it was facing the unscarred areas.) "A most definite overlapping of sorts. Like the imperfect folding of one slabbed layer upon another." At this point Sir Gus dismounted and walked towards the curiosity.

"Gus! Where are you going!?" These were the excited words of Joseph, who thought of the lumbering giant as a favorite older brother.

Sir Gus, without turning, gave a downward backward swat with his right hand as if to say, "I know what I'm doing," and continued until he had his right leg propped up on the *thing's* incline as he leaned in to look more closely at the curious fold and then down at the place where the mound seemed to violently erupt from the earth.

As the four sat on their fidgeting steeds (Rammak, especially, was ready to depart), Sir Gerald, who had been stroking the thin black whiskers on his recently born goatee, stopped, and, raising his ungloved left hand, index finger to the sky said, "I know what this curious formation reminds me of...a bird."

"What?" said Robert, taking his eyes away from Sir Gus who was now on both knees examining more closely the point where the soil met the mound.

"A bird...you know...when there is a need for protection, especially if there are young present...the bird folds its wings forward so that there is protection both in front *and* behind."

As Sir Robert and the other three contemplated this interesting conjecture, they saw Sir Gus stand and shout an observation of his own.

"It looks as if the plates (that's what he decided to call the many squarish sections) go *into* the ground...not up out of it! This thing, whatever it is, is *not* from below!"

At this point there was a rumbling...a stirring...as if a timer of sorts had gone off and the ground all around vibrated with the expectancy of who-knows-what.

"Gus...get back here!" yelled the four, their mounts beginning to buck and raise up...knowing something deadly was making itself known. But, before the oafish warrior could even *think* about running...the dragon...in a moment's time...had emerged. Yes...it was as Sir Jerry had surmised...the strange joining in the front was caused by the overlapping of what appeared as wings.

—Although these five had no way of knowing it, these *wings*—unlike the bird analogy—were *only* used for protection. This creature, though of a soulish evil birth, was nonetheless a living being like any other dragon. But...this monster did not retire to a cavern or hole when in need of rest. No...it had its own protection...a barrier no instrument made by man could hurriedly penetrate.—

Now, bathed in the early-morning rays, the huge wingspan of the beast was displayed and, as the five hesitated in momentary paralysis (much as the prey before the spider) the creature folded back these giant coverings and then lowered its head to inspect the insects it had heard knocking at its door.

"Depart!" Robert shouted as the giant dripping head of the creature twisted (somewhat like that of an owl) down to examine Sir Gus, who, instinctively, had drawn his sword, even as his knees knocked violently together. And, as he heard the sound of fading hooves, the monster turned its head aright and, coming down nearly to ground level, it briefly breathed in the scent of this morsel that had been so delightfully provided. For a moment their was no response…no apparent recognition. But, this monster was created to destroy and, as its slithering tail-tip made its way quickly to snare this little man, the creature raised high its head…making a straight path for its morning appetizer.

Then, there was a great avalanche of sound. It was a roar…a combination screech of pain and hateful fury. For, a mere second before the planned snaring and snacking…an arrow, a very *sharp* arrow, hit squarely in the slanted black pupil of the monster's right eye. And, although this sensitive surface is nearly as impervious to injury as the rest, nevertheless the creature raised up in momentary annoyance, brushing at the pesky sliver with its frantic right foreleg. But, this brief span of distraction gave Sir Robert (who had reversed course the moment the dart was loosed) and his powerful steed, Rammak, just enough time to swoop in, snatch the wayward knight (some feat, considering the size of the catch) and ride off to a place of higher vantage.

The creature, now fully awake and enraged, turned to pursue these insects but, as it stepped outside the line of its previous course, it stopped, as if some inner compass had sounded a subconscious alarm and, as the knights made good their escape, the dragon turned its head slightly and breathed in the intoxicating fragrance that wafted so heavily from the adjacent human settlement. The people of *this* city, having been fretting all night, were even now preparing to battle for that which was theirs and, as the dragon stomped in great heavy steps towards its purpose, it glanced, just briefly, at the audience of knights perched on a distant grassy knoll and, in their direction, it let out a disdainful, raised-snout blast of foul white smoke, as if to say, "You're not worth my time."

Chapter XV

Mercy is a stubborn thing
Though often pushed away.
It knows that hardship breaks the heart
And there reveals the way.

Sir Reginald, still very much aware of his prestigious position, stood at the barrier, barely noticing the king as his eyes were distracted by those in his company. Finally, however, after an extended period of time, the beauty and aura of the place began to chip away at his lofty facade until, from the tiny flame that flickered still in his heart…he felt again the yearnings of a young pre-knight. He remembered, ever so briefly, the joy of that first encounter…when he gave allegiance to his sovereign and was ushered into his presence. He experienced, for a moment, the wonder as the walls, in color and chorus, repeated the old and ever-new story of release and, as his attention was drawn to the center (as is the case of all those who yield themselves here) he looked, with unglazed eyes, towards his king. And, as he focused more fully on the great ruler…the restraining barrier quickly dissolved and there, immediately in front of him, a shining attendant stood silently…prepared to escort the *seeker* to a closer place.

But, old habits die hard (not that *this* habit was in danger of dying, but it was, for the moment…subdued) and, before stepping towards the king, Sir Reginald quickly glanced to his right and left to make sure none of his fellow knights had gone before him and, seeing that none had…he would have descended, except, just as he raised his right foot to take that first step he saw, out of the corner of his eye, in a place at the wall far beyond his company…one of the lowest servants of his entourage (in fact, it was the keeper of the stable) who had come in unnoticed (not that they were forbidden, but it was understood that their duties to their masters had to come first) and, with seemingly no effort…this underling walked seamlessly through the wall down towards the great king.

In a moment, Sir Reginald's countenance changed and, with the rising of his ire…so, too, the barrier also rose before him. Soon it became apparent to the others of his company that there would be no descent this day and, as the understanding spread…a universal sigh could be felt emanating from the elite. Yes, they very desperately needed guidance from the king…and now, with another delay, the danger to the inner quadrants increased all the more.

* * *

"It was a horrible screeching…one volley after another of piercing, ear-splitting blasts. But rather than just one tone," Sir Robert, the others of his company likewise kneeling before their liege as he recounted their encounter with the beast, continued, "rather than just one frightening note," he looked up into the serious expression of Sir Reginald, "…it seemed there was a chorus…like some sort of hellish choir encamped inside the dragon. And this united wail," he animated the telling with his hands, "seemed to gush out in wave after wave in a most unsettling melody and, from their behavior, apparently these sounds struck terror in the hearts of the warriors on the wall of *Philautos.*"

—Although he had no way of knowing it, the sound that Sir Robert heard was the very same heard by *all* those who had fallen prey to this beast before. However, to these…these who had contributed to its birth…the sound was *quite* recognizable. For, it was the cry of an unholy child to its parents…a cry of the most perverse and murderous affection. And to those to whom it was directed…when heard…it resonated sickeningly upward from that very dark and secret place in an unrepentant heart.—

Sir Reginald turned and, without a word, slowly made his way up the steps to his exalted chair and, after turning again to sit down he noticed that he had left the five waiting, silently, on their knees. "I'm sorry, my fellow knights…please rise," he said, as he gestured in an upward motion with his right hand even as he placed his weight upon the purple cushion. "Now, tell me of the battle."

"It was horrible, sire!" blurted out Sir Joseph before Robert could respond.

"Go ahead, young warrior," said Reginald, raising his fingers slightly to calm the complaint on Sir Robert's brow. "How did you view it?"

"Well, my lord," Sir Joe, restraining his gushing somewhat even as he stepped one cubit closer and looked squarely into the eyes of his master. "As we all know, the knights of *Philautos* are of superior skill." The others of his company nodded slightly at this statement and Sir Reginald, the unquestioned champion of the games, even he acknowledged inwardly that the skills possessed by these warriors were at least as great as his own. "Yet...the wall...the protection they had erected against man...when the beast had a mind to...it passed through it as easily as we through a divided veil."

"What do you mean...*when the beast had a mind to*?" Sir Reginald said, leaning slightly forward.

"He means that the creature," interjected Sir Robert, "though obviously more powerful than any dragon we've ever seen...instead of breaching at once the barrier of wood and stone...he seemed to take his time...as if extracting as much terror from his intended victims as possible."

Sir Reginald leaned back and, for a brief moment, measured this disturbing behavior against the limited knowledge that he possessed concerning the way of dragons. Then, with his right elbow firmly planted on its cushioned rest, he began to thoughtfully stroke the graying whiskers on his chin. "The wall...tell me of the wall? Sir Gustov..." he said, turning to the largest of the group, "...it has been some time since I've seen them. Remind me of their construct, good knight"

"Sire," Sir Gus, pleased that his knowledge of the subject had been tapped, stepped forward as he replied, "...as you know, the people of *Philautos* hired others to build and man their walls. Many of these mercenaries are, or should I say *were* from the province of *Misthotos*."

"Yes, yes...I know all this," Sir Reginald wearily prompted (he didn't want an in-depth exposition). "The walls, brother knight, tell me of the walls."

"Well, sire," Sir Gus said, withdrawing slightly (a bit disheartened that he couldn't lay an elaborate foundation), "the walls are not unlike our own...built merely to dissuade man."

"Granite blocks?"

"Yes, my lord."

"How high?"

"Similar to ours...perhaps four meters skyward adorned with parapet and platforms."

"Their defenses?"

"Only simple missiles from the arm and bow. Adequate to dissuade a human visitor, but totally inadequate to deter this beast."

"Tell me of the battle?"

"What battle?" This time it was Sir Francis.

"Go on," Sir Reginald turned his gaze to this latest orator.

"My Lord...there *was* no battle."

"What do you mean?"

"Sire," Sir Frank's expression intensified as the replay of the event made its way from his mind to his lips. "The warriors on the wall...after a few uncoordinated volleys...put their hands over their ears and escaped out a back entrance."

"What of the knights? Where were they?"

"They apparently retreated to their own, individual, fortified dwellings. And sire..." Sir Francis paused, the fresh remembrance twisting his emotions anew, "...they simply would not come to the aid of another...even when the children were dying."

"Children?" Sir Reginald, somewhat oblivious to those of the underdeveloped stature (except for his own...and these only in a limited sense) and, perhaps supposing that those of *Philautos* wouldn't even bother with this added care...asked the question anew. "What do you mean, *children?*"

"Sire," Sir Robert responded, putting his hand upon the shoulder of Sir Francis whose countenance, along with his head, were now bowed. "Sire...the beast, after spending a great deal of time screeching its chilling chorus as it paced and peered over the perimeter of the wall...it...without the least sign of effort...crashed through the barrier and began harvesting the children."

* * *

The party of knights, convinced that this day would not produce a closer place, followed the lead of their master and turned to exit the tabernacle. Robert, of course, being last in the column, waited as his brothers slowly followed Sir Reginald in the direction of the encampment outside the gate and, as he turned sideways, awaiting his step, he turned his head wistfully towards the sovereign he loved and there, just beyond the spot of the barrier where Sir Reginald had stood only moments before…was one of the king's shining attendants, standing, with arm extended *over* the wall, holding in his hand a parchment.

"Sir Reginald!" Yes, it was untoward for his voice to be raised in this fashion…especially in this place…and especially at a superior. But this was a desperate moment. "Sir Reginald!" he blurted once more and, when his disgruntled leader turned at the hearing of his name, he saw Sir Robert pointing in the direction of the attendant…and turning to this view, Sir Reginald's eyes fixed immediately on the parchment which he recognized at once as a message from the king.

* * *

"Sire…" This time it was Sir Gerald who offered his strength to the conveyance (the others obviously wearied by the telling), "our place of vantage was limited. But we could, with little difficulty, see a few of the inner dwellings of the people of *Philautos.* As you may recall, my Lord, the manor of each knight is, in itself, a fortress." Sir Reginald leaned back and nodded slightly as he rested his head against the high padded back of his chair. He remembered that the knights of *Philautos* were consumed with their own prosperity and protection. Yes, they were formidable fighters, and indeed, these warriors were forever sharpening their skills…but not, as was *his* case, in order to win and occupy a place of rulership and envy. No, these very self-centered beings didn't even have time for the adulation of others. Indeed, those who *had* children (of which there were few) had limited contact with the same…usually delegating their care to other, subservient souls. The reason being…they were continually polishing, primping, preparing, and building barriers for their *own* preservation. Indeed, the communal wall which encircled the place was merely a stopgap to hinder the curious. Each individual knight of the place thought his own little kingdom was impenetrable.

"After the beast easily breached the outer wall," Sir Gerald continued, "we saw it stop at the first compound."

"Did the creature use the fire?" Sir Reginald asked, aware of some of the ways of dragons (although, of late, he answered no calls beyond the river…but rather sent others to fulfill the decrees).

"Yes, my lord, but not at first."

"What then?"

"The creature stood and, as outside the exterior battlements…it began its accursed melody until the master of the dwelling, a knight, rode out in full armor. But…" Sir Gerald paused as the memory of the events came to life (or rather…death).

"What is it, man?"

"Sire," Sir Robert again came to another's aid. "The beast, instead of facing and battling the knight (although the warrior took the standard position and challenged the creature…yes, with the emblem of the king), it, after feigning interest in the contest, then turned and, after sniffing about like a hound after a hare…it began to frantically dismantle the dwelling and, with its most unusual tail…it reached in until it retrieved, kicking and screaming, a child from the midst."

"How horrible," uttered Sir Reginald.

"Yes, my lord, but this was just the beginning. For, after displaying this prize the creature—all the while screeching its wretched chorus—placed the toddler (in this case a little blond-haired girl) just out of reach of its father and, when the warrior came within grabbing distance, the monster would snatch the child from his grasp."

"How long did this go on?"

"Only a few minutes…although it seemed an eternity."

"The outcome?"

"Well, eventually the composure of the knight was in total disarray. The warrior, out of sheer frustration I suppose, charged the beast with lowered lance."

"And…what was the result? Any damage…injury?"

"Hard to tell, my liege. It did appear, from a distance, that their was *some* penetration (Sir Robert glanced briefly at his companions to assay their recollection of the event [among his fellows there appeared to be a consensus that there was at least the appearance of a minor success]), but (turning back to the intense gaze of Sir Reginald)…as there was no release from the monster (which dangled the sobbing child just above the knight's reach) the armored champion then dismounted and began flailing wildly at the scales which covered the demon's heart."

"What then?" uttered the lord of Alazon. He now rested his elbows on his knees and, as he began afresh to thoughtfully stroke his beard with the right hand, his distant expression revealed that, although the end result was obvious, he now was probing for points of weakness, vulnerability…already planning an attack and, if need be…a defense.

"Sire…" Sir Robert's gentle tone caused Sir Reginald to focus again on the story alone. "Sire…after the warrior was exhausted and had crumpled to his knees, the creature placed the child down and the poor thing ran to its father and sobbed at his neck. And then, although the distance was so great I couldn't tell, it appeared that it was perhaps communicating in some way to its intended victims. However, this only lasted a moment. It wasn't long until the creature's horrid tail wrenched the child from its father's arms and, after holding the beaten warrior down with one of its powerful forelegs…it dropped the screaming babe into its waiting jaws." The witnesses, save Sir Robert, all closed their eyes and shuddered at this remembrance. "Immediately after, as the beaten knight was also reduced to tears…he too was consumed."

"Where were the others?" Sir Reginald finally blurted out. "Why did they not rally and battle as one?"

"I don't know, my lord." Sir Robert said soberly. "That, I suppose, is the nature of *Philautos.* Each dwelling would not seek aid, nor offer any, to a neighbor. However," the knight paused before offering a conclusion.

"Yes?"

"Sire…" Sir Robert, known for truthfulness and frank honesty, continued, "I am convinced that even if the whole city had fought as one…this beast would have prevailed. Indeed, I know of no force, save the king himself, who can stop this creature from having its way. If I may be so bold, my lord…?"

"Yes, Sir Robert?" Again Sir Reginald's gaze was beyond this room.

"I encourage you to seek, immediately…counsel from the king."

* * *

The attendant, without expression, held the simple rolled parchment out, just above the barrier that separated the outer court from the inner. Sir Reginald hurried, pushing aside the others in his company and then, standing face to face with this curious being (curious, because although these attendants seemed human enough, they had a certain aura about them) he paused a moment before taking it. He looked down at the plain paper communiqué, and then quickly glanced at the king (who, at this great distance, seemed to be constantly moving). Upon focusing on the great ruler…a certain longing came suddenly upon the knight and, as he almost unconsciously reached for the message…when the attendant placed it in his palm…he thought he saw the king pause and glance his way.

As his fingers instinctively curled around the scroll and the attendant vanished from view, Sir Reginald was awakened from his trance and slowly looked down at, what he hoped, was the answer to his plea. It had been some time since he had had a direct communication from the king (not that none were offered…none were sought).

He looked at the seal (a spot of, what appeared, red wax…with the symbol of the king imprinted thereon). He quickly removed it, unfurled the parchment and, as all the knights looked eagerly on…Sir Reginald, after just a few moments, looked up, smiled and announced, "Gentlemen…as I had hoped…our answer is in the games. We shall announce and proclaim a tournament. The champion of which will destroy this beast." Turning to the one who had called him back, he said, "Sir Robert…"

"Yes, sire."

"Have many copies of this message made and send couriers throughout the realm informing of the coming contest."

"Yes, my lord," Robert said with bowed head as he received the scroll. "I shall attend to this immediately." And, as the others filed out quickly, following their jubilant leader…Sir Rob carefully unrolled the parchment to read this remedy that was sent from the king.

To conquer evil
Seek the one
The Champion in your midst
The one with sword…and shield…and song
The one whom God has kissed
But till you find
Hold not your place
But to the river run
And there destroy
The works of man
Until you find the one.

Sir Robert read the curious rhyme again and, yes…there did appear to be a reference to the games, but, as he leaned against the barrier (subconsciously rolling up the scroll even as his gaze was drawn to the great king), he found himself wishing that Sir Reginald had persevered a few moments more. Perhaps if he'd gotten closer, the king would have clarified and confirmed the message.

As he stood there, focusing on his redeemer, he suddenly felt the barrier dissolve and there, before him anew…was the stairway to the closer place. "Perhaps the king will talk to *me* about it," he thought as he prepared to join the king's attendant down this narrow flight.

"Sir Robert!" It was the voice of Sir Reginald, who had stopped, just before exiting the sanctuary, to see if all his ducks were in a row. Sir Rob, hearing his name, paused, turned, and waved to his master to indicate his compliance and, as quickly as it appeared…the opening to the closer place vanished. And, although he was too far away to be sure…when glancing back at the distant king as he slowly walked toward the exit…there appeared to be an expression of sadness on the sovereign's face.

"No," he thought to himself. "I'm surely too far to distinguish such a thing. This is a day of rejoicing. Yes…" he said quietly out loud (as if trying to convince himself)… "This is a day of rejoicing."

Chapter XVI

Beware the center's selfish view.
Let not its lies be heard.
For eyes turned inward cannot see
And ears despise true words.

Behind the creature…a burning. The walls of *Philautos,* once trusted for protection and peace, had been humbled to earth. Beyond these, the many dwellings that housed the knights and nobodies in this small city were seen to have been violently ruptured open and chillingly stripped of anything alive. These, too, were burning. Of course, as is the case of most attempted genocides…a few escaped. There wasn't yet in place the intricate snare necessary to capture *all* the harvest. A few of the prey had slipped past. But the creature knew, instinctively—even as he felt the remnants of the city churning in his belly—that his brutish destruction—his unique gift to destroy on a massive scale—would eventually be followed by a more intimate evil…a more detailed devilment…something you can't outrun and escape. The monster let out a burst of yellowish smoke from his nostrils. He did *not* want to share his quarry with another! But, as he lumbered on—his poisonous steps infecting and inflaming all that still lived in his wake—he knew that he was a part of a greater mission…a long planned and plotted desire. And though his tendency was towards insatiable selfish hatred…he knew there was a greater prize than just perpetual destruction. There was a goal that aspired to the heavens. Indeed, it was a horrible reaching that was anchored in the vile heart of a master he had not yet seen. A master who, even now, trembled with twisted delight as he heard of the daily conquests of his child.

* * *

It has been stated previously that from the moment of the rude revelation of the beast and the eventual inquiry of the king (by Sir Reginald and his fellow knights of the inner realm) that there was a span of some three years. One might suppose that the report of *Philautos's* grisly destruction (given by Sir Robert and his cohorts) would have inspired immediate communication with the monarch. But no, it is the nature of man (even those of the redeemed land) to first look to themselves for strength, and this was even more the case of those who walk the halls of Alazon. Presented here, and in the following two chapters, is a brief remembrance of the course and carnage that led to the eventual awakening (at least partially) of the haughty.

* * *

After the fall of *Philautos,* the creature continued on its counter-clockwise course in a steady, determined swirl that paused only to consume the intermediate dwellings that might be in its direct line of travel. As before, there was the screeching as it continually sought its *parents* and, if these hesitated to run at all (sometimes, and quite often in the inner places, there was a slowing attachment to *things*), these were quickly consumed and then the march would continue until a settlement of some size was met. These towns and cities, of which there were many, upon learning of the monster's intent, would seal off the settlement and await its attack. And, although a record of the creature's reputation would convince even the least sensible to flee, most of these inner burgs possessed an arrogance that prevented (or at least delayed) sound judgment.

* * *

Sir Warren pressed his bejeweled hands against his ears as the calling of his name wrenched his innards like a slow-acting poison that, though digested long ago, was only now overtly attacking the vital organs.

"*Warren…Father…Warren!*" The creature, its head bobbing slowly up and down—being horribly visible for only a moment at the zenith of its upward thrust—as it paced, with thunderous steps, outside the gate, was screeching a chorus that seemed to chillingly affect most who still remained within this vile city.

The forty-six-year-old knight, his hands still pressed uselessly over his ears (*useless*, for the words of the creature went past the hearing, into the very being), turned his head quickly to his left and right to observe that *all* his fellow warriors, spread out in front of their elaborate dwellings in this innermost city which bore the name, *Porneia*, were, every one, likewise affected. "Curious," thought this leader, lowering his hands as the creature paused from its *speaking* to take time to set ablaze yet another vacant parapet (the former occupants, as with the city of *Philautos*, were spineless mercenaries from the province of *Misthotos*...long since having escaped out a rear entrance), "though the creature utters *my* name, my brothers also dread its speech."

Sir Warren, long ago commissioned in the king's service and, not quite so long ago, given over, almost completely now, to a selfish hunger for things with which he sought to satisfy (an impossible task) his wayward members and mind...with his very life now in danger he began to react in a somewhat reflexive way, his polluted thoughts being parted to expose that there was still a remnant of that spark which once shone so brightly.

"Your weapons!" he shouted to his brothers (a gathering of like-minded men who, as is often the case, justified their selfish slide by grouping themselves with others who matched their descent). "Find your sword, shield, lance! Perhaps our lord will grant us victory over this thing that dare attack his chosen!"

The others, as if waking from a drug induced stupor, looked at one another and laid hold of the vision of their fellow dreamer. These, though wallowing for so long in what was obviously forbidden in the realm (indeed, *most* were known to cross the river in their pursuit, such was their lust for the dragon's things) seemed to shed, by their *own* strength—in just a few minutes—their garments of soiled silk and, having dusted off the former wares, they each reemerged clothed as a champion...as slayers of dragons.

Outside the granite walls, as burning timbers rained down and once-solid mortar crumbled from the sulfurous heat, the dragon paused, sensing a diminishing of *something*, and the strengthening of something else. As with all of his kind, the fear produced by human hearts—terror cultivated and coaxed by scale-clad demons—was an intoxicant. The waves of which, as it poured out of the little whimpering flesh-pods, gave strength and twisted pleasure to those who, with drooling tooth, prepared to complete the vile ritual by eventually spilling the life's blood of the pitiful creatures after their capacity for fear had peaked, or shortly thereafter.

—Terror, like every emotion, can only be sustained for so long. The dragons, being attuned to all things evil, could sense when the moment of optimum ripeness had passed. This was when the blood was let…unless, of course, their victims were true knights. These annoying creatures were to be dispatched as quickly as possible, as they were unlikely to exude anything but a calm reliance on the hated king.—

In a moment, as the small band of the wayward knights arrayed themselves in a line of defense on the far side of the grassy expanse that separated the wall from the town (a place for the grazing of cattle and sheep [formerly done *outside* the walls, but, as the population of the inner quadrants grew…so also grew acts of theft and butchery])…in a moment, Warren and his brothers—all mounted on fine white steeds, bred and purchased from the merchants of Alazon—these twenty witnessed the monster effortlessly step through the wall like the breaking of a paper ribbon or a loosely knotted cord at a sporting event. And, after the tumultuous sound of the curtain of rock being thus violently rent, faded, and, as the all-enveloping cloud of grayish dust and ash produced by this act slowly settled, the enormous crimson dragon paused from further advance so that all might see his terrible visage even as he, fuming, and nearly silent, calmly surveyed the tiny army of knights that dare oppose him. Curiously, behind these, there was also a rather substantial gathering of poorly armed rabble.

—Many, not all, knights of the king's commission are placed over a known number of subjects as protector and provider (by *provider* meaning: providing instruction in the ways of the great king). The *non-knights*— observed by the dragon—were those who had followed these back-slidden warriors in their gradual journey from the river to the inner realm. They were very poorly armed…and not *one* carried a full sword, and only a few had blades of any consequence.—

"Wait!" screamed *Sir* Warren as one of his underlings boldly (or foolishly, rather) charged, at full gallop, towards the monster that had so rudely disrupted their detestable lifestyles. The others, their mounts fidgeting and barely restrained, looked to their leader, wondering if they too should follow their overanxious brother (who, now with shield raised and lance lowered was steadily closing on the motionless beast). Warren held up his gloved hand, even as his eyes remained on the encounter that must shortly take place. The others, following his lead, calmed their mounts and looked towards the wall as the lance of the speeding knight neared the belly of the enormous dragon.

In a moment their curiosity was sated for, as the young warrior delivered a blow that would have obliterated any Ganab and fatally wounded any Shachath…against the scale of *this* behemoth the lance instantly shattered and the knight, thrown from the collision, lay prone, dazed on the once green earth beneath the dripping jaws of the monster. His horse, also knocked down and dazed, quickly regained a standing position and stood, obediently, near its master.

From the vantage of the town the scene of the next minute was most chilling indeed. For, as the dragon looked down on the flea that dare confront him, the tail, that long, adept, hideous appendage, quickly coiled around the midsection of the horse and, without taking its eyes off the knight, the monster threw the fully armored thoroughbred effortlessly in a high arch over the remains of the wall to its rear (where it landed in a broken heap, the impact killing it immediately). The knight, upon hearing the most unsettling screams of his valiant charger, then staggered to his feet and quickly drew his rusty sword. But *his* fate was like that of a small fish, flipped playfully into the mouth of one of the otters that inhabited some of the streams and rivers of the land and, as the sickening utterance of the wayward warrior and the loud crack of armor being chewed made its way to the ears of the observers, an old rhyme was grudgingly resurrected from the memory of Sir Warren.

> *To destroy the Muth…test the fire.*
> *If you skip this step…you will expire.*

"Brothers," said Warren as his fellow knights, aghast at what they had just seen, sat paralyzed with fear, "whatever type of dragon this is, it is surely a Muth, or more. Are you prepared to do battle on foot? Are your swords and shields ready?"

* * *

Sir Reginald surveyed this disheveled group of *knights* that knelt before him. They had obviously been through *something*…but he wasn't sure if their story of a valiant battle against an unbeatable foe rang true. "Nineteen…hmm," he pondered as he sat on his throne, his right leg crossed over the left. He seemed to remember that the compliment of knights in *Porneia* was perhaps twenty, or a little more. Here before him were nineteen, the many others, *so they say,* lay dead...defending the sheep of the city (meaning, of course, the lesser inhabitants of the town).

The ruler of Alazon rose from his lofty perch and slowly, thoughtfully, descended the polished stairs. "Arise, fellow knights," he said, with a gesture of open-armed welcome (although his mind certainly had a guarded stance). "I can see that you have been through much and I will arrange sustenance for you and your steeds. But tell me," he said, now standing directly in front of Sir Warren as the lesser stood to gaze into the eyes of his better, "why did you not go to one of the fortress cities closer to your home?"

—As has been stated previously, around and attached to the center, the many domains, fiefdoms, *kingdoms* (if you will) spread out like spokes on a wheel. However, of these many, there were three great cities...three great magnets that had around them all the many lords and lowlies that gravitated to their cause. Alazon, the strongest, oldest, most dominant, was one. Another was *Aphron*, a city that had its beginnings near the river. It was then called *Sophia*, but, having slowly drifted from the life-giving stream, it changed its name to *Daath*, and then, as it was seduced to the center it changed its name once more. The final anchor of the inner realm was *Sarx*, and it was from this tentacled city's region that the knights of *Porneia* had traveled.—

"Sire," Sir Warren nearly whispered, lowering his gaze, "*yours* is the city of the games...where champions reside...and *you*, Sir Reginald, are the Exalted Knight." And then, lifting his eyes to meet those of his now puffed up benefactor, "Indeed, where else *could* we go? We are in need of a place of unmatched strength. And that, my lord, is among the warriors of Alazon."

There was a moment of calculation as the pleasant words slithered from one heart to the other. And, even if these syllables—offered as delicate dainties to a hungry ear—were not sincere...they certainly resounded as true to the hearer.

"Very well," offered a smiling Sir Reginald after a few seconds' pause, while motioning with his hand that all those still kneeling should rise. "Sir Rob will see to your needs and accommodations." And, as he watched each stand, bow, and then turn to follow the last...the ruler of Alazon noticed that the swords and shields of these *warriors* seemed most devoid of luster...as if they had been bathed in a substance that had robbed them of their very purpose.

As this fleeting query dashed from his consciousness, the supreme ruler then quickly turned to attend to another matter of his kingdom, not knowing that the reason of this observed deadness was that although these knights had *indeed* fought in a battle, it was not the battle of their description. For these, after timidly testing the fire, they then, as one, turned and slashed their way through the horrified gathering of their ill-equipped charges. Indeed, they left a bloodied and wounded human populace to be devoured by a raging, billowing beast as they, the elite of *Porneia*, squeezed their way out a rear entrance and then, to secure their escape, locked the most narrow door behind them.

...And one might wonder, since knights are sworn to defend—to the death, if need be—those in their care...one might wonder why greater interest in this exchange of words was not paid as to the fate of the lesser...the lowly masses of *Porneia*? But, such is the nature of the center...the thoughts, desires, even worship, turn inward, and that which is meant to be given...is clutched all the tighter and, having been thus perverted, it begins to mutate and whither. Indeed, that which only thrives in the giving, when dammed, becomes a swirling vortex...drawing all things to the center. Whether it be of the inner realm, or the inner man...all things gravitate to the welfare of...*I*.

* * *

After the easy conquest of *Porneia* (though hardly a *conquest*—implying a battle of some sort—for this demon it could be compared to a trip to the market), after the plucking of the children, after the taunting, ripping, burning, crushing, and devouring of all who bore the king's mark...the beast effortlessly passed through the granite wall opposite his place of intrusion and continued in the circular pattern that served to cover and defile every square meter of the inner realm.

Along this line of travel were the lesser-walled cities of *Aselgeia, Teraphim, Kashaph, Eris, Qinah, Aph, and Shakar*. Each, famous (or *infamous*) for particular, distinguishing traits, was treated by the creature in the same way. First...the screeching, for, as its foul stench—that choking combination of sulfur, soul, and sewer—wafted over the walls much like a tidal surge over a dike, the loud guttural emissions of the beast would resonate unyieldingly in the wilting hearts of the city dwellers as it traveled round and round the perimeter. Indeed, each inhabitant would hear his or her name and would *know*, instinctively—though some went nearly insane trying to deny it—that there was a kinship to this horrible thing outside the wall. And, as their small children (who, due to innocence…could only hear a hideous roaring) clung to their garments and trembled, these residents filled the monster with their fears until, at the peak of despair, the creature would then burst through and then make short work of any resistance. And yes, though each walled city made varied and futile attempts at defense and attack, the dragon *always* prevailed. But…invariably…some of the knights, and lesser residents, of each place would escape. Some made their way to the river, but many sought the security of Alazon, where Sir Reginald welcomed their numbers and knowledge, and where he, as he gathered the pieces of this black-hearted puzzle…carefully made and executed his plans for defense and domination.

Chapter XVII

It grabs the eye.
Its taste is sweet.
A golden path for wayward feet.
But in the end...a horrid place.
Your food is shame.
Your air...disgrace.

"Look, Martha...isn't it as I described it?"

Martha, a frail, modestly dressed young woman with beautiful long reddish locks (that served, for the moment, as an amusement for their three-year-old boy, Philip—who sat sleepily on her left hip) shielded her eyes with her right hand and strained to see the dazzling reflective towers that gleamed in the distance as the eastern sun conquered the ancient peaks and lit up this area known as the inner realm.

"Yes, husband, I see them," she half-heartedly replied (still very unsure of this trek that took her tender family so very far from the river she loved.)

"Oh, *tulip*," said her slightly older mate in a condescending child-like tone as he place his arm gently across her shoulders and gave a playful squeeze. "It will be all right, darling. We'll only stay a fortnight."

—*Sarx* was one of the three great cities of the inner realm. Although it was along the same line as its sister cities *Aphron* and *Alazon* (meaning, equidistant from the center and thus on the same path of the dragon's way) it was enormous compared to its siblings. Known as a city of many gates and gatherings, with open arms towards all (as opposed to her relatives, who could be quite selective when it came to full time residents), yes, all whose desire led them to an inward place were welcome here…welcome to nurture and grow those things that the river could *not* nourish.—

> *The slope is gentle,*
> *Slight and sure*
> *That leads the simple down.*
> *The wise man often checks his way;*
> *The fool forgets…and drowns*

The *Carnal* family, mentioned previously, was one of the many who were making their move from the river…inland, most, to be sure, had every intent to make this just a passing fancy, a vacation, a sip from an intoxicant filled tankard that one never intended to drain. However, after the initial silencing of the inner alarm (this defensive mechanism was a warning of sorts that sounded from the river-bathed soul when encountering some destructive element and was usually overcome, not by brute force, but rather by a seductive dripping that wore away at the mechanism), when the alarm was adequately deadened, those who came to visit soon found themselves taking up residence.

Thomas, the head of this little family, had been, for some time, frequenting this inner cauldron. At first his visits were as a necessity for business (so was his thought), but of late it was a desire hard to contain. Indeed, this city—so geared for the satisfaction of the flesh—called to him much as a narcotic—after having been married to the human brain—calls evermore for a continual joining. Only the river could break this bond…and the river was something he did *not* want to see, let alone immerse himself in.

"Husband," said Martha cautiously as she and little Philip were led to all the *pretty* places of the city, "can you smell that?"

"What's that, dear?" said Thomas as he brought them, yet again, to another confectionary where his toddler and wife were offered free samples of the tempting wares.

"I'm not sure?" she distractedly said, concentrating now more on the delightful taste that danced with her tongue. "Something a bit unsettling…it's gone now." And then, having an appetite awakened, she swallowed, turned, and said, "What else is here, husband?"

179

"So very much, darling," he said, rising from the shiny white table at which they had been temporarily moored and, offering her his hand… "So very, very, much." The three, Thomas, Martha, and little Philip who, with one hand grasping Mommy's, and the other holding a rainbow-colored lolly, then strolled down the bustling main street of this most interesting metropolis…a city whose outward facade was mirrors and mirth, but when its shallow foundation was laid bare, it revealed a bedrock of greed and self worship. A fertile plot, indeed, for that which was sown from a dark and distant place.

* * *

"What is its name…again?"

Sir Robert, feeling very much like a peddler of pots and pans, took a deep breath and repeated, slowly, the name of the siege engine that he had towed, using four teams of the more durable horses of Alazon, to this field, not very far from the gates of *Sarx*. "It's called an Onager, Sir."

"Onager? Isn't that another name for a wild a…"

"Yes," the knight quickly interrupted, "but since there are ladies present we'll refer to it as a donkey…as you'll soon see why." Sir Robert, signaling to one of the lessers of his entourage (meaning one of the grunts, or foot-soldiers, who did all the labor intensive and less glamorous tasks in service of their masters…in this case: the hauling, preparing, and firing of this catapult) who then pulled the lever which set this unusual beast in motion.

With a loud THWACK the throwing arm (a large, stout timber [rather long, vertical, and moored at the base midst a twisting of strong flexible sinews] which had been wrestled to a horizontal state…and had been straining greatly to *not* remain so) was suddenly released from its anchoring chain and, flying blurringly upward it then stopped suddenly against an opposing cross beam. The sling—a great leather pouch held by two opposing ropes and attached firmly by these to the pinnacle of the rising wood—when the zenith was quickly attained one of these cords would release and the sling, which in this case held a fifty pound stone, then let fly the missile that went at least one hundred and fifty meters.

"Amazing," uttered the representative of the knights of *Sarx*. "And," then turning to see most of the feminine (and some of the not so) of his company cowering at a greater distance than when the demonstration had begun, "I can see why you call it a wild donkey. That recoil nearly threw this contraption on its face! Nevertheless," he said, walking up to the machine and patting gently the side of one of its rugged supports, "it could aid in the destruction of this dragon." And then, turning to Sir Robert, "How many do you possess? And what other strategies do you have for the completion of our common goal?"

* * *

Martha stirred from her drug-induced slumber. The sun was now at midday and its rays were demanding attention, and the *vacation*—that which was only supposed to last two weeks—had stretched into two blurry months. She, the once proper and prim manager of her little family, slowly swung her legs over the side of the soiled mattress, painfully sat up, and quickly commenced to place both dirty palms over the throbbing temples of her now somewhat swollen head. She, although from a sober distance appearing as a woman disgustingly destitute…she, nevertheless, found herself not desiring soap, or clean clothes, or even a decent meal, but rather her lust was for more of what had recently possessed her…and for this she began to rummage through the adjacent nightstand and the trash that had accumulated by the bed. This nearly reflexive response was interrupted and momentarily held in check by the sound of something deeper…her child.

"Philip?" she called, her voice rasping from lack of meaningful drink and nutrition. "Philip, where are you?" She could hear his muffled laughter coming from the adjacent room and felt, the way only mothers can, that something was terribly wrong. "Philip!" she spoke more clearly, stumbling to her feet. "Mommy's coming, baby!"

As she shuffled towards the doorless exit, leaning against the wall with one hand while cradling her head with the other, she heard another voice coming from behind her. "He's all right, Tulip. He's laughing, isn't he?"

Martha glance back for just a moment to see her husband, Thomas, sprawled over the other half of the bed. His condition was no better than hers, but then, she didn't recognize *her* condition, and his words weren't going to stop her anyway. She rounded the corner to the tiny living area of this rented space and was greeted by the simple words of her only child.

"Look, Mommy…pretty." Philip, obviously neglected (especially to the eyes of his *now-awakening* mother) was cradling something large in his two pudgy arms.

"What do you have there, honey?" she said, going over to the tiny window to open the light-restraining shade.

"It's an egg, Mommy…a big green egg."

Martha, her eyes adjusting to the light, stood there in shock for just a moment. For there, in the arms of her innocent child, was a glimmering orb! The sight of this, and another beside him, snapped her out of her stupor like a plunge into an ice-cold stream.

"No, baby," she said, rushing to his side and gently pulling the nasty thing out of his arms. "This can hurt you, honey. Mommy has to get rid of it." Martha quickly placed the dragon seeds into the canvas bag that they used for groceries, and then, pulling her son close to her she examined his hands…his perfect, innocent, little hands.

Thomas, who by now was standing in the doorway of the bedroom, scratching his belly with his left hand even as he began to lift a bottle of his favorite beverage with his right…stopped mid-pour as he saw his wife, sitting in the corner of the room, sobbing and rocking back and forth as she clung tightly to their little boy.

"*Tulip,*" he said, in that tone that she had begun to hate, "what's the problem? We'll leave those things for the collection…like we always do. Like we've done for the last month and a half."

Martha, looking again at the blistered hands of her baby and seeing in his eyes a sickness she had never seen before, blurted out, "NO!" and then rising to her feet she began to frantically dress herself and the boy in an obvious preparation for a trip.

"What are you doing, honey?" Thomas said between belches. "Where are you going?"

"I'm going back home…back to the river! I can't believe I let you talk me into this!" By now the lady was furiously awake and although her husband reached out to grab her wrist, she violently pulled it back.

"What's the matter with you!" he shouted, as even *his* fog of delirium was being lifted by an adrenaline surge.

"Do you see this?!" Martha held, palm up, the right hand of their ailing child.

For a moment Thomas leaned over and examined the now oozing blisters on his son's hand. Then, standing up, taking another drink, he replied, "There's nothing wrong with him. Lots of people in this city have those things. We'll buy him some ointment that will take care of it. Now, let the boy play and come back to bed."

The next sound he heard was the door slamming and the bottle he had just drained being broken against it. "No, I won't go back with you," he muttered to himself as he crawled his way back to bed. "I won't go back."

* * *

It was the wind that ushered the dragon's nearness from the point of conjecture to that of an unseen reality. A full day before the monster's plumes of fire could be made out in the midnight sky, the stench—that sickening smell of rotting flesh and sulfur—wafted over the new and improved bulwarks of a city that, heretofore, had no problem with decay and debauchery. However, this was a fight for survival. And it appeared, at least at first, that the many diverse, and often divisive elements of this huge metropolis would band together behind their many knights and attempt to accomplish what no other potential victim had done...to vanquish a dragon...a dragon like no other.

"Wake up, now." It was the hushed voice of Henry, an attendant to the wooden *spanking machine* (a name agreed upon by these two operators for this somewhat small siege engine recently acquired from Alazon). His slumbering comrade, now grudgingly stirring, had been dreaming of a family he had once had...and had traded away for *nothing*. But even this fantasy was interrupted by the gruff mumblings of his fellow soldier.

"Wake up," the voice said again, accompanying it with a shove. "It's coming...every now and again I see a glow...like a forest fire in the distance. But it doesn't last. It must be the creature using its flame."

Thomas, who had been forcefully conscripted to fight for this city he loved (and loathed), sat up, adjusted his crude helmet (no uniforms for these types, their own clothes and a hammered pot would have to do), and joined his partner peering over the granite battlement.

"There it is again! Do you see it!" Henry turned to look into the bloodshot (and now squinting) eyes of his fellow soldier as he pointed in the direction of the dull, distant glow.

"Yes, I see it," said Thomas, who desired greatly for another drink. "So what?"

"So what?" Henry said indignantly as they both turned and slid, backs against the wall, onto the oily platform which was their post. "It means that by the morrow we'll be pelting that lizard into oblivion," he said with an excitement compared to that of a hunter before the hunt.

"I'll tell you what it also means," said Thomas, who took a moment to clear his throat and aimed and launched a green nodule onto the pile of rocks that would be their ammunition. "It also means that the advanced guard couldn't do nothin' to stop that thing."

—The Advanced Guard: a hurriedly assembled force consisting of the most able of the knights of *Sarx*. These, in the annual games (always held in Alazon) had consistently done well and, it was the strategists *from* Alazon who urged that such a force and course be taken. Yes, the advisors from the Exalted Knight were quite persuasive, and why not? Better to destroy or disable the beast *before* it attacks a city, than to rely solely on untested battlements.—

> *Treachery has many forms,*
> *The blatant, and the coy.*
> *Beware a sudden friend's embrace;*
> *His motives may destroy.*

"Fifty of your finest!" The strategist from Alazon (*not* Sir Robert, who had departed after doing his little demonstration) spoke to the council that ruled the city. "Here's a list."

—Unlike Alazon, which prized greatly strong leadership and recognized the efficiency of one solitary voice, the cities of *Sarx* and *Aphron*, being loose-nit arrays of differing views, relied on many-tiered councils to make their important decisions...and this, the defense of the city, was the most important they had ever faced. Yet, even in this, delay and debate were unavoidable.—

The attendant took the curling parchment from the ambassador (named, *Ratsad*) and, bowing, handed it to the purple-robed statesman who was, for this season, the leader of this parliament. He slowly looked over the list and, having been satisfied, passed it to the next. Over the space of the next hour the list of names made its way slowly around the curved council chamber and, from the expression of each—after reading it—one could tell if there was sufficient representation on the list to either placate or *irritate* the holder.

"Well, gentlemen," said the leader, receiving the list once again, "what is your will? As for me...I find the list quite satisfactory."

"And why wouldn't you?" came a voice from an upper chair. "A fifth of those listed are from your quadrant!" And then standing and turning as he spoke, "I think there should be more names. I have many qualified warriors who aren't on that list!"

"He's right!" shouted one.

"Here, here!" joined another.

Soon all in the chamber were standing and, with voices raised and arms gesturing...there was chaos that left the ambassador (who stood quietly, with arms folded, sporting a slight, knowing smirk on his face) somewhat amused. He whispered to himself, "It's just as Sir Reginald said." And then, walking over to the leader, he tapped him on the shoulder (the gentleman had been turned towards the council...joining eagerly in the din) whereupon the ambassador, after motioning for an ear, whispered something that caused the leader to smile broadly and commence clanging the melon-sized golden bell that, theoretically, would signal an end to debate.

After a few minutes the representatives were in their seats, their expressions hardened and suspicious. The council chief then motioned for the visitor to speak.

"Gentlemen," he began, bowing lowly, "I apologize for this misunderstanding. *Of course* there are many more qualified fighters than those on this list. This was meant only as a suggestion. Please, by all means add to it as you see fit. It is only right that *all* the sections of your great city be represented in the victory that will surely take place against this common enemy." And, with this, followed by another courteous bow, the faces of those present softened and they began, in a more congenial chaos, to write their own lists to be added to the original. And, as the ambassador stepped back and waited quietly in the shadows, an idea was birthed that went far beyond the desires of his master.

"*Try, as best you can, to bring only those on the list,*" those were the vague instructions given him in the great hall of Alazon.

"Yes," he silently whispered to himself as he smiled and looked over the *new* list of names. "Yes, I have *just* the way to narrow the herd," his thoughts continued as he bowed and exited the chamber, "and, at the same time we'll see what that dragon is made of."

* * *

The mist was heavy on the fields adjacent the city of *Sarx* as the sun first lightly painted the clouds above and then burst, forcefully, over the mountain range which lay far opposite the king's castle. The soldiers on the eastern wall, wearied by lack of sleep and, although heartened by a chance to at least *see* this thing that had haunted half the night with its unnerving rasping (like a thousand snakes chanting, in monotone, the verse stated previously...*From the center, rounding round...*) and, added to this, every so often seeing a great plume of yellowish blue flame which evidenced just a hint of a towering dragon head…these civilian warriors hoped against hope that, with the day, would come their opportunity to vanquish this thing that dared disrupt their hearts' desire.

"I think I see it!" The words of Henry, who was ever peering over the rugged and hastily constructed battlements even as his partner, still sitting— back against the stones—chewed, with some difficulty, on a rather stale roll that had been donated by one of the local bakeries.

—*Sarx* had long had walls, but these, rather than serving as barriers of exclusion (for absolutely *all* were bid welcome by *Sarx*) these merely acted as gentle guides directing the curious to one of the many gates. From a distance the city, like a matron of royalty, appeared to be girded by a long shimmering ribbon, whereupon closer examination revealed that this delicate accessory was overlaid with but the thinnest layers of gold and silver, however, with the final realization that a dragon *was* coming (evidenced by a steady decline of its communication and commerce with the smaller, more vile towns closer to the center), additional height, of lesser stuff (as in *less* comely) was placed atop the old.—

"OW!" Henry looked down to see his partner pulling a fragment of tooth from the roll that had been, until a moment ago, only grudgingly yielding its sustenance.

"Perhaps you should add that *rock* to the pile," he said, offering his hand to his fellow soldier who, with the little finger on his left hand, was taking inventory of his ever diminishing cash of chompers.

"Maybe you're right," said Thomas as he harvested another fragment and then spat out some crimson at a cockroach that scurried nearby. Then, looking up at the somewhat mocking face of his accomplice (although, truthfully, Henry was the closest thing he'd had to a friend in quite some time), he accepted the assistance and soon the two of them were squinting to make out, as the morning mist quickly burned off due to the rising summer sun, a great reddish smoldering hill…a curious mound that had *not* been there the night before.

"Yes…that *is* the dragon." It was the voice of one of the generals of *Sarx* who had been schooled in the habits of this thing by one of the strategists of Alazon (who were all strangely missing) who had accumulated, over time, some insight as to the tactics of this creature that destroyed all in its path.

"How long will it stay this way, sir?" said the eager lieutenant who was in charge of the many batteries of catapults…most of which were stationed near the eastern gate.

"Hard to tell," offered the rather large commander (who was, in actuality a senior member of the council who had blustered his way into a commission). "We'll just have to be ready, lieutenant." Then, looking up and down the ranks that stood, in all directions, along the parapets and recently constructed towers, he continued, "You know what to do?"

"Yes, sir, but…"

"But what?" The general looked now into the face of this untested officer.

"It seems like a very strange strategy…sir."

"Yours is not to analyze or question the plan of attack devised by your betters…*Lieutenant.*"

"Yes, sir," barked the underling with a crisp repentant salute.

"Carry on," mumbled the general as he sloppily returned the gesture and then made his way towards a nearby descending stair. "Yes…" he thought to himself, minutes later as the growing urgency to retreat directed his steps, "a *very* strange strategy, indeed."

The dragon, somewhat larger than when first encountered by Sir Robert and his fellows, stirred as it sensed an invisible mist of fear emanating, barely, from the city nearby. Though its stomach was still somewhat full from the previous evening's consumption of a half hundred knights…its lusting heart, nevertheless, beckoned it awake and, as it stood—its huge protective *wings* casting, for a moment, a shadow on the distant wall of *Sarx* (much to the amazement and terror of those at their posts)—the *scent* of family filled its wide open nostrils and, like a wolf salivating before a kill, all the inner hellish processes of this creature began to bubble and churn and ignite in preparation for a great horrible feast.

"What shall we do?" These were the whispered and warbling words (due to fear) of the nearest battery attendant which he posed to the young officer who had just, an hour before, received a chastening from the commanding general.

The lieutenant, who had studied hard for this final exam said, calmly (a *total* facade!), "Wait, gentlemen." He held up high his right gauntleted hand (palm upward) to signify to those out of earshot that *all* were to hold their fire. Then, trusting that these barely-trained recruits would not forget their recent briefing (which told of the waving of a purple flag to signal the release of missiles), he turned to the original speaker and explained, *again,* the promised pattern of this invader.

"First," he said, squatting and using his right index finger to draw, crudely, in the dirt which had accumulated on the elevated walkway, "first the dragon will try to instill fear by screeching, or some such thing, as it travels, counterclockwise, around our perimeter walls. The monster will do this for so long (the lieutenant didn't know, and he didn't want to let on as to his ignorance) until he himself determines. Then the creature will choose a portion of the wall to breech…and then, once inside, it will dine. However," he continued, stopping his finger at the point that would be considered the easternmost gate and not noticing that the audience (of which there were now many members, and the number steadily growing) had turned somewhat paler at his reference to *dining,* "however," he looked up after placing an X on their present location, "we do not want this behemoth to determine its place of attack. That is why *we* will instigate the confrontation. Are the children ready?"

"Nearly," said an underling as he pointed to a long string of pre-teenagers who, looking rather confused, were being led up to their level. "They will be ready soon, lieutenant."

A few minutes later, as all eyes returned to the beast (which sat calmly, facing directly the eastern gate even as it, from time to time had been letting out great bursts of yellowish sulfurous smoke) the frightened observers, just as the officer had predicted, saw it slowly stand on all fours and, in an almost subliminal way, it began to rumble its traveling chant one last time before continuing on…

> *From the center, rounding round*
> *Father, Mother, bring*
> *Then to Master, we present*
> *The perfect empty ring*
> *The perfect empty ring…*

After this eerie recitation the dragon turned, slightly, and, coming just within projectile range (although all archers and artillery had strict orders to stand down), it then let out a nearly continual screeching as it plodded in great heavy steps around the city's skirt. Each man, *and* woman (of adult age) within the walls, almost instinctively slammed their palms over their ears.

For…it was a dirty calling…a reminder of something evil done…and *not* undone. Indeed, the dragon spoke in an almost continual haunting chorus to all its *kin* within the city, and all, even those whose ears had long been deadened due to age or injury…even these had a horrible hearing in their soul…a hearing that produced terror and an almost suicidal foreboding…and, as the creature, true to form, followed its counterclockwise way, the children (an even five hundred, some weeping, but many too young to be distrustful) were marched to an elevated platform that stood *above,* and somewhat back, from the eastern gate. These, whose parents had been assured of their safe return (though, truthfully, many of the guardians were far too absorbed in their own distress to notice, or care) were held, in plain view, by a small guard of sword-bearing soldiers. Yes, these tender human morsels were the bait…and it was essential that they remain on the menu *and* the platter long enough to be noticed by the hungry reptilian connoisseur.

The dragon…as it paced, and smoked, and screeched its chorus, could feel, with every passing moment, an inswell of terror…that nurturing substance that humans so delightfully exuded when properly motivated. It was a long way around *Sarx,* and the creature took note that there were many gates…none of which were large enough for this uninvited guest. But that didn't matter. No iron gate, *or* stone wall, had seriously hindered this demon before. And these, though appearing taller and more durable than any previously encountered…would be no different.

"It's coming!" was the call of one of the towered watchmen near the focus of the trap. And, upon his word all engines and arms prepared for a withering volley as the bait would *surely* be taken. But, as the children whimpered, (in plain view of *all*)…the dragon simply continued on…screeching and fuming as it had the first time around…passing by the *trap* without so much as a sniff.

"Thomas, Henry, and you others!" barked the lieutenant, signaling to those nearest the center. "When it approaches again…on my command…let loose a volley to grab its attention!" And these, as the children suffered yet another delay, waited for the watchman's call.

Then, as the monster, after another half hour's stroll, came once again upon the eastern gate (apparently intending to circle the city as many times as required to squeeze every last drop of horror from the inhabitants) its attention was drawn to the wall by a small barrage of stones passing by…and some careening off its formidable plates. This momentary annoyance produced its desired result for, turning slightly to survey its attackers it saw, on a raised platform above this most fortified entrance to the city…children! And not just a few children for which it usually had to delve and dig…but a whole smorgasbord!

Now…this was indeed tempting. The dragon, forever drawn to unite with its parents, nevertheless delighted in the consumption of those untainted by the soiled hands of the adults. And thus, the normal plan of attack set aside, the demon now walked directly—as its eyes widened and foul fluids dripped from between its jagged teeth—towards the dainty appetizers set before it.

"Fire!" It was the voice command of the lieutenant which was accompanied by a quick waving of the purple flag. A moment later a thousand projectiles (heavy stones, crossbow darts, longbow arrows, lighted firepots…rained down upon this lusting beast and, as these weapons (many missing, but many [surprisingly] finding their marks) showered upon the face and body of this dragon…for a brief moment it paused…and then, shaking its head as the missiles pounded and poured…it even stepped back! And, although this wave, which would have severally bloodied any army of man, did not appear to damage in any significant way this creature…it *did* cause it to retreat. And this gave the warriors on the wall hope and encouragement that if it could not be killed…perhaps it could be persuaded to travel on…to be dealt with another day.

"PREPARE!" shouted the lieutenant and, as the command was repeated down the line like an echo in a great deep-throated canyon, he, as he continued to have his eyes glued to the dragon that sat—fuming and still, nearly two hundred meters away—he then felt a firm tapping on his right shoulder and turned to see the general…the very same who had humbled him just two hours previously.

"Well done, Lieutenant," said the commander as the two traded salutes.

"Thank you, sir."

The general, walking to the wall and placing both hands on the uppermost granite (the platform upon which they stood was only four feet lower than the top of the new addition) said, while motioning for his subordinate to join him as they both fixed their eyes on this outer enemy, "From the council tower we were able to observe this first attack, and it appears that those missiles that struck the head, especially the eyes, were the most effective. You would do well to concentrate on this area, if possible."

"Yes, sir," said the lower officer smartly (although thinking to himself that such precision was difficult, as least for this bunch, to obtain).

"Very well, then," offered the commander, making sure he was *not* in the

SIR JOHN & THE DRAGON'S BOAST

vicinity for the next attack, "carry on."

The lieutenant saluted respectfully but then, as the general approached the stair, added, "General...what of the children, General?"

As the rotund and bejeweled leader slowly went down the steps (aided on each arm by a stout attendant and always hobbling down, right foot first), he said, "The children have to stay, Lieutenant. We don't want the creature to attack a weaker segment of our defenses." And then, pausing to look directly into the eyes of the artillery officer, "The children have to stay."

It was another half hour before the dragon (who simply could *not* keep his eyes off the innocents) advanced again and, as before, as it passed within one hundred meters...it was met by a now more accurate (practice makes perfect) barrage of stone and steel. This time, however, it, shaking its head as if a creature of the field engulfed by gnats, was able to come to within fifty meters before being turned back by the wave from the wall. And, as it retreated (to sit and stew as before) a loud cheer went up from the defenders and, throughout the great city the feeling of dread diminished due, in no small part, to the fact that with this distraction (the children) the beast had ceased in its familial call.

For the next two hours the dragon, ever desiring the morsels above the gate, attacked three more times. And, each time it was repulsed, coming no closer than it had in its second attempt. By now the sun had passed its zenith and, although there was no significant exhaustion on the part of the defenders...rumors did abound.

"I say it's just playing with us," said Thomas who, from time to time, couldn't resist putting a finger in his mouth to mourn his lost bicuspid.

"Nah," said Henry, who slapped the dust from his clothes (left over from loading one of the projectiles for the next volley) as he walked over to the wall to join his partner. "I think it's met its match. After all, we're not like those from *Misthotos*...we're here for the duration." Pausing to pick up a donated apple from a burlap sack nearby, he continued as he polished it on his soiled shirt, "*I* think it'll quit this little dance soon and choose, instead, a more agreeable partner."

"Like, *Aphron?*" said Thomas, pulling his finger from his mouth and reaching into the bag for an apple of his own.

"Eggsacly," said Henry between chews. "They'll probably try to debate the thing."

As the two laughed among themselves at the thought of this kind of confrontation, the dragon again stood on all fours and gave every indication that another attack was imminent.

"Lieutenant," the general, who, after seeing the earlier successes was now emboldened enough to join the *front line,* "Lieutenant, is everything prepared?"

"Yes, sir. All the catapults are loaded and we have ample ammunition to continue this course indefinitely."

"I've been told that even though this thing is like no other dragon we've ever heard of…it does appear to require rest." The general stood near to the lesser and motioned him closer so that he might whisper the council's last ditch advice. "If it simply will not be dissuaded, we'll begin—when the creature assumes its sleeping form—to evacuate the populace from the western gates as you and your men stand ready."

"Yes, sir," the lieutenant said softly, wondering why such a drastic action would be necessary when they were obviously doing so well.

"It's coming, sirs," a soldier from the wall reminded the duo. "In a moment it will be within range."

The dragon, as it had on each previous assault, advanced slowly, directly in line with its ultimate goal…the children. However, this time, just past the hundred meter spot…it stopped and, although many of the various weapons of man were well capable of reaching it at this distance…they had found it most beneficial to wait until another twenty-five meters had passed before ordering the volley.

"What is it doing?" the general asked, turning to the lieutenant.

Then, just below the murmuring of the troops, a faint clicking sound could be heard.

"QUIET!" yelled the lieutenant, and soon, as most peered over the wall and directed an ear in the beast's direction, they heard the final cadence of a most deadly countdown…

"H-U-C-C-C…"

Chapter XVIII

Costly is the wayward way.
Nothing to gain
But much to pay.

The visitor was again at the point of tears. Mary, ever compassionate, handed him a handkerchief and, as he held the cloth to his face, it softened, somewhat, the mournful sobs of this middle-aged fellow who had joined them earlier in the day (along with not a few others) at their weekly meeting down at the river.

"Thomas…that *is* your name?" said Sir John, seated directly opposite this stranger even as the knight acknowledged with a nod and a smile the two cups of hot tea left by Fredrick.

"Y-yes, that is my name," said this sorrowful figure as he removed the cloth from his eyes and folded it, neatly, besides the cup. "I'm so sorry. I don't want to be any trouble."

"Nonsense, Thomas. You are no trouble. However," said the protector, lifting his cup to take a drink and motioning to his guest to do the same, "I'm just curious as to your origin. Where are you from and what brings you here?"

Thomas, who had barely fled the city of *Sarx* with just the clothes on his back (several months prior) and, who had spent most of the morning repentantly weeping besides the river before finally—at the encouragement of his current host—stepping into the healing waves, asked, sheepishly, if he

193

might bare his soul to this *family* about his experience and, given permission, he, between waves of emotion and many more tears…recounted how he had fallen to the age old seduction and how it had ruined his life and almost killed him. We'll take up the account from his place on the wall.

"I, along with my companion, had been firing stone after stone at this huge dragon, off and on, for hours. I tell you, Sir John," he said, pausing to look at his benefactor, "I've never even heard of a creature of such size and strength, let alone seen one. And, as the day wore on and our aim improved…even when we could bounce a fifty pound missile off the monster's nose, it only seemed to deter him the least little bit."

"Go on, sir." It was the voice of Albert who had just come in from the field and always enjoyed a good story which involved combat.

"Well, as I was saying," said Thomas, standing for a brief moment to shake Albert's hand, "we had had some success against this thing. I don't know if we were hurting it much…although I can't imagine all that steel and stone doing *nothing* after so many strikes."

"You'd be surprised," interrupted Sir John, softly, as his mind revisited some of the Muths he had encountered and others he had heard about years ago (before the king had redirected his station).

"Excuse me?" said Thomas.

"Nothing, go on."

"Well, we had been at it several hours. The creature would attack, be repulsed, and then, a while later would attack again. After the morning waned the children were in a sorry state, but their crying and squalling, so it appeared, made the creature even more determined."

"What do you mean…children?" This time it was Mary, who had not heard all the sordid particulars of Thomas' life up to this point.

"Bait, Mary. They were using the children as bait," said Sir John as he brought the cup to his lips.

"Oh…I can't listen to this," said the matron and she departed out of the room, and with her, Fred.

"Please, go on, won't you?" said Albert, who found this whole discussion rather fascinating.

"Well," said Thomas, whose countenance seemed, at this final segment, to fall even more than from his previous confessions, continued, "Well, the creature made an advance, as before. We…all those who were prepared to launch stone and dart…we were waiting for the dragon to come to a certain spot that we had found most effective as to aim and intensity. The lieutenant, though he was a young fellow…he seemed to have this procedure down to a science, and we awaited his signal. But," Thomas shook his head slightly as he took a small drink, "but his signal never came."

"What happened?" asked Albert, who by now had his head resting on his hands (as was his usual habit when listening to a story.)

"Well, the creature came to the hundred-meter spot—perhaps a little closer—and just stopped. We probably could have reached it there, but we wanted it to come a little closer…as it had on the previous attempts. But this time it just stopped…and then I heard a clicking."

At this, Sir John's interest stepped up a good measure…as if something ingrained within his knightly make-up had been awakened…reminded.

"How did the dragon appear?" asked Sir John.

"It appeared almost rigid. It sat up and its two front legs looked as though they were fixed…perhaps even gripping the ground. And I could hear," said Thomas, leaning in, "I could hear a loud clicking…like something opening and slamming shut."

"The fire?" Albert, who had been through more than one training session with his father, interjected.

"Yes…that's it. But," and now Thomas held the handkerchief to his eyes once again, "but we didn't know it…at least not until it was too late." A minute passed and his understanding audience allowed this bereaving brother a few more moments to compose himself (although Albert wondered internally, *How many tears can one man possibly contain?*)

Putting down the cloth, he continued, "I heard a clicking, and then, as it continued on for a few moments…"

"How long?" By now Sir John's attention was fully realized. "How long?" he asked again, his eyes locking with those of his guest.

"Perhaps half a minute…probably less."

"Go on. What happened then?"

"Well," Thomas continued, his gaze dropping to his steaming cup which he held with both hands. "First," he said in a somewhat apologetic way, "you need to know that I didn't see everything that happened. If I had I suppose I wouldn't be here." He paused a moment more and continued, "After I saw that the dragon wasn't advancing, I decided to sit down with my back against the wall. All day I had been nursing my blasted tooth…what was left of it. So I sat there with my finger in my mouth feeling, for the hundredth time, the jagged remainder that stuck out from my gums."

"What did the dragon do?" Albert prompted. (He was used to keeping visitors on target from his many years of listening to Sir Peter.)

"Well, with most of the soldiers on the wall standing, and staring, and listening to that thing...well," Thomas took a moment to grab the handkerchief, "well...they didn't know what hit them."

"What? What hit them?" Albert raised up his head to inquire.

Sir John held up his hand slightly as a signal to his son to give this man some space. Then, after another minute, he himself continued the questioning. "Was it the fire? Did it send forth a blast of flame?"

"Yes, Sir John, that's what it was." By now Thomas was moving from remorse to rage, and in doing so the handkerchief was first clenched, then pushed away. "As I said, I was sitting there, tending to my own petty pains when WHOOSH!...an intense blast of yellowish blue flame, accompanied by a sickening smell of sulfur, rushed over the wall. Its force was incredible...I could feel the wall shake behind me, and the heat singed the hairs on my head." By now Thomas' eyes took on a blaze of their own. "The next thing you know, my partner Henry was screaming...and not only he...but almost all who had been unsuspectingly looking at the *thing* beyond the wall...each of these were blinded and their heads were ablaze—as if someone had grabbed them by the ankles, dipped them in paraffin, and then thrown them into a furnace. Many, my friend included (in hindsight, Thomas had attributed this title of intimacy to this last acquaintance from the city of *Sarx*), they were all soon dead. He writhed for a moment...calling out to me...but there was nothing I could do." Thomas paused, reliving the scene in his mind, and then he let out a great sigh.

"How far did you say the dragon was before it loosed the fire?" said Sir John.

"What's that?" said the visitor, thinking it a rather strange question.

"How *far* was the dragon from the wall when it loosed the flame?"

"Perhaps as far as one hundred meters...as I said, it wasn't yet close enough for the most effective use of our projectiles."

"Incredible," Sir John said half to himself. "Go on. What of the lieutenant, the general, the others who were defending the city?"

"Most...that I could see anyway...suffered the same fate as Henry. The general screamed and the last I saw of him was when he backed off the platform and fell to the ground beneath. And the lieutenant..." Thomas paused, raising his eyes to those of the knight's as he spoke of this youth whom he admired. "He, at first fell to his knees, but, as the fire consumed I could hear him shouting... 'Loose the stones! Shoot! Where is the flag?' And that's how he died…looking for the signal that was also destroyed by the same blast of flame."

"Were any able to fire back?" said Albert, softly.

"Only a few, son," Thomas almost instinctively associated this youth with the one he had not seen in many years, and the term, not meant to offend…did not. "Most of the siege engines were engulfed. Our platform was only four feet below the battlements. Whatever wood was exposed, burst into flame."

"What of the dragon?" asked Sir John. "What did it do next?"

"Well, with no wave of defense to deter it…it simply stomped its way to our most fortified gate. And now, as I think of it," Thomas looked up at the ceiling as if sifting through a jumbled memory, "although so much was happening around me…I *do* remember the platform shaking. It must have been the beast's heavy steps as it rushed upon the children."

"What *of* the children?" asked Albert (barely more than one himself), "were they far enough away to escape the fire?"

"Some," Thomas softened as he spoke of the innocent, "but most were partially exposed and these, the poor creatures, were writhing in pain as the dragon's head burst through the upper stones and, like a dog standing on hind legs and sliding its head sideways to steal a portion from its master's table…this merciless creature opened wide its jaws and, *using its tail*, it swept these poor babes to their deaths."

"How horrible!" uttered a now sitting up Albert as he put his right hand over his mouth. The young man then looked over to his father for some kind of anchor of solace in this conversation.

Sir John simply said, "What next?"

"Next," continued the guest, "the dragon clawed at the stones and these, to my surprise, fell easily before it. I suppose it's because the foundation, built more for sight than strength, could not withstand the heated blast."

"Then what?"

"By now I was nearly mad with fear. I ran to the nearest stair and, stumbling down and through a great chaos of citizens—citizens who, only moments before, had assumed an almost leisurely demeanor (such was their confidence in the wall and the warriors)—I cried out… 'RUN AWAY! RUN TO THE WESTERN GATES!!' But, as I heard thousands screaming as they were being cut down by the demon's tail even as whole blocks were incinerated by its fire…the sad truth was…"

"Yes…?" prompted Sir John.

"The sad truth was that outside each gate, *except* the eastern, was a toxic pool of some kind of poison. Apparently, earlier in the day when we *thought* the creature had not seen the children as it came 'round that first time…apparently it had. And, planning to set a trap for *us*, it, as it went by all the other gates…it secreted some sort of vile substance in front of each exit. Soon the bodies were piled so high that there was no chance of escape and, added to this, the dragon began its horrid screeching again."

"Screeching?" said Albert, looking to his father, whose countenance seemed to be hardening somewhat. "What does he mean, screeching? And what is this talk of poison?"

"Albert," said Thomas as the eyes of Sir John declared to the visitor that *he* should explain, "I don't know much about the poison except that everywhere this creature treads…behind it, in a great spreading wave…death follows. The trees, the crops, everything growing dies. And, although I've been told that wretched things can eventually take root…I'm not certain. As for the screeching…the dragon was calling *my* name. But," he added, pausing as if to add a new revelation to the thought, "…*all* the people that I could see seemed to be tormented. So, I suppose it was calling their names at the same time."

As Albert puzzled over this explanation, Sir John asked, "How did you survive? If this thing cut off your avenue of escape…how did *you* survive?"

"Sir Leslie," Thomas replied simply. "I survived because of Sir Leslie."

Sir John thought for a moment. That name sounded familiar. After a few seconds he retrieved a picture from his mind of some of the older warriors Sir Peter would associated with when not on an errand for the king. Sir Leslie was one of these. Sir John recalled that this particular knight was a bit of an outcast among the other protectors (meaning, he wasn't much on formalities, or for adding his name to some particular faction. He was, however, passionate about his service as a guardian…a passion that led him even to the gates of *Sarx*).

"Tell me what happened," he prompted.

"Well," continued Thomas, who pushed away his now empty cup, "Sir Leslie had come in search of me. It wasn't the first time, mind you. No, he had come several times over the years trying to persuade me to return to the river…to return also to my wife and child. But I, LIKE A FOOL!" he said loudly, closing his eyes and accentuating the words with a sharp nod of his head, and then, after a pause and a long, deflating sigh, "I…like an arrogant child, would refuse him. This last time I wouldn't even give him audience."

"How did he save you?" Albert chimed in.

"In the center of town," Thomas looked at the young man, "there was a very large open square. It was used weekly for markets and, on days of holiday it was used for great processions and parades. Eventually, having decimated the first half of the city, the dragon then entered this huge expanse intending, I suppose, to carry on until all the inhabitants were either buried, burned, or eaten. However, as it plodded its way, pausing only long enough to knock over the lofty tower that held the ruling council (the highest pinnacle of the place, very beautiful to the eye, but its foundation was weak), there came a point where it turned...as if something had caught its eye. And, sure enough, on the far side of the great mall, a lone figure held up a shield which bore the emblem of the king."

"Sir Leslie?" whispered Albert.

"Yes," continued Thomas. "He, alone, in the same simple armor he always wore, drove the dragon to madness by shining in its eyes the crimson sword. And, becoming enraged, the monster stoked its inner fire and tried to blast this *one man* into oblivion. But, time and time again, the knight would deflect the fire using his shield. Then, in the short time interval between blasts he would charge the brute and, even from my perspective it appeared that some damage was done."

"What happened...how did it end?" asked Sir John.

"Sir Leslie, from time to time, while running to the dragon or just before the fiery wave...he would call out for us to depart. One time," Thomas' voice softened a bit, "one time he used *my* name specifically. Well, a small number (comparative to the overall population) heeded his words and we made our way back *out* what was left of the eastern gate. And as for Sir Leslie," Thomas lowered his head, "one of the last to leave said the poor knight was backed into an area where a toppling wall—due to the dragon's flame—fell hard upon him. He *must* be dead. But..." Thomas looked up again into the eyes of Sir John, "But...because of *his* sacrifice...my arrogant heart was broken. I *had* to return...I had to."

For a sacred minute the three sat silently and then, turning to his son, Sir John instructed, "Albert, take our friend to the Common House." And then, to Thomas as he embraced him and walked him to the door, "Brother, due to the large influx of seekers from the inner realm we've set up a shelter where you will find a place to sleep and a decent meal."

From a distant room came Mary's voice, "If he wants a *good* meal...he can come here!" The two men at the door smiled, and Thomas reached for, once again, the handkerchief that the kind-hearted matron had earlier provided.

"Yes," said Sir John as he stood by the open door as his guest went outside to accompany Albert, "you're more than welcome to come visit us. In fact, I insist upon it. And," he added, giving a final wave as Albert and Thomas prepared to depart, "if we can assist you in the finding of your family…we will do this also."

Sir John sat down at the table and quickly let the previous tale play upon his mind. He, unlike his old mentor, had been hearing rumors from the ever-increasing numbers of refugees about an enormous dragon for quite some time. He, perhaps due to their usually abysmal state (physical, mental, *and* spiritual) normally didn't take their stories too seriously. But now, upon hearing this detailed account of the fall of Sarx—a well-known city (of course, well-known for all the wrong reasons)—perhaps a change of thinking was in order. And, as Sir John heard Amethyst's leisurely hooves clopping into the distance, he then arose and walked slowly over to a cupboard that he often used for items of immediate importance and retrieved a scroll that he had received some weeks before. It was the annual invitation to the *Games.* Normally he would ignore it (as he always did) but this time—written below the main inscription—were the words of the king. And *these*…he would not ignore.

* * *

"Tell me, my flying fool," the voice was, on this occasion, dark, cavernous, and its very sound seemed to rattled the bones of those who heard it, "tell me," it continued. "What is the status of the *seeding*?"

The Sower, prostrate before his Lord (and though deathly afraid that his cruel master might, on a whim, *kill* him, he, nevertheless, was overjoyed that he had been called into the throne room deep within the mountain).

"Master," he began, raising his head just a little without raising his gaze, "Master, the barrier above the river is strengthening, yet, once past it the seeds seem almost unhindered in their descent. In fact, my lord, the nursery in the center is filling again…much more quickly than before."

"Yesss," now the Dragon King's voice and body became serpentine. "I have seen it from below. Soon it will be time for a second birth."

"A second birth, Master?"

"Yesss," the great snake hissed as it coiled around the gold-plated throne,

200

"my child needs a brother…no…many brothers. And they will be ready soon." There was a slight pause as the monarch contemplated this next stage. And then, taking the shape of a dragon again, and seating himself on the copy of the royal chair destroyed long ago, he said, "Tell me of my son…where is he now?"

"Master, your child has recently destroyed the city of *Sarx* and is quickly making his way to the hive known as *Aphron.*"

"Pity," growled the *King*, "I'd almost consider letting that wretched place stand…so excruciatingly effective are its devices. However," he said, leaning back against the golden horror and letting out a foul puff of yellowish smoke, "they might return to the river…and we will not give them that chance."

The time-period of this little exchange was short—as it always was—and the Sower expected his dismissal and prepared himself to move quickly at its issuance.

"Tell me, Sower," the Dragon King said slowly.

"Yes, Master?" came the trembling reply.

"Have you tasted it?"

"Master?"

"You know what I mean, fool!"

The flying dragon paused a moment wondering if a truthful reply would cost him his neck. However, a prolonged delay in answering *surely* would.

"Yes, my lord. Sometimes, in the midnight hour, when I'm near the center…I see one of the worms making their way to the hatchery…and yes…I've had my fill."

There was another long pause and the groveling lizard braced himself for a bite or a blow…but none came. Only the words…

"You may go." Then, as the Sower slowly backed out of the door he heard one last instruction… "On the morrow, bring me one of *them*. Bring me, *alive,* one of those snatched from under his very nose…from under his very nose."

Chapter XIX

In zeal we promise lofty things
To make great conquests for our king,
But at the end, as from the start
The question is…
"Where is your heart?"

"Tell me again, Sir John…why exactly *am I* coming?" Mary, quite unsettled being away from her comforting knick-knacks and routines, asked the question…for the *third* time that morning…as they rode atop their humble wagon (Amethyst being the engine) that was heading for the city of Alazon, where both he and she were to engage in contests that would aid, supposedly, in the destruction of the *unknown* invader (unknown to them, that is).

"Because, *Mother*," the knight, sitting to her left on a paper-thin cushion (one of the reasons they—*they* being, Sir John, Mary, and Albert [who was snoozing on the baggage in the back] would make frequent stops) replied, "because singers are also required for this event. And, quite frankly, I know of none better than you." At this, Sir John released the reins from his right hand and gave Mary a comforting squeeze whereupon she patted the hand on her shoulder and gave her *son* the slightest of smiles.

"The river's right *here.*" These were the words of Fren, accompanied by an expression of utter confusion, upon hearing of Sir John's plans to attend the games.

"Fren," said the older brother. "Let me read you the letter again:"

—BY COMMAND OF THE KING—
IN ORDER FOR THE PRESERVATION OF THE INNER REALM,
AND THE DESTRUCTION OF THE EVIL BEAST THAT
THREATENS THEREIN,
THIS YEAR ALL ABLE-BODIED KNIGHTS MUST ASSEMBLE AND
PARTICIPATE IN THE ANNUAL GAMES TO DETERMINE HIGH
KNIGHT.
Also, singers will be needed for the exalted choir.
All of fair voice and form are encouraged to compete.

Fred leaned against his friend as they both stood sideways to the kitchen window (where the light streamed in) and followed Sir John's finger as the knight slowly read each word.

"You see?" said John, "*ALL ABLE-BODIED KNIGHTS*…that's me."

"Read down here," said Fredrick, pointing to the smallest print on the very bottom of the page. "I heard you read these words before. Read them again." Fren kept his index finger near the spot and looked his brother in the face until they both looked down together.

"Very well," said the knight, being somewhat amused that the very agreeable *Fredrick* was showing a bit of a stubborn streak. Sir John squinted slightly, cleared his throat, and continued…

To conquer evil
Seek the one
The Champion in your midst
The one with sword…and shield…and song
The one whom God has kissed
But till you find
Hold not your place
But to the river run
And there destroy
The works of man
Until you find the one.

203

Fren stepped back—just a little—then rubbed the graying patch of whiskers on his chin (he was attempting a goatee). He looked at the scroll, then up at Sir John. Then, pointing at the words of the king, he said, "He talks about the river. The river is right *here.*"

Sir John had to laugh as, after his statement, Fredrick folded his arms and then put a resolute expression on his face that seemed to suggest, *case closed.*

"All right, all right, old friend," surrendered the knight as he began to make preparations for an early departure the next day. "You don't have to come with us," he said, giving the gentle adult a smile and a wink. "Besides, I'm sure the garden needs tending."

Fren agreed. "It does. No one knows the garden like me."

The next morn, as the trio took to the main road after giving Fren his hugs and admonitions, they, when nearly out of range of both sight and sound…heard one last farewell.

"The river is right *here!*"

It took a full week for the three to reach the walls of Alazon. Closer to the river, when evening approached, they easily found refuge in the homes of other knights who, although many were not known personally by Sir John, and although their form, armor, and trappings were more elaborate…their spirit was the same. However, as they drew closer to the center, though the land seemed more fertile and productive (this was one reason that Mary's dead husband, Alexander, had wanted to move to the middle, but she would *not* abandon the river), the inhabitants were more guarded, suspicious and, on the last night, even though they *were* in the king's realm—the sound of unseen wings caused Sir John and Albert to alternate in standing watch.

On the seventh day, as Amethyst labored—just a little (he was a *very* strong horse)—to pull the loaded cart to the crest of a significant rise in the road…a youthful voice, full of excitement, rushed from the back of the wagon to the ears of the elders, whose own eyes widened with the sight.

"Father! Look at the walls!" In a moment the head of Albert was positioned between the other two as he laid a hand on their two inward shoulders. "I've never seen anything like it!" and then, turning to Sir John, "Have you, Father?"

"No son," he said calmly as they approached the first gated barrier, "at least not on this side of the river."

—Alazon, the greatest of the three inner cities (one of which was dead, and another's fate was in serious question), was a literal fortress, a citadel.

Smaller than the sprawling *Sarx,* though slightly larger in population than the curiously configured *Aphron* (more on this later), its protective barrier—once quite sufficient to keep out unwelcome men—now, with the addition of knowledge gained by the downfall of its sister, plus the added manpower for the task from the few thousand that fled the doomed city and were promised asylum for their labor—now this metropolis was surrounded by huge impenetrable walls that even this dragon (so it was thought) could not hope to breach. And this most envied of gatherings (for many sought citizenship here, most being denied) was known for a variety things…not the least of which were the *games.* However, along with the contest—as this trio was to soon discover—there was a peculiar atmosphere that permeated the place. Call it an air of superiority, of separation, of self-exaltation or blind ambition…this *quality* was evident everywhere…from those who pushed the broom on the street, or peddled flowers from a cart, or hammered iron on the anvil…it was everywhere. And, in this place, Alazon…it was most apparent among the nobility, the elite…the knights. For, as was evident by the signs of homage and adoration given—*even* to the visiting warriors (of which there were quite a few who had, apparently, like Sir John, answered the royal summons and were, even now, riding ahead of the humble wagon towards the grand main gate of the city), these were offered courtesies and honors that included, from the men…a removing of the hat and a lowered brow, from the women…a curtsy and a bowed head and, from the children…the lowering of the gaze and the kneeling on *both* knees.—

"Hold, there!" The harsh voice of a spear-bearing sentry (a rather stout fellow adorned in puffy purple linens and a face-enfolding silver helmet) interrupted the momentary sightseeing of the three. The soldier, whose expression conveyed that he was not one to mince words, rudely pointed his weapon at Sir John's chest as the knight gently pulled back on the reins and Amethyst, desiring a break anyway, let out a great snort and proceeded to deposit, with a loud *plop,* a somewhat unsavory package not far from the sentry's polished metal-plated shoes.

"What is your business here!" the soldier growled, somewhat perturbed that these backward-looking folk had not sought out the servants' entrance which was located far to one side.

As Albert and Mary, after a moment, once again turned their heads to and fro and pointed out to one another the many sights and sounds of this unusual place (such was their confidence in Sir John's handling of the situation) the guard, losing what little patience he had, thrust the spear within a hands breath of Sir John's throat. Whereupon, an eye-blink later, the spear was *now* in the good knight's possession and, the sentry, who then stood there with an expression of naked embarrassment…he finally (although only half a minute had elapsed) heard an answer to his query.

"My name is *Sir* John," said the warrior as he tossed the impotent weapon back to its owner and, understanding that this fellow might need more than a demonstration and a word to render belief, he added, "Albert…show the gentleman."

Albert, quite attuned to his father's methods, quickly uncovered and exposed the sword and shield of his parent's commission. Whereupon a most fearful expression descended upon not only *this* sentry, but also upon the eleven more who had come rushing to his aid. In a moment all twelve were bowing in respect and, in a small way, this little demonstration caused Sir John to sit up…just a little bit straighter.

"Sir John," the greeting, respectful, yet bearing just the hint of true welcome, came from Sir Robert as he entered the chamber where Sir John, Mary, and Albert had been ushered after the little *misunderstanding* at the main gate, just minutes before.

"Sir Robert, isn't it?" said John as he arose from the simple table where he and his fellow travelers had been offered a bit of refreshment.

"Yes," the visitor replied, smiling somewhat at being recognized by another warrior (in the city of Alazon, the most attention was lavished upon only the highest of knights…of which he was not). After shaking Sir John's hand he turned to the other two. "Your mother?" he said respectfully, bowing and taking Mary's hand gently.

"Yes," said John, pleased that civility was *not* dead in this most superficial place. "She adopted me a few years back. But," he added, "she is here to contend for a spot in the exalted choir."

"I see," said Robert in a somewhat condescending tone. Then, turning to Albert, "And this fine lad must be your servant."

"No," said the knight, walking over to the stout farm-boy and placing a hand on his shoulder. "This is my *son*, Albert." Then, as his child smiled up at him, Sir John moved his hand to the side of the boy's neck and gave it a playful squeeze. "He will, however, be my aide in the games."

For a moment Sir Robert had a puzzled, raised eyebrow kind of expression on his face (perhaps noting that the two did *not*—if physical similarity was an indication—seem to be related in any way) then, as if a small spark from the past flickered awake, he said softly, "I had hoped that Sir Peter would be here, at least to witness the event."

"No," John said quietly, glancing quickly to see if the mention of his mentor's name had any adverse effect on Mary (she appeared to force a little smile and then blinked repeatedly, as if trying to dissuade a rising tear). "Sir Peter is on a mission for the king beyond the river."

Sir Robert, turning away and slowly walking towards the door, added, thoughtfully, "I can think of no better warrior for the task…whatever it is." After a few more moments, filled only with the sounds of his footsteps, the messenger (for that was Sir Rob's function at this time) stopped, stiffened, and then smartly made an about-face as if he had suddenly remembered a task which needed completion.

"Sir John," he said, snapping his fingers to summon some attendants who had been busily polishing the visiting knight's armor in an adjacent room. "We have certain protocols in Alazon, and one of these," he continued, taking one piece of glimmering metal (the breastplate) from the polishers (who handed the rest to Albert, and then bowed lowly as they exited the chamber), "is that you, being a knight, *must*, while up and about among the general population (he then handed the very important piece to Sir John)…you must always *dress* as a knight."

Sir John gazed at the gleaming breastplate (he had never seen such a luster on anything but the shield and the sword) and listened on.

"Also," continued Sir Robert, as he walked over to a window and pulled back a revealing curtain, "we've arranged for you to have an appropriate mount. (Through the rather large opening there was, visible, standing in front of an unimpressed Amethyst [who was leisurely nibbling at one of the flowering vines that grew along the wall of this little enclave]…an elegant white stallion.) You are expected to ride this horse while in formation and, of course, you will need such a well-trained animal for the jousting competition." Then, after bowing respectfully to his fellow knight, he walked to the exit, made a simple hand gesture—whereupon a sentry entered (the very one who had been so rude to Sir John earlier) and Sir Robert, glaring into the face of this stone-like soldier, added, "This *fellow* will take your baggage and show you to your quarters, *then,*" he said with emphasis, "he will attend to your horse…being sure to wash and groom the animal."

As Sir Robert departed and the three stood to follow the somewhat downcast sentry, Sir John paused a moment to notice his own reflection in the polished armor. His infatuation, however, was soon disrupted when Albert, who carried the rest of the metal skin, came along side and whispered, in a whimsical tone, something the knight had heard many years before:

> *Pretty pictures are for the wall;*
> *Pretty pictures often fall.*

* * *

The dragon, fuming and plodding with poisonous steps relentlessly towards its next encounter, left behind it an ever-widening swath of destruction and corruption. In the beginning, upon exiting its birth hole, its influence extended perhaps a kilometer on either side. Now, as it grew stronger and more virulent with each bloody consumption, its wake spread out twice as far and, since its vile purpose was to *swallow* the whole land…this all consuming plague would, if not checked, accomplish its goal before another harvest season had passed.

The creature's next major encounter, to which it lustfully sped, would be the city known as *Aphron,* however, since the telling of the destruction of *Sarx* was incomplete, a brief revisit is in order…

After the few who were allowed a window of mercy by the actions of Sir Leslie exited the city and, after the good knight's silencing by the collapse of a wall, the dragon then proceeded, unhindered, to have its way with the remaining thousands who, to its vile sensory organs, exuded the most intoxicating scent of terror. The dragon, trumpeting with measured shrillness for an urgent joining with its parents, went from one block to the next, from one street to the next, calling, calling, calling. Some of the insects, too paralyzed to flee, were easily scooped up by the horrid tail. Others, running into any available structure, were soon flushed out by the fire and, if there were any children…these were the first to be seized. Thus, hour after hour, horrifying minute by horrifying minute, the dragon marched and munched and screamed its way to the back wall, leaving each area of a once prosperous city…in flames. Thus, most were destroyed, eaten, or burned and buried…but there were always a few who escaped. And one individual of note…*not* a natural native of this place…shall be remembered here.

After the dragon had exited through the western gate (after, of course, consuming the pile of humans who had succumbed to its poison) the creature continued, as the sun waned beyond the distant wall, towards its next banquet. However, as the fires diminished and the smoldering rubble filled the once great city—*turned cemetery*—with a foul gray fog, there arose, like delicate blossoms among the fire scorched earth…whimpers, sighs, and cries of anguish from the few who were able to somehow survive. Yes, from obscure cellars and holes they crawled (as many who could) and, having no thought for their former stations or class…they sought each other out. And these, having witnessed the full fury of the demon, these few decided to…if they possibly could…return to the river. However, there was one more gleaning…and this time it came from the sky.

The hour approached midnight. Many of the survivors had already exited the grandiose tomb, but there were a few who thought morning would be a more appropriate time to begin their trek. Then, as these huddled around various fires for warmth…there was the sound of wings. The people, unaccustomed to demons from the sky, were pounced upon quickly by a swarm of dragons that were of the same type as the Sower. The protective invisible shield—as had been discovered some time before by the bearer of the evil seed—had been pushed back to correspond with the goings of the great dragon, and this meant that this horrid feeding ground, once known as *Sarx,* was now available for these ravenous visitors.

—It should be noted that although the protective shield was greatly weakened, and therefore ineffectual wherever the beast had trod, it, nevertheless, rebounded somewhat with the daylight. This slight increase of presence was not enough to even phase the behemoth (due, in some part, to the fact that this creature found relation to the people of the realm). It was, however, enough to repel the much less armored fliers.—

Screams of terror filled the skies as those already horribly humbled, were now mercilessly taken away to be consumed in a more intimate way. However, as a pair of the winged demons paused by a now vacant campfire…there arose a conversation.

"I never thought it would happen."

"What's that, fool?"

"That we would dine in the realm of our enemy."

"Yes," said the other as he poked a talon between two fangs to extracted a morsel of meat. "It makes the meal that much sweeter."

"Wait," barked his companion, his eyes narrowing as his nostrils flared.

"What is it?"

"A smell," said the first between great draws of air, "I smell something amiss." Soon both of these *hounds* were searching the air currents for something out of place...something they had experienced before...yet something that shouldn't be *here* in this fallen place.

"It's a knight!" growled the first. "I've smelled that horrid stench before."

The other nodded his head in agreement and then added, "And he's alive...I'd swear to it."

"Well, my ugly accomplice (now the mood was almost jovial as the two imagined being able to devour [after the appropriate torture] a wounded killer of dragons), let's find this insect."

Before long the duo, using their fine-tuned sense for finding two-legged prey, were standing before a pile of stones that had fallen from an adjacent wall. They briefly looked at each other, displaying an excitement that comes when treasure hunters are about to make a choice find, and then, as they began to apply their joined strength and stamina, and with each subsequent hefting and heaving of the stones...their bubbling drool began to drip, and then run out in greater volume from their opened jaws. Finally, as they neared the very corner of the collapse they paused, focused, and then stepped back in horror. For there, wedged between the wall and the earth, was a great shield...a *knight's* shield. And on it, though dirt covered and dented...was the unmistakable symbol of their long-ago defeat...the crimson sword.

The two, having reflexively held their breath as worries from past encounters with *healthy* knights had momentarily taken hold...after an unanswered minute they both relaxed and the first, turning his head towards his fellow even as he reached for the shield to uncover the wounded warrior, said, "He's probably close to death. I was the first to sense him. I'm the first to bite. But don't worry, my repulsive friend, you'll have your..."

The final word was never formed. For, as this demon discovered...it is most difficult to speak with a knight's sword cleaving one's neck. And the other scavenger, having been temporarily paralyzed with fear...his fate was just as sharply defined. Then the warrior—yes, Sir Leslie—though wounded and weak...he nevertheless slowly hobbled his way towards the eastern gate...being sure, along the way, to render aid to any human who would listen. And now, not surprisingly, any who were still alive to hear...these listened very intently, indeed.

* * *

The games, held *outside* the walls of Alazon (due to the great area needed for the many events and the accommodation of the masses) were carried out with a precision that betrayed an ancient infatuation with the warrior and his ways…an infatuation that bordered on worship.

Sir John, lumped together with those predetermined to be less skilled (due, in some part, to his disinterest in the trappings of the royals) found himself most uncomfortable as he felt compelled to display his skills, time and time again, against fellow knights who could not long stand against his expertise with the sword and the shield. However, with each passing victory, and the adulation associated with the same, he slowly began to grow accustomed to the attention lavished upon him until…he not only tolerated the contest…he actually hungered for it.

"Albert!" The name was spoken gruffly, as a master might speak to a servant. "I need a smaller shield. This fellow has an advantage due to his smaller shield." Sir John sat, nearly out of breath, and took a draft of water before speaking again.

—They were now several days into the tournament and, what started as an almost forced compulsion to follow the king's *supposed* will, had now become something more. Albert and Mary had noticed it…the gradual change that was enveloping their loved one, but they, too, thought that it was perhaps a necessary rigor that would result in a more able defender of the realm. However, as Sir John slowly began to take on some of the traits of the host city (he added armor and frills, he began to practice the joust [heretofore considered a waste of time] and he began to associate more freely with the *highers* of Alazon, who were quick to encourage this rising star who was incrementally conforming to their mold), their concern that perhaps this path was the *wrong one* grew along with each of Sir John's successive victories.—

There was only so much time allotted between rounds of the match. The other knight (one of the citizens of this city) soon walked again to the center of the circle as an adoring crowd cheered and chanted his name.

"Albert!" Sir John threw down his cup and took his eyes off the warrior on the field. "I told you I needed a smaller shield…where is it?!"

His son, standing behind the old shield (the shield, upright, Albert's fingers curled slightly over the top, the bottom resting on the earth), gave his father a very questioning look, for, of *all* the superficial changes that had been made the last few days, *this* was a request of no small consequence, and thus he hesitated to exchange the long-trusted instrument of protection…for an obviously inferior model. This delay, and apparent disobedience, caused Sir

John's anger to rise and, as he raised his hand to strike his child—something he had *never* done—a few words from the boy's quivering lips caused him to pause.

"Father," the farm-boy said softly, tears welling, and then overflowing from his eyes, "Father...where is your heart?"

The blow was not delivered. Sir John stood motionless, as if pierced by a poison-tipped dart. These were words that *he* had been taught long ago, and had subsequently taught to others. "Where is your heart?" To the thoughtful soul it was to be a beacon, a compass, a light of self examination. *Is my heart in the sanctuary with my king? Are my zealous doings for His glory, or for mine? Where is your heart?* In his mind's eye flashed a thousand instances where he, as a protector and teacher, had said the words and now, as the crowd began to infer cowardice at his delay, he looked afresh at all the trappings and frills that he had so easily accommodated. Then, he lowered his hand and drew the hallowed sword of his commission—blessed and presented to him by the king himself—and held it up for close inspection. The luster, that shine and almost glowing that emanated from it when properly used...was gone. And finally, he looked again to his son...Albert. The boy...no...man...continued to look with compassion at his father. And soon the two were embracing and leaving the field as the taunts and jeers of the other participants fell upon their deaf ears.

"We shall leave tomorrow morning, son," said Sir John as he and Albert walked along, arms on one another's shoulders. "Where is Mary?"

"She's back at our quarters...praying."

"Yes," said the newly awakened warrior. "I have no doubt that you have both been praying much the last few days."

Concerning Mary, and the competition of voices, following is the brief account:

The day after their arrival, Sir Robert courteously came to the quarters of the three and then escorted Mary, in a delicate carriage, to the great symphony hall of Alazon. He then, taking the lady gently by the arm, walked her past a long line of glamorous dainties who were impatiently waiting their turn to audition. Finally, Sir Robert led her to a mark on the stage where she was to stand and, as she fidgeted with the buttons on her home spun blouse (a nervous habit) awaiting her cue, the knight walked over and whispered something to the sour-faced director. Soon, and without accompaniment (the musicians did not know the song), Mary was filling the great auditorium with beautiful notes that lifted high the work of the beloved king. However, after only a half minute, she heard, "*Thank you...that will be all.*" Then, as the director coolly took her hand to that of Sir Robert's, he added, "Perhaps next year, my dear. Perhaps next year."

Sir Rob, sighing inaudibly (such was his heaviness at *again* being required to do an ignoble task), patted Mary's hand (who, quite frankly, was just glad the whole thing was over) and dutifully escorted her back to her companions. And, as they left the large gathering of songbirds, there was a twittering among the gaggle concerning the gray-haired woman who dare compete with the others.

"The invitation said, fair of voice *and* form," hissed one.

"I thought she was the cleaning lady," giggled another.

"Some people have no sense of station," nasaled the last.

The morning following Sir John's revival the three exited the grand main gate of Alazon (the sentries being sure to smartly salute) and headed towards the direction of home. There was a lingering smell of rottenness in the air (due to the wagons full of dragon seeds which had preceded them on the road [a daily caravan which left at dawns first light]), but, since they themselves carried one such nodule (tightly wrapped for transport to be properly disposed of in the river), they barely noticed it. As Amethyst ambled along (munching an apple given as an incentive by Albert), the three were again treated to the sights of the ever-increasing defenses.

"Look, Father!" said the youngest, his hands again resting on the shoulders of those in front. "Look at the size of those machines!"

"Yes," said Sir John dryly, "they appear to be a most advanced type of catapult."

"I wonder why," continued the youth, slowly turning his head to take in the details as they passed, "I wonder why they would even inquire of the king...if they had such weapons."

"Yes," said the driver, reaching into a bag for some recently purchased breakfast breads and, as he passed these to the others, he said, half to himself as he took a bite and chewed slowly, "Yes, I wonder why Sir Reginald would inquire of the king?"

Chapter XX

Be wary how you touch the stars.
Your mind...your only tool.
For apart from heaven's living breath
Your wisest men...are fools.

The dragon rumbled awake from its necessary slumber and, spreading wide its protective wings, it raised its horrid head high and looked towards its next encounter...its next joining with its mother and father...its next family meal, so-to-speak...the city of *Aphron.*

Around the base of the creature, and spreading out rapidly behind it was the *rotting.* This foul residue was the poison decay that was its signature, its badge of ownership...much like a wolf or dog that marks its territory, so too this *thing* left its mark everywhere it traveled...and its mark was always death.

The city of *Sarx* was just a memory. The familial urge associated with *that* place had been satisfied...viciously, ravenously, lustfully...satisfied, and now there was another surge of desire, an urgency...an overwhelming *need* to consume those whose scent now abundantly filled its flaring nostrils. There it was, just a kilometer away in a placid plain...the city best known for its many ivory towers and the great maze that surrounded it.

—*Aphron,* the second of the three great cities of the inner realm (one of which was now a smoldering ruin, and the other a great hive of activity), was a gathering place for *thinkers*. Finding its origin near the river—many years before—it was then known as *Sophia*. Later, as ease led to leisure, and as leisure led to lunacy, some of the founders sought, craftily at first, to see through a prism *not* provided by the king and these, using the distorted light, moved closer to the center and established the town of *Daath*. Finally, having no compass (not all, but some) by which to gauge their shifting reasoning…the city ended up at this spot…not far from an all-consuming scale-clad monster that wanted nothing more than to fill its belly with their scholarly skirts.—

"I say there is no dragon!" The speaker, one of the venerated elders of the council of *Aphron* (Sir *Zed*, by name) held his arms outstretched as he spoke, giving—with the great excess of azure material in his doctoral robe—the appearance of a very large, bearded bat.

"Here, here!" parroted the others of his inclination (a sizeable gathering [in fact, the majority]) who also wore the light blue dress and congregated together on one side of the chamber.

"Honorable Sir," the speaker, Sir *Eirenikos*, who, like those aligned with *his* views, wore robes of a violet hue, countered, "of the creature's existence…there is no doubt. All our communications with the city of *Sarx* have ceased and besides," he now, having risen to speak (the custom of the place) proceeded to descend to the main floor to further expound, "…we have testimony…*living* testimony that there *is* a dragon and, because of this," he paused for emphasis, "because of this we must…MUST!…do something before it comes here and removes our station."

—This council chamber, fashioned much like the gathering room of *Sarx*, was circular in design with rising rows of seating. These, however, rather than indiscriminate places to park one's posterior…these were exalted *chairs*…and each delightfully cushioned *chair* was supposedly reserved for a particular intellectual who championed a great cash of knowledge in a particular area or field. In this chamber—corresponding to the many ivory towers (which were also arrayed in a circular pattern just inside the outer maze of the city)—there was a section for each *discipline*, and here, in this great room which was located in the one huge tower that occupied the very center of the city…it was here where, from time to time, the exalted members would come—not only to direct the affairs of the city—but, of a greater importance…they would come to offer debate and to render honor to one another for their many scholarly achievements.—

"Sir *Eirenikos*…" the tone of Sir *Zed* (who had also, while the previous was speaking, walked down to the main floor and was motioning with his hands for quiet) was condescending, like a wise parent trying to quell the fears of the little child who was convinced that there was a creature under the bed. "Of course," he continued, "we all are aware of the customs…the myths…the *traditions* to which you and your brothers continue, in spite of our many advancements, to desperately cling." As these words were spoken there was a gesturing towards Sir *Eirenikos's* dwindling number and, sitting besides these, an equally small cluster of those who wore magenta colored robes. "But!" he continued, raising a rigid index finger to go along with his stony expression. "We *know* that these dragons were invented to compensate for the ignorance of our predecessors." After this statement there was a pause filled with a general murmuring of agreement (not from Sir *Eirenikos's* corner, of course), and many nods in the affirmative from those who wore blue, black and white. "And!" He turned full circle and then faced the minority as he raised, rather dramatically, his voice. "We KNOW!" he said, his face reddening from the pressure. "…that the time to believe in such fairytales is long past!" Again, murmurs of agreement. "Therefore, being men of SCIENCE…being men devoted to TRUTH…and KNOWLEDGE…and WISDOM…" By now there was, along with the words, a loud punctuation from the like-minded audience after each emphasis.

"Being men of HONOR…" he continued.

"Amen!" shouted many.

"And INTEGRITY…"

"YES!"

"And DEVINE INSIGHT…"

"Here! Here!"

"We WILL NOT!…WILL NOT!"

"Yes!"

"Let ourselves be DISTRACTED!…DETAINED!…or DENIED!"

"Amen!"

"From our DEVINE DESTINY!"

By this time the chamber was in a frenzy. The few who wore violet and red looked to one another and quietly arose to exit the room. As they did, and as the chaos continued, they heard a chiming in from many of their *colleagues* that caused them to wonder why…why had they remained so long in this place.

"WE DON'T BELIEVE THERE IS A RIVER!"

"THE KING IS DEAD!"
"WE ALL DESCEND FROM THE DRAGON!"
"THE CRYSTAL SEA IS AN ILLUSION!"
"EVERY ONE OF US...IS THE KING!"

* * *

The journey home, as it often seems, felt quicker than the trek to the interior and, with each passing kilometer the atmosphere—that which weighed upon them—seemed to lighten and, as Albert again snoozed in the back (a rare gift...to be able to sleep anytime, anywhere) John and Mary, who had been each silently daydreaming themselves...these had no problem letting Amethyst amble on, nearly unassisted, towards the fields and fountains of home.

At first it was barely audible...like the remnant of a dream that lingered on for a few moments past awake. But, with each passing minute, the wisp of a sound grew louder. Like the sweet melody of an unseen lark coming from an ever closer wood, it bathed the soul and soon Mary, without consciousness, began to hum, and then softly sing to the tune. Sir John, who had been briefly revisiting, in his mind, snippets of his life, slowly rejoined the present as Mary's beautiful voice sang of the king.

From the back of the wagon there was a stirring, and then a kneeling, stretching, and scratching. Albert, whose *stomach* had awakened him, leaned between the two and then, after the loud crunch of a crisp red apple—followed by some sloppy chewing and a swallow—the boy uttered an observation that should have been obvious to all, "I hear Fren playing his flute...we can't be far away now."

Within a half hour (apparently the warm spring breeze had carried the music a great distance) they were in sight of the farm and, upon reaching the long rutted drive to the house...the melody ended, as if the player sensed that someone was near. Soon Fren was seen shuffling with open arms towards the people he loved and, after an extended period of kisses and hugs ("Fren...I'm too old for kisses!" Albert would say, all the while delighted) the four prepared to enter the house, but first Sir John had a stop to make.

"Fren," he said, unhitching Amethyst and handing the reins to Albert, "I need to take care of something. Would you like to come along?"

Fredrick was next seen holding, at arm's length, a bag that had something unsavory in it (as was evidence by his sour expression and the pinching of his nose with his other hand). Sir John took the bag and, motioning with his head for his brother to follow, he started walking towards the healing waters. Fren shuffled quickly to come along side his friend and, as they walked slowly across the sprouting field, he could be heard to say, "The river is right *here.*"

"Yes, my brother," said Sir John, placing his left hand on his companion's shoulder. "The river is right here."

* * *

The dragon—with each thunderous step growing more inflamed with desire for the joining—came within five hundred meters of its prize and paused to survey this *city* that would be its next feast. As pre-digestive fluids pooled and then ran out and down from between its razor sharp teeth, it scanned, from left to right, this peculiar place that seemed quite unready for a visitor such as he.

—As stated previously, the protective wall of *Aphron* (*restrictive* would be a more accurate term) was a large and expansive maze and, as the inner city was arrayed in a great circle, so too the puzzle that surrounded it. This structure, consisting of high brick walls (approximately three times a man's height and, on the outer facade…covered with ivy) stretched inward at least one hundred meters. The gates (open doorways, rather), of which there were not a few, each corresponded exactly with an ivory tower that lay directly opposite. The applicant had to merely navigate the mind-numbing twists and turns to make his way to his heart's desire. Most could not. However, atop the many partitions of the maze there was ample room for the knights of this city to stroll. In this way they could view—not only for sport—but also to carefully chart the progress of the *rats* (a term of endearment) and, if they so chose…they could drop little hints to facilitate the entrance of those deemed worthy.—

The creature, a bit leery due to its last encounter with boulders and brass, came within two hundred meters (supposing this to be outside the range of any larger weapons [as yet unseen]) and, after reciting, one more time, its traveling chant…it then began to circle, in a counterclockwise fashion, this settlement that filled its sensory organs with the hope of an ultimate communion.

"*Father…Mother…I've come for you. Join me, Father. Join me, Mother.*" The dragon screeched its blood-chilling summons and circled again and again this *city of the mind.* However, after expending much time and heart in the effort, the monster could feel no increase in the terror level. None. But, there *did* seem to be a gathering of the bearded monkeys on the outer rim and these, surprisingly, seemed to be *beckoning* the beast for a meeting.

"He's coming!" Sir *Zed* turned to face his many multicolored peers and the joyous expression on his face mirrored exactly that of theirs. These *distinguished* men of learning, fidgeting about as the dragon slowly approached, were on the verge of a *great* discovery. Obviously they were being visited by a divine creature (it knew their names!) and these *thinkers* couldn't wait to converse with it.

"Is it a dragon?" whispered, nervously, one of the white-robed leaders as the creature came within a stone's throw of the gathering.

"No...of course not," said Sir *Zed* through the clenched teeth of a pasted smile. "There *are* no dragons."

The demon, himself intrigued at the curious behavior of these worms, came right up to the outer wall (his height put his head somewhat above the prey) and, resisting the almost overwhelming urge to consume this plattered paté, he sat back and, as foul white smoke curled up from the corners of his closed mouth, he awaited a word from these smocked beings that bowed before him.

Sir *Zed*, briefly glancing up from his prostrate pose—and upon seeing that this visitor had paused long enough to converse—stood upright and began the dialogue.

"Oh, divine visitor," he began, spreading his arms wide (again, like a great bearded bat). "We are humbled that you would come to visit us. That you would stoop so low as to communicate with insects such as we." (Truthfully, Sir Zed and this crowd had much higher opinions of themselves. However, flattery was a tool...and genuineness need not be present for this tool to be effective.)

The dragon nodded its head down slightly, as if receiving this adulation and, parting its black lips, uttered, in a deep snakelike rasp, "Yesss."

As the creature spoke, and the other scholars stood upright, a sublime wave of delight flashed across their faces as their secret heart's hypothesis seemed to be confirmed now...right before their eyes.

"Oh, great being," continued Sir *Zed*, "we can see from your crimson hue that you must be from the very same source as an object of our study and investigation...the crimson sword."

At this word the dragon's head jerked back, as if struck by an unseen force, and its many scales—starting with those on the snout and rushing back and down like a rippling wave—clattered in a loud and violent fashion.

"THE CRIMSON SWORD IS A LIE!" screeched the beast as it pointed its teeth towards heaven, and then, for several minutes, it loosed a great volume of sulfurous smoke into the atmosphere while letting out deafeningly anguished cries and pounding the earth violently with its pillar-like legs. Finally, composing itself, the monster settled to its original state and, as it noticed that the humans were now cowering on their knees…it also noticed that there was not one sword between them. Nor any other weapon, for that matter.

—It should be noted that here, in the city of *Aphron*, although holding feigned allegiance to the king, the *crimson sword* and the whole story of the *Release* had taken on a mythological meaning. The knights themselves, although long ago receiving swords of commission, now put these in glass storage cases—along with their armor—and, although they debated about the usefulness of such things…the thought of actually using, let alone becoming skilled, was simply out of the question.—

Sir *Zed* was the first to stand and, being careful to remain in a somewhat hunched, submissive pose, he spoke again. "Oh divine visitor, please forgive our ignorance. Many of us had questioned whether the story of the sword was true (at this, many of his peers—slowly standing—nodded in agreement), please," he continued, "please enlighten us. For we, your servants…are seekers of truth."

The dragon, understanding that he was truly in the presence of *fools*, said in a deep monotone seriousness, "I…AM…TRUTH." Then, focusing on the leader, he said, "Come closer…and *behold*."

Sir *Zed,* almost giddy with the invitation, slowly walked to the demon's mouth which—being aligned exactly with the edge of the wall—opened slowly. There, as the bearded scholar leaned in, over, and between the two lower blood-streaked fangs—he saw—coming from the depths of the creatures throat…a light! Then, stepping back, he bowed and asked a question.

"What have you shown me, Master?"

The monster, closing his mouth, said with emphasis, "*I* am a portal. In me you find a door to true wisdom. Only through *me* will you attain the goal you all so richly deserve."

Sir *Zed,* almost flush with pride, asked, "How, Master? Are we to go *into* you?"

"Yes, my child," the dragon said in a velvet soft tone. "It will take a step of faith, but," there was a pause as the eyes of the creature scanned those who stood before him, "but, by entering into me…you will discover the source of the light…you will become one *with* the light."

Sir *Zed,* ready to be first in this endeavor, excitedly asked, "Now, Master? Now?"

"Wait, my child," said the *thing* as it raised its dripping head high and looked *beyond* the educated gathering. "Are there any others? Are there any…*children?*"

The leader, awakening slightly from his fantasy, responded, "Yes, my lord. Many of us have wives *and* children."

"Excellent," whispered the beast. "These, *too,* must be rewarded for being wisely associated with beings such as you."

* * *

Down at the river, having properly disposed of the wretched *seed* that he had nurtured, Sir John and Fren sat on the edge—their bare feet just below the shimmering surface. As Fren lay back, hands behind his head…appearing to blissfully gaze at the reflective clouds that danced above, Sir John couldn't help noticing that in the brief span that he had been gone…the waves of power—that evidence of the divine—now seemed to be stirring the mist once every minute.

"Fren," he said, now joining his brother in the restful repose, "I've noticed that the power comes more quickly now."

"Mm hm," said Fren, pulling a strand of grass and placing it in the corner of his mouth. "The king said this would happen."

"Oh, I see," said a skeptical John, turning his head towards his companion and being somewhat amused at how often Fren thought he had a direct line of communication with the monarch.

Fredrick turned his eyes to meet those of his friend and said, matter-of-factly, as he pulled the grass from between his lips, "He said they would soon come so fast…we wouldn't be able to tell one from another."

"*Oh,*" said a condescending John. Then he and his brother, before rising to walk slowly to the arms of home, spent the next few minutes lost in the display of the Crystal Sea that reflected…hopefully…off the billowy parchment high above.

* * *

"Are there any more?" the dragon purred to Sir *Zed*, who had just arrived leading a rather large contingent consisting of women and children (each family being lead by their individual head [each father glowing as if leading his loved ones to a discovery of treasure]).

"No, Master," said the leader, bowing. "There *were* some unworthy others…but they left the city before your arrival."

"Pity," rasped the dragon. "I may have to punish them for being so foolish."

Sir *Zed,* upon hearing this, swelled up a bit more…feeling his positions had now all been vindicated.

The dragon, lowering its dripping jaws to align with the edge of the wall, asked the question, "Are my faithful ones ready to ascend to the next level…to become one with the light?"

All those in robes nodded in the affirmative. Many of the wives—most who were quite attuned to their husbands' ways—also whispered, *yes.* But, *all* of the children (those old enough to distinguish evil) clung to a parent's leg—many shuddering and weeping—and shook their heads *no,* or simply buried their faces in the clothing of an elder.

"Now, now, children," whispered the creature in a fatherly tone, "there is nothing to fear." The dragon raised its head so that all could see. "I know that my appearance is fearsome," it continued, "but this is only to drive away those who are unworthy…the cowardly…the impure of heart." There was a brief pause as minds were weighing the words. Finally, the demon said, "Look here." At this it drew in a great draw of air and then, for a period of some minutes, proceeded to puff out smoke rings of various sizes—much to the delight of the children.

After this playful demonstration the dragon lowered, once again, its jaws to the edge of the wall. "Sir *Zed,*" it whispered, "come here."

The leader, *very* honored that the creature had called him by name, went close to the beast and leaned down to hear its command. Then, seen nodding as the dragon spoke words that only he could hear, he stood upright and returned to the gathering. "My fellow chosen ones," he began—again spreading wide his arms—"this divine being would like to ultimately demonstrate that there is nothing to fear. He says that once someone slides into the light (*slides*…an accurate term since this was the method whereby one traveled down the throat), that they may, for a brief time, communicate with their loved ones from the beautiful place of the shining." Then, scanning all the faces of his like-minded comrades, he said, "Although I wanted to go first…the visitor wants me to pick another. Who will volunteer to be the pioneer into glory!"

Quickly, all the hands of the robed ones went skyward. After these…many of the spouses. But, from among the children…even here there were a few. Sir *Zed*, bypassing entirely the adult volunteers, singled out a beautiful red-haired lass who was perhaps six or seven. The lead knight, crouching down to her eye level while he was positioned next to the open dripping jaws, motioned with his right hand for her to come. She, named *Zaku*, looked up to her two parents who stood behind her and, having received their nod of approval (accompanied by a swelling of pride in their breasts) they gently ushered her to the waiting arms of Sir *Zed* who now (although previously having little regard for what he referred to as *troublesome trolls*) greeted her as a beloved uncle.

"What is your name, child?" he whispered after placing her on his left knee and purposely brushing his gray whiskers against her right ear.

The little girl, delighted at this kind attention (it was quite foreign to her), let out a joyful squeal and answered, "*Zaku.*"

"Well, Miss Zaku," said the scholarly scoundrel as he stood and, grasping her left hand in his right, they both turned to face the ominous chasm, "are you ready to be the first to go to a magical land? Are you ready to lead us to a wonderful place?"

The little girl, upon seeing the jagged teeth and the heaving black tongue, began to stiffen and whimper just a bit.

"There, there child," cooed the elder, taking her in his arms. "You must look *beyond* the doorway. This is just a test to see if we're brave enough." Then, putting his cheek against hers, "See, see there…way in the back. What do you see?"

The little wisp, through a sniffle, said, "I see…a light."

"Yes…you're right. It's a light, and…" he turned her little face so that their eyes could meet, "we both know that only good comes from light. Isn't that so?"

The little girl, after wiping her nose on her sleeve, nodded and said, "I guess so."

"Well, Miss *Zaku*," he said, putting her down again. "In that light is where the good stuff is…and…after you go, Mommy and Daddy will be right behind." As Sir *Zed* said this, both he and she looked back at the proud couple who nodded in agreement (the mother wiping a tear of joy from her cheek).

For a moment the two stood before the gaping jaws—not noticing that the eyes of the beast were opened their widest and vibrating with anticipation. Finally the little girl looked up at the kindly gentleman and said, softly, "Will you go with me?"

"I'll go with you right up to the slide?"

"Slide?" she said with excitement. "I like slides."

"Oh, didn't I tell you," he purred. "It's like a wonderful slide that takes you to the light."

A moment later the two were seen walking into the dragon's mouth—the elder balancing himself on the infirm tongue by, from time to time, reaching out with his left hand to push against the slimy meter-length teeth that adorned the upper jaw. The little girl held tightly, with both hands, to the knight's right hand and, a half minute later they stood before the gaping throat where a yellowish, flickering light could be seen dancing far below.

"It stinks in here," said the little mite, looking up at the kindly gent, while crinkling her nose.

"Oh, I hadn't noticed," he said, smiling. (Of a truth, many of these robed scholars had made the dragon seeds an object of their study. The smell in this cave was very like the orbs.) "Are you ready, dear?" he said, grasping her beneath the arms.

"I guess so," she whimpered.

"Remember," he said, holding her over the pulsing hole. "Remember to talk to us after you get there. Don't get too distracted with the wonder to let us know how it is."

"I won't," she said, nodding her head side to side as she kept her eyes fixed on the light.

And then she was gone. Without a sound the darkness swallowed her and, if any had cared to notice…the dragon's eyes began to roll back into its head. Sir *Zed,* confident of what he had been told, calmly walked out of the mouth and, as others greeted him with questioning gazes (especially the parents), he stood next to the jaws and quietly raised his hand.

"Just a moment," he said. "She'll speak in just a moment. After all, the shock of the beauty takes a few seconds to overcome."

And, just as he predicted, as they held their breaths for an additional half minute their silent wonder was rewarded for, coming from the depths of the beast came the little girl's angelic voice. "Oh, Mommy, Daddy…it's wonderful here! The colors are so pretty! Everything sounds so good, and smells so good, and I seem to know so much more than I did before! Please,

Please hurry! I'll be waiting. Hurry!"

As the voice faded...all remaining fears took flight. And soon there was a clamoring to get in line for this ultimate ride to paradise and, as each family entered—and then jumped enthusiastically into the pit—the eyes of the creature rolled completely back into its head and, as each human submitted itself wholly to the beast...it seemed, that from the center of its being...with the registering of each additional surrender...the monster would quiver with a most evil and perverse delight.

Finally, after some hours of an almost party-like atmosphere—punctuated, from time to time by messages from beyond—there was only left Sir *Zed* and the beast. The creature, before this last morsel could enter, closed its mouth and raised its head high to speak down to its slave.

"Well done, faithful one," said the bulging brute. "You have served me well."

"Thank you, Master," said Sir *Zed,* bowing low and wondering what special reward must surely be his.

"Rise, favored one," said the dragon as he unfurled his huge wings and let rise his hideous tail. "For your unselfishness...for your willingness to lead the many to their just destination...I will share with you the greatest truth of all."

Sir *Zed,* almost bursting with anticipation, saw the beast open wide its devouring jaws one last time and heard, from its hellish depths, the *true* words—starting with the child, *Zaku*—spoken by those who had believed him.

"MOMMY!...IT HURTS!...DADDY!...HELP ME!"

These *words*—and ten thousand more—always enfolded in the blood-chilling screams caused by excruciating pain, poured out of the beast. On and on—for some minutes—a horrible chorus from those who had splashed into the flaming acid and, as they saw the previous fools thrashing, bobbing, and decaying before them—they often remembered Sir *Zed* in their last heartfelt invocation.

After a short time of hearing this *truth*...the scholar's countenance collapsed and, though his knees were weak...he turned and started to run. But, before a full step was completed, he was held suspended, the tail of the dragon firmly wrapped around both ankles and, as he dangled, pleading—with his scholarly smock draped over his face—the creature spoke once more, "Also," it hissed, "I will give you the privilege of joining your brothers. You, however, will enjoy the journey...*twice*."

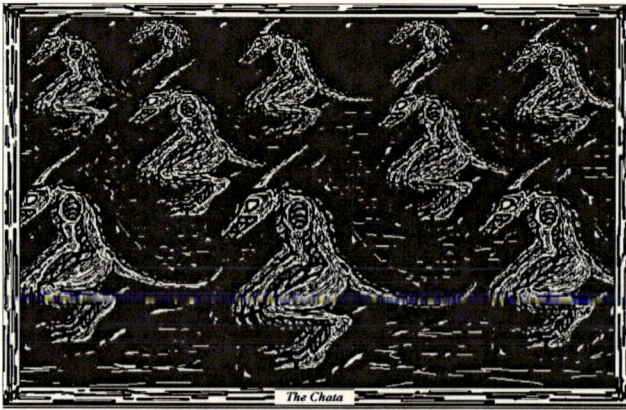

The Chata

Chapter XXI

Pride not checked
Unguards the door
Then soon resides
Ungodly more.

Ssssssppt...

The delicate and deadly sound of a knight's sword...wielded well.

Ssssssppt...

The two brothers, *Chammad* and *Shalal*—as they heard the muffled noise—paused from their bagging of the booty to look at one another and smile as if silently acknowledging the wisdom of acquiring such an able partner for such a profitable endeavor.

Ssssssppt...

Sir *Nabal* sheathed *again* his dripping blade. Before him, in this rather large and ornate chamber (it was a treasure room, the precursor to the vault where his companions were busy)...lay the draining bodies (with the heads separate) of at least five of the flying devils that roamed so freely in the inner realm when the darkness swallowed the day. *Yes*, he was well aware that, at any moment, another of the disgusting monsters would be coming down the narrow tunnel from the outside (he could hear an even score of them cursing at the mouth) and yes, it *would* be easier to keep his weapon at the ready...but...he found this somewhat boring...and not *at all* challenging. So, as yet another of the Sower's brothers lunged from the shadows at this human (the knight illuminated only by a single oil lantern) Sir *Nabal,* in one fluid motion, drew the sword and—while crouching somewhat—sliced powerfully upward, whereupon the dragon's head was neatly separated from its shoulders and it then did an interesting twirl as it careened away from the falling and flailing body.

"A brilliant acquisition, brother," said Chammad as he continued to stuff gold coins into one of the many burlap sacks they had brought for just this purpose.

"The musings of a genius," agreed Shalal as he opened a new sack of his own.

The object of their flattery, of course, was Sir Nabal...and the story behind his partnering with these two is an interesting one. It is the tale of glory sought...and not found. And, if one was not destined to be well-known...one could at least be *well-fed.*

On the very day—only earlier in the morning—that Sir John and his company had left the city of Alazon, another knight—Sir Nabal—had also departed. This warrior, like many, had answered the call to seek and crown a champion for the defense of the kingdom (although, truthfully, his secret motive was to *at last* receive recognition for his hard won prowess). However, he discovered—after winning several preliminary battles—that the *ultimate winner* was already known. And this knowledge (though some sought to ease his despair with consolation promises) led to his unsolicited departure from this city. And it was this departure that coincided with the daily transport of the wagons.

—*The games,* though tending towards purity in their origin, were now not only a test of the blade and lance...but just as much (more so, really) a test of the tongue and of the mind. Thus, Sir Reginald, though advancing in years (still, an excellent fighter) maintained, without pause, his control of the reins of Alazon. And, this was due, in large part, to his skill at negotiating allegiances and alliances. Indeed, when *threats* to his dominance arose...the following was his instruction to his minions:

If you cannot cool his craft, then slow his blade with guile and graft.

Those who could not be bought or coerced...would ultimately leave in disgust, or somehow lose due to lower means. Thus, Sir Nabal, whose great skill *was* recognized early on...was made aware of *how things are.* And being so informed, he chose rather to depart from the charade rather than kiss the tainted ring of the *High Knight.*

And so, when this young disheartened knight slowly began to pass two wagons carrying foul orbs from the city of Alazon on their way to the center (although, after this brief stretch of road that led from the city they would have soon parted ways) it was the comforting words of one of these haulers that caused him to pause and consider a detour...a *momentary* detour to at least profit in some way from this failed crusade.

"Good knight," said Chammad (the younger of the brothers who, from his perch behind the reins controlling a dozen of Alazon's lesser [though stronger] horses, and who was at eye-level with the blonde-haired warrior as he slowly passed on his left). "Good knight," he repeated, as the young fighter's mind was obviously elsewhere.

Sir Nabal, summoned to the present by the hearing of his title, turned his head to the right to gaze into the squinting dark-colored eyes of a *lower-classer* who smiled a jagged tooth smile and grabbed, with his right hand, the rim of his peasant's cap in a show of respect. Sir Nabal, not one to readily associate with the masses, couldn't help noticing, however, that this repugnant fellow...was adorned with *much* gold.

"Yes," said the knight, as a sour expression washed across his face. (The wind had changed direction and the stench from the huge cargo of orbs [even though tightly covered with oil cloth] attacked his nose.) "What do you want?"

"Good knight," said Chammad, thrilled that a door was slowly opening. "I see that you're leaving the games early. I saw you fight," he continued, playing to the despairing expression that accompanied the subject. "I must conclude, since your skills are unmatched, that there is some kind of funny business going on."

Sir Nabal, now with a sympathetic ear, seemed to forget all about protocol and eagerly said, "Yes! You've got it exactly right! The games are fixed!" Then, looking straight ahead and raising the volume considerably, "I was a fool not to see it!"

"Good knight," stroked the bejeweled commoner, "You are *no* fool." Then, as the knight turned a softer expression towards the hauler, he added, "Your leaving the games *proves* that you are no fool. In fact, only fools would remain."

This was the beginning of the brief partnership. The knight, finding temporary solace in these refuse removers, listened to their proposition...which was a simple one. However, first a history: The haulers (these two, and many more before them [their lifespan was brief due to the toxic load]) would, daily, take their foul cargo (the many dragon seeds collected early each morn [of which there was one presently from the quarters of Sir Nabal]) directly to the center dumping place. This, though meaning a traverse over the deadened ground where the giant dragon had formerly trod in its circular route, could be accomplished, just barely, in the hours still lightened by the sun. In times past, before the behemoth emerged, the wagons would travel in the night. But now, since the flying dragons were a growing menace (many a lone human had, by this time, been carried off and consumed), the trip had to be done quickly. There was little time for any delay. However, as these two had discovered, there was just enough lag time to explore, briefly, the remains of some towns and residences where the former inhabitants had either fled...or been fed. And these explorations accounted for the gold that they flashed without reserve. However...and here was the proposition...these vile characters knew, that if they had more time, they could raid the inner vaults of the small cities within. And, if they could survive the dark hours (when the winged ones appeared) they could make a substantial haul indeed. Enough to retire and be done with, at last...Alazon...and its large quantity of refuse.

At this point of the story—by now all three (the two brothers and Sir Nabal) had paused to allow their horses to drink—and at this juncture the knight finally understood his piece in this puzzle.

"You want *me* to defend against the dragons," he said matter-of-factly, taking a drink of wine from a skin the brothers offered.

—Sir Nabal had traveled many times beyond the river on the king's business. These important rescue operations (usually done with a pure and sincere heart) had caused him to face many a demon. Of these, the flying ones...once you acclimated to their ways...were discovered to be quite easy to dispatch.—

"Exactly," said Shalal, nodding his head and smiling, "If you allow us time to explore and gather," he turned his head towards his brother and then back to the knight (all the while reaching into a pocket in his dark leather vest), "then we *all* can be well supplied with these."

At this he held out three precious coins and, as the warrior grabbed one to examine, the giver added, "Enough to finance your missions for a lifetime. Imagine," he purred as he saw contemplation working in the warrior's expression, "imagine *never* having to be dependant on anyone else again. Imagine all the good you could do...what you could do for the *king*."

Sir Nabal closed his hand around the golden bait and, looking up at the brothers (who stood very close together), he asked, "Where do we begin?"

"A city named Philautos, good knight," said Shalal.

And, as the three prepared to depart, the younger brother added, "We know of a gold-filled vault...strong outer walls, and only one narrow way in." And at this the three departed...a knight on horseback...and two commoners with *empty* wagons.

Ssssssppt...yet another of the arrogant flying beasts lay in pieces on the—now getting congested—floor. "You'd think they'd get the message by now...the idiots," mumbled the knight as he sheathed his sword, walked to and then stooped over one of the older decapitated heads (*older*, as in longer on the floor, therefore less fluids to deal with) and, picking it up—using one of its forward four inch fangs as a handle—he calmly walked over to the narrow passage (only enough room for one) and stood there a moment...listening and, as he heard the creatures outside questioning, with wild cursing, the fate of their last *brother* (they were brother in kind, but certainly not in sentiment) they began, *once again,* to stir themselves to action, which meant the stronger of the demons would send in those deemed more expendable.

Sir Nabal slowly shook his head. "As predictable as the sunrise," he whispered. "Speaking of which," he said, beginning to swing the weighty skull back and forth to build momentum for a throw, "I'd better help these imbeciles make up their puny minds." And with this he threw the head the twenty meters required to reach the outer door.

As expected, there was, for a moment, complete silence as the grisly part wobbled into the gathering of taloned feet that congregated at the entrance. Inside the chamber, holding in a laugh, the knight walked quickly and stood, once more, by the rather large oil-filled glass lantern that was positioned on a sturdy marble pedestal on the far side of the room. As he heard the dragons begin to curse anew he figured the decapitated head would have one of two results. Either they'd see the folly of this attack (unlikely) and fly away, or they'd enter into the fray with greater ferocity and frequency. Both conclusions were acceptable to the knight but, being a warrior, he wanted the latter. But what he got...was something totally unexpected.

Ssssssppt...Ssssssppt...Ssssssppt...Ssssssppt!

"Oh my," said a near-joking Chammad, "our friend is having a merry time of it, isn't he?"

Ssssssppt...Ssssssppt...Ssssssppt...Ssssssppt!

"Wait a minute," said Shalal, standing upright with a concerned look on his face. "Something's not right. There's no way that more than one of those creatures could get into that chamber at a time…unless he *let* more come in."

Sssssppt…Sssssppt…Ssssppt…Sssssppt…CRASH!

A moment later, running in and turning to attempt to push closed the large vault door…was a *bleeding* Sir Nabal! "HELP ME, YOU FOOLS!"

It took the brothers a moment to process the words but…they could hear…coming down the inner hall the bone-chilling sound, like fifty pairs of shears…scraping, scraping, scraping.

Soon all three of the men were pushing frantically on the rusty iron door and, just as it came within inches of closure…six small dragon arms—each with tiny sharp talons—thrust through the crack and thrashed wildly. "KEEP PUSHING!" shouted the knight and, as the refuse haulers pressed their considerable weights against the cold metal, Sir Nabal hurriedly unfurled his blade and, with a lightning-quick downward slice…severed all six arms and…the time this maneuver purchased from *whatever* was outside the door…allowed them to finally close—and bolt—the barrier that was, for the moment, their only protection.

"What happened out there?" panted Chammad, as all three were sitting, with heaving breaths, with backs against the door.

"Dragons," said Sir Nabal finally. "Dragons like I've never seen." He stood up (the other two…in much worse physical condition…stayed down and listened) and continued. "I was dispatching the flying ones…that was easy." As he spoke he went over to one of the two oil lanterns (these were made of tin) and, after looking at some of the gashes on his waist and legs, he turned one completely off and then went to the other to turn it down. "I had just prepared myself to finish them off. I had thrown one of the severed heads out the door…to rile them up…to cause them to come more quickly."

"What are you!" screamed Chammad, "…some kind of moron!"

Sir Nabal slowly drew his blade and held its sharp point to the offender's Adam's apple. "Those *things* outside the door are *not* flying dragons. They're something different."

"Go on," said Shalal, gently pushing the blade downward, "my brother is sorry. Please…go on."

The knight put his sword to rest and slumped down on a pile of bagged gold that the brothers had just stacked. "I heard them cursing, plotting, urging one of the younger ones to be the next to avenge. Then," the warrior paused, rethinking the sequence, "then there was a commotion of sorts."

"What do you mean, good knight…a commotion?" This time it was Chammad, who had softened his tone as he rubbed his neck.

"I mean it sounded like a confrontation. As if a third element had entered this equation. And then, after a few minutes…I heard the sound…that disturbing sound like blades scraped along the stone. Then, instead of seeing one of those impotent birds…I saw instead a handful of *tiny* dragons…things without wings, but with teeth and talons…and they ran quickly into the room. Understand," he continued, pausing to reach for a flask of water, "…they were no problem to kill. My blade halved them easily…but…there were too many. They swarmed like ants. Like ravenous rats. Finally I had to break the lantern to slow them with the fire."

A full minute passed as the three considered the words just spoken. (Meanwhile, faintly, the horrifying sounds of the *little dragons* could be heard through the door.) Finally, Chammad and Shalal stood and walked over to their partner and, as the dim light accentuated the hollows in their faces, the elder spoke, "What do we do, good knight? What do we do now?"

"Well, my repulsive friends," he said, as he tied a cloth around his bleeding right calf. "We wait for the dawn. Perhaps these demons are like their flying cousins. Perhaps the light will drive them from the door. But," he raised his head and motioned to Chammad to bring him another bag to be used as a bandage, "I suspect that these are closer in kind to the Great Dragon and," he said, cutting the bag to ribbons with a borrowed blade, "if that be the case, then the light will not affect them and you," he pointed with the knife to the younger, "and you," then to the older, "and I," he pointed to himself… "are destined to die in the midst of *all* this gold." His minor repairs done, he handed the ivory handled blade back to its owner and then, removing his helmet, he said, "Do we have any food for a last meal?"

* * *

Chata…that is the proper name for the things (what Sir Nabal had referred to as *tiny dragons*) that—even as the air grew thin within the vault—continued to scrape, tirelessly, their teeth and talons against the metal door that separated them from their lusts desire. And yes, the young knight's suspicion that these creatures were in some way related to the great dragon…was indeed terribly correct. For…just hours prior to this incident…in the darkness of the midnight hour…like a great pulsing puss-filled sore, the dumping place…*again* filled to capacity (so much more quickly than before) it had, once more, given birth anew. This time, however, having an unhindered touching from the lower lord…a production of millions of individuals squirmed out...instead of just one. These—nearly mindless, except for their uncontrollable desire to murder—like foul maggots from a great gaping wound, oozed outward in huge heaving waves to fill the saucer-shaped valley that surrounded the hole and, as each, with tooth and claw, ripped the membranous bubble that was their hellish incubator...these small fiendish imps (never taller than a man's chest) began to swarm and cover the inner realm. And these, unlike their enormous predecessor...these *could* easily outrun a man. And these...unlike their self-worshiping relatives from beyond the river...these thought not of personal preservation or power, but rather willingly became the vile legs to the bloodthirsty thoughts of their evil king. And yes...these, as Sir Nabal suspected, these found their mix from man *and* dragon. Therefore the sun—whose rising brought pain and banishment to the winged ones—to these it simply brought greater sight...a keenness in order to kill...and a discerning in order to destroy.

Chapter XXII

If you prepare the weapon
But not the heart
You may lose the battle
Before you start.

The games were over. As predicted…Sir Reginald, though more than double the age of the younger contestants, *somehow* managed to win one spectacular victory after another. He was, without a doubt, in his own mind—and to all that mattered—the undisputed champion or, as stated in the king's decree…*the one.* Surely, so he thought as he stood on the gilded balcony (the golden helmet again firmly affixed) and waved to the adoring masses…surely all the requirements for victory were met. The walls were impenetrable. The engines of war…unmatched (on *either* side of the river). The exalted choir…without peer. And he, the king's chosen one…was resting in divine favor.

The report from the outermost scout was that the great beast was only one day away. And, as Sir Reginald, who now walked among the defenses and contemplated the great army at his disposal (and how it would come in handy *after* the dragon's death) he couldn't help but laugh at how he had been, just a few months prior, so worried as to seek some mystic solution from the king. His concern at that time arose from a meeting with one of his servants and, for purpose of clarity, it is related here…

"Ratsad! You old weasel, come here!" Sir Reginald, having just concluded a quite serious meeting with the fifty knights that had recently arrived from *Sarx* (*serious*, meaning that these knights, who were most grateful to be invited by the *High Knight* of Alazon, and had bowed and genuflected and absorbed readily the words that he graciously shared), motioned that his trusted servant, the *ambassador* to the now dead city (although, at the time of this meeting the fate of *Sarx* was yet unknown) slink away from the shadows (where he had been silently standing during the lengthy warrior love-fest) and divulge to his liege the particulars of his success.

—Ratsad was an older gentleman (although still rather nimble), gray of beard, green piercing eyes, and he liked to dress in reddish hues. Lately his choice in color was the brownish red... like that of dried blood. Ratsad was an administrator of sorts. He was quite skilled at filling in the details of the desires (spoken in generalities) that dripped so readily from Sir Reginald's lips. He was rather good in this role... it was his place. However, his long desire was to be a knight (in some degree because these were readily lavished with honor and praise), but, since this *calling* was determined by the king and, therefore, he never could, by his own efforts... become one, this planted a seed of resentment. And it was this seed, no doubt, that birthed the terrible plan that served both his master's ends... and his own.—

"Come here, old friend," said a smiling Sir Reginald as he motioned with his bejeweled right hand (although the term *friend* would certainly *not* be used if there were any other knights present.)

"Your servant," said the older, bowing respectfully having walked to the base of the polished steps that led up to the throne of rulership.

The High Knight, still smiling, walked down the stair and, beckoning that his representative rise, they both walked over to a silver table that held a decanter of some rather strong spirits... which Sir Reginald poured with an obvious expertise.

"Tell me, you sly dog," said Sir Reginald, bringing a golden goblet to his lips and offering one made of a lesser metal to his aide. "Tell me... did not the council have anything to say about the leaving of these fifty?"

"I told them that this was an advanced guard, sire," replied Ratsad with the slightest of smiles as he raised his goblet and sipped a significant portion. "I told them that these could destroy the beast *before* the city was in jeopardy."

Sir Reginald turned his back to his servant and slowly walked and sipped while his companion filled his own cup afresh. "I knew they would fall for that," said the High Knight as he stopped a few meters away and turned again to face his guest. "But having dealt with this self-important rabble before," he took a draining drink and headed back for a refill (Ratsad already holding up the exquisitely carved receptacle), "I was *certain* they would squabble about the number." The two men—now a half meter apart—drank in unison, then Sir Reginald completed his thought. "How did you convince them that only these fifty were necessary?"

"Oh, I didn't do that, sire." Ratsad poured afresh into the leaders goblet and then his own. "In fact," he continued, holding his cup chest high while looking squarely into the face of his superior as his master reached the dregs once more. "In fact, they insisted on fifty *more* be added to the list, and I," now *he* drained his vessel before completing *his* thought, "encouraged them to do so."

A heaviness, like a blanket, descended on the room. Ratsad attempted to pour again, but Sir Reginald would have none of it. He took the decanter from his servant's hand and placed it on the tray along with the goblets. Then, standing in front of his *old friend*, he said dryly, "Where are they, Ratsad? Where are the other fifty?"

"Quite dead, your majesty…quite dead." Now the old statesman, feeling somewhat empowered, poured himself another drink as Sir Reginald walked slowly up to his throne and sat heavily upon it.

The *Ambassador*, goblet in one hand and bottle in the other, walked to the base and continued. "Since I had your directive to bring *only* the ones chosen, and since I knew the council would not oblige…I simply allowed them to pad the list to their hearts' content."

By now Sir Reginald had an elbow on each armrest and his face buried in his palms.

"Upon leaving the city I simply told the undesirables that they must *prove* themselves on the field of battle." He continued, "I then sent the others on ahead and watched with interest to see what would happen to these *inferior* ones. I thought," Ratsad paused as he poured again and took yet *another* drink, "that you, being a great warrior yourself, would be interested in a report of how they fared."

The High Knight slowly lifted his head from its cradle and then leaned back into the soft cushioned chair. This wasn't the first time this servant had completed his desire in an odious fashion. Then, leaning, elbows on knees, he asked calmly, "How *did* they fare?"

Just then a messenger, quite exhausted, burst into the room and ran to the vicinity of the two men, all the while begging forgiveness for the interruption.

"What is it, man?!" barked the administrator.

"The city of Sarx..." the young man, now on one knee, looked up at Ratsad and then at Sir Reginald (who was now standing).

"Yes?" said the High Knight, walking down to stand before the obviously troubled youth.

"Sire," the boy said, looking up to his leader, "the city of Sarx is fallen. The wall is breached and the dragon...the dragon is even now consuming the inhabitants." After this revelation the messenger hung his head even as a look of astonishment washed across the face of the ruler.

"You may go, son." Sir Reginald, after a few moments, kindly said to the youth. "Go to the kitchen and tell them I said prepare a meal for you."

"Yes, sire. Thank you, sire."

After the messenger had left, the two schemers were left alone for a silent minute. Sir Reginald paced slowly in a circle, ending, again, at the table where he retrieved his goblet.

"Old friend," he said, walking to Ratsad and holding his glass for another draft. "I must hear of how the weapons and walls of Sarx were overcome." He took a swift drink. "And I must hear *exactly* what transpired when the dragon met a knight's assault."

"Yes...*your majesty*," said his aged companion as he bowed lowly. "I am most honored to serve."

* * *

Mary stirred, with a stirring spoon the size of a canoe paddle (actually, it *was* a canoe paddle...provided by a scavenging Albert), the delicious simmering contents (a stew consisting of donated vegetables and meats) that filled an enormous iron kettle that was positioned just above a wood fire which burned, incidentally, some of the now well-seasoned leavings of that giant maple that had fallen...what seemed so long ago. She, who was used to doing her culinary artistry in the confines of her kitchen...she was now forced to be outside (because of the sheer volume of fixings), adjacent to Fren's beloved garden (handy for the needed spices) and, as she made other preparations for the daily ration that they so willingly offered to the many refugees that were streaming from the interior, she paused, wiped her brow with her apron, and listened, just a moment, to the beautiful melody which drifted so lightly from the flute her son played from the simple bench not far away.

Once upon a dark and fearful time…

She, never having been taught lyrics to this simple tune (which her son seemed to repeat over and over of late), had words come forth which seemed to bubble sweetly up from her spirit. In fact, it was this very song (such was her familiarity…needful in a position of forgetful stress) that she had used at her audition in Alazon.

Imprisoned by the wall of our design…

Mary began to stir the steaming delight afresh and, as she did, pieces of carrots, potatoes, green beans and onions surfaced in the swirl.

Traitors to our God, so good and kind…

Mary paused, seeing some strangers approaching the way to their home from the road. She, who had seen many an unfamiliar face these last few weeks, lifted the paddle, rested it on the rim of the kettle and, as she straightened her attire in preparation, she, without thought, whispered one more line…

Worthy of tears…

"Good day, madam," said the lead gentleman (a somewhat haggard fellow dressed in strange attire [flowing long robes with peculiar markings]) as he bowed low before the still-primping matron.

"Good day, Sir…Sir?" Mary held the question aloft. She knew these were knights of some sort…but who…and from where?"

"Sir Eirenikos," he responded as he stood erect. "We are from the city of Aphron…and," he said, lowering his gaze just a little, "we have come to seek the river…and a fellow knight…Sir John. Do you know where he is, dear lady?"

"Yes…oh, yes," she responded, a bit unsettled having heard (bad news travels very fast) that the former home of these *elite* was now an empty husk. "Sir John is at the river, even now." She pointed in the direction of the life-giver, but, being a compassionate sort, she *had* to offer more. "Won't you please stop to refresh yourself? Have a drink…a meal?"

"No, no, thank you," said Sir Eirenikos, still somewhat amazed at how generous these people closer to the river could be. "We have ample supplies. We simply need to go to the river. Perhaps another time." Then, as he, and those with him turned and hobbled in the direction they were given, Mary stood watching for a moment…pondering the urgency that seemed to be enveloping the kingdom. Then, being awakened by her motherly drive, she grasped again the paddle and began to stir in a lazy figure-eight pattern. Soon the flute music was restored and, before long she could hear the words rising from within.

Once upon a dark and fearful time…

* * *

"What is its name again…Captain?" Sir Reginald, standing next to the moorings of a giant wooden catapult, asked as he ran his right hand along the rough-hewn timbers that were fastened together, in various locations, by large iron bolts.

"A trebuchet, sire," said the attendant smartly (having already been— along with his crew—standing at attention, he took one step forward to correctly give a reply to a superior.)

The High Knight, although normally well-pleased with such displays, at this point he had his mind on loftier things. "Relax, soldier," he said, looking the fellow in the eye even as he patted the nervous underling's right shoulder. "In fact," he continued, sweeping his gaze beyond the captain to the other half dozen *tenders*, "go on about your business, gentlemen. Make sure this darling is ready for tomorrow's dance."

The grunts behind the captain—displaying now a look of utter relief and offering heartfelt *Thank you, your majestys*—went back to their preparations for tomorrow's encounter and, as they did so, Sir Reginald—standing beside the leader of this band—gently put his right hand to the captain's back and the two then walked around the giant engine as the ruler sought to further his own education.

"A trebuchet, you say?"

"Yes, sire."

"Tell me, Captain, how is this weapon different from those we sold to the city of Sarx?"

"Oh, your majesty!" began the soldier with enthusiasm, "…great in many ways.

"For instance," he continued, "the catapults, of which we sold many, were very limited in range and quite unwieldy. These, however," the captain looked up at the great chamber that distinguished it from the other, "these use a counterweight…a system that does not rely on the tension of various sinews for power."

"So," interrupted Sir Reginald, "these can launch a missile and," the two walked up a narrow stair to a platform built along side the weapon, "I assume that the amount of ballast and, of course, the weight of the projectile," he looked (as both leaned against a waist high railing) into the captain's face (which took on the enthusiasm of a teacher who had successfully transferred knowledge), "…that these two factors determine the distance that the round carries."

"Exactly!" nearly shouted the young soldier. Then, remembering to whom he was speaking, he said, in a quieter tone, "Exactly, sire."

Sir Reginald smiled weakly at the bubbling commander (pleased that there were, at least on the surface, those whose motives were not as duplicitous as his own) and, offering to the soldier the opportunity to descend the stair first, he continued the conversation as the two set foot on the stone foundation, "I presume you have been given and are prepared to follow the directives that are most important for the success of this coming battle?"

"Yes, your majesty," the captain said smartly, snapping to attention. "General Ratsad has made it very clear as to our mission. We are ready, sire!"

"Very well, Captain," said Sir Reginald, offering a nod to acknowledge the salute, "carry on." And, as he and his small entourage walked along the battlements to another of the many engines (there were at least thirty on this section that straddled the main gate—the *only* gate), he said to himself as he rolled his eyes upward and sighed, "*General* Ratsad…indeed."

The Great Dragon

Chapter XXIII

When worship takes the inward path
It ends in bloodshed, pain, and wrath.

"Well, *General*...what are your thoughts?" Sir Reginald, standing behind the granite parapet constructed atop the southern gate of Alazon (again...the *only* gate), said, having just lowered from his right eye the gold-plated spy glass and now handing it to the bowing *counselor* who had just answered a summons to appear before the Exalted Knight.

"I beg your pardon, your majesty?" said Ratsad, taking the offered instrument and bowing again...more lowly this time.

Sir Reginald, still somewhat perturbed at the scheming of this servant, waved away his entourage of other knights (a half dozen of the chosen) so that he could speak more intimately with the *old man*. Then, bidding the *ambassador* rise, he pointed between the posts towards the huge, steaming, crimson mound that was their enemy and, as the servant was directed, and then placed the glass to his left eye, Sir Reginald feigned assistance and, coming very close to the gray-hair tufted ear of his most senior advisor he caustically whispered, "Listen, you old fool. You are *not* a knight...and you *never* will be. You are *not* of the nobility...and you *never* will be. And you certainly are *not* a general. Let me never hear of such insolence again...do you understand?"

Ratsad removed the instrument from his vision and bowed, again, very low. "Yes, your majesty. Please forgive your servant. I meant nothing by it."

Sir Reginald looked down at the pitiful creature before him and let the displeasure slowly drain from his countenance (after all, his greatest victory was at hand) and, turning to look again to the field, he said (after letting the ancient one stay in that position another minute), "You may rise, Ratsad. Come here beside me and reveal your thoughts."

Ratsad, with some difficulty (the awkward position had caused his old knees to tremor) stood erect and shuffled to be at his ruler's side (who was again peering through the glass). "Sire," he said, "it appears that the door to your desire and destiny has come at last." Then, as the easily flattered leader lowered the glass and looked, without malice, to the one he had just stepped upon, Ratsad added, "Sire, you are the *one*. It is the king's will that you take your place beside him."

—Alazon, the oldest and most dominant of the three great cities of the inner realm (of course, at this point, it was the *only* one remaining). It was from this place, so long ago, that the idea of the center sanctuary (that later became the *dumping place*) was birthed. It was here where distinctions of the people were discerned and decreed. It was here where *nobility* was exalted and the common were abased. And it was here where the *games*…the contest that perpetuated the persuasion of human-worship…thrived in an unnatural cycle of mutual, carnal, admiration.—

Sir Reginald, having dismissed his old accomplice (and toying with the idea of ending their relationship *permanently*) turned towards *his city* and scanned the breadth of it from west to east, even as he breathed deeply the crisp morning air (which, due to a northerly breeze, had not yet tasted of the wretched fumes arising from the beast.) As his attendants again joined him as he strolled—hands behind his back—upon this *command* platform, he felt a great rise of satisfaction as he looked upon a metropolis that, through his lengthy tenure, had taken on many of the attributes that he himself valued.

—"Distinctions," was one of the words that he had coined long ago. "There are distinctions in men, and animals, in vegetation and in stone," he would say. "As gold differs from granite, and as the purebred differs from the impure…even so there are *distinctions* between men. Some…the knights…are as the gold. Others are of lesser stuff. We shall not," he would bellow, "we shall not pretend the distinctions are not there. But, rather, we shall embrace them and render to each the honor due."

Thus, Alazon, of all of the king's realm, became a place of approved divisions. The highest class, naturally, were the knights…and these were to be recognized as such. Other classes (of which there were many) also received varying degrees of favor. And, to those of no calling, or talent, or perhaps afflicted with some limiting condition…these were the lowest of all…and rightly treated as such.—

* * *

The dragon, feeling the warmth of the rising sun and, to a greater extent, feeling the inner burning of lust not yet realized…*hatched* from its protective posture and—as the amazed distant defenders looked on (though truthfully they *knew* what was coming) the creature, screeching—with its head towards heaven—spread wide its protective wings and, having folded these back, it settled, after some minutes, into a stance on all fours facing, directly…the southern gate of the city and, as the gentle morning mist (nudged along by a rising breeze) caressed the monster's dripping nostrils with the fragrance of *family*…it opened slightly its mouth and uttered, before it began the circling…the traveling chant that was its devilish directive and drive…

> *From the center, rounding round*
> *Father, Mother, bring*
> *Then to Master, we present*
> *The perfect empty ring*
> *The perfect empty ring…*

But…before the last hiss of this incantation had a chance to travel any great distance, a swarm of—what appeared as a cloud of swiftly rising gnats—darted up from behind the towering granite walls adjacent to the gate, coming in a high arch. In a moment the mystery of these was solved as, with uncanny accuracy and powerful sledgehammer blows…stone after stone (all at least two hundred pounds in weight!) slammed into creature's torso, head, feet, and immediately adjacent…causing it to recoil in pain and bewilderment.

Now, it needs to be understood that, although this monster was armored like no other…it was still a creature of earth (although, to be sure, mixed with spiritual stuff that had its origin in hell) and, as such, it was *not* eternal. And, being caught totally off guard as to this sort of weaponry and expertise, the dragon shook its head slightly and looked down at some of the fragments of its protection that had been chipped off by the blows. And, as it also peered at the *things* which dared lend themselves to such use…there was, for the briefest moment—intermixed with the sunlight—the appearance of ever increasing dot-like shadows which came from nowhere...yet grew quickly...culminating in yet another chorus of slamming thunder as stone upon stone crashed into the behemoth's body.

"*Five hundred meters...amazing,*" Sir Robert, although scheduled to join his lower brothers in the formation that was, even now, coming together on the inner parade grounds, said in a monotone whisper as he watched one volley after another fly and apparently do damage to the monster he had seen, close up, these many months before.

A few moments later, after a quick reload, the whistling of wood and leather and boulders sent aloft filled the air once more and, as he again put his own spy glass to his eye he then saw, *and heard*, the pounding of the plates and the guttural screams of pain that emanated from a dragon that had never faced such an onslaught before.

"Sir Robert! Come here!" It was the voice of Sir Reginald (who was standing squarely on the command platform fifty meters away). The lesser knight, hoping that perhaps he hadn't been truly recognized, sought to press himself more closely between the rising of the granite posts in front of him. "Sir Robert, come here, man!"

"I suppose I'd better go," Sir Rob thought to himself as he straightened his attire and, smiling (as if he was *supposed* to be there all along), walked briskly to join his leader.

Sir Reginald, obviously *very* pleased with the progression of things, beckoned his knight-servant to come to a better vantage place. "Look," he said excitedly, handing Sir Robert the more powerful instrument.

"Simply amazing, sire," said the lesser, removing the glass from his eye. "I'd have never thought this creature could be so easily affected."

"Oh, my simple fellow," smiled the exalted knight, taking the glass from his bowing brother—even as another well-coordinated volley violently sailed into the morning sky, "this is just the beginning," and, looking again at the distant destruction, "...just the beginning."

* * *

"Gold is the key, my young captain...gold is the key." The words of a darkly caped and hooded Ratsad, traveling with some of the more able of the non-knights as they rode, on horseback, in the midnight hour, across the river that separated one kingdom from the other.

It was a mission of some importance…a mission of life and death and, although the Exalted Knight, Sir Reginald, had traveled to seek wisdom from the king, he had also let his most capable and crafty negotiator know that wisdom *from all quadrants* was welcome…and that the money bag was open and without limit.

—At the time it finally registered with Sir Reginald that the threat of this beast was indeed real and that, if not defeated, it would mean the end to his dominion and, at the *very* time when he, in desperation, briefly retraced his steps to the sanctuary of the king, he had, before leaving, also sent out this representative to the *other* side…to see, if possible, if there were any *other* remedies available for the disposal of a giant dragon…a dragon like no other.—

The young captain (who would later command a small crew that tamed an advanced catapult) looked over to his *leader* as both their horses struggled up the gently sloped embankment that led them in the direction of the Dragon Lord's domain. "Gold, Sir? This will buy us the secrets we need?"

"Oh, my naive fellow," laughed the old master. "It was gold that bought us the plans for the engines of war, and the construction of the walls (both of which were being furiously accomplished—with much help from the many refugees that were flooding the city) and," he continued, "gold will open the door to a more destructive substance…something I had heard rumors of for quite some time and now, through the confessions of a dying dragon (an interesting account involving the *chance* encounter of a dead Shachath and a *nearly* dead Ganab—both of which had been mortally wounded by an unknown weapon), I now know of the location where it can be had…and *gold*, my youthful inquisitor…will buy us the recipe."

After some days of travel (curiously devoid of trouble by dragons of any kind) the group of fifty fighters (not a knight among them…but all skilled with the bow and blade nonetheless—save Ratsad…whose ability was with the tongue) came across a valley of bones and skulls…dragon bones, mostly…although, upon closer examination…there were remnants—if one were to sift the ancient sands—of many human skeletons, as well. In the center of this grisly enclave was a walled chateau…manned by a small contingent of archers…men greatly skilled in the crossbow. Though barely visible at first glance (such was the distance) these marksmen made themselves known by accurately planting—mere meters from the leading horsemen—a cluster of twenty steel bolts. The landing of which caused the horses to rise up and the unseasoned warriors to gasp. Upon closer observation, however, one of the darts had a small parchment attached.

"What does it say, Captain?" said Ratsad (who seemed unmoved by the whole thing).

"It says, sir," said the youth, who scanned the message briefly, then handed it up to his leader, "*Only two beyond this place. Two with gold may see my face.*"

"General," said the warrior as he held the reins of Ratsad's mount (to calm the beast as a few more crossbow bolts buried themselves a few meters away), "who exactly have we come to see?"

"A famed alchemist, my curious tot," said the old one with a slight grin. (He rather enjoyed the stolen homage he had garnered from many of the *grunts*.) Then, signaling to his loyal aide to again mount up and, at the same time hearing (his aging ears were still quite acute) from the ranks behind, some grumblings, he quietly asked, "Tell me, Captain…are there any of your legion that give you concern as to their loyalty?"

"No, Sir," said the companion in an almost reflexive way. "Of course all our men are loyal to me and our cause." But, as the elder's silence and stony stare conveyed the message that a closer examination was needed (all the while, more grumblings from the back), the captain finally divulged the names of three.

"Call them forward, Captain."

"Yes, Sir."

Soon, three of the background complainers (rather excited to be chosen) were sent to explore ahead and, as they left with the leader's blessing—riding three abreast and closing slowly on the spot where the warning was given—the captain pressed his horse next to the *old man's* and said with hushed urgency, "*General*…the message said *two*!"

Ratsad held up his right hand for silence (without giving the underling the courtesy of a glance) and, after a few meters more…one of the riders lay dead…a dozen bolts in his armored chest.

The other two…bewildered, frantic with fear…raced back to the group where an angry (on the surface) Ratsad questioned their return.

"Why have you come back so quickly?" he fumed.

"General," both men had dismounted and were bowed to the ground. "General…our brother…dead."

"Stand up, you cowards!" the old one scowled. "You knew before you came that your lives were forfeit." Then, motioning them to stand aside and that gold-filled bags be brought forward, he added, "The captain and *I* will go on ahead. If we return alive…you must, before we go back to the city of heroes…you must prove to me your worthiness. Now go! Out of my sight!"

A few minutes later, the captain and *Sir Ratsad* (a title he encouraged when the true knights were not around) easily passed the pruning place and made their way to the opening gate of the citadel.

"General," asked the younger, coyly, "your method…could you explain?"

"Ah, my young student," said Ratsad, turning to smile at the curious expression on the other's face. "You must look beyond the present to see the goal…always the goal." The lad's questioning brow remained and the old one continued, "We…you and I…needed to see if those who sent the message could be trusted. Thus…they *commanded* two…so we sent three. Also, since it is very important that we always have the absolute loyalty of those who cover our backs…you wisely suggested three who were questionable. Thus, my young scholar," he said, nodding in respect to the dark-clothed attendants at the gate (noticing also many on higher places of vantage with weapons at the ready), "we proved that the message was accurate (two were left alive) and we also removed one of the troublemakers and the others…well," he chuckled slightly, "well, these will amend their ways and prove themselves, ultimately, to be the most loyal of all."

* * *

The dragon, as wave upon wave of crushing blows rained upon it (without a doubt a more than adequate onslaught to kill any Ganab, or Shachath, and certainly enough to drive away even the hardiest Muth)…the beast—being pushed on by the overwhelming desire to consume that which beckoned it from within the walls—decided to begin the circling. "…for surely," it thought, "such a defense could *not* be mounted throughout the length of the perimeter."

"It's moving, Sire."

Sir Reginald grabbed the crude telescope from the attendant, looked for himself, then acknowledged the words with a nod.

"Sir, what are your orders?"

"Lieutenant," said the High Knight without concern, "have these batteries prepare for the next phase. Then inform the choir director that the singers will be needed shortly."

—As recounted earlier, Alazon—like the other walled cities of the inner realm—originally only had adequate defenses to deter man. These sturdy walls—much too low for such a beast—*now* served as the platform for the mighty engines of war and *another*, higher wall was built outside the first (a man's length gap between the two). This imposing structure was such that even the creature's greatest upward extension (as evidenced at the destruction of Sarx) would be incapable of reaching the top. Also, the uppermost edge of this sturdy granite wall had adequate openings for archers and the observers that directed the catapults but, if the need arose, it provided ready protection from the fiery blasts. There was also, two meters below the rim, a broad walkway where the choir would attend. The choir that, in their own way, offered *another* weapon the creature had not previously encountered.—

* * *

"The gold, gentlemen." The speaker, a rather distinguished looking (though cold in expression) individual—great in age, wearing a long white robe which had smatterings of scarlet and—as he had apparently just left his alchemist's layer—as he spoke he also removed some protective gloves which were bright crimson in color.

"The gold, gentlemen," the master of this place repeated and, as he did so, some somber attendants—from the shadows—stepped one step closer, weapons drawn.

"Forgive us, my lord," groveled Ratsad (he was certainly used to this) as he, and the captain bowed low and then quickly placed four hefty bags of Alazon's finest on a battered oak table (which had a polished copper overlay).

The alchemist—whose name was *Phoneus*—sat down at the table (one of his associates quickly providing a padded stool), pulled closer a flickering oil lamp (itself made of gold), and meticulously pulled each of the many gold coins individually from the bag…treating every one with the delicacy of a newborn babe. Finally, after nearly an hour's time (there were *many* coins) he disappeared into a back room and, after the sound of keys and locks, came back with a small rectangular wooden box (the size of an infant's coffin) and placed it before the outsiders.

For a moment there was silence as the visitors were quite uncertain as to the expectation of their host. The alchemist (whose mood had brightened to match the luster of the gold) finally blurted out… "Well…open it…it's what you came for!"

The armed attendants were waved away by the lord of the place and Ratsad, and his young accomplice, were offered drink and a morsel as the three sat down at the table of commerce and the elder visitor gently pulled the mysterious box to himself and then slowly lifted up the hinged lid. Then—the captain peering in from one side—Ratsad reached in and pulled up, with tremoring fingers, some grayish, sand-like powder…which he then let run through his appendages back into the box.

Obscured by the lid (which Ratsad now slowly closed)…a low, rolling, chuckle could be heard coming from the seller (who was leaning forward, head down, elbows on the table). Phoneus, lifting his gaze, looked at the two and said, "What did you expect, gentlemen? A magic wand? A lightning bolt? No!" he leaned forward and pulled the box to him (twisting it quickly). Then, grabbing a great handful, he held it high and let the grains fall like a silky curtain.

"No," he continued, "what you have here is *power*. This harmless-looking substance is a powerful intoxicant. No, not for you or I…it would do little to us…but, to a dragon?!" he closed the lid and stood, "To a dragon this is a drug which, when administered correctly, will cause drunkenness…drunkenness to the point of *death*."

"Drunkenness?" whispered the captain to his leader. "I don't understand."

"Listen, young man…and learn," said the alchemist as he began to walk about the room (much like a professor in a classroom). "There are two ways to defeat an enemy." As he spoke the words he raised his right arm and, as if blowing out a match, he quickly extended vertically the arthritic right index finger and held it inches from his mouth. "The first way is from the outside…such as overpowering force, or," he paused and leaned, palms down, directly in front of the youth, "second…from the *inside*…where the weaknesses—and we all have them—can be exploited." Phoneus stood upright and slid the box over so that it was between he and his guests. "The dragons thrive on the flesh and souls of our kind. They play and prune us like a vineyard. This powder, when administered correctly, overloads their systems and," he sat again on the stool, "just as a man can die from too much drink…these *too* die from drunkenness."

This was all very strange to the visitors and, wanting the conversation to end, the alchemist asked the next question *for* his guests, "How do we administer it, you might ask? Well, my friends…the answer has been before you since you visited my territory."

"The bolts...the crossbow darts," said Ratsad in a quiet monotone.

"Yes...exactly. Bolts, when laden with this substance, and shot in adequate number (depending on the dragon) will first incapacitate...which gives opportunity for a more traditional dispatching...or, if the dragon is small enough...it will kill it outright."

"But what about a Muth?" blurted out the captain. "We are faced with an enormous dragon...it's at least a Muth...if not more."

Phoneus put his right elbow on the table and rubbed, slowly, his mole-spotted chin. "Muths are more difficult. That is why your archers must be the very best. The only," he spoke with deliberation, "*only* place that is vulnerable to the poison laden dart...is the eye. Then...and I don't care how big the creature is...if there are enough darts in place...the creature will, at least for a time, be incapacitated. Then you have time to flee."

"Flee?" said Ratsad, who was getting the uneasy feeling of being fleeced. "*There is no fleeing.*"

"Then you must," said Phoneus slyly, "while the creature is down...you must use the methods of *your* knights to breach its heart."

"But didn't you say," asked the negotiator, cocking his head slightly to one side, "didn't you say that if there was enough poison administered...that this, too, would kill the beast?"

"Quite right...but...the question is...especially for a creature of great size...how much is enough?" Then, standing, and beginning to don, again, his crimson gloves, he added, "I recommend, in order to be sure, that you couple the darts with the knight's sword. Now, I urge you two to join your fellows quickly. The dragons, by this time, know you are here. You'll find your exit much more difficult than your entrance."

Ratsad and the youth stood and bowed, courteously, to their host then, as the door was opened and they prepared to step, Phoneus (himself prepared to continue *his* work) said, "One more thing," at which both visitors turned. "Please send your associate," he said to the elder, "to prepare the horses."

Then, with the captain gone and Ratsad very attentive, Phoneus continued, "You did not ask *how* the poison is attached to the darts. What medium is needed?"

"I didn't think it was important," whispered the schemer.

"Oh...it is vital," said the alchemist, nodding. "In fact, it is essential. You need a medium of such purity that it can slice easily through the demon's outer layers and this, my like-hearted fellow...involves very small children. You *do* have small children in your city, don't you?"

"Yes…" said Ratsad as his face paled slightly. "Yes…we do."

The *ambassador*, feeling that he was descending to a new and horrible low, turned after a moment of contemplation to go but, out of a nagging curiosity he asked, "Sir…one more thing…I noticed the graveyard without…the many dragon bones, and below these…human."

"Yes," said the alchemist with a sigh. "From time to time the dragons attempt to attack this place…they aren't very wise."

"And the humans?"

As Phoneus walked towards his grisly work-chamber, he said, "Years ago my profession was opposed by the fools of this realm. They sought my head. But now," he laughed as he slowly disappeared into the darkened doorway, "now they accept me…some," he continued, barely audible, "…even worship me…the *fools*."

* * *

The dragon, shaking off the effects of the torrential pounding, slowly began its counterclockwise circling of Alazon. As was its custom…every few steps it raised its head and called, mournfully, for its *parents*. *"Father…mother…I've come for you. Join me, Father. Join me, Mother. I've come for you!"* The sound, as before, was piercing, soulish, dripping of hellish oil…but…it seemed to be somehow neutralized before it penetrated the city. Something was diffusing the horrid stream…and that something arose from the *Exalted Choir*.

—The Choir…the very best and beautiful of the land…walked along the platform that was constructed below the outer wall's rim. These talented ladies and gents—dressed in sparkling garb—strolled, step for step, in parallel symmetry with the beast and, as it lifted high its wave of devilment, these (under the direction of a gentleman named, *Eritheia*) lifted eloquent songs that spoke of the knights' power as they fought bravely in the name of the king.—

At first, due to the wariness born of the bombardment, the creature stayed a great distance from the wall. But, as no other missiles were launched…it angled, slowly, towards the center. When it reached three hundred meters, however, again stones of even *heavier* weight were launched (not as frequently, as the greatest concentration of catapults were by the southern gate) but with just as much uncanny accuracy.

—Alazon, if nothing else, was a place of order, law, and the demand for perfection (indeed, *worthiness* was closely tied with how well an individual followed predetermined guidelines). Long before the creature's arrival the defenders (meaning the *grunts*) were drilled unto exhaustion as to the perfecting of their technique…whether it be the use of the catapult, or the accuracy of the crossbow.—

The monster, sensing *no* rise in fear and, being plagued with the occasional bludgeoning boulder…now, as it continued in its course (it was a slave to its task)…the heavenly words of the choir were weaving between its own and, as these penetrated its brain…an anxiousness, an uneasiness, began to percolate from its center.

"Ratsad."

"Yes, your majesty."

"Are your archers prepared?"

"Yes, my lord…two of the finest are in position on the walls opposing the gate."

"Very good. Now…you're sure about this elixir…this poison?"

"Yes, my liege. Its effectiveness was witnessed by the great dragon graveyard that surrounded the alchemist's lair."

"And…it will *kill* this thing, you say?"

"Yes, my lord…if administered in adequate quantity."

"You have enough darts, then?"

"Oh, most assuredly, your highness. We'll make certain the creature is supplied with more than enough venom to still its wretched heart."

"And, you say there will be adequate time for me to administer the *lethal* blow?"

"Yes, *Exalted* Knight. The dragon will fall and its life force will slowly ebb. But, before that distant point you will have, *your majesty*, all the time you need to administer the lance in front of the masses. More than enough time to convene the grand assembly."

"Good, good (short pause). The *eye*, you say?"

"Yes, *Master*, on such a beast as this the eyes are the most vulnerable spot. A quick thrust with your lance will, with one strike, destroy the last obstacle to your proper ascendancy."

"*Yes*…my time *has* come…it is here at last.(The servant bowed and turned to go.) Ratsad."

"Yes, your highness?"

"Get the children in position."

"Yes, my lord…as you wish…as you wish."

The dragon, though of fiendish intelligence, was in a state of perplexity as—mixed in with its lustful desires—it was assaulted by the constant barrage without, and the heavenly anthems which wounded within. Nevertheless…it was driven and, as it continued its plodding pursuit it came, once again, to the place of its beginning…the southern gate.

—As stated previously, there was now only one gate in or out of Alazon…the southern gate. Having learned the lesson from the dragon's assault on Sarx, the framers of *this* defense, when they constructed the outer wall, did *not* want the creature to have opportunity to despoil any other exits as it had done so masterfully before. Also, the well-spread knowledge that there *was* no plan for defeat…no way of escape…this would give the defenders all the more reason to succeed. Yes, Alazon was now surrounded by a towering impenetrable barrier except…except for the southern gate. This—the *only* exposed portion of the old wall (though built up to equal height with the new)—this entry—which sported two huge polished copper (over white oak) clad doors (hinged on the side, meeting in the middle with more than adequate bracing behind) being set back from the new structure (the new tapering to meet the old) so that if one were to look down where the new wall met the old it would appear very much as a large letter *V*, although, truthfully, future plans included a landscaping to make the entrance resemble the first letter in the name of this greatest of all cities…the letter *A*.—

The behemoth, fuming, screeching, and its head twisting side to side as it tried to shake off the most annoying sound of praise rising from the choir—suddenly, without explanation…felt relief. For, all at once the anthems stopped…and the stones from the sky…ceased. And, sensing something sweeter than fear…something more succulent than terror…the monster turned (as if it were a giant lodestone drawn in the direction of the polar star) to face the southern gate where, assembled in a jubilant mass of innocence…were at least *one thousand children!* And these, unlike the rigidly held trappings of Sarx, these were playing, singing, laughing…all in the confines immediately outside the entry to the city, all waiting for a plucking from a very hungry beast.

To be sure, the trap…the snare…the noose…all these, when examined by rational beings…these can easily be recognized and avoided. But—and this applies to *all* parties in this conundrum—there comes a place where the *rational* is smothered by the raving. Of course this is an ambush! Of course there is destruction in the wings! But, with the temptation comes a twisting, a turning, a slithering, a sliding…a lever that prods, repositions, and, when all is said and done...the rational course becomes the course of desire...always desire...always lustful, selfish, soulish, damnable...desire.

The dragon...drooling, chest heaving, weary of mind yet ravenous of hellish heart...lunged towards the morsels that lay a little less than three hundred meters away and, though not a creature of speed, it came quickly nonetheless, matching the gait of a man at a medium trot...and the distance passed quickly, all the while the children—those pure bubbles of innocence—seemed unconcerned, unfettered by the approaching doom.

Then, as the moving mountain reached the two hundred-meter markers (there were colored stones placed at various distances in the surrounding fields which served as aids to the spotters) it was hit by a deluge of *five-hundred-pound* boulders. These—the first wave in unison coupled with the loud songs of praise from the choir reborn—stopped the beast dead in its tracks. Then, as it wobbled from the concussive blows, it let out a great thunderous ear-splitting scream of pain and anguish as *something*, time after time, caused its hideous head to quiver and recoil. Finally, after some minutes (all the while giant rocks slamming into its body, neck, and head) the creature resorted to a reflexive tactic it had used with success before.

As the Choir sang, and the boulders flew, and the children swirled about as if in a great whirlpool of delight...the forelegs of the enormous demon became like huge, rigid pillars of stone. At the same time the face of the monster took on a hellish expression which was fixed straight ahead—the eyes (every so often wincing from an unseen onslaught) were bulging and glowing ever brighter and, for the briefest of times, below the sound of the choir and the stones, and just above the clamor of the children...there could be heard the clapping of the inner valve that meant the all-consuming fire of the creature was building and its release was imminent.

WHOOSH! The flame, like a geyser of super-heated steam bursting from the confines of a volcanic chamber, rushed forward—devouring all that was green and alive before it. Ten, thirty, seventy, *one hundred meters*...it flashed forth in one horrific instant. But, as the expanding plume reached this great distance it, like a vicious charging dog on a strong chain tether...stopped. And beyond this lethal length...there was nothing but a scorching foul wind and, beyond this...just a warm breeze and...beyond this...were the children...unaffected, unmoved—though certainly applauding the spectacle. (They had been told that this affair was to be as a play, a circus.)

"Another, General?"

Ratsad, watching the creature expend itself and then pivot (the tail whipping about, brushing aside the grounded stones like pebbles before a massive broom) and, finally facing forward once more (although appearing very weak and subtly off-balance), he replied, "Yes, soldier, one more from you and your fellow."

The archer, who, along with the elder, were on the eastern side of the gate, gave a one-fingered hand signal to his counterpart on the western side. Then, nearly as one, they both let fly a crimson bolt and these, in a split-second, entered each of the half opened eyes of the dragon. Whereupon the poison, coupled with the two-dozen other injections, caused the great behemoth to stagger and—as Sir Reginald and the other elite looked on—finally, with one last ineffectual lunge, its once powerful legs succumbed and it crashed to earth…its neck and snout thrust straight out and, a moment later, the hideous head slowly turned on its right side as its black tongue unfurled to lie dormant on the charred earth.

As a great cry of victory arose from the wall and those around the High Knight congratulated him with boisterous salutes, the archer asked, "General…shouldn't we fire a few more bolts…just to make sure?"

"Now, now," said the smirking statesman as he slowly turned to go and grovel before his lord, "we don't want to be wasteful. Besides," he said in a barely audible voice," the *Exalted Knight* wants to finish the job himself."

* * *

It was the *Grand Assembly*…the gathering of the knights. All the elite of Alazon, along with all the visiting refugees of station (meaning, of course, *other* knights) made a great corridor (parallel lines) leading from the hundred-meter point up to the dragon's hideous head. Along with this boisterous gathering (this was a day of celebration!), portable stands were quickly in place (such was the pre-planning) for the wives and children of the upper select, along with a raised platform for the Exalted Choir.

Ratsad, being the High Knight's all around spokesman, very slowly (he had discovered long ago that *delay* was often a source of irritation to those who were *his betters*…thus he was never want to employ it) shuffled between the rows of the upper crust and, standing just in front of the monster's snout (a low death rattle still barely evident even as a warm putrid mist moistened the old man's backside), he lifted high his left hand for silence and then, raising a parchment in his right…began to loudly proclaim… "The words of the king!"

> *To conquer evil*
> *Seek the one*
> *The Champion in your midst*
> *The one with sword…and shield…and song*
> *The one whom God has kissed.*

He continued, "Having thus fulfilled the prophetic words…I give you, (a respectable pause) the champion!…the most High and Exalted Knight…Sir Reginald!" As the old conspirator spoke these *final* words he pointed towards the opening doors of the citadel (they had been temporarily closed for effect) with his parchmented right hand and, at the same time, he bowed lowly…holding his left hand over his heart.

The gathering, knights and elite all, turned their gaze to the southern gate and, as a regally festooned Sir Reginald came out (wearing polished silver armor [front and back], supporting with his right arm a towering, glistening white lance [strangely tipped in red], his left arm sporting a small, decorative, round shield which bore *his* emblem—a knight on horseback—a crimson cape flapping triumphantly behind and, of course, the brilliant gold helmet…all this while on his most noble, high-stepping white stallion [equally attired] named, *Reqam*)…the *Grand Assembly,* upon seeing their hero, burst forth in cheers and accolades and the *Exalted Choir* enthusiastically sang of conquests to come.

Sir Reginald made his way slowly through the glorious gauntlet, nodding, from time to time, to acknowledge individual acclaim and, reaching the barely breathing beast, he gazed down at the exposed left eye. This large orb…nearly a man's size in length—aside from the very dilated black pupil—appeared as the milky yellow of an egg that had been overly seasoned with pepper. These dots, of course, were the blunt—barely protruding—ends of the many crossbow darts that had been so expertly launched, and the crimson medium in which these were bathed (of which just a tinge remained)…this gave them ready entrance past the steely outer layer and then…the poison did the rest. Now, as the high knight glanced confidently up to the red tip of his towering weapon which pointed towards heaven…it was now up to him to make the demon's end—and *his* beginning—all the more sure. But first…a speech.

"My brothers!…My fellow knights! (Of course, there *were* ladies present, but he considered the fairer gender as little more than garnish.)" he said, slowly directing his steed forward, away from the beast (preparing for the final charge). "This is a great day for truth, honor, and the exaltation of Alazon!" As he spoke the words with punctuated emphasis, the gathering of five thousand (an impressive array of warriors...all on horseback, armored, polished, and ready to obey) would let out hearty calls of affirmation. "The God of the Crystal Sea has shown his favor (cheers)...the king of the crimson sword has shown his will (cheers)...and, after this day, *I*, your *champion*, will lead our legions to the reclamation of *not only* the inner realm (wild cheering)...but also the civilizing of the entire wayward kingdom of *Ekklesia!*" At this final remark, as the crowd continuously yelled their favor (in jubilant disarray) and—having reached the end of the gathering (roughly one hundred meters from the dragon)—Sir Reginald turned, secured his faceplate and, for a few minutes (before lowering the lance for the final attack) simply remained statuesque...absorbing the praise and the highness of the moment.

Meanwhile, on the western side of the assembly...milling about...being a herdsman of displaced children, the discourager of the curious ignoble and, on occasion, the collector of litter...Sir Robert, and the four (three of which were on the eastern side) were doing what they always did at these gatherings. Yes, being the lowest of the knights they were assigned the tasks listed above and, as Sir Rob paused from his wandering to view the undulating forest of skyward lances as the High Knight prepared for the final thrust...Rammak, the exceptional mount on which Sir Robert sat...suddenly became quite disturbed.

"What is it, brother?" said the elder softly as he held the reins firmly in his gloved right hand and patted the troubled beast's neck with his left. Rammak (they had been facing the spectacle) began to slowly back up, shaking his head in a twisting fashion up and down.

From experience, Sir Robert knew this behavior meant there was danger on the path...whether a viper or some other beast or, on one occasion, a bridge not passable (although to the *human* eye, it certainly had appeared so). The knight looked down, and what he saw caused a terrifying chill to run through his frame.

"Sir Gus!" he screamed. "Tell your brothers to disperse the crowd! We must return to the city!"

"What is it, Captain?" Sir Gustov, riding quickly along side his leader, asked.

Sir Robert, understanding the urgency of the moment, simply pointed to the earth and, as it took only a moment for his fellow knight to comprehend he yelled—as he sped towards the gate—"NOW, RIDE!!"

Sir Gus hesitated just a moment more to stare. For, below him, in a subtle expanding circle of decay, the *rotting* (that poison that emanated from the beast) was spreading quickly. When the creature had first fallen and the knights had assembled (all on the charred earth from the flame) there was no remnant of the poisoning. But, on the fringe, where the grass was still green...*now* the blades were quickly disappearing in a sickening dissolve. This meant that the creature was certainly not as near death as Sir Reginald believed. In fact...it *appeared*—if its expanding pool of deadly secretions was any indication—to be recovering!

Sir Robert, having reached the polished copper doors of the city in a flash (Rammak was unmatched in speed), began to pound the formidable barrier with his right hand and forearm.

"OPEN UP!" he desperately screamed and repeated between groupings of blows. "THE DRAGON IS REBORN! OPEN UP...ALERT THE ARCHERS!"

After a half minute of this, and just as Sir Reginald prepared to lower his lance for the final victory charge...Sir Rob heard a familiar voice wafting down from the fortifications above.

"Sir Robert! Is that you, old friend?"

At his master's gentle prodding, Rammak sidestepped slowly away from the gate so that the elder knight could see, for certain, the owner of the voice. A few moments later, as a graying head (accompanied now by a gold crown!) poked out from between the stones...Sir Rob's curiosity was duly sated. "Ratsad! What are you doing?! Open the gate at once!"

"No...my brother," said the deceiver, slowly nodding his head side to side. "The creature must be dead before entrance is admitted. I suggest therefore...*old friend*...that you and your elite fellows simply do what knights do." Up to this point the corrupt counselor had been even of temperament, but, seeing no movement on the part of the astonished Sir Robert, he concluded... "NOW GO! AND BRING NONE OF YOUR KIND BACK BEFORE THE DEED IS DONE!" At this—like dominoes neatly positioned in a row—archers were seen lining up on the wall (spreading out from the center). And, to add credence to the crowing...*all* of these skilled warriors had Sir Robert in their sights...and it appeared (as their eyes were filled with hate) that they would have no trouble at all in happily extinguishing his solitary flame.

As the knight turned—his heart wounded by the betrayal in the midst— he spurred his charger to try and intercept his leader before it was too late.

But...as he saw the ineffectual strivings of his brothers (*none* of the bystanders took seriously their pleadings) he heard the final thundering of the hooves, the cry of the crowd and then...a great and terrible hush as something horrible beyond his sight was taking place.

Back on the wall *Sir Ratsad* couldn't help but snicker as he saw—through Sir Reginald's *own* spyglass—the unfolding of his elaborate plan. For, as his *master*, the Exalted Knight, leaned and lowered his lance and sped towards his destiny with greatness...his *slave*, his *servant*, his *never-to-be-anything* puppet...it was *he*, Ratsad, who now controlled the keys to the kingdom, and it was he who would redefine the foundations of Alazon. Foundations that, very soon, would *not* include the former gentry.

"That's it, you little fool," he mumbled to himself as he focused on the coming impact. "Surely the bloodied tip of your lance will penetrate even as the archers' darts," he whispered mockingly. "But, oh my (he fought to restrain his laughter), you don't know that *your* weapon was bathed from the butcher's pan. But, how could you? One blood looks like another, eh?"

The crowd cheered as Sir Reginald (*very* skilled at the joust) aimed the sharp point of his lance for a perfect cleaving of the eye. But, as his huge dagger's tip touched the orb's outer layer...instead of piercing the eye and then penetrating the brain...the lance acted as though it had struck a rock-hard crystal globe and his weapon—that which was his favorite—it then forcefully pushed up (without so much as scratching the outer layer) and violently rammed open the protective eyelid (which had been drooping somewhat due the demon's drug-induced stupor) and stuck there in the crease. The High Knight, unprepared for the sudden stop, flipped over his mount's bowed head and, after falling onto, and then off of the creature's lower jaw...he sat, dazed, leaning back against the underside of the monster's craw. His steed, Reqam, quite unused to such a result—and slightly injured in the collision—hobbled over to his master.

A moment later, to the horror of the bystanders, the dragon's dilated pupil focused sharply and, as each of the imbedded darts slowly (as if pushed by an unseen hand), was expelled from the eye's yellowish field, the creature turned its head aright and, looking directly into the face of the *Champion* (Sir Reginald was close enough to touch it), the demon said in a cavernous monotone, *"Where is your sword, good Sir knight?"* And then, without ceremony, in one grisly motion, it swallowed both the High Knight *and* his horse and then, raising its snout skyward (while with one quick head-shake dislodging the lance [which fell, point first, into the adjacent choir, impaling a soprano]) it made, while the thousands of attendees screamed and stumbled over each other to escape, a complete circle. Having done so the dragon's long, cable-like tail, went through the hysteric crowd like a sharpened scythe through standing grain. In a great circle of destruction, the horses, men, women and children, fell. Those closest to the beast, due to the slowness of the collision, were simply crushed, broken and bruised. But those on the outer edge, where the thinning, whip-like tail traveled at an accelerated pace…these where cut in two, sliced asunder, decapitated, and mortally laid open.

The choir director, badly injured (as were most in his charge) nevertheless had the presence of mind to have his singers try to launch one more debilitating (to the creature from hell) song of praise. But, as the remaining sought to compose themselves and coalesce for one more anthem, they didn't notice that the dragon had become rigid, its eyes fixed with hatred, and the inner cadence begun.

"H-U-U-C-C-C," the director raised his right arm (his left was broken) to bring to focus the remaining singers but, as the sound of the creature (which was to his back) was mixed with the screams of the dying…it was the widening eyes of the choir that alerted him. Slowly, just before waving for the first note, he turned his head to see the dragon cock its head back and then, in lightning quickness, shoot forward. There would be no more singing today. The choir, along with many in the same path, were incinerated by the flame.

On the wall, Ratsad, and the many who had had their fill of the elite, were elated at the events. And, as they suspected, many who had avoided the dragon's attack, rushed back to the city they loved.

"Greet them, Captain," said the general nonchalantly. And, with this, a thousand arrows darkened the sky. But, these skillfully aimed instruments of death were *not* directed towards the dragon…no…these were the *thanks* and *returns* from a populace that was tired of being considered *inferior*.

And so, thousands fell from the dragon's rage, and thousands fell from the rage of man. And among the first were the knights from the town called *Porneia*. Their leader, Sir Warren, once content to slaughter his own in order to elude harm, now lay dying from a crossbow dart to the throat…but his end came not from this…but rather from the boots of others who used him as pavement to seek their own escape.

On an on the carnival of carnage played. As the morning sun slowly reached its zenith and the shadows withdrew to none, those of the elite whose roots were so firmly planted in Alazon (and who could not bear to leave her), these tried incessantly to return to their place of honor and, when seeing those in front falling from the wayward dart (so they thought) they would temporarily turn to face the beast (which itself was held at bay by the catapults that did not remain silent). And so, back and forth in mindless hysteria the remaining herd of knights went from one form of death to another and—as there were very few who sought another escape (of which there was *one*...back to the river)—before long the number of living was a mere handful. It was at this moment that the general again commissioned his *special* archers to loose the crimson bolts. But, *this time*, when the dragon (who had been lustfully consuming the prey) perceived the first intrusions— and rather than staying for a lethal dose—it turned and lumbered away from the city until it was out of range. From this distant spot (though an occasional stone could reach it) the dragon began to circle and scream once more. This time, however, with no choir to dissipate its call...the chilling summons began to have an effect. Also, being so heartily fed, the monster exuded vast amounts of the *rotting*, which pushed its way quickly up to the city walls.

Round and round it went...calling, calling, calling, and, even when the maddened children were placed outside the gate (amid the decaying dead) even these could not tempt the beast to risk the crimson darts.

Into the evening the dragon called, feeling, with each pass, the terror level of the humans rising (just a little...such was the confidence of the *new* lords.) And, as the pitch of night made the creature's eyes glow all the more (now a dull red), it knew that it could not chance an inward foray. But, as the moon began to dominate the midnight air, the dragon was content to enfold itself in its protective wings, understanding (and it let out a snort of yellowish fume at the once foreign thought) that it was the fiendish foresight of its evil master that would now aid it in its desire. For, as its consciousness slowly succumbed to slumber (a sweet sleep aided by the still digesting knight-flesh), it could faintly hear the sound of a hundred dragon wings. These puny cousins would, no doubt, raid the city...plucking morsels and instilling fear. But—and the dragon had almost reached its place of ultimate rest and recovery (this dormant time brought healing as well as renewed strength)— it could feel and hear the touch of a thousand little talons...like very small side-walking crabs scurrying over a bolder. These, the Chata, would scale, like columns of ants, the *impenetrable* walls and, no matter how many defenders (and there were *very* many) these humans would at least be too distracted to do *him* harm. Then (now the demon's mind's eye was nearly closed) he would burst through the gate...and the final consumption would begin.

* * *

It took nearly a full week. The onslaught of the tiny dragons against Alazon was as the wind-driven tide...wave after wave after wave. But the defenders, still heady after being released from their chains, fought fiercely and with precision. However, the smallest of cracks can doom the strongest of dams and, on one cloudy eve the flying demons combined with the hungry hordes at the southern gate and these, though themselves decimated by arrow and sword...they prevented, just long enough, the weapons that could dissuade the greater threat from coming close enough to burst through. Once this was accomplished...all was lost.

"Sir Ratsad! General!" It was the desperate voice of one of the captains...out of breath, bleeding and bruised. "General! They're coming! You must escape!"

Ratsad, dressed in Sir Reginald's purple robe and sitting on his former master's cushioned throne, tilted the gold goblet in such a way that the last drop of elixir dribbled down (half into his mouth and the other half onto his beard.) He then leaned back and let the emptied glass slide from his fingers onto the polished steps (where it then mournfully clanged down till it rested alongside the equally empty decanter). "Let them come, Captain!" he mumbled. "Let my subjects come and worship!"

The soldier paused a moment to look on with disgust but, not being content to die a fool's death...he unsheathed his sword and, running into the outer chamber...there was then heard the sound of slashing steel and beastly squeals until, at last overcome, the captain's own cry of agony briefly mingled with the din.

Sir Ratsad, the *High and Exalted Knight of Alazon,* slowly arose and staggered down the steps. As he stood at the bottom—weaving slightly as if on an ocean barge—he leaned over and fumbled for the empty vessels. Grabbing one in each hand, he then stood and raised his head to behold—with blurred vision—the things which now (a vast number!) slowly pushed the doors apart accompanied by the sounds of shears...scraping, scraping, scraping.

"Come in! Come in!" he warbled, raising high the useless containers. "We have much to talk about...you and I. Come, bow before your king. Come bow before *Sir Ratsad.* Come bow before the *High...*"

Chapter XXIV

Great neglect...and evil grows
Defiling all the land
Until, with nowhere else to run
The dead must take a stand.

Sir John knelt upon the hot and charred earth. The soil—still retaining heat from the recent blast of flame—burned his knees as he struggled to pull his upper body erect by grasping the hilt of the sword he had just recently inverted and thrust—with the little strength he had left—into the place where blossoms once flourished. "Funny," he thought to himself, "this place, before *I* instigated the battle (hours before) was a blessed field of sweet clover. Now," he shook his head slightly, "it is a blackened landscape, a sterile plain...a place that is dead...and a place..."—he leaned in against the battered weapon—"...because *I* have failed...it is a place where *our* ending...begins." Then, as he heard the final clacking of the dragon's inner valve (by now—such was the length of the struggle—he had, with only a subconscious counting, a sense of *exactly* when the fire would come) he whispered outloud, "It is only fitting that I be the first to die."

* * *

With the fall of Alazon…with the fall of the jewel and the scepter of the inner realm…with the consumption of the haughty and the heinous and the heretic…the creature, the monster that slithered from the hole in the center so many months prior…now…with renewed desire, and its goal within sight (the goal of swallowing the *whole* kingdom) the dragon lustfully set out on its counterclockwise course. But now, instead of the relatively tight overlapping that had been its method…now (such were its emanations—plus the assistance of the more intimate plague behind) its line of destruction angled much more sharply towards the rim. Indeed, the area targeted, though greater in expanse, would be defiled at a very quick pace and, since so greatly nourished by the fears and flesh of its *parents*, the need for rest and repair was substantially reduced. Thus, the crimson-scaled curse could plod on, hour after hour, and day after day…coming in the night…and coming in the light…coming to kill, and destroy, and steal with fire all that which its master had ripped from his clutches the thousand years before.

* * *

"There's a dragon, brother! A dragon!"

"Hm? What's that, you say?"

"A dragon, Sir *Perispao*, a dragon!"

—The great walled cities of the inner realm were gone, destroyed, and subsequently picked clean by the winged dragons and the locust-like Chata. Now, having consumed *most* of its parents (the few that remained had escaped towards the river, but were *still* greatly desired), the crimson dragon's influence continued on to defile the countryside that led to the shimmering flow. These lands, and those who lived there—though having no business with the hellish hole in the center—these, nevertheless, were subject to this monstrous maelstrom which, having begun, would consume *all* in its path…all…until *all* was no more.—

Sir Perispao took off his small, round, wire-rimmed reading glasses and looked up at his assistant. "A dragon, you say?"

"Yes, brother!" said the younger, following the gesturing of the elder (who, slowly rising from his chair had pointed with his right hand—without looking—towards his armor in the corner while with his left he reached under a large pile of parchments to retrieve a message ignored…a message that *had* contained the words of his king).

Sir Perispao stepped out into the center of his study and, as his attendant began to strap his heavy armor upon legs and torso, the knight held the parchment at arm's length and read, out loud, the admonition.

To conquer evil
Seek the one
The Champion in your midst
The one with sword...and shield...and song
The one whom God has kissed
But till you find
Hold not your place
But to the river run
And there destroy
The works of man
Until you find the one.

True, originally this message had been attached to the blabberings of the *inner circle* but (he transferred the paper to the other hand as the dressing continued) even in his own pilgrimages to the sanctuary he had overheard (though he was not one to eavesdrop) the words spoken to others who were, for whatever reason, troubled with this matter.

"I thought it just another twisted misinterpretation," he whispered to himself as, upon sitting on a dressing-stool, his aid affixed the heavy, feathered helmet.

—As a reminder: The simple armor of Sir Peter, Sir John, and most of those closest to the river was by no means the only attire of the knightly class. Indeed, it seemed the greater the distance from the *life giver,* the more the additions.—

"What's that, Sir Perispao?" said the attendant, helping with the chin-strap.

"Nothing, my brother," said the elder, standing and swiveling to settle the plates into their final mold.

Just then another, *very disturbed* member of this community burst in. "Sir Perispao!" This fellow, a farmer, whose expansive holdings were south of town, had the look of sheer terror on his face.

"What, brother?" said the elder, ushering the troubled member to a chair. "The dragon?"

"Yes...I mean, no!"

The brief conversation which followed told of the horrible influence which emanated *from* the monster. This farmer…who never actually *saw* the beast…instead saw his crops wither and rot, his livestock sicken and, upon the horizon…a single, unbroken moving…as if some sort of ghastly horde of *things* were following in the dragon's wake.

"Go! Take the people straight to the river," said the knight to his assistant as he, with some difficulty, mounted a gold-colored palomino, named *Thorubazo,* (a horse used for travel, *not* battle) and, as the fuming, terrible head of the creature (having just loosed a blast which was evidenced by yellowish smoke freshly rising from its nostrils and—being dispersed back along the ridge of scales—it went up from the frightening face like the trails of a dozen incense candles) came into view, the courageous leader (as the mount was urged to a medium gallop) turned his head to the side and shouted, "Tell them to take nothing! Leave *all* possessions! Run to the river! To the river!"

There was a pause in the dying that day. An older knight…one who had been terribly distracted with all the details of his flock…too distracted to drink his fill from the river and to bask frequently in the presence of the compassionate king…this noble servant, for a two-hour span (enough time for many in his care to escape) shone the symbol of the king boldly in the demon's face. And, as he ran—with wearying legs—again and again to the creatures expanding breast, he could not (and before long, he knew it) significantly pierce the armor. Nevertheless, he persisted…and because of it…most of his own—those whom he tirelessly served…lived. But he, finally knocked down and broken by the tail, was last seen struggling to stand one more time (an arm and leg broken, the helmet dislodged, blood running down the brow), whereupon he was lifted high by the snake-like appendage and then slammed, unmercifully, upon the hardened earth. And, although knights are desirable feed for such as this creature, the dragon (stepping upon the corpse) traveled on, leaving the morsel for the irritating rabble that was swarming to its rear.

And this is how it went as those dwelling closer to the river became aware that there was *indeed* a danger. Many, in unbelief (and confident of their prowess) would take a stand and—regardless of tactic and configuration (though brave, noble, and *experienced* at killing Muths…and though they would sometimes combine their skills with *other* knights to lessen the burden)—these, every one, would ultimately be destroyed by the dragon's fire, or tooth, or tail and, for those who avoided the single-minded beast (thinking that *destruction* had only one means) these (again, regardless of ability) would be overwhelmed by the Chata and—if surviving till darkness—the flying fiends. And so…the great fear-driven migration began. And soon, possessions, places, positions and partitions were abandoned. "To the river! To the king!" was the universal cry. And, as the land adjacent the shimmering bead sighed from the great weight, nevertheless the dragon came, and as it came (the land burning in front and withering behind) it spoke.

> *From the center, rounding round*
> *Father, Mother, bring*
> *Then to Master, we present*
> *The perfect empty ring*
> *The perfect empty ring…*

* * *

"Have you seen my son, fool?"

The words, spoken coolly—as if enquiring of a misplaced sock—caught the Sower entirely off guard. One reason…the location. The winged demon, having just filled his sack with the spores of defilement, had only now emerged from the mountain chamber to take his place on the ledge before flight. But there, on the edge of the precipice, was another (so he thought) of his kind. But, when this intruder spoke, and the words were accompanied by the hideous glowing eyes…it was clear that this was no ordinary flying lizard, but rather another (for whatever reason) manifestation of the Lord of the Dragons.

"My lord!" the Sower gasped, prostrating himself quickly lest his flight to earth begin *too* soon.

"You won't be needing those, *idiot*." With the words a razor-sharp talon sliced through the leather belt and the heavy sack flattened against the rock…some of its contents spilling out.

"My lord?" whimpered the lower demon, hoping his neck was not the next target of the claw.

There was a clicking as bony points tapped the granite…the Dragon King walking away and towards the launching place (his massive membranous wings wafting in the gentle twilight breeze.) "There are none in the interior…are there?" he rasped, standing on the very edge.

"N-n-no, Master," stuttered the underling (chancing just a glance upward to see more). "All the humans are dead."

"And," the King spread wide his massive sails, the myriad of visible veins pulsing (in an off-crimson transparency, due to the waning sun) with fluid from its wretched heart, "none of the seeds survive near the river?"

"No, sire," said the Sower in a near whisper, "the barrier is as strong there as it's ever been…*stronger,*" now the flying one had drifted into boldness, "in fact, it is almost impossible to breach it even at our highest limit."

There was an unsettling pause just as darkness quickly blanketed the hated land as the remnants of the red sunset evaporated in the western sea. Then, suddenly, there was the stench of foul breath and the Sower immediately found himself flying (as in *thrown*) against the wall behind and, as he slid down (knowing, though in pain, that it was *not* meant to kill) he saw his master—with one taloned finger—pick up and toss the ancient bag over the edge and into the deep.

"Yesss," said the King, licking remnants of the spores off his appendage with his forked, black tongue. "It is a *final* defense. He knows I have him!" He clenched his claws into a tight fist. Then, turning towards the other—who was again wisely prostrate—he said, "What of the curtain? What of that accursed veil?"

"Sire," said the Sower, his eyes vigorously closed. "It is as you said…it is receding…it cannot withstand the press."

"Yess," hissed the ancient evil as he walked over to his servant and, with one clawed hand picked up the Sower and placed him on his taloned feet (his scaly knees knocking). "This is the night of our victory," he added, turning and walking again to the edge. "Tonight they will fight or flee…and both paths lead to victory." There was a slight pause as the dark lord seemed to be rummaging through his memories. "I've seen the mist before," he said with purpose as the horrible wings were stretched wide again. "It is always a temporary thing. He cannot sustain it…and tonight…my faithful fool," the Lord of the Dragons turned and appeared to be sporting (if possible) just the hint of a smile, "I need all of your kind unhindered. This is the night of reclamation. Now go!" The command was accentuated with a pointed head-gesture. "Summon your brothers. We descend at midnight…we will feed till dawn."

* * *

Sir John, having resigned himself to submit to death's coming blow (there was nothing more *he* could do), saw, through the eerie, gray, sulfurous mist (the sun had set hours before, though the stars and a nearly full moon lit the field) that the eyes of his foe were burning brighter with each successive draw (much like a coal in the blacksmith's hearth). It wouldn't be long now. A deafening noise...a crush of intense pain...and then death would come. But, it wasn't the thought of physical pain that weighed so heavily upon him. No...the pain that tore at him *now* was the thought that he had failed his beloved king...and that he had failed those in his care.

It was nearly time for the dagger's thrust. (The dragon was just to the point when its head would cock back and then loose the torrent.) Sir John, his mind now relaxed and free from the rigor of battle (when wits are at their sharpest) thought back, weeks before, to the moving of the mist. It was at that time, when the dragon made its final tack towards the rim (having just passed the castle's shadow in the west—the sight of which caused the monster's hatred to seethe), and, as its foul poisoning (the *rotting* which fanned out quickly in a wide swath behind and, not far behind this...*millions* of Chata) rushed towards the terrified inhabitants who chaotically gathered at the bank. It was then that the mist which *always* hovered over the middle of the Living River (which—as Fren had predicted—was now one continuous rush of power)...moved. In an instant...as the dragon destructively plodded ever closer and as its evil emissions consumed to within one kilometer of the river...it was then that the mist—as the people wept in despair—rushed *through* and past them and became a wall...a impassable wall that stopped the evil...a little under one thousand meters from the river.

As a result, the poison that crept along the ground, when it came to the veil, it violently became vaporized as if water thrown to a red-hot skillet. The Chata (not known for deep thought, but rich in guttural instincts) would—for a brief time (they were not *totally* ignorant) throw themselves lustfully at the white. These, too, would become as air, leaving no corpse or cry...but just a foul stench. Eventually the millions of fiends, as the dragon plodded its final circuit, would spread out all along the perimeter and, as there was just enough transparency in the veil to catch the sight of human flesh from time to time...these demons would constantly be at the point of frenzy, waiting to lunge...waiting to kill.

Sir John, as he saw the red orbs of his conqueror quickly become smaller (meaning the head was now at the point immediately before destruction's rush) and, as his mind seemed to distance itself from the weeping of his body...he, in this briefest of moments, encapsulated all the incredible events of the last days. For, as the fearful, and frightened, and hurried, and harried, and humbled subjects of the king abandoned their holdings to run to the river's edge (and it was the same *all* along the stream, not just in his quadrant), Sir John saw knights of every persuasion strip themselves of all their feathers and fancies, their habits and handicaps, their additions and add-ons, their clutter and control...and these...driven to the river's rest, would submerge themselves in its healing flow and, as their tears mingled with the divine...these would then purpose to visit the king. Thus...in the brief weeks prior to this event...there was a constant flow, a great habitation, a continual pilgrimage along the banks of the Living River...going into and out of the castle of the great king. And these thousands, who entered homogenous—indistinguishable from one another in their station or status—would exit with the glow of the royal presence upon their faces, and the knights...who were once singular and self-centered...these became collectively zealous as they hurried themselves in the honing of their skills and in the instruction of those in their charge.

But...and now the resigned and restful knight (his body numbing, but his mind still scrolling) could see—though the shadows dictated sight—the eyes of the dragon suddenly disappear (meaning the mouth was now open) *and* Sir John, unmoved by the imminent, then thought back to the press...the pushing back of the veil. It was (and he didn't understand why...and the king wouldn't reveal, in fact, when in the sovereign's presence—such was the atmosphere of peace—that the worried wondering *never* manifested itself), it was as if the great gathering of ghouls and the constant unholy wash emitted by the dragon caused, slowly, the veil to retreat before the onslaught. Thus, what was one kilometer, over a few weeks...became half...and then half again. And, though there was a continual renewal, and refining, and rejoicing in the king's presence and in the water's flow...the king *never* offered another solution save the one compassionately given to Sir Reginald, so long before. And now, at this culmination, at this ending, on this day when Sir John felt compelled (even as the thousands upon thousands of his brethren were pushed to the point where most were abiding in the river and the rest occupied that delicate sliver of bank where *no* evil—veil or not—could come) to make a stand. On *this* day, when—such was the retreat of the curtain—that even the blessed entrance to the bridge (which could now be seen protruding from the mist on the far western side of this once green field) would be (and was *now)* blocked. At *this* moment (even as a bright hellish light—in this millisecond of time—illumed the dragon's blood-stained mouth) the meaning of the horrid creature's boast became clear...for *all* the remaining humans—being spirits encased in flesh—and even though there had been a resounding rush to repentance, and a returning to the river, and to the king, and to the God of the Crystal Sea…still, these were servants who required simple sustenance. And *now*, as *all* farms, fields, fruits, and foliage (not to mention the animals used for food) were either destroyed or out of reach…it became abundantly clear that since the king's *champion* could *not* be found…*all* humans along the river would either starve or flee to the other side (where a literal army of demons stood ready) or try, in vain (as he had), to battle the dragon or the locust-like Chata. Thus…and a slight tear welled and rolled down from the outer corner of Sir John's left eye (even as he saw the great ball of licking blue and yellow flame, coming)…the blessed kingdom of *Ekklesia*—that which was born by the ultimate bloody sacrifice—would become…as all the children of the king died…*the perfect empty ring.*

Sir John was braced…kneeling erect, his hands (palms down) on the hilt of the king's sword, his head slightly bowed. He was weary, worn, his left arm bleeding and nearly broken (such was the force of the tail when it—through an exhaustion induced misstep on his part—ripped his shield from him). He had never lost his shield before (*meaning*…in battle. Once—a few winters past—his *son* had used it as a sledding device and its whereabouts—at a very inappropriate time—were unknown to the frantic guardian for over half a day), but…he had never battled a behemoth such as this. And, as the all-consuming onslaught neared (here…in this briefest of time-spans) and he sensed the fury of the flame, he recalled the compulsion, the absolute resolve (against the advice of many of his peers) that he must…must!…confront this destroyer. Many, as he had prepared to enter the veil, begged him to reconsider. "Perhaps the king himself will come," said some. Others whispered, "Who does he think he is…the *Champion*?" But he *had* to do battle…this was his call, and now, on the point of becoming dust…even now he did not regret it.

With his death only a breath away…he recalled the struggle. He remembered when he had exited the curtain (which, at the time, was white as a cumulus cloud…but now, hours later and in the night, it flickered with the radiance of the Crystal Sea) how he had stepped out into this field that lay adjacent the rugged bridge. Up until this day the people had streamed in and out of the castle over this blood-stained conduit but, with the protection of the mist diminishing…the flow had ceased. Thus, seeing *no* alternative and urged on by an overriding compulsion to give, *literally*, all…he exited the veil, shield and sword high, prepared to immediately step into the fray.

But, though around the confines of this gentle, clover-blessed (for some reason the *rotting* was not as effective here) arena a thousand Chata fidgeted (their fangs ever sharpening) and though, when they collectively saw this lone human step—as a fox upon the snare—into their overwhelming presence, it only took Sir John a moment to understand why they delayed for, on the far side (easternmost) of the field, the Crimson Dragon sat, placidly, yet its eyes pulsing with hate as it continually gazed upward at the great king's castle that towered just beyond the river...immoveable...ever breaching the horrible black Wall of Separation. Yes, as the knight saw the creature of his intent (it was huge!) he also saw, along the edge of the field (and a few literally *in*—and quite flat—such was their compression) that the dragon had set boundaries for these lesser demons by killing a fair number of them. Indeed, it was abundantly clear that they were to be spectators *only*...spectators of redeemed man's last gasp.

—Unbeknownst to those in the struggle...when the conflict between Sir John and the dragon began it was seen—through some strange refraction of light or (more likely) a divine intervention—played upon the river-side of the anointed veil. Thus, when the two battled...when man and monster met this last important and horrible time...*all* the humans—those in the river and those beside—saw it as if witnessing from the clover's edge.—

Sir John, no novice to the slaying of even the largest of dragons, used (even though this creature was twice what he had ever seen before) the same techniques taught to him so long ago. First, the testing of the fire and, as he had been told previously and was, this day, readily confirmed...this creature could send out a withering blast of flame a full one hundred meters! This meant, of course, the knight had to stand much closer than he would have preferred (in order to assault the monster between blasts)—and thus be subject to a much higher degree of hellish heat and pressure. Plus...there was the tail. Remembering that a normal Muth's tail was not nearly as long, and he had always been able to position himself just beyond its thrashing reach. This *thing,* however, was of a much greater length and, in order to do battle at all, the knight had to either duck, or jump, or roll, to avoid the whip-like recoil. And it was this action—after making minimal headway against the creature's scaly breast—that caught him off-guard. Yes, the tail, after several hours of missing, finally knocked Sir John violently down and, at the same time, it powerfully stripped the shield from his left arm.

And now...it was time to die. Sir John, eyes closed, head bowed, peacefully (though he tearfully acknowledged to himself that he, in his own strength, had failed, *nevertheless*...his foundational reliance upon the compassionate king gave him, even now...*peace*) awaited the blast of all-consuming fire that would rip his life from him. His ears—the only organ probing beyond his position—heard the horrific roar of the flame. Like an avalanche of hate it rushed to, and then strangely *around*, and over him. Yes, he felt the heat, like standing directly in front of a freshly opened and glowing red kiln, assault his exposed areas. But, in the brief timespan of the rush (approximately six seconds) his pain did *not* increase. However, without time for his weary mind to comprehend the event (his eyes were still closed), he suddenly felt an arm strongly push him (from the left side, both he and the sword) down to a prostrate position. A moment later he heard the scythe-like tail whistle past...mere inches from his skyward gaze. Then, turning his head forward again he saw...ALBERT! Who was lying beside his father (nearly nose to nose...and sporting an enormous crooked grin) and who had the knight's shield protectively atop them both.

The older man, still very much dazed, deliberately blinked several times (trying to erase this vision from his sight). However, the teenager, who then quickly stood and lifted (with very little effort) his *father* from the ashes (at the same time patting some of the residue off his guardian's armor) calmly remarked, "Father, it's past time for our tea. I thought it good if I come fetch you."

There was only time for one quick, joyful embrace (Sir John, tearfully smiling and, with his right hand—the left was limp and blood covered—jostling the youth's hair as if he were still a four-year-old) for the dragon, after the mist had cleared and the moonlight revealed there were now *two* humans to deal with, lifted its head skyward and let out a high-pitched hellish screech and then commenced, with thunderous steps, to charge the two insects that dared inconvenience it by living.

Albert, who now carried the shield, followed directly behind Sir John as the elder easily evaded the moving mountain. The teenager, always inquisitive, yet truly unafraid as he joined his will with his father's (he had, in a sense, sacrificed his life before entering the veil) asked questions as they ran.

"Father?"

"Yes"

"Why is this field surrounded by all those red lights?" The Chata (mentioned earlier) like all dragons, emit a reddish glow from the eyes at night.

"Tiny dragons."

"Excuse me?"

"*Tiny dragons!* Remember, *Sir Nabal* mentioned them?"

"Oh, yes. (a ten-second pause) That was quite a story he told, wasn't it?"

"Yes...quite a story (beginning to puff slightly as they weaved away from the fuming volcano). Are you staying close behind me?"

"Yes, Father. (another slight pause with only the distant sound of the Chatas' teeth and the thumping of the dragon's pillar-like legs) Father?"

"Yes, Albert...what is it?"

"How long do we dance like this?"

"Until it stops for a moment...then we show it the king's emblem once more. Hopefully then it will send the fire."

"I see." (For another ten seconds the sound of two sets of feet—one light, another labored—on brittle remnants of clover.) "Father...so tell me...how goes the battle?"

Sir John, smiling slightly (although unseen by the youth as he was still running in front of the farm-boy) replied, with a bit of playful sarcasm in his voice, "How does it *look* like it's going?"

"Well," said Albert—who had begun running *backwards* (such was his vigor) along his elder's left side. "It looks like your arm is a bit banged up...but I'm sure some of Mary's porridge and a day or two of rest will fix you up."

"Get *back*," said John along with a punctuated head-nod, "if you don't pay close attention, our *next* meal will be at the king's table."

After a few more seconds had passed—as they made a wide arc around the still plodding beast—Sir John heard the voice again, "Father?"

"*Yes.*"

"Seriously...how goes the battle?"

"Wait!" Sir John, suddenly aware that the beast had stopped, turned to face his son and then, with his right hand (the sword was sheathed) spun Albert to face the dragon. "The shield, son! Raise high the shield!" For a moment the dragon, whose eyes were captured by the sight of the crimson emblem...roared as if in pain. "To answer your question," Sir John spoke, his mouth near his son's right ear, "I've carved through more than enough armor to reveal an ordinary Muth's heart. But this thing," the dragon ceased its venting and began to become rigid, "this thing," he continued, "is like none I've ever encountered. Now listen," his voice took on a battle-tested urgency, "when the creature begins to stoke its fire I will run up to it and strike.

274

You...ARE YOU LISTENING?" Sir John had noticed a glazed look of distracting fear awash his son's face.

"I'm listening," said Albert with a nod.

"You must come with me half way. I will not be able to retreat beyond the flame. You must hold the shield and protect us both." John, tenderly pulled Albert's chin so they were face to face. "Do you understand, son?"

"Yes," the calm look in his father's eyes reached out and touched his own. "Yes, Father, I understand."

As the two warriors stood poised for movement (Albert holding high the shield and Sir John, just to his right, with sword in hand), they at last recognized that the dragon was preparing to loose the fire.

—During daylight hours the creature's overall visage (and, for that matter, *any* Muth's) clearly gave evidence of the fire-building, but at night, it was the resounding clacking of the inner valve that was the surest sign.—

"Run with me!" shouted Sir John as he lit out toward, what appeared, a fool's sure demise. He—his son in tow—was a few steps ahead, when, approximately halfway to the beast, he shouted back, "Here (pointing with the sword—without looking back—towards the earth), stop here!"

Albert—his light expressions now absent (along with some of his sense)—went *further* than his father directed. So that—after striking the plates with three swift strokes (little damage)—when the elder returned and crouched behind his son, it took a few moments more to realize the error. Just before the next expected onslaught, John (feeling something wasn't quite right) gazed around the right side of the shield to estimate the dragon's nearness. "Albert!" he screamed. "We're too close!"

But it was too late. The blast, like all the others, came like a powerful rushing geyser and, even as the elder quickly positioned himself behind his bracing son, and as the first initial onslaught hit like a sledgehammer, he truly thought that they would be bowled over and, if not killed outright...then surely injured beyond repair. However, after the time of flame expired, the two were still there...apparently unscathed! Albert, whose youth and strength had not been previously tested, now—in a discovery made quite by accident—afforded the knight additional time (since they could regroup at a closer vantage) to hack away towards the demon's heart and—as Sir John said nothing, but merely smiled as he raced again to attack—he had not noticed that his son (not proficient with the shield, plus his girth was greater than that of his father's) had left himself, when the fire came, slightly exposed. Albert's left foot was now badly burned (the pain excruciating)…but he would not tell of it. Nor…in the hour to come (as blast after blast was endured and, *every time* the fire came…the boy suffered harm) would he speak of his other injuries. He had determined, as he saw his beloved father hobble off (blood streaming from his wounds) to fight again and again, that he would—at *all* costs—protect this king's knight. And if it meant dying in the effort, "Then," thought the youth as he put his aching shoulder against the shield, "so be it."

The nearly full moon slowly crept towards its zenith and the stars—like hundreds of distant oil-lamps with the wicks freshly trimmed—gave this desperate night a brightness not often seen this time of year. The warriors—two humans, and a dragon of joint heritage (earth *and* hell)—continued to exchange blows…and one side, as midnight approached, seemed decidedly weaker.

"Father," said Albert as the elder hobbled back to the protection of the shield, "surely you're close to the heart by now?" The words, reflecting weariness and worry for his parent, were not answered immediately for, as soon as Sir John had positioned himself (crouching behind the youth) another withering blast engulfed the duo and, while the knight gathered strength for another run, his son was using *all* of his to withstand the force. And, since this particular episode was lengthy (meaning: many blasts without chase), the boy's left arm and shoulder were being severely burned as the shield (which could withstand only so much) did not have enough time to dissipate the cumulative heat.

Fortunately, *this* time (although it meant no progress could be made with the sword), when the fire was ended and the tail again missed its mark…the creature charged them once again and, as the two hobbled just ahead of the monster, Sir John finally answered his son…their conversation accentuated by gasps for breath (as both were near collapse).

"Albert…I've sliced and struck through nearly a meter of armor."

"How much further can it be, father?"

"I…don't know, son. Follow me!"

"I'm sorry…I'm so tired."

"As am I. (a five second pause) I'm sorry, son."

"W-why, Father? Why are you sorry?"

"Because I should have known." The two circled left as the dragon began to slow down.

"Known what?"

"That with a creature this large I should have cut a wider swath."

"What do you mean?"

"I mean I have to keep backtracking to compensate. I'm sure if I had been thinking I would be through by now. Wait! It's stopped! Raise the shield!"

As the midnight hour struck, a great armada of flying dragons launched from the cliffs of the accursed mountain. This time the barrier over the river seemed weaker (perhaps due to the despair which accompanied the revelation of the war) and the many traversed it easily. On, far ahead, near the western wall and the horrid breach, the eyes (especially those of the lead demon) could see the flashes of the conflict. It was here that *he* would go, and the others? Their directive was to spread to all quadrants by the river and, as the mist was beaten back (as it surely would be this night!) these winged devils would aid in administering the long-due human slaughter. Yes, this night belonged to the dragons. And the day?…well…the day belonged to the dead.

Five more blasts and when Sir John barely returned to the very small zone of safety, he saw, as the fire yet blazed around them again, that his son's body was quaking violently (though *still* holding the shield). This time, instead of running to the fray (even as the valve tolled in the background) the elder gently turned his son into the brightest light. There, he saw the black streaks on his child's face left by an hour of tears, when the pain inflicted was too great. And, upon closer examination, he also discovered that the injuries of his brave son would have no remedy…save the touch of the king.

"Father," Albert said meekly, seeing the tears caused by a father's tortured heart, "I have to brace myself…it's almost time."

Sir John, who was too weak to help, crouched behind the teenager as he withstood, *yet* again, another fiery blast. It became clear, however, that for this spent shepherd (as his body began to shut down)…that attacking once more was out of the question and, as Albert slumped to earth (and his father along with him—the tail bounding high above) that there would not be another defense, as well.

Suddenly, as the dragon began to prepare itself yet again (perhaps sensing the sweet end of its labor), there was the sound—behind them!—like an explosion, a cracking of a glacier, or a violent tearing—as when a mighty oak is cleaved by the lightning strike. The two brothers, nearly dead, turned their gaze away from the dragon's eyes and there, fifty meters arrear…was a massive boulder which had a sizeable cleft (enough for one man to enter, and a depth unknown) which *must* have been caused by the extreme heat of the fire.

"Albert, come on!" Sir John tugged at his greatly injured child. "Come on, let's run to the rock. Perhaps we can find safety there…at least for a few minutes."

And, as they reached (nearly crawling the last few meters) and squeezed themselves into the gap (wedging the shield in the opening as they, without holding it, crouched behind) the fire, without effect, glanced off the shield and the stone which was now the holder

The dragon, expecting to see smoldering flesh, now (when the smoke had cleared) saw a great rock of unknown origin and, upon closer examination…it perceived there was a small fissure, and in this crack was the accursed sign of its enemy! The monster, enraged that his victory had again been delayed, rushed upon this defiant object determined to—if it could—somehow claw the human vermin from their little hole. But, try as this behemoth might, it could not—either with talon, tooth, *or* tail—penetrate the tiny enclosure and so, backing up for maximum spread, it determined to turn the stone into a glowing coal. "Either they will flee the heat," it thought, "or they will cook." And so, the fire was loosed…again, and again, and again.

"Father," said the son as he and his elder tried to *not* touch the sides of their little cave as the walls became hotter and hotter, "what shall we do?"

Sir John, nearly unconscious due to loss of blood, smiled weakly at his child as the quivering flames illumed the young man's face and replied, "I…don't know, son." And then, touching gently the cheek of the one adopted years before, "I truly wish we had time for that tea. I've so enjoyed those times together."

Albert returned the smile, his injuries also removing most of his strength and, as they were at the point of defeat…at the point of succumbing to a restful release…they heard it. Muffled and distorted slightly by their vantage in the rock…it was as if an angel had alighted and pierced the veil of darkness with a radiant beam of sun. And the words…they were words of a song that spoke of victory…words of a battle fought and lost…a battle where winning was birthed from what appeared…the greatest defeat.

"It's Mary!" shouted Albert. "Mary is singing!"

…Once upon a dark and fearful time,

The dragon, who *had* been drooling, preparing to pluck the shield from its place (previous attempts were met by the tip of a sword), recoiled backwards as the sounds of heaven repelled his hearing of hell.

...Imprisoned by the wall of our design.

The massive creature, forgetting, for the time being, the two that *had* been its desire, scanned beyond the rock to try and find the source.

...Traitors to our God, so good and kind...worthy of tears.

"There she is," scowled the eater, "behind this accursed rock." And, with the seeing came a slow deliberate walk to attain. However, as the dragon sought to coordinate his movements to vanquish this most frail opponent...he found her lifting of the king as a piecing dart...a most painful distraction that kept his strength and motion limited. "She must die!" were the demon's thoughts. "Of the three...this one...*this one* must be sure to die!"

Mary, shaking with fear (yet resolute to help those she loved more than life) paralleled the hideous beast as it stalked her around the rock. Gray of head and feeble in body, as she struggled to keep the boulder between she and the beast, thoughts of dragons past and her former life of terror and bondage began to well up from a forgotten place in her soul. But, as she rounded to the eastern side of the stone...she saw the shield...and from behind it came voices...voices that were music to *her* ears.

"Mary! Come here!" Sir John removed the shield and waved her into their tiny spot of safety (which, strangely, now had room for three). She, weeping with joy, rushed to enter and—seeing with only the faintest of lights—these dear ones, she hugged and kissed each but...as her wise embrace revealed their condition...she stepped back and began to weep for another reason.

The dragon, his senses sharpening (as the song had ceased) deliberately took position facing the three. As he had begun (before this last interruption) he would do again. The fire would be sent until the three were dead.

"Mary! Mary!" Sir John gently shook his mother's shoulder with his right hand as she knelt next to the wall, weeping in great mournful sobs. "Mary...there is still hope. You have to sing!"

The matron, who combined sorrows past with sorrows present, continued to cry. John, seeing her like this, remembered their first time of introduction. *He* was the teenager then, and she...she was in the same position he found her now. However, there was a difference...and he had to, somehow, make it clear. "Mary," he knelt beside her and spoke gently into her left ear. "Mary...there *is* hope. But *you* have to do something. You have to sing. When you sing it hurts that thing. Your words injure it. I *need* you to slow it down. Mary...Mary...if *you* fight...we can still win."

The old woman never thought of herself as a fighter. *Always* defenseless. *Always* in need. But, as she uncovered her eyes and saw the faint smiles of the men...she (with John's tender help) stood, brushed off her dress, walked to the entrance and, standing behind the shield, continued the story set to song.

The dragon was halfway through its hellish preparation—the fire building, the breast swelling, the eyes blazing—when the first notes of the second wave hit.

> *Crying out for hope...deserving none.*
> *Reaping what we'd sown...what we had done.*

And these words...weapons that struck into the very soul of the creature...these acted as a dragging weight, an anchor, a scattering prism, and, where before the creature could quickly rush to the point of explosion, now its journey could be compared to a heavily loaded and speeding wagon entering a *deeply* flooded road. The song...this sweet melody sung by an *old lady* that lifted high the work of the great king...hindered the process *so much*, that though the monster was still able to surge to eruption...the building to the blaze took over *twice as long*!

> *Is there none to help...not even one?*
> *O, save us from tears.*

Sir John, who stood directly behind Mary as she fought, gently (but surely) pulled her back and down behind the shield as the fire was eventually loosed. And this, being her first experience with the flame, she—as the fire roared and licked all around them—screamed—holding her hands over her ears. But, as it ceased, the knight quickly stood (his strength somewhat renewed) and nodding to Albert (who was pressed against the wall—half reclined—his legs nearly useless) the youth, with one hand, pulled the shield from its station and Sir John hobbled towards the dragon, sword drawn, and, as Mary's eyes widened in fear and unbelief (why would he go!?) her other child firmly, but respectfully, spoke.

"Mary...Mary!...you *have* to sing! Sir John is weak, but if you sing he will have time to fight. Sing, Mother! Sing NOW!"

There was only the slightest of hesitations as the matron understood what her men were saying. And, as the dragon's rage built and the figure of the wounded knight diminished, she quickly stood and sang again.

> *Then, beyond the wall...you heard our call...with your love.*
> *And, you sent your son...your only one...you gave your all.*

In the blurry distance (the knight, now in the shadow of the quaking beast and thus, could not be clearly seen) the slow clapping of the valve was suddenly overpowered by the sound of steel violently striking against scale. One...two...three...four...five! times it struck and then Sir John could be seen returning through the mist, bowed somewhat and shuffling in small awkward steps—using the sword as a cane.

Mary, just prior to the dragon's head jerking forward, went out and pulled her son to safety (Albert, again with one hand, quickly replacing the shield just before the rush of fire.) This time, however, as the flame illumed the crevice...Mary saw John (whom she held by the arm) turn his head and, between great heaving breaths, he smiled broadly. And, though the roar of the fire made speech impossible...the expressions on each of the three faces communicated precisely what had to be done.

And thus, the three fought as one. Mary, suppressing her fears, would stand and sing of the king she loved. John, bleeding, broken (the tail had done as much internal damage as outward), would follow behind the triumphant anthem and, as the anointed words slowed the assault of the enraged demon, the knight would strike, again and again and again, at the deepening gash that neared (he hoped!) the point of final penetration. And Albert, badly burned...*he* was the keeper of the gate...the shield and, as his charred members cracked, bled, and stiffened...he still could quickly remove, and put in place, the saving barrier that bore the king's emblem. And, as the morning crept into the darkest portion of the night...as the luminescent veil which held back the frenzied hordes of Chata slowly submitted to their press...as the thousands upon thousands of the king's faithful retreated and coalesced in the river and on its delicate edge (seeing the battle as if in person...which, at this point, mixed hope with despair) there came a revelation after Sir John's last slow return, that caused a cheer to erupt from the two he told…and the multitude that he could not see.

"Mary! Albert!" Sir John was beside himself (so much so that he let a full cycle of flame build *and* come so that he could speak). "I can see the *glowing*!"

Albert, who had been taught of such things, smiled weakly (such was his pain) but his eyes brightened with the news. Mary, who *always* left the room when talk of fighting dragons occurred (as was not uncommon when warriors gathered) had a puzzled expression upon her face.

"Mary," Sir John gently grabbed her left shoulder as he came very near to speak. "It means I can see the glowing from the demon's heart. It means I am very near the place where, if I can but pierce the two chambers, the fluid and the flame will mix and that thing will *die*!"

At the words, Mary…weak, filthy, some of her hair singed away…as the words brought understanding her expression became firm, resolute, triumphant. And, if Sir John had not restrained her…she would have stood up right then (just as another blast came) to continue her part. But, as the flame roared overhead (and in a very small portion around the sides of the shield) the matron looked surely into the eyes of her protector. She knew what she had to do and, like her two preparing partners…she was ready to do it.

And, as quickly as it came, the fire ceased. Without prompting, Mary stood, took a deep breath and, as the first muffled hammer of the valve began (the sound, like a very heavy cloth-covered board struck against a large stone—even louder now, due to the removal of so much shielding) Mary, with all her being…sang.

Then for us a king became a slave.

Sir John hurried toward the quivering shadow, now seeing three red beacons…the eyes (which were *very* bright) and the dull pulsing light from the rendered breast.

Bearing our just due…His life He gave.

As the warrior neared the familiar spot (so much time had he spent there) he was oblivious to the huge pillar-like forelegs on either side which gripped, so tightly, the charred earth below and—quickly bracing his weary legs, the knight—without thought, raised the king's sword to strike…also ignoring the almost deafening thunder of the valve within and the tornadic sound of air being sucked in to aid the hellish combustion, above.

Dying for our sin, our souls to save! Worthy of Praise!

One! Two! Three! Four! Five!...with greater strength and precision (not known, due to weakness and injury, since the beginning of the fight) the human warrior carefully chipped away at the armor which still covered the raging inner chambers. The *glowing,* when uncovered while opposing *normal* Muths, was a sure indication that the most vulnerable covering was near (a thick, leather-like skin). This, once found, was easily pierced with an anointed sword but, as the knight delivered blow upon blow (the chips of the dragon scale darting sharply and cutting into his face even as the mountainous creature seemed to involuntarily quake with each delivery) and he, excited that *this* could be the finish (finally!) of this deadly contest, Sir John, sadly, found that this, again, was no ordinary Muth. And, as he forced himself to turn—for his own preservation—towards his waiting family (and he, without resolution) he...along with the burden of pain, and the shadow of death...he also carried the news that this last layer of defense would take even *more* time to breach, and time...for the wounded and weary...was in very short supply, indeed.

Nevertheless, the three continued (what else *could* they do?). However, such was Sir John's deteriorating condition (and Albert was no better) that the knight began to attack every *other* cycle of the flame and, as the night crept slowly on, the rock that protected them became hotter, and its restraining sides (that which held the shield)...became more brittle and, as the brave elderly woman saw, bit by bit, the strength of her once robust men...wane, she realized that it was now up to her—she, the *keeper of the kitchen*—it was up to her to be the encourager.

"Sir John!" she yelled as the warrior's expression took on that of a drunken man about to submit to delirium's sleep. "After this next fire...you must go!" She shook his shoulder as the clapping of the valve neared culmination. His eyes seemed to brighten (just a little) and he weakly smiled indicating that he understood. Just before the rush of flame she directed her biting words towards her *other* son. (How many times had they heard this tone before?) "Albert! Albert! Wake up! I need you to be ready with the shield!" The teenager...in great pain...desiring the end—opened his eyes and turned his head towards the source of the rude intrusion. Then squinting (as he used to do after peering out from under a comfortable blanket) he smiled broadly…indicating that he, too, was ready.

The fire, no less intense (*How much hellish fuel does this thing contain?*), burned hungrily above them, then, as it ceased and the next beat of the valve began, Mary shouted, "GO!" At this Albert quickly removed the shield and Sir John slowly staggered out, sword drawn.

> *Then when blood was spent, the wall was rent…our debt paid!*
> *You received our pain, our filth and shame…only you!*

Mary sang as loud as she could. The words…which vexed greatly the demon (not to mention the smaller versions in audience) seemed to carry otherworldly strength and she…as she desperately looked into the blurry shadows…this gentle woman hoped that this was enough to aid Sir John and that perhaps, *perhaps*, this would be the last time that he would have to venture out.

"There he is!" she thought to herself (not pausing the song) as he hobbled from the mist. Then, after the three had endured *another* onslaught and waited for the bursting of the next (so that the knight could rest) Mary and Albert heard the words that they had sought for hours.

Sir John, breathing heavily, yet his voice alive with anticipation (even as the valve hammered in the background) said, "I've reached it…on the very last strike…I've reached it!"

"The last layer?" Albert said weakly.

"Yes!" said the knight who reached out to touch his son's soot-covered cheek. "Yes," he said tenderly, turning to Mary (also cupping the left side of her face as fresh tears welled and flowed). "One more verse, dear lady," he said. "The opening is very small…but, with God's help, I believe one more verse will buy me enough time to destroy that demon."

WHOOSH! The fire rushed over them like a huge wave over pebbles on the beach. But, as it quickly abated (the stone—now oppressively hot—and the sides that secured the shield—crumbling still) and as they prepared for the next signal to advance…not only did the resonating thud of the valve *not* immediately sound…but there was suddenly an unseen presence (perceived by a cringing of the redeemed spirit) of something very evil…and something very old.

Mary, who stood behind the shield awaiting the cadence that prompted her to sing…she was the first to see something different in the distance. "Sir John, look at the dragon," she half whispered. And, as the crippled warrior stood beside his mother and looked towards the east, he saw the head of the monster convulsing…as if wrestling with an unknown force. Finally, after another half minute the thrashing ceased and the eyes of the demon (already bright) became as beacons from hell itself and, though they were obscured from its view due to distance and darkness…the creature seemed to look right into their *very* souls…and then it spoke.

"*Mary! Mary! It's me, Allen! Mary, come and see me. I'm alive…come here…come to meet me. O, how I've missed you.*"

Mary, who—only a moment before was rigid in her defiance and determination, now—upon hearing the voice of her long-dead brother (but maybe he wasn't dead!) she then began to breath in shallow irregular breaths as something deep and dark within was made alive by the counterfeit words.

"*Mary, help me! You can help me! Come to see me. You shouldn't have left me alone that night, Mary.*"

Now (and Sir John and Albert could see it) it became abundantly clear that if this attack of lies was not restrained…there would not be another covering verse and, as Mary wilted to earth and began to weep, the two men could distinctly hear—in the distance—the sound of the demon's hellish valve as the fire was again being enraged to the point of explosion.

"*Mary,*" Sir John sat down beside her and put his right arm around her quaking shoulders as she sobbed. "Mary, that thing is a *liar,*" he spoke gently into her ear. Just then the flame rushed upon them and as it did she screamed a muffled scream into her ragged dress.

As the dragon continued for another blast (as the cleft where they hid became more and more oven-like) the warrior spoke again. "Mary…this is the same tactic the dragons used against you years ago. Do you remember?" She lifted her head slowly and barely nodded. "They took Allen from you once, and now they want to use his memory against you. Don't let them, Mary. We need you to sing. We *all* need you to sing!"

Another wall of flame rushed to, and over the trio. Mary's expression, however (as the fire ceased and the hammering of the valve began anew) revealed that there was an overcoming strength in her that must have come from a higher place and, as the force of the next avalanche of flame caused the anchoring points on the walls to give way (lasting just long enough for the shield to withstand this last onslaught…and then it fell—emblem side down) she stood, understanding that this was their last chance. And, waiting a teary moment (as Sir John prepared to venture out and Albert struggled to remove the shield altogether (there would be no one able to hold it next time) to hear if the monster would begin to stoke the fire once more, she said to herself between sniffles… "I wish Sir Peter was here."

There was only a moment's pause when, from the inky black that now concealed the beast…a low cavernous voice slithered. *"Peter? Did you say, Peter?"* The three in the enclosure looked at one another in puzzlement. Then the dragon continued twistedly on.

"I know Peter. He's DEAD! He died a coward's death and even now his decaying parts are within me!"

Mary, *knowing* that this thing was a liar, nevertheless pressed her hands over her ears even as she was still resolved to sing when the clapping began. However, what the dragon said next reduced her—even though she had a palm of flesh over each ear—to a quivering ball of fears and tears on the crevice floor. For, in the perfect imitation of the grizzled knight's voice the deceiver said, *"Mary, I never loved you! I felt sorry for you! I had to get away from you. You drove me to my death! You killed me, Mary! You killed me!"*

Then, in the distance, as all hope vanished…H-U-U-C-C-C…

Chapter XXV

No greater love
No nobler deed
Than to give one's life
And for others...bleed.

"Excuse me, Sir Peter...I...er...mean, *Peter?*"

The old warrior smiled slightly as he stirred (in a lazy figure-eight pattern) the dying embers of the once robust fire that had become—over the long, cold night—just a non-threatening mound of warming coals. "Rather like myself," he had mused out loud a moment before and the young man, Nicholas, who had—from their first meeting, weeks before—been drawn to the old teacher like an only child to a dear uncle...heard it.

"Oh, nothing, Nicholas...nothing."

"Please...call me, *Nick.*"

Sir Peter turned his head and smiled at the gangly, crimson haired youth (at the same time gently tossing the speckled birch branch he had been using to stir into the emaciated blaze) who was sporting a wide-toothed grin and a mischievous twinkle in his eye that the old knight had seen many, many, times before from other dear ones...both past and present.

The elder—having slowly stood and arching backward (hands on hips) to stretch his tired frame—then put his burly right hand on the shoulder of the barely-twenty-year-old—who was among the few that had answered the king's call to go on this mission—and said, "Well, *Nick,* let's awaken our brothers and prepare. Today, in the king's name and strength, we will set free the captives…and by God's grace…his light will shine in this very dark place."

The youth, who had been hungering for a leader of this stature, looked up with resolve and nodded sharply at the command and, after a few minutes of nudges, jostles, and, *It's time to get up*s…the gathering of twenty (that's all who could be gleaned from the thousands of requests) were soon busying themselves in preparation…preparation to dispel and destroy a horrible practice…a practice that grieved the heart of their beloved king.

—At the time of this account it had been several weeks since the farewell of Sir Peter and those of his heart. He had, for whatever reason, been given a commission by his Lord and, though it was obviously not important enough for many of his fellows (they ignored it)…he felt honored, *and* humbled that he would be chosen to serve at such a great age.—

The initial meeting of the like-hearted (on the kingdom side of the river, parallel to the land of their destination) was a bit awkward. First of all, there was *not one* other knight among the willing and, since those gathered were prone to simple zeal (and thus *knew* of the substantive service of the often-maligned redhead [now gray]) it was all he could do to get them to drop the title and homage and understand (although they instinctively knew it) that they were a team…a unit…a body to be used for the king's pleasure.

Second, there was need of training. Since those who traditionally wield the sword were not to be inconvenienced, others of different callings had to be quickly equipped. Unfortunately, the old warrior only had time to teach the fundamentals (such was the urgency) but, observing the selflessness of these *less noble*…he soon found an even greater appreciation for *all* of the king's subjects…an appreciation which added substantially to the measure he *already* had…a measure that was quite unheard of in those called *knights*.

At the time of the above conversation the expedition had already been several days into the territory of the deceiver. Ironically, this wicked place had been, at one time, a land once greatly influenced by the king's ways. It had been a country oft traveled by the knights and, indeed, the hollowed out sanctuary where the cold night was spent…had been an outpost…a well-spring…a place of refuge and refreshment. However, with the passing of time, (O, the predictable pattern!) the temporal was magnified and the eternal trivialized and now…a once blessed land (like so many before it)…had slipped into gross error. However, though civilizations and nations are wont to slowly slide from any height attained in the area of righteousness (some quicker than others)...the heinous practice to which *these* volunteers were desperately sent...was a vile deception initiated *not* by the general consensus of a degraded population, but rather this *evil* was birthed in the minds of a few of the willing *elite* inspired by the tongues of the Ganab who had readily nested in their midst. These demons—crafty creatures that they were— understood that *words* hold the power. And, when definitions are changed...so, too, are the results. And the results of this *change*...to the tune of millions, upon million, upon millions...was blood.

"Do you hear that, Nicholas?" Sir Peter, who fell naturally into the role of mentor, had the small band stop and, for a brief minute, be very quite. The young attendant (that's what he considered himself) along with the others, slowly turned their heads from side to side trying to discern a sound that their leader so readily acknowledged. Finally, after a minute of quieting the brain and the brawn...a most disturbing, heart-troubling wail could be heard coming from the northeast direction.

"This way, gentlemen," said the old warrior as he pointed with the sword in his right hand and waved ahead with the shield-bearing left. The others, also bearing weaponry and armor of a lesser degree, fell in behind as they seemed to be going from a densely wooded area and entering a more barren landscape. (Truthfully, it had the appearance of once being fertile farmland...but, for some reason, it had become a desert...devoid of all life.)

"Peter," said Nicholas as he sprinted a bit to get alongside the bristling knight. (It seemed the closer this band came to their ultimate destination the more robust and ready was the elder.)

"Yes, my young Nicholas," said the warrior who, though his sights were fixed beyond the horizon (the band had now left the wood and fanned out in a V pattern behind the knight), he still could have a little fun with this apprentice.

"Nick."

"Yes...*Nick.*"

"Why is it that we could not hear the sound as you did at first?"

Sir Peter quickly scanned a 180-degree swath and, noticing that the lifeless soil was rife with Ganab tracks and droppings...he yelled back, "Be alert! There are many dragons ahead! Mostly Ganab...remember what I've taught you!" Then, turning to look at the laboring youth (due to a shorter gait compared to Sir Peter's substantial stride) on his left, "What did you say, *Nick?*"

"Sir Peter, (the elder noticed that the expression on the younger's face was quite sincere and as such…there would be no more teasing today) why could *I* not hear the sound as you did at first?"

"Because, my young seeker of truth (O, the memories this conversation invoked!), in order to hear the beating of the heart…you must place your ear very near the breast."

The two walked on (getting closer to a gentle rise which, when peaked, would no doubt give view of their ultimate destination) and, seeing that the question on Nick's face was still there…Sir Peter gave the verse…*That his concerns might be your own…spend time with him…and him alone.*

This seemed to shed *some* light and, as the younger's eyes brightened and the elder's watered (just a bit), Sir Peter…without word…turned and signaled (crouching, slowly pushing his hands toward the earth) to the others that they would *not* be charging over this rise…but rather, they would lie down at the crest for a few moments…and observe.

"What are they *doing*?" whispered one of the few on Sir Peter's right as all of this small expedition lay, belly-down (so as not to be seen) and peered towards a distant focal point that was alive with dragon *and* human activity.

"They're slaughtering the innocent," said the elder, coolly (though his inner emotion was anything but). "They are murdering their own in order to feed the dragons."

—Perhaps three hundred meters from these volunteers was an unbelievable sight. There was a small hill…a mound perhaps two meters high, the summit of which covering an area of no more than one hundred square meters. This curiosity was surrounded by a simple chain fence. Atop this rise (which was relatively flat) there could be seen in the center— hovering over what appeared as a butchering stone—a human dressed in azure garb…the same attire, incidentally, which mirrored that of healers…physicians. However, *this* creature's actions proved that *healing* was not his intent for—to the horror and disgust of the observers—a multitude of small, defenseless children were brought, one by one, by their mothers (each adult being charged for the service and each one accompanied by her own personal demon) and then these poor, defenseless, innocent souls were placed trustingly upon the flat stone, whereupon this *doctor* (whose name was *Prodotes*) would then proceed (in machine-like fashion) to heartlessly slaughter the helpless infants and, as the attending Ganab would screech in delight (and other human attendants greedily divvied up the spoil) the woman (none the better) would then be cast aside…she to live out her days with nothing more than the promise of a lifetime of torment and regret...and thus becoming a constant source of nourishment to those whose birth was from Hell.—

As Sir Peter described in detail what was taking place (and *had* been taking place for years) in front of them, the color seemed to drain from his young friend's face. "How...how can they *do* that!" he stammered as small streams descended from his eyes to drip off his chin below.

Sir Peter patted the young man's back (the youth's face now on crossed arms as he gently convulsed with grief). "It's deception of the vilest kind," he said and, as Nicholas looked up again to view the carnage, Peter also turned his gaze forward and continued, "Through the lie of the enemy the women are convinced that their children do *not* exist...but," he paused a moment, "their hearts tell them otherwise. Eventually...their hearts tell them otherwise."

"Sir Peter," said a voice just to the left of Nicholas, "who are those *other* humans gathered at the gate. Are they *knights*?"

The elder squinted to make out more clearly the colorful and shiny gathering of dignitaries that appeared to be aiding in the task of ushering the deceived into the demon's den. "Yes," he said, his voice bathed in contempt, "they *are* knights...*false knights!*" Sir Peter spat forward as if even the mention of the imposters defiled his lips. "They are the most loathsome of the creatures below," he continued. "Pretending to be about the king's business...they, *in fact,* work for the *other* king and, though they mimic true knights in their appearance and mannerisms...their deeds betray them as deceivers, charlatans, totally devoid of the spirit."

For another silent minute the gathering looked on as the long line of women and children (again, each accompanied by a drooling dragon) slowly marched to their doom. Then, from a place *behind* the mound could be heard the thundering steps that could only mean one thing...a *Muth.*

Soon, lumbering around the far end of the slaughtering place, a huge ashen-brown Muth (obviously very old) named *Shachat* positioned itself (as if it knew!) between the foreigners...and their goal.

As the gathering from the true kingdom watched the hellish mountain plant itself in one spot (fuming and snorting and screeching—as if boasting of its own power [the Ganab, who hissed nearby, couldn't care less and were, in fact, quite willing to berate the behemoth behind its back]), the elder turned his expression towards his newest student and asked, "Nicholas...what is your ambition?"

"*Sir*?" said the youth, a bit surprised at this detour of focus.

"What is your ambition, son? What is it you wish to become?"

"Why, I...I wish to become a knight," he said quietly.

"Why?" asked the elder, tenderly.

"Because," and with the words there was a fragility in his voice that seemed to be asking approval from the beloved warrior, "because knights are the ones who do the most for the king."

"Nick," said the elder as he looked with a father's care into the younger's eyes, "it is *God* who determines worth...not man. Seek the path *he* has for you...this will be of the greatest use for his kingdom." Then, speaking slowly, he accentuated one last rhyme, "...*for loving service of the king...find first the way where* your *heart sings.*"

Then, standing, he shouted to the rest... "Remember what I told you," and, at that, he quickly made his way down, not *only* into the sight of the huge Muth, but also into the clear view of *all* the other demons that cared to look. (Most, however, were so busy in their lustful pursuits, they did not pay heed...or...perhaps such was their confidence in the unbeaten giant that an approaching *old* knight seemed inconsequential.)

What then ensued was a classic battle between a true king's knight and the armored giant dragon known as a Muth. There was the *Testing of the Fire*, and then, after the monster's weaponry had been coaxed to exhibition, Sir Peter (his age not appearing to be a factor at all) made charge upon charge and, as the behemoth fumed and screeched and thrashed about as the emblem of the king was forever in its face, the knight, like the mongoose and the snake, always knew when to strike and when to retreat. Meanwhile, as the battle raged on past the hour mark, the Ganab which swarmed nearby (as the slaughter of the innocent went on unabated) began to show signs of agitation and fear as it became obvious that this *insect*—an old, washed-up figure of a knight—was lasting far longer than the younger, fancier kind that usually made there way to this spot.

Finally, as the time of warfare approached the second toll...there was a loud, deafening screech of pain as the dragon—its heart and fire chambers pierced—raised its head straight up and then—as a mighty sequoia felled by a tiny axe—it slammed to earth. And, as a dust cloud temporarily enveloped the scene, only a slow, sickening gurgle gave evidence that the monster was dead.

But, what of Sir Peter? The Ganab...who *now* were very much attentive (most contemplating life-persevering flight...which would involve, of course, taking their human slaves with them) shivered with fear as the air slowly went from opaque to crystal. But, instead of seeing a triumphant knight brandishing the sword and the accursed shield...they saw, instead, Sir Peter kneeling, with his right hand upon the imbedded sword and the left (devoid of the shield, which lay prone nearby) clutching his side as if gravely injured.

As the implication of this development became clear, there was great excitement on *both* sides of the field. The Ganab, sensing an easy kill, gathered quickly and rushed, like hounds to the hare, upon the wounded knight. Meanwhile, Sir Peter's brothers on the hill *also* wanted to attend to the fallen but—and Nicholas made sure his fellows understood the knight's last command—only upon *his* summons should they come.

And so, as the humans looked helplessly on, a swarm of Ganab descended upon the feeble dragon-slayer. And he, apparently wishing to delay the end—as he saw their drooling fangs approach—he quickly lay upon the ground and pulled the shield over his exposed body.

For a few moments the scene appeared as if a morsel of meat had been thrown into the jungle stream and immediately encircled and chewed upon by ravenous piranhas. Or, from the air it might be likened to a wretched bloom...the center being the barely seen shield, surrounded on all sides by disgusting black petals. And, as many of the dragons as could wedged in for their fill...there was, waiting behind, a multitude of other fiends...all lusting for a piece.

It was perhaps thirty seconds...claws were clawing, fangs lunging, tails flailing, but then, suddenly, the analogy took a different turn. It *now* became like an apple being cored...*from the inside out!* The anointed sword of Sir Peter thrust instantly skyward (at a forty-five-degree angle) and, with one powerful, fluid, circular motion...*all* the surrounding Ganab were at once in pieces and, as these fell and quivered in grotesque gushes...the knight (somewhat soiled and slimed) stood erect...the shield, bearing the king's crimson mark...glistening in the sun on his left arm, and the sword of his commission...it was raised triumphantly, perpendicular to earth and, as there was a moment of hesitation and unbelief amongst the vermin (of which there were still many) the old knight then pointed the sword to his brethren on the hill and these, acknowledging the command with a shout...rushed valiantly upon the confused rabble and, with Sir Peter in the lead, they courageously carved a path towards the human herd and the hated hill.

In only a few minutes (the Ganab have no stomach for open battle) *all* of the dragons had fled for their lives and—reluctantly leaving their precious *treasures*—they gathered in a fearful frenzied mob to a place far beyond (although still within sight) the three lines of humans. Now there were only the *false* knights to deal with and these, upon seeing (as Sir Peter and company arrayed themselves in a single line directly opposite the imposters) the true symbol of the king and the radiant swords which showed his pleasure...these lowered their lifeless wares and stepped back, allowing the very many in bondage (horribly, some were recognized as being from the *king's* side of the river!) to gaze unhindered upon the bearers of truth. Soon— as the deceivers and liars had lost their hold—the eyes of the women were at last opened and they began, one by one, to stoop down to lovingly embrace their innocent children and then, with one heart, these reunited pairs tearfully came to the arms of the waiting rescue party and, as they were escorted away from this awful place, only Sir Peter remained a few minutes more.

"Peter!" exclaimed young Nicholas as he saw the dragons and their allies becoming emboldened beyond. "Let's go! It won't be long and they'll be upon us!"

The old warrior slowly shook his head from side to side to relay his unwillingness and, as he held high—immoveable—the shield and the sword...his apprentice followed his mentor's gaze to see, incredibly, that atop the wretched mount the murderer...the slaughterer of hundreds of thousands...was himself trembling under the terrible weight of revelation. Soon, this creature was looking at his hands and as he did so he began to weep uncontrollably. And, if not for the intercession of the knight, this man would have taken his own life. Instead, he *too* was directed towards the river and, as Nicholas and Sir Peter followed behind, the younger (seemingly filled with anger) whispered to the elder, "Surely not him! Surely...*Sir Peter!*...Not him!"

As the dragons and deceivers, enraged at their defeat, slowly (but with increasing speed) advanced towards the invaders, Sir Peter turned and faced his confused companion. "Nicholas," he said with the tender tone of a beloved teacher. "*Nick*," he continued as the young man finally met his gaze. "The king's decree is that *all* be invited and," the younger jerked his sight towards the physician who walked, slumped shouldered, ahead. "And," the elder placed his right hand on his friends shoulder (even though the youth *would not* look at him) and said, "*no matter how tarnished is the soul...the blood makes clean, completely whole*."

Nicholas had no time for any more *silly* rhymes and he quickly turned and stepped briskly away from the *old man*. But, as he approached the crest of the small hill that preceded the wood, he heard the whistle. It was the sound of something terribly fast, slicing through the air. A second later the young man heard a guttural cry and then the clatter of a shield and sword falling to earth.

"Peter!" he cried, as he turned and rushed back to see his elder companion on all fours, head bowed, a crossbow dart deeply imbedded in his back.

"Help me up, brother," said the elder weakly, struggling to right himself with the kneeling aid of the youth. A moment later another dart slammed deeply into the knight's flesh.

"The shield, Nicholas," Sir Peter whispered as the frenzied youth simply clung to his friend as more darts landed all around them. "Place my shield behind me."

The young man, regaining some soundness of mind, quickly picked up the large protector and propped it behind the kneeling knight. "Good," said Sir Peter, still clinging to the lad and slowly raising his head as he spoke, "very good."

The expression on the youth's face, as Peter looked into his eyes, was that of utter fear and despair for, running freely from the elder's mouth and coloring his matted gray beard was a bubbling crimson wash that evidenced, at the very least, a punctured lung.

Sir Peter smiled at the lad as he, leaning heavily upon him, wiped his mouth with his gauntleted left hand. "I should have heard that coming," he weakly laughed (blood flowing anew and he, coughing between words). "A few years ago I would have swatted those like flies."

"Sir Peter! Let me help you...the river will heal you!" the boy struggled to raise the mortally wounded knight.

"Settle down, Nicholas," wheezed the elder as he resisted the attempt, and then, smiling... "I mean *Nick.*"

The young man peered over the shield and saw in the distance one of the false knights being congratulated by his fellows even as these beckoned the dragons to advance.

"Listen, Nick," said Sir Peter, weakly patting the young warriors shoulder with his right hand. "I don't have much time. Please, do as I say."

At this point the elder rested his brow upon the young man's right shoulder and, because of lack of strength, he leaned heavily upon him. "Nick...Nick...can you hear me?"

The young man, tears streaming down his face and falling upon the elder's mane, nodded yes and finally spoke, "Yes...I hear you."

"Listen," the words were airy, labored, interspersed with desperate gasps, "the dragons will come. They will be leery. They remember the deception from before. Nick...do you hear me?"

"Yes, yes, I hear you."

"I need you to imbed the sword...I need to lean against it...I need you to rest the shield against me. Do you understand?"

"Yes." The words were accompanied by gentle quaking as tears could not be restrained.

"Do it now...my friend...do it now."

Nicholas, still holding the elder, reached behind and picked up the sword. Then, pivoting slightly, he thrust the king's weapon deep into the earth. "Sir Peter," he said, gently grabbing the elder by the upper arms (the knight's head deeply bowed), "it is done, Sir Peter."

The old warrior, with a last summoning of strength, raised his gaze to meet that of his weeping companion. "Call me, *Peter*," he smiled and, as the distraught young man smiled in return he then helped position the knight so that he could grasp the hilt of the sword while leaning against it.

"Thank you, Nick," said the elder as the youth, once more, touched the knight's brow with his own. "Now, go. This charade will buy you perhaps a half hour...and Nick...one more thing."

"Yes, Peter," said the sorrowful apprentice as he leaned back, preparing to depart.

"Tell my dear lady...tell her of my undying love...and tell her that I will toast her beauty until our meeting at the king's table." There was a slight pause as the knight's final breath was drawn. "Will you tell her that, my friend?"

"Yes...I'll tell her," said the young warrior as he stood to depart, but, as he looked beyond to the creeping advance of the demons, he could tell that his dear mentor had not heard his reply. The old *wall-builder* had traveled on...on to the place prepared by the King.

As Sir Peter had surmised, the previous deception caused great caution on the part of the dragons. However, approximately thirty-five minutes later (just long enough for the departing rescuers to get safely away), the Ganab finally fell hard upon the knight's lifeless body and, as these, like ravenous sharks, ripped apart the corpse and then gave the armor and weapon (which had lost their luster) to the false ones...they then set about to continue the horrid practice of the place. Soon another executioner was found...and soon the web of deception was woven anew. But, as a small grisly morsel of the knight was carefully preserved, wrapped, and then taken by a winged creature to be consumed by the Lord of the Dragons…there appeared on the spot of earth where the knight expired…on the portion where his life's blood was spilled…there seemed to be now in place an invisible beacon…a calling…a silent siren that cried for an end…an end to an evil practice…an evil practice that grieved the heart of the Great King.

Chapter XXVI

To conquer evil
Seek the one
The Champion in your midst...

"Mary! Mary!" Sir John spoke forcefully (even though near collapse himself) above the tormented lady as she—with hands over her ears—shook her head from side to side in a visual sign of denial as more and more tears streamed down the many paths of her soot-blackened cheeks.

"Mary," his words were tender now as he knelt beside her (she still shaking her head with her eyes pressed tightly shut). "Mary, you know that thing is a liar."

—In the background the C-C-C-C- of the dragon's death knell— signaling their doom—approached its zenith.—

"Mary," offered Albert who, though mortally burned, found enough strength to reach out and touch his mother's trembling knees, "you know that Sir Peter loves you. Remember his words at your parting."

The matron, as the clacking of the valve took on the deliberate sound of its final strokes, looked up and, as she slowly absorbed the loving words just spoken by two of her dear ones, a peace seemed to wash gently across her face and, at this very late time when all was obviously lost (at least as far as they were concerned)...this was all that Sir John and Albert had hoped to accomplish in these final seconds. For, unfortunately, Sir Peter's final farewell—left with young Nicholas at the time of his death—had not yet been carried to the woman he loved (such was the chaos of the time) but at least now these three could be swept away, in peace, by the torrent of flame that they...in themselves...had no way to prevent. They were ready to die.

Meanwhile, as the luminescent billowy barrier that held back the frenzied Chata retreated ever nearer the river (and with it the king's subjects pushed more and more into the flow) there was, in the very center of the blessed stream (as all other eyes were fixed on the sorrowful happenings without) a lone individual who wept the tears of a tender grieving child. He, though by all appearances a grown man...was of a delicate mind and, although he had often played at the feet of the king he could not...he would not!...give himself rest while all those he loved were at the point of death.

"O God!" he wept, his hands covering his eyes as tears flowed down and the tiny drops caused rainbow-like ringlets as they fell into the surge below. "O God! O God! please help my family...please...please...please...save them!" Then, with a deep heart-emptying sigh... "In the name of my friend...the king...I ask."

And, as the place for words was gone, and as the final hellish clacking of the valve ceased and the horrid head of the beast withdrew and, as the three in the crevice of the rock held each other's hands for this final journey...something stirred from deep within the Crystal Sea. There, beyond the castle, in the depths and currents of the unsearchable sea...a single crystal...a lone, shimmering, glimmer of light—one wondrous, solitary, divinely birthed entity—compelled by a love that would *not* be denied—shot up and then...as quick as thought...this singularity exploded above the thrusting and gushing head of the creature from hell. And, from this tiny, barely seen crystal, a great storm-cloud—replete with swords of lightning and crashes of thunder—suddenly filled the sky above the dragon with a reservoir of rain that fell...in one torrential sheet!...upon this blackened valley *just* as the unquenchable flame speedily exited the bowels of the beast.

Mary, John, and Albert, bravely bracing for their end and seeing just the first glimmer of the monstrous fireball were, along with all the stunned spectators, amazed that the geyser from the creature (in a huge explosion of chaotic steam) was thoroughly *quenched* by the washing from above...a washing that was birthed, only moments before...from a cloudless sky. Then, as quickly as they came, *both* waves were ended and, as a gentle descent now replaced the downpour over this once fertile field, the dragon—seeing that its quarry *still* lived, raised its teeth towards heaven and, after spewing forth great and terrible curses towards its enemy of long ago…it then focused piercingly, once more, on the representative lambs in the rock and, with all the bile and hatred and rage of a millennium of remembrance…it stoked its inner fire in order to finally, triumphantly, vanquish the water-drenched little *insects* and, after these were cinders…*all* others would either suffer the same fate…or they would die from the fangs of the many…or they would expire due to starvation as they huddled in fear on the banks of their *blessed river.*

"Sing Mary!" shouted John who, dripping and drenched could barely believe what had just happened. "Sing Mary!" he shouted again. "The Lord has given us one more chance!" Then, stumbling through the mud and the choking heavy mist the knight ran towards the glowing as the final verse of the hymn, sung by an exhausted and still weeping elderly lady, preceded him to the dragon's heart.

Then you rose and donned the royal crown!

At the words the dragon's concentration was shattered. What was to be a quick fire-building, now slowed ever down as the song of his enemy vexed the monster's black soul.

All before your throne must now bow down!

Sir John…weak, wounded, nearly bloodless, sloshed through the residue of the saving torrent and, gasping for breath, he saw, just ahead…the glowing. It, like the blaze from the dragon's eyes, pulsed a voracious eternal rage and, as he positioned himself between the quaking monstrous forelegs he realized, too late, that the depth of the final layer would require him—in order to pierce it— to throw himself into the breach. This would mean his sure death…but, without a second thought, and as the final verse of the triumphant hymn coincided exactly with the last slamming of the valve…he dove…*with all his remaining strength*, he threw himself—his right arm extended with the anointed sword of one of the king's chosen protectors pointing straight at the demon's heart—into the hole that had been carved deep into the dragon's chest.

The serpent's head was crushed into the ground. All glory to you!

And, at the time there *should* have been a controlled explosion that would have instantly sent forth the all-consuming gushing of hell, instead…as the demon opened wide its hideous jaws…*nothing* emerged, for, far below—near the commonness of the soil—the point of the sword, having been mightily thrust *through* the thick leathery skin and past the chamber of lusting flame, it finally, just barely (the poor knight now immovably wedged and being overcome by fumes and flame) nicked the protective layer on the other side. And this incursion, this slightest of violations…produced the smallest of holes…a minuscule breach…a tiny opening of opportunity that allowed the fury of the furnace to claw at the hate-filled fluids of the heart and, as the blood and fire explosively mingled, the tiny hole (in an instant of time) became a dam hopelessly rent.

KAWOOSH!! the flood, as the contents of each hideous chamber tried to dominate the other…this produced a mammoth collision of opposites which sent forth—at first—a huge concussive wave, and then it was like a large iron furnace being mercilessly gorged with fuel until, unable to control or contain, the sides of the vessel itself begin to melt and succumb to a fire which knew no restraint.

At the initial blast, the knight (now unconscious, such was the concentration of poison) was thrown—sword and all—violently from the breach and, as his limp and twisted body arced and then slammed down mere meters from the protective enclosure—the other two humans (Albert, crawling, and Mary, hobbling) went out and, using what little strength they retained, they were able to drag their brother into the rock and, between these two, they were able to lift up the knight's shield for at least a little protection from—*God only knows what*—was coming.

The dragon, its eyes betraying a sickening bewilderment as its innards began to war with one another…at the moment of the first substantial explosion (in the process there were several punctuations of power as other sources were greedily swallowed by the flame) its neck and head, like the end of a smartly cracked bull-whip, shot straight up and, as the horrid orb was violently flung—and was then suddenly stopped at the end of its tether—something small was seen to be thrown high into the dark canopy (save for the frequent lightning discharges) above.

Now there was no stopping, no saving, no quenching of the hell that had been loosed in the belly of the beast. As the Chata that surrounded the field scattered…as the humans that beheld the drama in the mist awakened…as the three in the rock held on to one another beneath the battered shield (John had barely regained consciousness) the monster, unable to resist, or deter…succumbed to the eating within. The flame, like a rise of volcanic magma, caused *all* tissues and sinews encased by the armored walls to explosively burn. The eyes, once windows to a fury below, *now* these were windows…opened. Now, instead of just portals of refraction, the fire *itself* consumed the hateful spheres and then licked furiously out past the barren sockets.

And, for perhaps five awful minutes, the hellish blaze screamed and raged and gnawed at all that could be eaten within the dragon's thick armored casing until…evidenced by a sudden silence and a sickening gray burst of smoke…the dinner was done and the hollow head and neck…like a towering brick stack—after a brief moment of false exaltation—it then suddenly broke off at the base and, as this great weight slammed into the earth with a loud *BOOM!* (the place of contact shattering) the rest of the neck, like falling dominoes, unraveled in the direction of the trio and, as each section burst into pieces on the earth (the intense heat had compromised the strength of the armor) with a frightening cadence of *boom! boom! boom! boom!* The hideous head…that which devoured and lied and cursed and uttered the dragon's evil boast…this grotesque sphere flew with hideous smoke-trailing sockets and fang-toothed mouth agape—in one last act of defiance—directly at the protecting rock and, upon the violent meeting of these two…the dragon head shattered irreparably into a great rain of tiny harmless pieces which buried the three sheep in the fold.

Meanwhile, as this final scene played out upon the protective mist and was beheld with humble awe by the next participants, there was, among the viewers…a sifting, a sorting, an almost unconscious shuffling into position. These, who had—everyone—their lives reduced to a place of dependence by the river. These, many who were—when fleeing here—encumbered with trappings and treasures and trivialities…now these simplified folk took on a oneness, a common resolve, a universal understanding of what they *must* do and, as the revelation of the battle ceased and the outside dragons (in great anticipation) rubbed their fangs furiously together as they paced…

Suddenly, as quickly as it came the first time—the mist…in one brief second immediately after the total destruction of the great dragon was revealed…the protective barrier then rushed swiftly away *from* the Chata, *through* the humans, and back to the center of the Living River.

The Chata, the millions upon millions that took their place all along the perimeter (most were oblivious to the fate of the Great Dragon—most not *even* the least bit concerned), these, in a rampant frenzy (now released from the hindrance of the accursed veil) rushed upon the morsels that had been so long their only desire. But, as these lustfully lunged towards the *helpless* humans the sky (which, for some reason, was now being quickly covered by the very *same* storm-cloud that had centered over the field of the dragon and the three) gave way to a huge flash of lightning which, as the horde of red-eyed demons hungrily scurried forward, reflected off—not a chaotic, cowering mass of victims—but rather, a multifaceted *wall* appeared before them...a wall where each tiny section, as the lightning—for the briefest of moments—made darkness, day...each section bore the emblem of the great king! The Chata stopped, repulsed and enraged by the sight. But, as successive flashes filled the sky—making discernment possible—that which appeared as a single barrier was revealed to be, rather, a wall of *shields*...shields exactly as those born by the king's knights! There, stretching out before them towards the horizon on either side, as far as their wretched eyes could see...were nothing but shields! Shield, touching shield, touching shield, touching shield and, as the lightning flashed, and the rain fell, and the ground reverberated with the percussion from above...it became clear that each shield was carried by a warrior...and each warrior appeared to be attired as a king's knight!

For a brief moment there was a stand-off. The dragons...the millions of maddened murderers...were, at first, confused at this simple human barrier, but, after a few seconds of low-level contemplation (not to mention the pressure of the ravenous horde behind them) the beasts succumbed to their evil hearts' directive and rushed upon the would-be defenders. (After all, these toothsome terrorists could *easily* scale vertical granite walls...how much more this insignificant and arrogant wrinkle?) And, as the seemingly unbroken first wave of claws and teeth and pulsing red eyes rushed into the bracing band of humans (none of which wavered at the press) the Chata discovered that though they clawed and gnawed at the emblem of the king...they could *not* grip the polished metal. Then, as these in front screeched and frenzied against the immoveable, a *second* wave—in a great unified cresting of demons—followed quickly behind and then washed *over* the tops of the first, preparing to fall ruthlessly upon the defenders below. But, as these...*all* along the circling wall...reached the zenith of their attack...they all...without exception...were thrown back by an unseen force! For there...standing somewhat back from the sword and shield bearers...was a choir...an unbroken line of anointed singers who lifted high, and with one voice, their hymn of praise concerning the great triumphant king and the all-powerful God of the Crystal Sea!

Now, with the millions in disarray, the human warriors opened slightly the hand-held gates and loosed—striking nearly as one—sword after sword after sword into and through the dragons that dare stand against them. And these *little ones*—wretched creatures that were lightly armored (though their weapons of talon and tooth were deadly to the unshielded)—these were easily sliced asunder by the well-placed blade and thus, in a matter of minutes, one hundred thousand lay dead and dying as the great army of the king, as one, stepped forward and, as wave upon wave of the desperate evil tried to push back, or separate, or breach the wall of metal and men...such was the discipline of these troops that there was no variance due to selfish ambition or sloth and thus, as the rain fell and the lightning flashed and the triumphant hymn of the king reigned above...the dragons (who knew nothing but to lustfully attack) continued to fall.

Meanwhile, circling high above the fray, as the line of the bloody conflict below slowly contracted towards the center...legions of flying dragons (under the direction of the *Sower* who remained at the highest point just below the churning thunderclouds) swooped down to rewrite the equation in favor of the murderers.

"Behind the lines!" he hissed. "Make the defenders turn!" was his command to the multitude as they spread to every corner and prepared to distract the human warriors in order to allow the ravenous horde of Chata— like swarming ants—to divide and conquer. But, as these vile ones angled sharply downward with swept-back wings and fangs and talons at the ready...when they came within a half kilometer of the earth they—to the horror of their leader—burst into flame and, like a brilliant meteor shower, they filled the sky with the bright yellow glow of their incinerating carcasses even as their anguished screams filtered up to the bewildered ears of the second in command.

The Sower, hovering in disbelief as his comrades violently succumbed to an unseen force, suddenly felt, rising up from the depths of his black heart...an ancient dread...a remembrance of a time, long ago, when the barrier, the shield, the protection that covered this accursed kingdom was, at *all* times, and everywhere...so powerful that to challenge it was suicide. And, as these subconscious memories bubbled up, his eyes—which moments before had the brilliant glowing sharpness of the hunter...now his reddened orbs had the quivering flame of fear and, as he felt the quick and terrible coming of the force that had killed his brothers, he, with all the strength that terror could muster...flew high and fast to return—if he possibly could—to the lair of his master.

The storming dark night gave way, reluctantly, to the gray of day. The clouds, which now—for some reason—covered the *entire* kingdom, continued to release a healing rain (it would be discovered later that this liquid balm reversed the poison emitted by the now dead dragon) even as the front line of human warriors, though the battle had waged for hours, continued to advance without tiring. However, closer examination of this army of the king revealed that the front line was *not* made up of superhuman swordsmen...requiring no rest or refreshment. No...a more intimate view revealed that after so many waves of the demons were dashed and destroyed (the ignorant beasts knew only to attack...and die) that there was a constant *changing* of the human guard. Thus, as one tired, he would, before the next encounter, be seamlessly replaced by another. In this way, as the weary were replenished by those who supplied this need, the combined effort of the many...never faltered. And, it should be noted, that although *all* the warriors on the front line appeared to be knights...most were not. For, over the course of the last few refining months, the knights—feeling compelled to train the many in order that they might fight as they (and the *many* feeling compelled to receive such training)—these knights had unselfishly emptied themselves into their charges. Thus, an army nearly of equals—acting in unison with the warriors unseen—marched on against, what appeared, an insurmountable enemy...an enemy that was quickly (though there were so many) being vanquished by what was supposed to be their victory feast.

On and on battle raged. Past the morning bells and the striking of noon the relentless Chata charged again and again. And, each time, without exception, they were mowed down and then, as the dragons hissed and gurgled their last, the humans would step forward to await another onslaught.

—It should be noted that in this bloody encounter the citizens of the kingdom did *not* have to hunt down or pursue the enemy. No...these basest of dragons *only* knew to attack. But the main reason the king's army advanced after each vanquished wave (although as the circle contracted there became available more warriors for relief) was to step away from the great quantity of fallen dead.—

As the front line continued in its mission, a short distance behind there was another line doing battle. These, the singers (consisting of all shapes and sizes and ages and appearances) sang hymns without ceasing (again, there were others in standby at all times) and provided cover for those forward and…in addition to these…far to the rear…as the warriors battled and the singers sang praises…there was *another* kind of warfare going on. For, being careful to stay in the flow of the river, a great multitude of citizens (again, all shapes, sizes, ages, and appearances) interceded passionately on behalf of the many and, through the benevolent answer to these constant petitions…the rain fell…and the invisible barrier above was restored. Plus, in addition to those who fought with blade and with song and with prayer…there was another unseen multitude that did all the necessary work that sustained the other three. And one of their tasks…a rather distasteful duty…was to gather the dead Chata and throw them into huge heaps for later disposal.

One tiny dragon, thought dead—but really only knocked temporarily unconscious by the glancing blow from the hilt of a sword—found itself (as the battle line moved away) nearly smothered by the many oozing corpses of its brothers that had been quickly piled upon it. The creature, desperate for air *and* revenge, pulled and squirmed and shoved its way to freedom on the edge of the gruesome mound and, as it, breathing heavily, lay in one of the sticky puddles at the base…it turned its hateful squinting gaze towards the enemy that marched against his brothers. The dragon, unwounded, quickly devised a plan whereby it would slash its way effortlessly through the singers (they had no armor) and, when reaching the sword-bearing humans…it would then fall upon the weakest and perhaps, *perhaps* this would provide an opening for a breakthrough, but, just as the drooling lizard stood and began to hungrily sprint towards the unsuspecting, a little figure of a knight stopped it cold in its tracks.

For a moment the two enemies gazed at one another. The dragon, used to facing opponents of greater stature, turned its head quizzically to one side as it hissed *down* at this armored human that he concluded must surely be some kind of runt or reject. Then, in contempt without caution the dragon lunged at the miniature and, a moment later, its lifeless body was *again* thrown to the heap…this time to rise no more.

"Well done, little one," said an older knight (who was taking a short break from the front line) as he took a drink of water from a flask and then offered it to his fellow warrior. "What is your name, son?"

"Mark, sir," said the child as he smiled a gapped tooth smile and squeaked out a chuckle. Then, taking a drink, wiping his mouth on his right sleeve and handing it back to the adult, he asked, "And what is your name, sir?"

The elder, smiling and patting the lad on the helmet said (as he turned to again take station on the front line) "My name is Sir Leslie. Thank you, *Sir Mark*, for your service." And then, as he walked slowly between the singers he shouted back, "Continue to watch our backs, Sir Mark!"

"Yes, Sir! I will," said the lad excitedly. And then, pausing a moment to professionally straighten his armor and unsheathe his sword…he then, with purposeful steps and keen eyes, continued to faithfully execute his task of patrolling the growing piles of demons and, to be sure, before this day was done…before the last wave of the Chata were ultimately destroyed (as twilight approached) there would be more than one occasion when a dragon who *thought* he had escaped death to fight anew…wished, after meeting a child of the king, that he had died properly…the *first* time.

The Sower collapsed on the well-worn granite ledge that had been his launching place for a thousand years. His body, drained of strength due to hours of forced flying in the higher altitudes (plus the constant buffeting from the *shield* that pulsed upwards all along the route) caused him to lie, immovable, for an hour as he, facing the enemy's land, finally heard a distant human cry of victory as the ocean of thunderclouds then gave way to a brilliant crimson sunset.

The flying dragon…weak and wounded…struggled to his feet and began to shuffle slowly towards his demon's lair where, perhaps, he would find a human morsel suitable for a snack. It had been a terrible night. It started with such promise and he…*he* who had been given command of so many of his brothers…well, since most were dead the old flyer surmised—as the sun disappeared completely behind the western sea—that he would be demoted, at the very least, to the task of his name.

And what *of* his master? What of the architect of this fiasco? The Sower didn't care and, as he bowed his head to enter the foul cave he called home…he inwardly hoped that the Lord of the Dragons…that hateful creature from which all their vileness emanated…was dead. Then, perhaps he…*he*, the wisest of the remaining…would reign over this realm. "I know I could do a better job," he mumbled, a bit despondent that there was nothing but bones to choose from among the pens. Then, as he grudgingly shuffled towards the exit (planning to gather a morsel from the humans still in bondage) he walked through the opening onto the outer plateau (noting that the sky was completely clear) and, nearing the edge he paused, becoming aware and seeing—from the corner of his eye—a bent figure perched off to his left...apparently a flying dragon which seemed to be cradling his wounded head with his claws.

"Brother," offered the Sower (a bit surprised that one of his underlings had lived), "are you all right?"

For a moment there was silence as the intruder slowly lowered his dripping forelegs and, as more cheers of human victory wafted up from below, this creature then turned its gaze to the inquirer and, as he did, the Sower—seeing the fires of hell raging in this unknown dragon's eyes—he knew, at once, that the master...the one he had hoped was dead...*lived*.

"Your highness," groveled the Sower, now prostrate before his Lord. "You're alive...I'm so relieved."

For a few moments the flying dragon, eyes shut, being very still, heard the scraping of his ruler's talons as he purposely walked towards his servant. Then, as before, the sound became that of scales slithering on the stone. And, as the trembling *second in command* smelled the rottenness of his king's breath and the flick of his tongue he whispered, "Master...shall I begin the seeding runs again?"

The Sower hurtled down as he had done countless times before, launched moments earlier from the well-worn ledge high atop *Dragon Peak*. This time, however, instead of the well-executed darting descent...instead of carrying the bag of leaven-like seeds for a horrible, hateful harvest...*this* time his limp body tumbled and twirled and dashed again and again against the jagged outcroppings which violently ripped large portions of his flesh until, at last, his broken body slammed into and draped lifelessly over the unyielding rocks below.

Above, two hate-filled eyes watched intently as the winged dragon took its last hapless flight. "Yessss..." a cruel voice whispered as the figure paused and then turned and slithered away towards the bowels of the mountain. "Another seeding run *is* in order. Take care of that for me...will you...O faithful servant?"

Epilogue

It was a summoning…a calling…a yearning concerning all…and literally *all* responded to it. The king…the *Great* King of the universe who—so long before—had provided release through his own blood; this all-powerful benevolent ruler desired audience with the subjects he loved and, in front of these…he desired to honor the *one,* the *champion,* the very same who had destroyed the crimson dragon and inspired the host to victory.

And so they came…the thousands upon thousands, the *hundreds* of thousands…from all quadrants of the kingdom. And, though the distance was vast, and the trek on human legs would normally be long…this, however, was a journey of the heart, and thus, *this* ingathering took only moments. And so, as the sun cleared the eastern peaks on the morn after the battle, and just before the time of concerted labor was to begin—when all things good would be repaired and renewed and all things evil would be properly disposed of (in the river)—they, all the humans of the kingdom who had survived…gathered. Past the rough-hewn bridge and through the rising mist of praise…past the outer gate and the flowering inner courtyard…through the simple doorway with the blood-stained lintel they came. And, as the multitude streamed into the inner sanctuary and, as they were greeted by the sounds of a great triumphant choir singing—in a fullness not possible with human voices—a rendering of the very same song that came from Mary's lips…they, without one exception (such was their focus and desire) passed directly into the king's presence without pause or hindrance at the inner wall. Indeed, it was as if the wall did not even exist.

Finally, as all eyes were fastened on the Great King...he, attired in a brilliant multicolored robe and standing before his golden throne, held high his open right hand and the multitude became silent awaiting the proclamation. Then, with another hand-gesture towards two of his shining attendants, a throne—exactly like his own—was brought in and placed approximately two meters from where he stood. Then, smiling down into the gathering, he pointed again and—with the aide of the two who had brought the throne—Sir John...weak, wounded, and still attired in his rent armor and garments was brought before his lord.

The knight, barely able to kneel on his right knee and with head bowed while cradling his useless left arm with his right, he then, while feeling only the pounding of his heart...heard the crimson sword slowly unsheathed and, a moment later, he felt its powerful touch upon his two shoulders. Then, as the multitude explosively cheered at the honoring, he felt a strong healing power flow throughout his body and, as he looked up in amazement (tears beginning to well as he, with mouth agape, gazed into the loving eyes of his king) his body was restored and he couldn't help but raise his left hand and turn it back and forth before his watering eyes. Then, looking again past his healed appendage he saw the king, with arms wide, and the now *healthy* knight stood and was embraced by the sovereign, who said (as he gestured towards the other throne), "Thank you, my friend, for your sacrifice on behalf of the kingdom."

Sir John, humbled by the recognition, bowed before his lord and made his way slowly to the duplicate throne.

"O, John...one more thing," said the king as he removed his robe and handed it to the very surprised knight, "I see you are in need of raiment...here...wear this today."

And the champion, as the king motioned for another robe, was (along with all who noticed) struck with awe at the glimpse (for the king wore a pure white silken undergarment...slightly open at the breast) of the sizable purple scar (as if fresh) located directly over the sovereign's heart.

After Sir John had donned the royal robe and sat down (the multitude cheering wildly) the king, who did *not* sit down, raised his hand once again for silence. Then, as only curious whispers could be barely heard...the king motioned for *another* throne to be brought, and this golden seating—an exact replica of the other two—was placed next to Sir John's...slightly closer to the king. Then, without hesitation, the lord sent his two aides into the gathering to retrieve *another* warrior, and this fellow…a teenager, terribly burned—Albert!—had to be carried due to the horrific trauma his body had undergone. And, as the young man—in great pain—knelt before the king of all, he *too* felt the touch of the crimson sword and, as before, the power of this instrument drove all infirmity from his body. And, the boy, who had been staring at the king's feet (even as his body was quaking due to uncontrollable waves of agony) when the healing suddenly came he, with an expression of utter amazement, looked up—with grateful tears in his eyes—to see (as Sir John before him had seen) the Great King with arms open and a look of tender compassion on his face. As the two embraced, the king said, "Thank you, Albert, for your sacrifice on behalf of the kingdom."

Then, as the crowd acknowledged that it really *did* take the two to do the deed they—as John also stood with applause—cheered for the young man as he—now *also* adorned with a royal robe—sat beside his father. But still, the king did *not* sit down.

Then, a few moments later, the king again raised his hand for silence and yes…*another* throne was brought in and was placed beside the other three. Then, as many in the gathering looked to one another in utter amazement, the king's hand pointed to an elderly lady near the front who had been weeping for joy because of the honor given her two beloved men, but now—seeing that *she* was the focus of attention—she began to shake with a paralyzing fear….so much so that the two assistants had to gently coax and assist her in order to bring her to the platform.

"Mary," said the king, having anointed her with the sword and now embracing her as she wept upon his shoulder, "thank you for conquering your fears. Thank you for your service on behalf of the kingdom." And, as Sir John and Albert greeted their tearful mother with kisses and hugs she, on a throne still closer to the king's, sat down (she also wearing a robe) even as the great throng cheered wildly at the three who, together, had fought the terrible beast.

Then, as jubilation ruled and joyful celebration ensued, the king, after scanning the multitude for a brief moment, he then, without a word, stepped down from the platform and began to ascend towards the distant exit. The gathering, quite shocked at this happening, became suddenly silent as they parted (bowing as he neared) before the Great King as he walked purposely towards the outer courtyard. And, upon entering the enormous flowering expanse—the blooms made all the more brilliant by the blazing morning sun—the Lord then made his way to a far distant corner where a rather large

Rose of Sharon created a canopy of purple and white.

For a short time the king stood patiently in front of the flowers with his right hand tenderly outstretched. Then, after a minute of suspense (as many had gathered to witness) a frail looking, stoop shouldered man with bowed head, reached, timidly, to take the hand of the king who then led this bashful fellow past the great multitude to take his place of honor on the platform, and, as yet *another* throne was brought in (this one placed immediately next to the king's) and as the gentle soul kneeled (with face to the ground) and trembled before the mighty sovereign...he *too* was touched by the sword and, as the king held the weeping figure he said, "Fren, thank you for your petition. Because of you...the battle was won. And," he continued, as he grabbed Fredrick by the shoulders and looked into his face, "I very much enjoy our daily visits...next time don't hesitate to come." Then, cupping Fren's face in his hands, the king kissed him on the forehead.

"**...the *one* with sword...and shield...and song. The *one* whom God has kissed**." The answer to the king's riddle, mouthed quietly to himself by a smiling Sir Robert (who stood near the exit), soon was birthed in the hearts of all and, as the multitude, with understanding, cheered and praised the God of the Crystal Sea *and* the king, the four on the platform...John, Albert, Mary and Fren—all adorned with a royal robe—all sat down as one, and the king...he, in a final display of honor, bowed before the *Champion* and then he, too, sat down on *his* throne.

Sir Robert, still shaking his head and grinning at the revelation...he then—as the enormous gathering continued to loudly celebrate—turned his gaze to his immediate left. There, beside him, dressed as he—in the simple armor of the king's knights (and smiling just as much), were Sir Gustov, Sir Francis, Sir Gerald, and Sir Joseph. But, beyond these, standing at attention against the back wall, were at least two hundred *more* knights (among these: Sir Eirenikos, formerly from Aphron, and his two associates, Sir Rak and Sir Yatab. Also, Sir Nabal was in the mix and, standing very straight at the end of the line...Sir Leslie, and, although *this* elder should have taken command...he chose instead to fall in with the others [*less thought...more fight!*])...all awaiting Sir Rob's signal. Then he, gazing one last time at the king and the four, raised high his gauntleted left hand and, with a quick, forward, throwing motion, he then led the warriors out. For these, of one soul and purpose—these were answering the call of their great king to try and end, if they possibly could, an evil practice in the land beyond the Living River and, as a guide, their hearts were being directed by an invisible beacon...a beacon planted by the blood of a beloved brother not long before.

Then, as the knights silently exited the building and the people continued to celebrate, four small, white-robed children—two boys and two girls—could be seen toddling out of the river's archway and into the waiting arms of the king. And, after hugging and kissing each of these innocents, the sovereign then directed them to the open arms of the four.

And, as a beautiful blonde-haired girl with chubby pink cheeks and deep blue eyes crawled lightly up into the lap of Sir John and then commenced to squeeze his neck tightly as she nestled against and repeatedly kissed his left cheek...he, holding her snug with both arms—his eyes closed even as great tears began to well and flow down and drip upon her delicate white robe—he then heard Mary emotionally say to him as she leaned forward while cradling a black-haired boy (who was fascinated with her ears)... "O, Sir John...isn't it wonderful?"

The knight, at the words, opened his eyes and looked into the innocent depths of the darling on his lap and then—knowing that soon his arms would be empty as she would have to continue on to the far-distant place of the sanctuary he, glancing quickly that way, thought he saw, just for a moment—in the moving blurriness of the other side—a quick, but recognizable flash of matted red hair. Then, smiling and laughing as he squeezed the child tight one last time, he then looked at Mary and said—as more tears flowed—"Dear Lady...call me John. From now on...just call me...*John.*"

Song of the King

Once upon a dark and fearful time
Imprisoned by the wall of our design
Traitors to our God, so good and kind
Worthy of tears…

Crying out for hope, deserving none
Reaping what we'd sown, what we had done
Is there none to help, not even one?
O, save us from tears

Then, beyond the wall, you heard our call
With your love
And you sent your Son, your only one
You gave your all

Then for us a king became a slave
Bearing our just due, his life he gave
Dying for our sin, our souls to save
Worthy of praise

Then when blood was spent, the wall was rent
Our debt paid
You received our pain, our filth and shame
Only you

Then you rose and donned the royal crown
All before your throne must now bow down
The serpent's head was crushed into the ground
All glory to you!

WHAT THEY MEAN

(Words loosely defined using NASEC 1981)

Ganab......*thief*
Shachath......*destroy*
Muth......*kill*
Tebel......*world*
Ekklesia......*church*
Sathar......*secret*
Emunah......*faith*
Yachal......*hope*
Alazon......*boastful (pride)*
Kolleb......*kol (all)* plus *leb (heart)...all heart*
Rammak......*royal stud*
Philautos......*self*
Misthotos......*hireling*
Porneia......*immorality*
Aphron......*fool*
Sarx......*flesh*
Aselgeia......*sensuality*
Teraphim......*idolatry*
Kashaph......*sorcery*
Eris......*strife*
Qinah......*jealously*
Aph......*anger*
Shakar......*drunkenness*
Ratsad......*envy*
Daath......*knowledge*
Eirenikos......*peaceable*
Zaku......*innocent*
Chammad......*covet*
Shalal......*spoil*
Nabal......*foolish*
Chata......*sin*
Phoneus......*murderer*
Eritheia......*ambition*

Reqam......*empty*
Perispao......*distracted*
Thorubazo......*to disturb*
Prodotes......*traitor*
Shachat......*slaughter*
Rak......*gentle*
Yatab......*reasonable*
Zed......*arrogant*
Sophia......*wisdom*

The Dragons

In the land beyond the Living River known as Tebel, where chains and sorrow are woven tightly around the souls of human kind, there are four main manifestations of evil that walk, slither, and fly. These, the ready representatives of their cruel master, the Lord of the Dragons, seek to punish and pillage, burden and break, torture and twist, disease and debase and, ultimately, crush and consume the vast multitude of two-legged *insects* that, for some reason, are so adored by the God of the Crystal Sea and his representative...the Great King.

The Ganab:

Smallest of the *Earth Walkers* (never more than three meters in height when standing erect), this villain is usually dark in color (mirroring the deadness of the shadows) and very lightly armored. Although capable of flame (a small amount, sometimes used as a tool of intimidation to demonstrate what is to come via its larger cousins) the main weapon of this dragon is its tongue...and its vile intellect. Able to discern the weaknesses of its prey, it slithers, almost hypnotically, into the thoughts and heart of its enemy...unlocking the door to terror, and bringing to ripeness the fruit of despair. Although many a human warrior, if not watchful, will eventually lower their defenses after the subtle prying attack of the Ganab (this patient dragon is usually in *no* hurry), the experienced knight quickly recognizes the source of the poison and, with a swift thrust from the anointed sword...the Ganab either flees...or flails.

The Ganab

The Shachath:

A destroyer, a bearer of disease, a walking plague, a destructive storm. The Shachath is the *husbandman*, the gardener of the human crop…destroying readily those things in which the pitiful creatures give attachment….wealth and health. Able to outrun its two-legged prey, it prefers, as its main course, to feast upon the despair and foreboding that accompany its wares. This monster, usually no taller (measured to the shoulder, the neck adds considerably more) than four meters, its color borders on the hue of green pond-scum. Its fire is substantial, but its powerful scythe-like tail—in combination with the flame—are usually enough to dissuade the average warrior from solitary combat. However, a true knight (if able to coax the fire) takes little time to dispatch this villain. Also, being a beast of limited armor, a well-placed lance is just as effective as the sword.

The Shachath

The Muth:

A Slayer, a killer, a merciless consumer of human flesh. This behemoth is the ultimate harvester of the crop. Beginning at a height of five meters (also measured to the shoulder) and upward (depending on age), but of great weight and girth, this creature knows little of the delicacies of preparing and pruning. Heavily armored, this villain is impervious to the lance and other such *long-distance* weaponry. However, since its primary attack is with the all-consuming fire (spewed great distances) the preparation of this affords the true knight time to whittle away at the wall. This creature's defeat, however, is dependent on a warrior using *all* of his skill coupled with the adornment supplied by the king.

The Muth

The Flyer:

The last class of dragon found beyond the Living River, this creature, slightly larger than the Ganab, has huge bat-like wings in which to swiftly and powerfully manipulate the airy firmament as it darts in and out of the human cauldron…dipping, nearly at will, to retrieve a portion of screaming flesh. Lightly armored, this monster, nevertheless, is quick of claw and tooth, plus, to the dismay of many a warrior, it has the added advantage of a long, adept tail which serves as another grasping appendage. However, once knowledgeable of this dragon's ways, a true knight has no problem in defeating this reptilian foe.

The Sower

The Hybrids

After the breach in the Wall of Separation and the subsequent establishment and encircling of the kingdom of Ekklesia by the Living River, provision was made by the warrior knight for his subjects that, if followed, would prevent any dragon's print to be found ever again in the soil of the redeemed land. However, with the passing of time, and the neglect of the children, creatures of mixed blood began to emerge to again torment the subjects of the king.

The Sathar:

In the liberated land provided by the substitution and sacrifice of the Great King, dragons (those of pure hellish lineage) have no right to exist. However, as at the beginning, the seed of rebellion is still present and waiting just outside the individual citizen's sphere and, if he or she should choose to entertain this bobble for any length of time…an orb of destruction appears. This *dragon seed*, if not properly disposed of (in the river) and, worse yet, if gathered and hidden…these, over time, will coalesce into a dragon hybrid known as a *Sathar*. This monster, having many of the attributes of its distant cousins, is also infused with the individual traits of its human *parent* and, when born, it seeks to unite with the same. A knowledgeable knight can make short work of this creature. Unfortunately, by the time this incubated intruder is manifested, often the human nurturer is too self-absorbed to avoid destruction, not only of themselves…but of most of what they hold dear.

The Sathar

The Great Dragon:

When the mingling of *dragon seeds* (the massive quantity of unrepentant leavings of a rebellious host) are allowed to simmer unresolved over an extended period of time (literally *hundreds* of years) and these, being primed and prodded from below via the influence of the evil lord…an enormous dragon is produced that seeks not only its *parents* (of course, over the long period of time needed for the incubation and birth, many of the parents are dead…but their lineage will do) but also *all* whose ways are opposite those of its master. Having *most* of the attributes of the other dragon types (and more beside) this monster is *nearly* unstoppable. Measuring fully twice the height and girth of the largest Muth, the fire and fury of this creature seem an impossible hurdle to overcome. The king says "the Champion" can prevail…but who is he?

The Great Dragon

The Chata:

The smallest of the hybrids, this *tiny* dragon never attains a man's height, but its small size affords it other advantages. Born quickly of individual seeds of rebellion (as opposed to the Great Dragon which took nearly a millennium to nurture) its lust for consuming its individual parent—due to the *greater* influence from the Dragon Lord—is dispersed to include *all* humans. Very light of armor, but deadly of tooth and talon, this creature, like the swarming bee or the army ant, finds its strength in overwhelming numbers. Able also to scale vertical walls, no stronghold of man can long sustain a defense against these dragons that do not sleep.

The Chata

Printed in the United States
58159LVS00003B/193-240